T0123276

He groaned against her mouth, and triumph roared through her. Then he took over the kiss, forcing her head back, overwhelming her as he poured heat into her that filled her entire body, head to toe.

He removed his hand, and she whimpered. Embarrassment flowed through her, and she straightened, still feeling intoxicated. As if she'd sipped too much of the aged wine she wasn't supposed to have unless it was during her study of society dinners.

"Are you okay?" He released her hair, once again looking too big and too dangerous.

"I think so." It took her a second to realize that tears filled her eyes. One spilled over to slide down her cheek.

He caught it and rubbed the droplet between his thumb and forefinger, looking thoughtful. "Who are you, Dessie?"

"Nobody that matters," she told him, giving him honesty again. The wind tossed fallen leaves across the stone wall, and cheerful daisies waved. It was late for them to be blooming. "Um, Garrett? I feel messy."

He lifted her off the wall, yanked her bag over his shoulder, took her hand, and towed her back around the building. "Go inside and clean yourself up, and then get your ass back out here. We're not done." His face was set in a hard mask, and his tone was unrelenting. "By the time you return, be prepared to give me the full truth."

Also by Rebecca Zanetti

GARRETT'S DESTINY

By Rebecca Zanetti

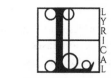

LYRICAL PRESS
Kensington Publishing Corp.
www.kensingtonbooks.com

To the extent that the image or images on the cover of this book depict a person or persons, such person or persons are merely models, and are not intended to portray any character or characters featured in the book.

This book is a work of fiction. Names, characters, places, and incidents either are products of the author's imagination or are used fictitiously. Any resemblance to actual events or locales or persons living or dead is entirely coincidental.

LYRICAL PRESS BOOKS are published by

Kensington Publishing Corp.
119 West 40th Street
New York, NY 10018

Copyright © 2022 by Rebecca Zanetti

All rights reserved. No part of this book may be reproduced in any form or by any means without the prior written consent of the Publisher, excepting brief quotes used in reviews.

All Kensington titles, imprints, and distributed lines are available at special quantity discounts for bulk purchases for sales promotion, premiums, fundraising, educational, or institutional use.

Special book excerpts or customized printings can also be created to fit specific needs. For details, write or phone the office of the Kensington Sales Manager: Kensington Publishing Corp., 119 West 40th Street, New York, NY 10018. Attn. Sales Department. Phone: 1-800-221-2647.

Lyrical Press and Lyrical Press logo Reg. U.S. Pat. & TM Off.

First Electronic Edition: October 2022
ISBN-13: 978-1-5161-1078-0 (ebook)

First Print Edition: October 2022
ISBN-13: 978-1-5161-1083-4

Printed in the United States of America

This one is for all the readers who have been with the Realm since the beginning and saw Garrett come into the world. I hope you love his story.

Acknowledgments

Thank you to the readers who've been with the Realm since the beginning, and those who have jumped in with this new era, starting with *Vampire's Faith*. I have many wonderful people to thank for getting this book to readers, and I sincerely apologize to anyone I've forgotten.

Thank you to my supportive family, Big Tone, Gabe, and Karlina; as always, I love you and appreciate you so much.

Thank you to my hardworking editor, Alicia Condon, as well as everyone at Kensington Publishing: Alexandra Nicolajsen, Steven Zacharius, Adam Zacharius, Vida Engstrand, Jane Nutter, Lauren Jernigan, Elizabeth Trout, Samantha McVeigh, Lynn Cully, Arthur Maisel, Renee Rocco, Rebecca Cremonese.

Thank you to my wonderful agent, Caitlin Blasdell, and to Liza Dawson and the entire Liza Dawson Agency.

Thank you to my awesome assistant, Anissa Beatty, for her excellent social media work as well as the fun with the Rebels, and thanks to Rebels Jessica Mobbs, Heather Frost, Kimberly Frost, Madison Fairbanks, Suzi Zuber, Asmaa Nada Qayyum, Amanda Larsen, Karen Clementi, and Karen Fisher for their assistance.

Thank you to Writer Space and Fresh Fiction PR for all the hard work.

Thanks also to my constant support system: Gail and Jim English, Kathy and Herb Zanetti, Debbie and Travis Smith, Stephanie and Don West, Jessica and Jonah Namson, Chelli and Jason Younker, Liz and Steve Berry, and Jillian and Benji Stein.

Chapter One

Garrett Kayrs settled his bulk in the booth, reaching for a glass of beer from the iced pitcher on the table. Raucous laughter poured throughout the diner as motorcycle clubs converged on the way to a festival. Not one he and his brothers were attending, but they were along for the first part of the ride to camp for a weekend.

"Would you stop frowning?" Sam Kyllwood snapped from across the booth, his green eyes showing irritation.

"I'm not," Garrett growled, frowning at his friend.

Honor Kyllwood, Sam's mate, slapped him on the arm. They'd been mated for over three years, and she was definitely one of the best-natured people Garrett had ever met. "You two behave. Garrett, I'm sure you'll find somebody to play with when we get to the campground and, Sam, give him a break. It's the first time we've gone on a ride in years that he hasn't had a female on the back of his bike. He's lonely."

Sam cut the pretty woman a look, his powerful body protecting her since he'd positioned her next to the window. "The last woman he dated tried to rob you—at knifepoint."

Honor chortled. "Yeah, but I kicked her ass. Those training sessions have gone well."

Garrett hid his grin. She was correct. He'd been searching for the right female to ride behind him for years, consumed by the quest, and he hadn't found her. Prophecy claimed she'd be dangerous, even deadly, and would probably try to kill him. It was time to get on with it.

The beast inside him, one that had slumbered beneath the surface for so long, was now stretching awake. Pissed off and ready to kill. At least now he had a job to do when they arrived at the campground.

The outside door opened, and a vision walked in. Well, more like the girl next door. She wore a frilly green blouse, white capri jeans, and sexy tan wedges that showed off her dainty pink toenails. It was autumn, and she should have been wearing a jacket. A slouchy bag looked heavy over her fragile shoulder. Her auburn hair curled down her back, and an air of pure irritation emanated from her.

Looking like an indignant kitten, she stomped right into the middle of the diner, next to Garrett's table, not seeming to realize she'd walked into a den of wolves.

The man behind her definitely noticed. Young, slick brown hair, pressed beige pants, and thousand-dollar loafers on his feet. He looked around at the various motorcycle club members sitting in different areas of the diner, all hungry, all possibly dangerous. "Let's get out of here," he muttered.

The kitten turned, her hands going to her waist. The scent of something fresh and sweet wafted from her. What was that? "You just don't get it." She leaned toward the man, anger turning her peaches-and-cream complexion into cherry-blossom pink. "The answer *was* no." She swept out her arms. "The answer *is* no." She clapped her hands. "The answer will always and forever, until the *time of the rapture*, be no." She threw her arms up. Then she shook her head. "I quit."

The man reared back. "You can't quit."

"I just did," she sighed. "I'm out. I'm not finding what I need in this job anyway." She nodded, her shoulders stiff in the flimsy blouse. "I'll send your father a nice email later today tendering my resignation. Please extend my gratitude to him for the employment opportunity." She turned away from him.

The man made the mistake of grabbing her arm.

Garrett was up in a second, towering over them both. "Let. Go."

The man jerked back as if he'd been punched in the gut.

A slight gasp came from the kitten.

Probably one of pure terror. Oh, Garrett knew what she saw. He was six and a half feet of raw muscle in a torn and dirty black motorcycle club jacket, with shaggy hair to his shoulders, a couple of bruises across his jaw, and cracked knuckles he hadn't bothered to heal after a fight the night before.

He cut her a look and then rocked back on his heels.

Her crystal-clear blue eyes were full of delight...and wonder. "You," she whispered, reaching out to touch his whiskered jaw. Her tongue darted out to lick her luscious bottom lip. "It's you." She tilted her head, adoration in her liquid gaze.

The touch shot straight to his balls, making him throb in a way he hadn't in years. He growled low.

Then she withdrew.

"No." He didn't know what he was denying, but he didn't want her to stop looking at him like that. Nobody in his entire life had looked at him like that. With adoration, need, and...hope? More than anything, he wanted that touch again.

The blush blossomed into full-on rose, and she clapped her hand against her bag. "I, ah, um, I'm sorry." She frowned. "That was, well, that was..." She looked around, no doubt noticing that every gaze was focused on her. She shrugged delicate shoulders and looked up at him as if forcing herself to meet his gaze. Black lashes, natural and thick, enhanced those incredible eyes. "I apologize."

"Let's go," the man said, backpedaling toward the door.

She frowned at him. "No. Go away, Aster. I'll find my own way home."

Aster looked around, paling. Then the asshole left the kitten in the den of wolves.

Her hands fluttered together. "Oh. Well." She caught sight of the empty row of barstools at the counter and started to move that way.

"No." Garrett angled his body just enough to stop her. He was at least a foot taller and a hundred or two pounds heavier than she was, basically making him a solid wall. "How do you know me?" There were many bounties on his head, but there was no way the kitten was a bounty hunter. He could read people well enough to know that.

She glanced down at his monstrous boots and took a deep breath before looking up and meeting his gaze. "I don't know you." Then she smiled, and sure as shit, it was like the sun had appeared over the mountains after the rainy season. "That was weird, and I apologize. There's no way I could know you, correct?"

"Right." He grasped her arm, careful not to bruise her. "You're sitting with us."

"No, I—"

He nudged her into the booth, putting his body between her and the rest of the bikers in the place.

It was time for some answers.

* * * *

Well, she'd just gone and done it now, hadn't she? Dessie settled into the booth, her entire right side warmed by the man sitting next to her. Make that the formidable block of muscle sitting next to her. Would it be weird if she asked him to remove the tinted glasses covering his eyes? "You're the highwayman a'comin," she whispered.

"I like poetry as well." Why did that sound like a threat from him? How could he be real? He couldn't be. It wasn't really *him*.

When he lifted one finger, a waitress came out of nowhere so fast her thighs hit the table. "Yes?" she asked breathlessly, her ample breasts straining against her black tank top.

He didn't seem to notice but instead turned his head slightly to Dessie. "Order."

She gulped. Order? She didn't have enough money for lunch as well as a ride home. "I'm, um, I'm not hungry." Her stomach rumbled, but quietly enough she was sure nobody heard it.

Now he turned his head all the way toward her, and even through those glasses, she could feel his intent. His hair was dark, with some natural highlights that showed he spent time in the sun, and his facial features were rock-solid angles that tempted a girl to run her fingers across the masculine bone structure. "Don't lie to me again." Her body wanted to back away from him, but she was already pressed against the windowsill and wall. "Order, or I'll do it for you."

Maybe she could hitchhike back to the motel or just leave her meager possessions there. She had everything she needed in her overlarge bag. "I'll have a cheeseburger, no onions or pickles. Thank you." It was a diner, and she'd learned that they usually had burgers, so it was a safe bet. Besides, she loved cheeseburgers. They were a warm new comfort that probably would go straight to her thighs, but who cared?

"Drink?" His words were clipped. Her unfortunate choice of words earlier had apparently angered him. Or, at the very least, irritated him. She had a feeling that he was only allowing her to see his emotions because he didn't care if she knew he was not happy.

"What's your name?" The question popped out of her before she could stop it.

He didn't so much as twitch, instead keeping her captive with his gaze. If anything, more tension rolled off him. "Order. A. Drink."

Her knees trembled, and her breath quickened. Once again her body reacted without conscious thought. These feelings were new and all for him. She didn't appreciate the sensations at the moment.

She shifted her weight, trying to find a comfortable position. "You're very bossy." While she'd tried soda and didn't much like it, water wasn't appealing to her in this moment.

Apparently, his patience had ended. "Bring another mug. She'll have beer."

The waitress sprinted away. Probably so she could return quickly.

At least if they poured from their pitcher, she wouldn't be charged for the drink. "That would be lovely," Dessie said primly to nobody in particular.

His grin was slow and more devastating than a train crash.

The smile warmed her more, and she was grateful he didn't look so scary any longer. If being polite charmed him, she'd draw on every etiquette lesson she'd ever learned.

She finally broke eye contact and looked across the booth. Another overlarge man sat across the worn wooden table, and he also wore a leather jacket. His hair was black, his eyes green, and his expression tense. Next to him sat a truly beautiful woman with tawny skin, rope-twisted black hair, and sparkling dark eyes. She had curves Dessie would love to possess. "Hi," Dessie said, focusing on the woman, sensing she was the safest person in the booth, if not the entire diner.

"Hi." The woman tilted her head, curiosity in her gaze. "What's your name?"

"Dessie. Yours?"

The woman glanced at the man next to her, and he barely nodded. "I'm Honor, and this is Sam." Had she just asked permission to give their names?

Dessie frowned. These people were obviously on guard, and her touching the guy next to her as if they were old friends was a mystery they apparently didn't like. Why would they?

A shuffling sound alerted her, and she looked around to see several of the patrons rearranging themselves in this half of the diner. She liked patterns, and she quickly discerned this one. The biggest and meanest-looking of the leather-clad men were now all seated closer to them. Surrounding them in booths and the closest tables—forming a wall of protection around them. How intriguing.

She noted on the back of their jackets the outline of a large grizzly bear, sharp teeth flashing beneath the word GRIZZLIES. "Why do you all have matching jackets?"

Even Honor wore a black leather jacket. She played with a stunning diamond engagement ring on her finger. "We belong to the Grizzlies, which is a motorcycle club." Then her gaze narrowed. "You've never heard of a motorcycle club?"

"No." Dessie shrugged. "I haven't been in California very long."

The woman's gaze cleared, and she barely nodded.

What was going on with the almost nods? Perhaps that was just how Honor and Sam communicated. Or maybe Sam couldn't speak. Dessie looked directly at him, wanting to shrink beneath his sharp gaze. "Are you mute?" Somebody coughed in the booth behind her, but she didn't turn. Her eyes widened. "Oh my. Is that a rude question? If so, I do apologize. I didn't mean anything hurtful."

Sam blinked. Twice. "No. I'm not mute." He drew a phone from his pocket and texted with one hand, not looking away from her. "Told Bear to skip the diner, and he's covered on all sides."

"Good," Garrett said. "His new enforcers are doing well. I don't feel so bad leaving him now."

Dessie reminded herself that she was strong and free, but these men would probably only answer a limited number of questions. So she wouldn't ask about the mysterious Bear. Instead, she steeled her shoulders before partially turning in the cramped booth to face the man taking up all the oxygen. For some reason, she could barely breathe. "What's your name?"

"You don't know?" He hadn't stopped watching her. Not for a second.

She shook her head.

"Garrett." Then he waited.

Why was he waiting? "That's a nice name," she hastened to say. Was there some sort of social convention she was missing here? It was entirely possible.

"Thank you." The amusement had returned. She definitely enjoyed it better than his earlier irritation. "Now how about you tell me who you are and how you know me."

Two waitresses arrived with a mug and all of their food. Somehow, Dessie's meal was already prepared as well. She waited until the women stopped fawning over the two men before reaching for a fry. Fries were the best invention she'd discovered lately. "My name is Dessie. I am now a freelance reporter, and I do not know you. At all. I didn't even know your name until you gave it to me." Unable to help herself, she reached for the cheeseburger.

Garrett did the same, and his cheeseburger was a lot bigger than hers. "Very well, Dessie. Eat your lunch. Then you and I are going outside for a little chat."

Chapter Two

As possibly Dessie's last meal, it had been delicious. For the first time in a week, she forgot the fact that somebody was following her. Well, probably. She'd seen the same man several times, but he'd never approached her. Perhaps her mind was going.

She began to protest when Garrett tossed bills on the table to pay for her burger but stopped when he turned that gaze on her.

"Let's go." He grasped her hand and tugged her rather gently from the booth.

She dragged her bag with her and then stumbled, quickly finding her balance when he planted one strong hand on her shoulder. Her lungs seized, and her stomach roiled. The luncheon had been so bizarre that this was the first time she'd felt fear. They'd eaten mostly in silence and very quickly. A desperate glance around at the remaining diners confirmed that nobody was going to help her. So much for continuing to pack as much life into her remaining hours as possible. Time was not her friend. She clutched the bag to her ribs.

"Do you have a weapon in there?" Garrett asked mildly.

"Yes. A knife." There was no reason to lie to him, considering he could easily take away the bag.

He kept his grip on her hand and began striding toward the exit. "Okay."

Should she be miffed he didn't try to confiscate the knife? Probably. She had to hasten her steps to keep up with him. His hand around hers felt warm and solid, so big she wished she had time to just compare their hands palm to palm. He was a very large man who, nonetheless, managed to move surprisingly fast. Within seconds they were outside the diner, where people milled around different bikes, packing things in compartments and igniting the loud engines. Based on the various names on the jackets, there were several different clubs present.

Fall colors lit the world on fire around them, the trees shedding their bright red and gold leaves. The sky was a mellow blue, and the sun bright but not warm.

Garrett continued around to the rear of the building, which was a surprisingly quiet area. A crumbling rock wall crusted with moss held back a grassy hill. In one smooth motion, he released her hand, grasped her hips, and lifted her onto the wall.

She yelped and then settled, surprise filling her. She was still several inches shorter than he, even on the large wall. "Why is any of this necessary?" She planted the bag next to her, calculating how quickly he'd just moved. There wasn't a chance to get to her knife. And could she really stab somebody?

"Who sent you?"

The fact that he hadn't answered her question shot a chill through her body. "Sent me?"

He instantly tangled one strong hand in her hair and planted the other next to her hip on the stone. "Yes. Play dumb, and you won't like the results. Is somebody after Bear?"

"No." Bear was an odd name, but he was obviously important to Garrett. "Well, let me clarify that statement. I don't know Bear and thus have no knowledge of whether or not somebody is after him. I assume Bear is a him, though I could be wrong. But—"

"Stop." His grip on her hair tightened with a firm tug that shot sparks right to her breasts. Well, that was interesting. "Baby, I don't want to hurt you, but I will. I'm not gonna ask again. Who sent you to find me?"

She blinked. "Take off your glasses."

He paused. "You want to play? We'll play." He slowly whipped off the glasses, revealing gray metallic eyes that shouldn't exist in the real world. It had to be some type of genetic mutation. "Talk."

Her mouth opened, but no sound emerged. "Your eyes. They really *are* metallic." How was it possible? She'd seen him just like this.

"You've seen a picture of me?" His eyes went cold. Flat. Frozen metal.

She swallowed and tried to move away, but he held her firmly in place. Heat blew through her.

His pupils narrowed, and he leaned in even closer, his lips almost touching hers. He forced her legs apart and moved in. Watching her. Studying her. Awareness lightened his unreal eyes. "Maybe I won't have to get violent." He nuzzled her mouth and nipped her jaw, twisting her head to place a gentle kiss behind her ear.

Fire lashed from that small touch, zinging to her breasts and then farther down between her legs. She shuddered, and she could feel his firm lips form a smile against her skin.

"There we go." The rumble of his voice rolled throughout her entire body.

She'd opened her mouth to speak, to say something, maybe even the truth, when his mouth took hers. Shock thrilled through her as she realized what was happening, and her eyelids closed on their own. If she could have moved, she would've swayed toward him. Instead, with him holding her in place, she just let herself feel. His lips pressed against hers, demanding a response, and she gave it to him. Tentatively at first, she let instinct rule and followed his lead.

Pleasure oscillated through her, scorching each nerve on its path to her core. She grabbed his shoulders and fell into passion, stilling when his tongue swept inside her mouth. Her eyelids opened to find metallic gray watching her. Not wanting to lose the heat, she closed her eyes again and met his tongue with her own. It was decadent. Like triple-chocolate melted lava cake mixed with fine wine. She moaned, wanting more. So much more.

He partially drew back. "Who sent you?"

"Nobody." She leaned forward and kissed him, wanting to keep going wherever that feeling went.

He returned her kiss, pushing her head into his hand. "Who wants me dead?"

"Nobody who's ever kissed you." Just speaking against his mouth, her lips moving over his firm ones, shot tingles beneath her skin.

His grip tightened, and even that slight pain was erotic. Then his hand was on her breast.

She gasped, leaning back, her face heated. The sensations were so much stronger than she'd read about in those novels.

Through her blouse and bra, he pinched her nipple. Pain and pleasure flashed together, and she cried out, arching even closer to him. She ached. Between her legs, she needed more. Him.

Deep color stained his cheekbones, making him look more dangerous. Like a predator that had just trapped prey. "How do you know me?" He flattened his hand and caressed her breast, taking away the pain.

"I dreamed about you," she said honestly. "I did not believe you to truly exist." At least in her more realistic moments of thinking. A girl could always wish, however.

His chin lifted. "Dreamed about me?" His fingers trailed between her breasts and down her torso, lighting fires along the way.

"Yes," she gasped. "Just once, but you saved my life. Or the image of you did. I didn't think you were real." He reached the button of her pants and flicked it open. Was she going to let him do this? Her body angled closer to him. These feelings were good, and they were temporary. She truly didn't have much time left, and she wasn't going to pass up any opportunity. It was her mantra. "I would say it's a coincidence, but he was you. You were him."

"Right." He leaned in and nuzzled her neck, his hand sliding easily inside her panties.

She gulped. Even though she could understand his not believing her, she didn't care right now. She held her breath, and her abdomen tightened.

"You want this?" His fingers found her, easily sliding through her wet folds. She was so wet. How did that happen?

"Yes." She didn't know what he meant, but whatever it was, she wanted it. Was pushing into his hand for it.

His grin was feral. "So this is how? You're supposed to seduce me?"

"No." But if she knew how, she definitely would. His finger slid inside her, and the other one pressed on her clitoris. Electricity sparked through her. Oh, she'd studied anatomy carefully just like all of her subjects, and she understood what a clitoris was, but she'd had no idea what it could do. Or maybe it was just Garrett. He flicked her, and she jerked, her thighs quaking. "I don't want you dead." Never.

"Right." He leaned in, licking her neck. Then he inhaled, his powerful chest moving. He frowned. Keeping his fingers right where they were, he leaned back slightly to stare at her. "You're human."

Even in desperate need of something she didn't understand, amusement filled her. Life was bizarre. "Yes. I'm only human, Garrett. Not immune to your charm or abilities or bad-boy vibes. You're human, too." And by the size of the bulge in his jeans, her lessons on anatomy hadn't prepared her for much at all.

Something sizzled in those eyes. Something dark and unidentifiable. "You're fucking human. I don't sense any enhancements."

Enhancements? "No. I'm in my early twenties. You're kind of a jerk thinking I'd have plastic surgery or something." She wasn't all that well endowed, and it hadn't bothered her until now. Had that waitress with the D-cup sized breasts interested him? Her desire, if that's what this was, began to wane.

He kissed her hard this time. Hard and angry, his fingers started to move again. She opened her mouth and let him take, opening her legs to let him give. She was climbing. High. Something was there, out of reach. Her body began to gyrate against him, following his pattern, surrendering to him. Those fingers were magical. Then he halted.

She groaned and opened her eyes, smacking him on the cheek. "You have got to *stop* stopping." This led to an orgasm, she was fairly certain, and she wanted one. A big one. Her body craved it. "My pain is your fault, and you need to fix it."

One of his dark eyebrows rose.

Realization trembled through her, and she paused. Most people probably didn't hit Garrett in the face.

"You want me to fix your pain?" His voice was a seductive low roll with a hint of danger.

She gulped, fully aware that his hand was in her pants. "Yes." This was definitely something she wanted to experience before she died.

He sniffed her again, his face against hers. "You're not psychic? Empathic? Telekinetic?"

She fought the urge to hit him harder. "Stop being ridiculous."

He leaned back and cocked his head. "You really aren't."

Was he crazy? She'd read that crazy sex was the best, so perhaps he was touched in the head? At the moment, she didn't care. At all. So she clamped both hands on his cheeks and yanked his mouth back to hers. She sank her teeth into his bottom lip, wanting that bite. His shoulders jerked, and she slid her tongue inside his mouth, trying to mimic what he'd done to her. Attempting to give him the pleasure he'd swamped her with, wanting him to feel as good as he made her feel.

He groaned against her mouth, and triumph roared through her. Then he took over the kiss, forcing her head back, overwhelming her as he poured heat into her that filled her entire body, head to toe. His fingers slid in and out of her and then he angled her farther back, controlling her with the hand fisted in her hair.

Sensations bombarded her as wild as the waves crashing against the rock wall of her home so far away. Powerful and deep, they took her under while forcing her to climb, inch by deadly inch, toward a ledge she didn't understand. She was helpless against the pull. She climbed higher, her body shaking, his fingers magic against her.

With a sharp cry, she fell over the cliff. Wildfire crackled through her with whip strokes of impossible color and electricity. The waves bombarded from within this time, rippling out into the universe, taking her voice with them. She rode the waves, undulating with ecstasy until she finally came down.

He removed his hand, and she whimpered. Embarrassment flowed through her, and she straightened, still feeling intoxicated. As if she'd sipped too much of the aged wine she wasn't supposed to have unless it was during her study of society dinners.

"Are you okay?" He released her hair, once again looking too big and too dangerous.

"I think so." It took her a second to realize that tears filled her eyes. One spilled over to slide down her cheek.

He caught it and rubbed the droplet between his thumb and forefinger, looking thoughtful. "Who are you?"

"Nobody that matters," she told him, attempting honesty again. The wind tossed fallen leaves across the stone wall, and cheerful daisies waved. It was late for them to be blooming. She hurriedly zipped up her pants, reality returning with the sound of motorcycle engines gunning in front of the restaurant. "Um, Garrett? I feel messy."

He lifted her off the wall, yanked her bag over his shoulder, took her hand, and towed her back around the building. "Go inside and clean yourself up, then get your ass back out here. We're not done." His face was set in a hard mask, and his tone was unrelenting. "By the time you return, be prepared to give me the full truth."

"I did," she mumbled, so confused she wasn't sure which way to go.

Opening the door, he nudged her inside. "Seduction didn't work. That leaves pain. Neither of us wants that."

She stumbled inside, so off-balance she wasn't sure the planet was still spinning. "My belongings?" She reached for the bag.

"No. You have two minutes, kitten." He shut the door before she could protest.

She'd try to run away, but she needed that bag. Needed everything in it to live her short life before she died.

Time was definitely mocking her.

Chapter Three

Garrett moved toward his bike, which was guarded by club prospects. Though he shouldn't have let her go before getting his answers, he needed a minute. The sound she'd made when she'd climaxed, so pure and real, was one he'd hear in his dreams for a very long time.

His hands shook, and he covered the reaction. What the hell was wrong with him? He dumped the bag's contents out and caught the few items that didn't land on the seat. No cell phone. What kind of a woman didn't have a cell phone?

He opened the wallet just as Sam approached, his gaze serious.

They'd bonded as Grizzly brothers, as well as enforcers, more than prepared to take down any enemy. Most of the Grizzlies were actual grizzly bear shifters, so as the only two vampire-demon hybrids in the motorcycle club, they would've bonded anyway. Of course, Garrett's sister had mated Sam's brother, so they were true family as well.

"Destiny Applegate," Garrett read from her license. "Address in Texas." He looked closer. "The license looks genuine." There were no credit cards or pictures in the wallet. Only nine dollars and three cents. She'd been traveling with a man she didn't trust, and all she had with her was less than ten bucks? Irritation flooded through him, with anger—real anger—right behind.

"G? What the fuck?" Sam asked, his gaze sweeping the entire area around him.

That was a damn good question. Garrett folded up the wallet and tossed it at one of the prospects guarding the bike. "Shot? I want a deep dive on this. Everything you can possibly find, and tell the techs they might need to just start with the picture. Discover who she is and when she acquired this. Call Chalton at the Realm—he's the best, and I don't have time to fuck around."

If Bear was in danger, Garrett wanted to know it yesterday. Bear was the president of their club, happily mated, with triplets in the back of his SUV as they took this run.

Sam watched the prospect jog away. Many of the other clubs had already taken to the road, but the Grizzlies hung back, waiting patiently. "She's human. Like, genetically human and not enhanced." Immortals could mate enhanced humans and often did, but normal humans held no appeal for them. Normal humans couldn't be mated, and they were fairly uninteresting except when they made scientific advances. "What's happening?"

"I don't know." Garrett wanted her. His entire body rumbled with hunger for her, and that made no sense. As a vampire-demon hybrid, he could scent an enhanced female five miles away. That woman inside, with her fragile bones and sharp wit, was all human. He'd been wrong about her eyes. They weren't just blue. They had gray flecks through them, giving her a wild look. An untamed and wild look that no human should ever have.

"Well, what did she say?" Sam asked. "Did she explain?"

"No. Said she saw me in a dream." Garrett looked at the rest of the contents. Two romance novels, one in French and the other Italian, an older book written in Greek hieroglyphics, a bottle of water, a notebook with no notes, a pen, a toiletry bag, and a set of clothing, including a light jacket. No laptop.

And one more thing.

He'd expected a pocket knife. Instead, he found a military tactical combat knife with a six-inch, stainless-steel blade about six millimeters thick. The silver was deadly sharp and angled on one side, with serrated barbs on the top. The handle was zinc alloy and made for a woman's hand. One word graced the glinting steel. *Destiny.*

Sam scratched his head. "She doesn't look like a woman who'd have her own custom-made knife."

Garrett examined the weapon. "It's handmade. There's no way to trace her from it." As a woman traveling alone, it made sense to have a knife. What didn't make sense was her name on it. His brother was correct. Dessie was not the type of woman to own a knife. She wasn't enhanced and thus had no way of protecting herself from him. He could smell a lie, and he hadn't scented one on her. But a human wouldn't dream about him. "This doesn't make sense."

"I couldn't detect falsehoods, and neither could Honor, but we could have Honor sit down with her," Sam offered. Honor was an enhanced human female who'd become immortal when her chromosomal pairs increased after mating Sam. Her enhancement, even as a human, had been the ability to detect lies.

Garrett slid the knife into the sheath and replaced the contents in the bag. "Some enhanced females have been able to mostly mask their enhancements."

Sam winced. "But there's still a slight vibration. I get *all human* from her."

"So do I," Garrett said softly, his gut clenching for some odd reason. "How could a normal human dream about me?"

"She has to be lying," Sam said, frowning. "With the knife and the girl-next-door good looks, perhaps she's trained in deception? We would never expect any of our enemies to send a human after us, which would actually be smart and might work." They had so many enemies.

But it didn't feel right. None of this felt right. Except when Destiny Applegate had been in his arms, in his control, falling apart. That had felt more than right. That had been sunshine and good scotch all wrapped up in one, warming him from within, hitting places he'd thought frozen cold forever.

For months, maybe years, he'd been slowly going ice-cold inside. The power inside him and the pressure on him, the fates pulling at him, had all conspired to keep his mate from him, and the absence had been killing him.

Slowly, ride by ride, inch by inch. He had a very real fear that by the time he found her, his powerful goddess, he'd be dead inside. It would be too late for them both.

But this little human, with her innocent eyes and sassy remarks, had warmed and thawed those dark places. Even if only for a few minutes. Garrett tossed her bag in with his belongings. "Find me a helmet and boots for her. She's coming with us until we figure this out."

* * * *

Dessie rushed through the diner to the restroom, her head down. There were still some motorcycle club people in booths finishing their lunches. Had she been loud? She'd experienced a spectacular orgasm, and she was fairly certain she'd cried out. Possibly noisily. The man of her dreams was even better in person. Although her dream hero would've believed her when she told him the truth.

Garrett most certainly had not.

She pushed open the door and hurried to make use of the stall, trying to fix her panties as best she could. Then she moved to the sink and stopped short. Her eyes were deeper than usual, her mouth rosy and swollen, and her hair a wild mess of curls. She looked the way she felt—like she'd just had an incredible orgasm. As if she were truly the captain of her own soul, as she'd read in "Invictus." Her romance books had not described the sensation well at all. It was so much more than she could've imagined. High color, close to a candy red, splashed across her cheekbones.

Her legs shook, and she forced her knees to hold tight. Then she washed her hands and dried them with a paper towel. Now what was she going to do? She couldn't exactly run away while he held her bag.

Just as she was about to exit, the door opened, and two men walked inside. They were rough-looking but young—maybe her age. Both were taller than she, and they hadn't been sitting with the Grizzlies. "This is the ladies' room," she objected. Neither looked anything like the man she'd thought had been following her that week.

The guy on the left was blond with a goatee, and his belly fell over his belt. "But you're no lady, are you?"

"I've taken lessons in manners." It was unfortunate the men were between her and the door.

The other guy had dirty brown hair, parted in the middle, but was clean-shaven. He was thin and very pale. "I'm Trout and this is Plot. We're with the Alite motorcycle club, and we're looking for somebody to party with us for the weekend. Heard you screaming good outside and thought you might want to hop on a bike and go for a run. We'll treat you nice."

She wasn't entirely sure what a run entailed, but she knew she wasn't interested in accompanying either of these men. "That's kind of you, but contrary to my recent behavior, I'm not a lot of fun."

Trout grinned, showing a piece of bacon caught by his upper incisor. "You would be with us. Come on. A run is totally cool. We ride down the coast and will end up around Tahoe for a three-day party before continuing on to Phoenix. It's wicked. Tons of drinking, good food, great sex. I promise we'll take care of you."

There was no way either of these men could match the orgasm Garrett had provided with just his hand. "My answer is a polite no."

They lost the smiles. The energy in the room changed.

Plot glared. "Listen, whore. We're totally fun, and you're going to miss out. Why would you go out back with a Grizzly for a quick feel and not come have a whole weekend with us?"

He did not just call her a derogatory term. "Did you see that Grizzly?" she asked. "Did you get a look at him? If asked, the table would've grown girl parts and gone out back with him." It wasn't kind, but she didn't appreciate the way they were looking at her. Even so, when Trout appeared more hurt than angry, she sighed. "Listen. It's like—"

The door opened, and Garrett strode inside, with Sam next to him.

She'd misread them at lunch. They weren't slightly dangerous but good-natured guys. They were killers.

Garrett still had the sunglasses on his head, and his metallic eyes had gone flat. Deadly. Furious. "What the fuck is going on?"

A shiver stroked through her, and this time it had nothing to do with desire. She chilled, her instincts flaring awake, like small prey in a forest when a predator has gotten too close.

Sam edged to Garrett's side, and if Dessie had thought he'd be the voice of reason, she'd been wrong. His shoulders were back, and anger darkened the sharp angles of his face. "I was hopin' to try out my new knife on this trip."

Trout swiveled next to Plot, shoulder to shoulder, slightly blocking Dessie.

Garrett could see her over their heads. "You. There." He pointed to the far wall.

Her legs carried her to that wall before her brain even caught his meaning. "There's no need for consternation, everyone."

Sam cut a look at Garrett. "Consternation?"

Garrett pinned her in place with his gaze for a long second and swept her entire body with it before focusing on the other two motorcycle club men. "If you so much as scared her, you're dead."

"I'm not scared," Dessie whispered. Well, she wasn't scared of Trout or Plot. Garrett was another matter entirely.

Trout puffed out his unimpressive chest. "We heard you out back with her. She ain't wearing your colors. Any colors."

Dessie frowned. "What are—" At Garrett's look, she shut up. The look *clearly* said to shut up. She might be free and brave, but she wasn't stupid.

"She sat with the Grizzlies for lunch. You knew this. You were in the far right corner, and you saw her. Therefore, colors or not, you fucked up." Garrett's voice was low and soft, full of unmistakable menace. "Dessie? Did they hurt you?" He didn't look at her.

"No, not at all," she said quickly. "Honest. They just invited me on what's called a run, and I said no."

Sam set his stance. "How did they take your refusal?"

She blinked. "Um, good? It's fine, Sam. None of you belong in the ladies' room."

Garrett now focused on her, and she felt like a specimen tacked to the wall. "What did they say?" When she started to lie, his chin lowered. "Told you once not to lie to me, baby. You don't want me to tell you again."

Her throat went dry. Like she'd eaten sawdust. So she told him, word for word.

Garrett's expression didn't change, and he looked at Plot. "Did you call my woman a whore?"

His woman? She tried to swallow so she could talk, but her mouth was a desert. Finally, she cleared her throat. "It's fine. They were more hurt than angry, Garrett. And to be honest, I did go out back with a man I'd just met and have a fairly loud orgasm." She had to be fair. "It's not like they knew that the situation was unique and that you're the only one."

He paused and then looked directly at her again. Did he have any idea how powerful that gaze was? Yeah, he probably did. "The only one what?"

Her lungs felt as if somebody was squeezing them. "That's been inside me. Mouth or anywhere else." Her confession should've calmed everyone in the room.

It did not.

Chapter Four

Garrett plunked Dessie on the seat of his bike, keeping his hands gentle on her waist. He'd spent years hooking up with the most dangerous females he could find in an effort to locate his mate, but he'd had no luck. Unexpectedly, this female was all human, and he could break her in two accidentally. He would not allow that to happen.

She gulped, her cute wedges swinging and then settling. "Your motorcycle is very nice. What kind is it?" The wind fanned tendrils of her hair against her smooth skin.

"It's a Harley-Davidson Fat Bob." Customized to within an inch of its life. "This is her first run, actually." He'd needed something new.

"Oh." Her tongue flicked out to touch her pink bottom lip.

He inhaled her scent but still couldn't identify it. The smell was a cross between strawberries and oranges, and it was driving him crazy.

"Please stop frowning at me." Away from the buzzing lights in the diner, there was a lot more gray than blue in those eyes.

His frown deepened. "Listen. I don't want to hurt you, but I will if I have to." He'd never been more full of shit in his life. Oh, he'd find out if there was danger to Bear, but even that goal wouldn't make him harm someone so fragile. While he was far from his roots right now, his mama had taught him better. "So tell me the truth."

The angel rolled her eyes. "I have. I haven't lied to you once." She glanced around as his brothers finished packing up, joking as they prepared to ride again. "I see you must be going."

"Didn't you just quit your job?" He moved to the side to allow the meager sun to continue providing her warmth.

She sighed. "Yes." Then she bit her lip. "I worked for a small newspaper, and that job wasn't what I need." For some reason, she still didn't appear too frightened of him.

He studied her, in no hurry. Bear and his family had plenty of cover as they drove toward Tahoe. "I just talked about hurting you."

She leaned back to study his face. "I know, but I don't think you would." Her shrug beneath the light blouse brought his attention to her breasts. They filled out what appeared to be a plain white bra. Filled it out very nicely.

He straightened. "Why not?" Most people looked at him and thought *danger*. Then, if they had the balls, they looked in his eyes and thought *death*.

"I don't know. You protected me from those guys, and every time you touch me, you make yourself be gentle. There's something in you I can see. Something kind and good, even though you have all of those muscles. Are your eyes some sort of genetic mutation?"

"You could say that," he said dryly.

She looked around again. "Where did you put my bag?"

"Somewhere safe." He thought about the contents. "You read several languages?"

"Yes. I majored in different languages and also long-forgotten texts. I love deciphering ancient languages." Her eyes glowed with happiness at just saying the words.

She was stunning. If there was a chance to gain her compliance for the run, his life would be a lot easier. As would hers. "Do you want to come on the run with me?" He wasn't accustomed to asking for anything. Usually, patch bunnies just jumped in front of him when they arrived at a campsite, and he gave them a good time, always hoping to find that mate haunting his dreams. This cute human wasn't his mate, but she was compelling, and she was in need of protection. He could provide that.

One of her finely arched eyebrows rose. "You're inviting me to ride on your motorcycle to the weekend of debauchery?"

Humor ticked through him, and he almost smiled. "Yes."

She studied him, thoughts flitting across her delicate face. Then she pursed her lips. "I am between employment opportunities."

His heart gave one hard thump. What the hell was that about?

"I have never ridden a motorcycle, and I would like to do so before I pass on," she murmured, her hand caressing the leather seat.

He waited her out. She was going with him regardless and would stay right where he wanted until he figured out who she was working for or, more likely, who had used her to get to him. Or who was trying to use her. He didn't know. None of that made sense, so she wasn't going anywhere.

She looked him up and down. "What would my responsibilities be for this weekend?" Now her tone had turned suspicious.

"To obey me and stay out of trouble," he grunted.

"I'm not the obedient type. I've tried, and I just can't do it," she said just as honestly. "Would you expect sex?"

He appreciated her directness. "No."

She reared back. "I'm not familiar with motorcycle club norms, but I assume most women on the back of your bike would be expected to perform."

Perform? Was she from the last century or what? "I don't want a woman who doesn't want me." His voice turned gravelly. His body was pounding, and it was for her. A human. One he would probably crush with a decent hug. What was wrong with him? Maybe he had finally tipped into insanity.

"Oh, I want you. I just didn't know the requirements."

He actually had to fight to keep his expression bland, even though he knew she wanted him. Her color was heightened, her eyes bright, and her legs restless. The scent of her was still on his skin. "Sex is never a requirement with me." What was her game? She seemed innocent and honest, but her questions were odd.

She cleared her throat. "What if I'd like to engage in sex? With you?"

His cock sprang wide awake, hitting his zipper with such force he sucked in air. "If you're on the back of my bike, I'm your only option." He wanted to laugh as well as rip off her clothing. He controlled himself and did neither. "Virgins aren't my thing."

Her face fell. "I can understand that. Yet I don't feel right being on your bike while you go off to find a nonvirgin to play with. You know?"

Was she meaning to throw him in circles? "I guess you're saving yourself for marriage. Or at least a forever somebody," he said, trying to be as gentle as he knew how, even though his hands were itching to tunnel through that thick hair.

"Oh, no." She brightened. "I mean, I would, but I don't have that kind of time." Her smile was both sweet and rueful. "If I were worried about my future, I wouldn't be contemplating such a crazy weekend with you. However, I have no future, so there's nothing to risk."

His gaze narrowed. He felt it. "You have no future?" Damn it, she'd pulled him completely in. She was good. "I'll take care of whatever threat is after you, darlin'. Easy." He meant it. Slight vibrations of fear and sadness wafted from her, as well as a sense of hopelessness. "You aren't going to die."

"I am." Acceptance lit the blue hues of her eyes, pushing out the gray for a moment. "Not because of any person, Garrett. I don't have much time left."

He leaned in, ignoring her sharp intake of breath. Her scent was unique, sweet, and intriguing. There was no hint of illness. "I told you not to lie to me." He leaned back, anger shooting through him. "You're not sick."

"No, I'm not." She pushed a wayward curl out of her eye. "I have a brain tumor. It's inoperable. They gave me eight weeks at first diagnosis, and four of those have passed. Now I have approximately four weeks until my brain gives up the fight and shuts down my body."

He swallowed. There was no hint of deception in her. "You're sure?"

"Yes. I saw three different doctors on my way to California and another when I got here, and the diagnosis is the same. They get so sad when they have to tell me." She shook her head.

Damn it. He wasn't going to let her die. "I have access to doctors you can't imagine. Are you sure you have only a month left?" What was he doing? He didn't have time to deal with a human problem. Yet now, remembering the sound of her falling apart in his arms, he couldn't help it.

"Yes. There are specific markers I'll show when I begin to decline, and I've felt none of them yet. I'm hoping for more than four weeks." She sat straighter. "I planned to head south, so riding with you toward Tahoe sounds like a lovely time. And I would like to engage in sex, if you're amenable."

He nearly exploded. This was pissing him off to a degree that wasn't safe for anybody. He felt energy and looked up to see Sam staring at him from across the lot, sitting on his Harley, his gaze concerned.

From the opposite side of the parking area, Honor moved beyond several motorcycles and stepped up beside Garrett. "I found boots that should be about her size, as well as an extra jacket from Marla. Mine wouldn't fit her." She handed them over, along with a pair of pink socks, and smiled at Dessie, her gaze sharp. "I overheard you say that you have a brain tumor?"

Dessie nodded. "Yes. Sometimes it gives me a headache, but most of the time, I don't know it's there. Well, except sometimes I do get a little dizzy. It's not bad."

Honor leaned in, her nostrils flaring. "I see. Do you want to hurt Garrett, Bear, or Sam? Or any Grizzly?"

"Of course not," Dessie said quietly. "I know you think I'm weird, and I probably am, but I had a dream once about a man who looked like Garrett. That's all. I'd never heard of any of you before today."

Honor exhaled, her shoulders moving. "I get the truth from her. Not that it makes any sense. We can talk more on the way. Sam's itching to get going and make sure Bear's family is all safe." She patted Garrett on the arm and then turned, loping toward Sam's bike and hopping on the back.

Garrett handed the jacket to Dessie. "Put this on." He leaned down to unbuckle her wedges.

She accepted the jacket and held up the soft black leather to read the back. "Property of Grizzlies?" Her startled gaze met his.

"Yes." He sifted through their conversations for a way to explain. "It's a motorcycle club norm. Wearing clothing that states you're property means you're protected by my entire club. Nobody else will bother you. No other man will make a move, and you'll be safe. So you'll wear it."

She mulled over his words and then pulled the jacket over her blouse. "All right."

He finished with the other wedge and slipped the socks up to the bottom of her capris. "Also, I'm on a job for a bit, so you need to do as you're told. There could be some danger. If I tell you to do something, you do it. No questions and no arguments." Her skin was soft against the calloused pads of his fingers, and something dangerous heated inside him.

"Will there be bad people at this event?" She looked down as he slipped on a pair of black leather boots that almost reached her knees.

"Yes. Dangerous and deadly." He shoved the second boot into place, not liking how perfect she looked in the gear. Like a librarian out for a wild time. "Are we clear on the rules?"

"I don't obey well." She didn't seem to be bothered by that.

He *was* bothered by the statement as he zipped up the jacket. "You don't obey and there will be consequences you won't like." He let the beast inside him show.

If anything, her lips twitched. "Okey doke."

A lesson would need to be taught, he could already tell. Fair enough. He wanted her with a hunger that should prompt him to leave her here, showing what a bastard he could really be. "There's something else. I want to help you, and I will. After the run, we're pivoting and heading north to my hometown. There I'll take you to a doctor who can heal you, if it's at all possible. But that's all there is for us. Even if we fuck like rabbits, it's temporary, and we're done when I move on. There's no hope for a future between us." He chose the expletive on purpose to show her who he was, and it wasn't some savior. "Tell me you get me."

"I most certainly agree." She held out her feet, admiring the boots. "Even if your doctor is a miracle worker, there's no future for the two of us."

Should it piss him off that she was so accepting of that fact? "Why the hell not?" God, he was a moron for asking the question. He knew why not—she was human, and he wasn't anywhere close. But she didn't know that.

"Don't be silly, Garrett." She gestured around them at the rough-and-tumble riders. The woman didn't even know that most of them were grizzly bear shifters, but her instincts were spot on.

He settled her back and straddled the bike. "Arms around my waist." She complied, and her small thighs pressed against his. Fire speared through him, and he fought a groan. Maybe he was the one who should see a doctor. His other hand snagged a helmet out of the air thrown by a Grizzly riding by. "Just plaster your body to mine and let me move us both." He handed it back to her. "Put this on."

She obeyed and then settled closer against him, doing as he'd ordered. Her hands were tentative and clamped together near his waist.

He unclenched them and pressed them against his shirt beneath his jacket, her touch almost undoing him. Then he concentrated on the road and pulled out with his brothers.

This ride might actually kill him.

Chapter Five

Dessie had thought she was free before, but she'd been wrong. There was no sense of freedom as strong as riding with Garrett on a motorcycle down an open road. The wind blew into her, and she snuggled against him, feeling wild and safe at the same time. Exhilaration rode her, and for the first time, she knew it was okay to die.

No matter how good Garrett's doctor might be, Dessie had seen the medical images of the mass in her head. It had tendrils that extended in every direction, and the only way to take it out was to remove her entire brain.

One of the reasons she'd agreed to the ride was to avoid the man who had probably been following her. He'd been stocky and bald, and she'd seen him too many times. There was something not quite right about him. Although he hadn't approached her, so perhaps she'd just read him wrong. But why had he been following her?

At the moment, she no longer cared.

She turned her head to the side, her ear picking up Garrett's strong heartbeat through his leather jacket. Strong and sure, just like him. Then she closed her eyes so she could just feel and was drawn back into the night. That night when she met him—or somebody who looked just like him.

It was a time of mystery, a time of depth. The sea crashed mercilessly beneath the cliffs, spraying onto the rocks with dark glee. Oh, it was a time of destiny.

She glanced at the rising moon to gauge the time. A time of destiny? Nope. It was just another darn Tuesday. A chuckle escaped her at her fanciful thoughts, no doubt brought on by a fantasy story she and a couple of the other girls had dreamed up that morning at breakfast before the headmistress had arrived in the dining hall.

Now Dessie sat on an ancient stone bench only a few yards from a drop-off to the churning sea far below. It was an area off-limits to everyone in the enclave, but sometimes, she needed space. Trees behind the forgotten spot hid her from view, although she'd need to report for bedtime soon.

Her lessons had been unusually tough that day, and her body hurt. Even her brain ached. Worse yet, her heart hurt. Right in her chest, pain radiated out, proving to her that freedom was only an illusion. She'd turned twenty and had now graduated. It was time for her to venture into the world and find her way.

But she'd been chosen.

Why? She wasn't remarkable in any way compared to some of the other girls. In fact, it had taken her two extra years to graduate, but she'd shown potential with languages, so two years had been added on. She'd completed them without complaint and now wanted freedom. A life.

Yet she'd been chosen for four more years of education, so she could attain the equivalent of a college degree and study the languages of the world. Because she had an aptitude.

There was no refusing.

She was trapped, and she could barely breathe. There was no way out of the enclave without permission, which for her had never been granted. She felt like a cat trapped in a world of turtles. Nobody wanted to play, and there was no laughter. Not really. Hopelessness was a new feeling, and one she didn't much appreciate. Plus, she was always exhausted. No matter how much sleep she got, she was still tired. It was the gloomy weather. Had to be. What if she finished her four years and they tacked on three more? Or ten more? Perhaps she'd never leave the island.

Fog rolled up from far below, its fingers crawling over the rocky ground and winding up into the trees.

A chill arrived with the uncoiling mass, and she shivered, watching the moon through the haze. She couldn't stay here another four years. Her legs wobbled, but she stood, inching toward the edge. Perhaps there was a way down the cliff. Even though this was her spot, her very secret place, she'd never ventured too close to the edge. The ground softened as she approached.

Her feet slipped. She regained her balance, slowing her pace. There was only a foot to go. She could peer down into the darkness.

The ground moved away, and a strong hand grabbed her, flinging her back to the bench. She hit hard, the breath whooshing from her lungs. Her eyes widened.

A man stood between her and the cliff, the fog swirling around his legs, his eyes a devastating metallic gray.

She struggled to breathe, unsure if it was the impact or the vision that stole her breath.

He settled his stance, his chin lowering. Dark hair fell to his shoulders in waves. His bone structure was masculine and rugged, yet sharp and somehow dangerous-looking. He stood at least six and a half feet tall, and his body was one long line of muscle. Power emanated from him and glittered in those impossible gray eyes. "Do not." When he spoke, his voice was a guttural rumble.

She couldn't move.

For the longest time, she could do nothing but stare at him. Then he slowly faded away.

For days, for months, for years, she'd convinced herself that she'd fallen asleep on the bench. Now, holding Garrett, she wasn't certain. He was exactly the image she'd seen that night. How was it possible? That was the true reason she'd agreed to accompany him on this glorious trip. While she craved adventure and a sense of life, it was that dream that had her pressing her palms against his rock-hard and surprisingly warm abdomen.

If it was a dream.

She was shaken out of her memories as he pulled into a small camping area with the rest of the riders. They all cut their engines, and the silence pounded in her head. Reluctantly, she released him and pulled off her helmet.

"You'll be sore." He reached back and helped her off the bike, holding her arm until she gained her balance.

Her butt and thighs ached. "I am." Then she looked around at the myriad of picnic tables, and her stomach rumbled.

He swung off the bike with a catlike grace, standing so tall he blocked the entire camp from her view. "We'll stop here for a quick dinner and get back on the road so we can make camp before it's too late." His gaze was veiled, his tone mild.

For some reason, she shivered. If the man in her dream wasn't real, then she'd just driven to the middle of nowhere with a broad and muscled man she didn't know. At all.

What had she been thinking?

* * * *

The drive to the campground had been pure torture with the tiny human all but wrapped around him. Garrett gently took Dessie's hand and led her to a picnic table near an outcropping of rocks. The wind rustled fall bushes with surprisingly full red flowers. "We'll eat here." He had to get away from her, if only for a few minutes. His abdomen remained heated, as if he could feel her small hands still pressed against him.

She swallowed and looked around.

Honor rescued her. "The outhouses are this way." She tucked her arm through Dessie's, and they made their way along the rocks toward wooden outbuildings.

Sam tossed riding gloves on the table, but there was no heat in his tone as he said, "What are you thinking?" His thick hair ruffled in the light breeze.

"I don't know." Garrett scouted the entire area, looking for threats. "There's something about her I can't figure out."

Sam's gaze flicked around as well, and then he settled, sitting on the bench. "You might have to be a little more firm in questioning her. I know—giving her an orgasm and then making sure your mark has a safe helmet is one way to go. Perhaps you'd like to continue and wrap her up in a blanket and snuggle her to sleep? Read her a bedtime story?"

"Shut up," Garrett said, also without heat.

Sam lifted sandwiches out of a cooler.

"Uncle Garrett!" a small child yelled, running full force toward him from the parking area, her hair flying in the breeze.

He crouched and patiently waited until she smashed into him, catching her arms at the last second so she wouldn't be hurt. Then he lifted, spun her around, and settled her at his hip. "How was the ride, Lyssa?"

Her curly hair was a combination of wild colors down her back, mostly dark brown with all sorts of natural highlights. Her eyes were a violet-blue, and her features fragile. Her bottom lip pouted out. "The movie quitted. We only got to watch Little Kitty *three* times." It figured her brothers had let her choose the movie. Although three times had been pushing it.

Garrett watched the other toddlers make their way toward him. The three-year-olds were triplets, their parents a witch and a grizzly bear shifter who had some dragon blood in him. Immortals could have lineages from different species, but their inherent nature could only be of one. Lyssa was all witch, like her mother. "Here come your brothers."

She turned to watch them. "Tack brung my kitty."

"He did." Garrett watched the shaggy-haired boy trudge along, kicking every rock on the way but being careful of the stuffed animal. He was his father's son, all bear shifter. Stocky and strong already.

The final triplet, Elijah, seemed to have inherited the dragon traits. Elijah stalked to the side and slightly behind his brother, his young gaze scanning the area, his hands free. Garrett had no doubt Elijah had shoved the kitten into Tackle's hands, thus leaving his own hands free to defend if necessary. The trait was inherent in the kid—he'd never been attacked. None of them had.

Tackle reached them and handed his sister the toy. Then his gaze caught on Sam setting out food, and he jumped that way, reaching for a sandwich.

Elijah was slower to reach them. "Did runnin' hurt your foot?" he asked his sister.

"No." Lyssa cuddled her kitten closer and laid her head against Garrett's chest. "It don't hurt no more, Jah. It's okay." She looked up at Garrett. "I bumped my toe, and I cried."

"I always cry when I bump my toe," Garrett agreed.

The little girl grinned and kissed his whiskered chin.

"Is that my girl kissing some yucky guy?" Bear stalked their way, carrying two coolers and appearing as powerful as the leader of the entire Grizzly nation should.

"He's not yucky," Lyssa yelled, kissing Garrett again.

Elijah shrugged as if he didn't agree and walked over to accept a sandwich from Sam.

Bear dropped the coolers by Sam and straightened, looking like a full-on bear shifter. Shaggy brown hair almost reached his shoulders, which were wide by anyone's standards. His chest was a barrel, his hands made for breaking pretty much anything. At the moment, his honey-brown eyes were frustrated. "The movie died. Completely. They sang at the top of their lungs for a hundred miles. A hundred." Without looking, he snatched the beer Sam tossed to him right out of the air.

"Where's Nessa?" Garrett asked, turning to look. His gaze caught on Dessie, who stood near Sam, her eyes wide on Garrett.

She looked shocked, actually. Seeing him with the toddlers probably was a surprise.

"Here." Nessa strode up behind Dessie and Honor, no doubt having just used the facilities. The witch had long black hair, violet eyes, and an amusing penchant for creating fire out of the air and throwing it at Bear. "At the top of their lungs, Sam." She held out a hand for a beer.

Garrett strode toward them, easily holding the toddler. He made the introductions.

Bear's nostrils flared. "She's human."

Dessie frowned.

Nessa slapped her mate's arm. "It's nice to meet you, Dessie." She held out a hand.

Garrett's phone buzzed, and he tugged it from his pocket, looking down. "I have to take this." Handing the toddler to Bear, he strode past the rocks and kept going as he answered the video call. "Garrett."

"Where are you?" Dage Kayrs asked, gaze steady on the camera.

Garrett gave their location. "We'll be at the camp in a few hours." He leaned against a rock and studied his uncle. "Is all good?"

The king's silver eyes revealed nothing. His black hair was pulled away from his face, and he looked closer to thirty than centuries old. "That's up to you, G. If you can't negotiate peace with the feline shifters at this meeting, we're going to war with them. I like the cats as allies, not enemies."

Not for the first time, Garrett felt loyalties pulling him in opposite directions. The feline nation was angry with the vampires and demons because of Garrett and his blood brothers. Not the Grizzlies, but brothers forged in blood and bone and a shitload of pain, whose mission was to save the world. Seven immortals. In order to prepare themselves, they'd altered the known physics of this world, and the cats were pissed. They had been for years, and they were about to make a move. "I'll take care of it."

"Afterward, I'm calling you home. You've ridden with the Grizzlies for years, and I know you thought you'd find your mate with them. But enough is enough. You're needed here with family. The world is heating up, as you know. We're about to go to war again, even if the feline nation doesn't attack."

"I'm aware," Garrett said, the idea of leaving the Grizzlies feeling like a punch to the gut. They were his family, too. And he hadn't found her yet. His mate. The one he dreamed about. His gaze lifted to see Dessie sitting on the ground braiding Lyssa's hair with the little girl snuggled in her lap. Tackle sat next to her, his elbow on her thigh as he ate. Elijah stood nearby, watching her carefully, almost seeming to be guarding Dessie as much as his sister.

A low tug pulled at Garrett's chest. "All right, Dage. I'm coming home, and I'm bringing a friend. She needs to see the best doctor we have, which means your mate." He clicked off.

Chapter Six

Dessie stretched beneath the sleeping bag, surprised at how comfortable the ground could be, even though she was freezing. In fact, with gathered leaves beneath the bag, it was more pleasant than the thin mattress she'd slept on at school for so long. The stars twinkled above her. She tried to count them, but her eyelids grew heavy. The autumn air swept across her skin, chilling her even more, but she didn't care.

The stars were too beautiful.

They'd reached the charming meadow in time to unpack and set up in an area next to outcroppings like the ones earlier. A fire roared in the middle of their small camp, and Grizzly members had bedded down all around them. Other groups could be heard in the distance, each with their own fire. She noted absently that anybody who wanted to get to her would have to go through the entire Grizzly encampment.

Garrett had helped her get settled in and then had left with Sam to cut through a group of pine trees, saying he had a meeting.

What kind of meeting did one take after dark?

She stared at the stars again, shivering until her teeth chattered. Was he with a woman? If so, why had he brought her along? Jealousy felt like fire ants beneath her skin, and she didn't like it. She took several deep breaths and calmed her heart rate, as she'd been taught. This was an adventure, even if Garrett abandoned her. She deserved an adventure before she died. Plus, she'd been warned by Garrett that many of the people around them were dangerous, so perhaps staying safe in the sleeping bag was what she wanted.

She missed him. How silly was that? She'd known him for less than a day, but she felt as if he'd been with her for years, ever since the dream. Riding behind him on his bike and touching him for so many hours had been more than she'd ever hoped to feel. He was more frightening than her dream man, and she knew he'd only brought her along because he wanted to solve the mystery of her initial statement to him, but even so, he'd been both kind and gentle with her so far.

And that orgasm. She'd never imagined feeling so close to the sun, but she'd reached that point. Not the heat but the absolute brilliance of the moment.

She wanted that feeling again, and right now, she felt bereft. A line from a Poe poem filtered through her mind. A dream. The heartbreak of life. She'd been heartbroken when she'd learned of her condition. Each time she'd been examined by a new doctor, she'd felt a slim hope. No more. Acceptance was the final step of any seven-step program, and she had reached that state.

Even so, her heart sped up as Garrett emerged from the copse of trees. She didn't even know his surname. The firelight cast his features into contrasting light and darkness, so many sharp crooks and angles. His steps were sure, and the play of his muscles graceful, leaving no doubt of the predator living within his skin.

Her breath stuttered, and all poetry flew out of her head. The brilliant masters she'd studied for so long had never viewed this man. Never. Not one of their lovely lines neared the beauty inherent in him. Was he an angel? A dark one to take her to Heaven? A fleeting thought and a silly one. Even so.

He toed off his boots, the metallic glow of his eyes piercing the darkness. "You're cold." His shirt came next, revealing raw muscle highlighted by the fire. In one smooth motion, he removed his jeans, opened the sleeping bag and slid inside, bringing warmth and the scent of leather and motor oil. "Should've put you closer to the fire."

She turned toward him, drawn by his warmth. His hand cupped her head.

"I should be afraid of you," she whispered.

"You most certainly should." A flash of his white teeth lit the darkness.

"Is your business concluded?" His tempting flesh was so near, and she'd never touched a man.

He sighed, his breath smelling of fine whiskey. "Not even close." A shriek shattered the evening, and it took her a second to realize it was a cry of ecstasy. He grinned. "There's some playing going on two camps over. We tried to put you and the kids where you wouldn't see too much, but I can't control sound waves."

"I don't mind." She tentatively reached out and flattened her hand over his heart. His skin was heated and so silky, and the muscles beneath her palm made her stomach flutter. "Are you finished considering me a threat?"

"You're definitely a threat." He gently pushed a piece of hair away from her face. "Where did you get that knife, Destiny?"

Oh. This was an interrogation. Fascinating. She'd expected pain and fear. Not muscles and warmth. "You don't like to hurt people smaller than you, do you?"

"No, and I really don't like to harm females." His fingers curled around her neck.

She tried to swallow, but her throat forgot how. "Seduction is your weapon?" Not that she cared. When one faced death in less than four weeks, being seduced sounded like a fine outcome.

A slow chill wandered down her spine, surprising her. The entire day had felt like another dream. But this was real. She was in a sleeping bag with a man. Not just a man. This one was twice her size and heavily muscled.

He propped himself up on one elbow to watch her. Even the moonlight seemed to gravitate to him, caressing his skin and illuminating those high cheekbones, while leaving the darkened hollows at peace. "You okay?" he rumbled.

She bit her lip. "I'm realizing my precarious position."

His smile was slow, and his chest moved as if he'd chuckled. "Just now?"

"Yes." She swallowed, acutely aware of the heat rolling off him. At least she'd stopped shaking. "I became caught up in the romance of racing away from all of my problems, and there was such an incredible feeling of freedom riding behind you." But now conflicting feelings caught her. She wanted to know more about him, and she wanted to touch him. To have him touch her again. Yet what was she thinking? She might only have a month left to live, but she wanted those four weeks. He was much stronger than her, and if he wanted to hurt her, he'd probably succeed.

"We can go to sleep if you wish." His legs were bare and her feet cold, but she remained still.

The urge to touch him was a physical burn. "Do you believe me? About the dream?"

"No," he said softly.

She blinked. "You don't?"

"It doesn't make sense to me, so no, I don't believe you once had a dream about me." He didn't sound too concerned.

Her spine stiffened. "You think I'm a liar, and you still brought me on this trip?" The truth hit her. "You brought me *because* you think I'm lying." Wait a minute. It had been her decision to accompany him. Hadn't it?

"Listen. Your reaction to seeing me was genuine. I'm definitely in your head—I just have to figure out how I got there. I think somebody is taking advantage of you to get to me."

Heat flushed up her neck. Wait a minute. He not only didn't believe her but thought she was some simpleton who'd been manipulated? The insult awoke her normally dormant temper. "That's it." She started to shimmy out of the bag.

She didn't make it.

One broad hand gripped her hip and pulled her right back in with a sharp tug. She lost her balance and fell, surprised when his free hand caught her head, cupping it. "What's your plan here, princess?" He sounded even more amused.

Her breath deserted her. "I'm leaving."

"No, you're not," he said softly. Too softly.

She shivered. "You can't make me stay here."

He didn't bother to answer.

"I'll scream," she threatened.

"Go ahead." His fingers threaded through her hair. "I'm not going to hurt you, Dessie. But you are going to answer some questions."

That's what he thought. She bunched her fist and punched him right in the throat. But instead of coughing or pulling back, he just looked at her. All of her fingers ached. What was his neck made of, cement?

"Hitting isn't nice," he murmured, his gaze dropping to her mouth.

She shifted to clap both of his ears between her palms, but he rolled her over onto her back before she could make contact. One of his hands pressed against her abdomen, holding her in place.

"Knock it off." He looked down at her. "Why do you have a fake ID?"

"I don't," she said. "My license is authentic." At least it was supposed to be authentic. "Why do you think it's a fake?"

"I think it's probably authentic." His hand felt heavy on her stomach. "But you don't sound like you're from Texas."

"Well, I am. Now, if you want me to answer any more questions, I suggest you let me out of this bag." She tried to sound as proper as possible.

"Where do you think you're going?" He looked around. "In every direction there are camps with heavy drinking and partying going on. By leaving, you're either going to freeze to death, or you're going to walk right into danger. How is that a plan?" He still didn't move his hand.

"I already walked into danger," she muttered.

His grin was a quick flash of teeth. "Yeah, baby, you did."

She shivered from head to toe at his tone. His sexy, dangerous, intriguing tone. Why did she respond to him like this? She turned her head to see his face better. "If I said I'd take my chances, would you let me go?"

"No."

She huffed out a breath.

"Why don't you have a Texan accent?" he asked.

"I grew up in a boarding school," she said quietly. "My parents died when I was young, and my father's sister acquired custody of me. She sent me to boarding school the second I was eligible, at six years old. It wasn't as bad as it might sound." She tried to keep her voice flat, but the hurt still flared hot and bright.

The hand at her nape began to knead gently. "I'm sorry, Dessie."

She shrugged, but the hurt remained. "I liked school." Although it took forever for them to set her free.

"What boarding school?" he asked.

Apparently the interrogation had begun. She didn't see much of a reason to be stubborn. "I attended Chapel Hill for Girls for grade school and then junior high. After that I attended Stoneton Hills Academy for high school as well as college." She had worked hard but had yearned so badly to be home in Texas.

"Where are those schools located?"

"Oh, no." She pushed his hard chest, not surprised when he didn't move. "You have to be fair. What's your last name?"

He studied her for a moment. "Kayrs."

She blinked. "Is that Gaelic?"

"It's a lot of things," he said. "Location of the schools?"

"First New Hampshire and then Maine," she said. "What do you do for a living?"

His thumb caressed her jawline even as he continued cupping her head. "The Grizzlies own a garage, and I work on bikes. Sometimes cars. For now." He leaned down and kissed her nose. "Why are you a virgin?"

She jolted. That was direct. "It was an all-girls school with a university component, and I've only been out on my own for a brief time. A doctor at the school was the first to diagnose my tumor." Which was probably why they'd finally allowed her to leave. Oh, she knew they liked taking her aunt's money, but they had to graduate her sometime.

"Why didn't you go home to Texas?"

"There was nothing there for me with my parents both dead." She frowned. "Apparently whatever money my father left has been tied up in a trust all these years." She rubbed her chest, feeling oddly safe for the first time in years. She should be terrified of him, but what scared her more was dying without ever living at all. This was her one chance. "Garrett? Do you want to kiss me again?"

"Yes."

She reached up and slid her hand over his chest. Even his neck felt strong. "I'd like that. One kiss."

Chapter Seven

Garrett barely heard her soft words. The woman was a beguiling mixture of laughter, innocence, and spunk. He would've bet his lips had rusted into a permanent frown, but she'd made him not only smile but chuckle several times in one day. A kiss? Yeah. He could give her that.

Her beguiling gaze skimmed to his mouth.

He leaned down and pressed his lips to hers. He wasn't a gentle male, but he'd try to be for her. Her lips were soft, full, and already curving beneath his. She was a fast learner.

She made a little sound in the back of her throat, pouring fire throughout his body. Every nerve lit up, her essence spreading through him, searing his torso, arms and legs, even his hands and feet. It was as if she lived inside him for the briefest of moments, filling him with light.

It wasn't possible that this tiny human could make him feel so much—he'd been going dead inside for years. Oh, he'd planned to do his duty, his many duties, but joy had left him long ago. The dreams that plagued him had leeched parts of him away.

Now he felt alive again. It didn't make sense, but he needed to protect her. Part of him desperately wanted to shield her. The other part, the primal being at his core, wanted to lose himself in her.

Her hands slid up to tangle in his hair.

He broke the kiss and slipped his hand beneath her shirt to flatten across her abdomen. Somebody had apparently given her a pair of leggings and a cotton shirt to sleep in. It was a good thing he'd asked Honor to take care of her—he owed her big-time. Dessie's skin felt impossibly soft against his work-roughened palms. He couldn't mistake her sharp intake of breath.

She leaned up and nipped his neck. "I love your neck. It's so strong." The need in her voice spurred the beast inside him.

Unfortunately, he never went into a situation blind, and now he wanted to protect her as much as himself. "Why do you have a tactical knife with your name engraved on it?" He leaned down and nuzzled his way from her neck to her clavicle, which he licked.

She shivered and angled her head to give him better access. "Professor Samuelson handcrafts them and gives them to every graduate." She sighed and arched against him, effectively pushing his hand closer to her breasts. "He says we've been protected by the school for so long that we don't understand the outside world and that every girl needs a knife."

Garrett gave in to temptation and set his palms on the undersides of her breasts, letting the fullness warm his fingers. He couldn't disagree with Professor Samuelson. "Did he teach you to use it?"

"Yes." She arched against his fingers, her nails scratching down his bare chest. "He also joked that he didn't want us to stab ourselves. The college is so small that he can hand-engrave the silver for every graduate. Oh, and he also sells them across the world and is the wealthiest professor at the college. But he loves teaching."

"What does he teach?" Garrett would need to do a deep dive on the good professor once he heard from Chalton about Dessie.

"Art, sculpture, and art history," Dessie said, her voice breathless.

He caressed one breast, cupping it. Her soft moan had him struggling to stay in control. He encircled her nipple and then pinched, at first softly and then with more pressure as he heard her heartbeat increase. At the same time, he slid his other hand down into her leggings, tapping her mound but not coming close to where she needed his touch.

"Garrett," she moaned, her reactions so honest his chest hurt.

"How good are you with the knife, kitten?" he murmured, sinking his teeth into her earlobe. His fangs started to drop, and he shoved them ruthlessly back up. The last thing he needed was her learning about immortals.

"I'm okay," she whispered, her voice sounding distant. Her little body tried to gyrate against his hand, so he flicked a quick finger along her clit and then moved on to her thigh.

Her whimper of frustration had him smiling against her skin, although he felt the same way. His cock throbbed, and the blood rushed through his veins too fast to hear. "How did you end up in California?"

"I've been seeing different doctors in the hopes of a better diagnosis," she said, widening her legs and obviously taking matters into her own hands as she tentatively scraped her nails down his chest to his abdomen, where she began tracing each ridge. "The latest one was in California. Could you stop interrogating me now?"

"Sweetheart? This is nowhere near an interrogation." He slid one finger inside her and was suddenly close to heaven again. Just like earlier. He leaned up and kissed her again, going deep, taking everything she was. Her sweet taste, strawberries mixed with oranges and something so pure it'd never leave him, propelled him right into full-on addiction.

He shouldn't be getting this close to her. He couldn't get lost in a woman, a human woman, and he knew it. His fate lay elsewhere.

Her small hand slipped beneath his boxers, the movement both cautious and curious.

He jolted, then froze. His heart pounded, and thunder bellowed in his ears. Her innocence and misplaced trust thickened his blood and burned electrical sparks across his skin. He removed his hand from her panties, manacled her wrist, and drew her hand out of his shorts. "Take a minute." Then he leaned his forehead against hers, trying to control his breathing. "This isn't what you want."

She clutched his hip, her eyes wide. "This is exactly what I want."

He gripped her jaw between his thumb and forefinger, leaning back to see her eyes. "Listen. You don't know me. I'm a killer, baby. I won't hurt you, but I'm not the kind of guy you want to waste yourself on. You deserve better. A house, kids, a full life with peace."

Her eyes filled. "I don't have a full life ahead of me, Garrett. I've seen five doctors, all specialists. I want to feel and live every moment during the time I have left."

"I know better doctors than you do, and I'm going to help you." His cock jumped against her thigh, harder than steel. "Let me make you feel good but stop pushing me to go further."

Instead of agreeing or even thanking him for being so fucking chivalrous, she rolled her eyes. "You're not in charge. The last thing I need is for some oversized biker to tell me what's good for me. I'm not afraid of you, Garrett Kayrs. I may not know a lot about men, but I can tell you want me." With that last statement, she reached for his dick again.

* * * *

Her body felt like it belonged to somebody else. To a wild and free, not to mention healthy, woman. Dessie ignored Garrett's warning as her hand cupped him, or part of him. He was unbelievably hard.

"Not gonna warn you again, kitten." His low rumble was so soft it made her shiver.

Even so, when his penis bucked against her hand, she smiled. Yes. He wanted her, and she wanted him, and it was time to see what the big deal about sex was. "I don't think your body is listening to you."

"I've noticed. But you *are* going to listen to me." In one lightning-quick movement, he had her up and flipped over onto her stomach.

The breath whooshed out of her lungs. Then his hand descended on her butt.

Hard.

"Hey," she protested, shoving her arms out to turn herself back over.

He almost casually slid a muscled leg over both of hers, effectively pinning her. Then he shoved the bag down to their thighs, and chilled air kissed her skin. "You're lucky I think you're cute." He smacked her butt several times, spreading warmth through her entire lower body. "Most people don't get even one warning from me—you've had two." He swatted her again, his palm spanning her entire bottom.

Pain lashed through her, followed by an intense wave of heat. Her sex clenched, and mini-explosions detonated inside her. Nerves she didn't know she had sparked to life throughout her body. "Stop it." Her voice was weak.

"You sure you want me to stop?" Dark amusement and need lowered his voice to guttural. He gave her two hard smacks on both cheeks to punctuate his question.

No. She wasn't sure at all. What was wrong with her? Her body shouldn't react like this. Shouldn't be even more aroused. "Yes. Stop it?"

He swatted her right in the middle, fanning more flames. "Tell me you understand me. That when I tell you to stop something, you do it."

She blinked, trying to get her brain back in charge. Even so, her traitorous body arched into his scalding palm. "I don't require you to protect me from myself." Her voice was breathy with unbelievable need.

"You need more protection than anybody I've ever met." To prove it, he smacked her again. Then again. "Tell me you get me."

"Fine. I get you." She'd wear his palm prints for at least a day, if not two. Why did that arouse her?

He rubbed her abused butt, and she moaned, needing more. What, she wasn't sure. "What do you get, kitten?" he asked.

She blinked. "Um, I'll listen to you."

"It's a good start. How about you just obey me? Life will go a lot easier if you choose that path now." His hand was driving her crazy, and he probably knew it.

She tried to swallow, but her entire nervous system was focused on the pleasure of his rough caress. "I don't intend to obey anybody."

He swatted her, and she cried out, her breath catching when the pain burst into pleasure. "Then you're going to have a rough couple of weeks until we get your health figured out." His hand pressed against her skin as if keeping the heat inside her. "I'm going to help you, and you're not going to make my life more difficult while I do it. Period."

She couldn't make that promise. It would be a lie. "Maybe I'll just leave." Her stomach rolled over. Not one part of her wanted to leave him.

He was quiet for a moment and then gently turned her onto her back. His metallic gray eyes glittered through the night. "No."

Her heart snagged. "No?"

"No. Just decided. You're not going anywhere until you see my doctors." He gently gripped her chin, stopping her automatic protest. "You have a choice right now. You can stay with me, on the back of my bike and in my bed, or you can sleep in your own bag closer to the fire and ride in one of the SUVs when we head out in the morning. I'll take care of you either way, but make sure you know what you want. I'm not having this discussion again."

Her mouth opened, and her brain fuzzed.

He moved his thumb across her mouth. "If you need, you can take the night to decide. But I do want your answer first thing tomorrow."

She knew her answer. "I want to stay with you." That commitment was more terrifying and exhilarating than all of the experiences she'd been trying to shove into what little life she had left. "But I can't promise to do what you say all the time."

He leaned down and kissed her. "So long as you understand that, if you disobey me, there will be consequences."

"I understand," she said breathlessly, her butt on fire.

He chuckled. "They won't be pleasurable like this was, trust me." He nibbled her jawline.

She shifted her body restlessly, a near-pounding between her legs. "Garrett? I need, um, something..."

"I know." He licked down her neck and sucked one breast into his mouth, lashing her nipple through the thin material of her top. He shoved up the cotton and kissed his way down her torso and abdomen, smoothly sliding her leggings and panties down her legs with one hand. He tugged them off.

She couldn't breathe. His mouth was devastating. Then he kissed her, right on her sex. Pleasure burst through her, followed by panic. What was he doing? She grabbed his hair to pull him up.

He growled against her. She stilled. Vibrations spiraled from his mouth through her. "I don't understand." The pressure inside her might kill her.

"You will." He licked her and then seemed to devour her. His mouth, his tongue, his fingers all went at her, propelling her right into the second orgasm of her life. She cried out, shuddering, as extreme pleasure whipped through her. Finally, she settled, but he didn't stop.

Not even close.

He added the scrape of teeth to the sensations bombarding her, taking complete control of her body. She was helpless against him, and even her brain shut down. She didn't feel the chill of the night any longer. Only such raw pleasure that she had no choice but to ride it.

She tipped over into another climax with a rough cry and shoved her hand against her mouth. Her body bucked against him. He cupped her butt with one strong hand, forcing her even closer to his mouth.

His whiskers were abrasive on her thighs, only adding to the sensations.

She desperately tangled her fingers in his thick hair as he continued with his onslaught. No way could she orgasm again. "Garrett."

He ignored her and sank his teeth into her thigh before returning and sucking her clitoris into his mouth.

Her head thrashed back and forth on the small pillow. She'd had no idea this was even possible, but she was climbing again. So high and so out of control. His rough hand squeezed her abused butt, and she broke wildly. This time she did so silently, her mouth open in a muted scream.

Finally, he paused to look up at her, his smile wicked.

Then he went at her again.

Chapter Eight

Garrett felt like his entire body had been put through a meat grinder as he signaled for two of the prospects to keep an eye on the sleeping woman in his bag. A fragrant patch of wildflowers bloomed nearby, and he'd almost picked her a bouquet. He was losing his mind.

He'd worn her out without taking advantage, and his cock was pissed. No doubt his balls were a hideous blue. Although dawn was just now streaking pink across the sky, somebody had already stoked the three fires, and he circled one to reach Bear and Sam. They sat at a picnic table near the tent where Nessa and the triplets still slept.

He arrived at the table. "Stop giving me that look."

Bear crossed his massive arms. "Stop being a fucking moron."

Garrett's temper stirred. After a night with Destiny Applegate, he felt marked. Her scent and taste were all over him, and he wanted more of her. All of her. It had taken every bit of his impressive self-control to keep from fucking her silly the night before. "You've been on me for years to stop picking up dangerous females to ride on my bike, and now you're pissed I have a nice girl? Make up your mind."

Bear rolled his honey-brown eyes. "At least I understood the vipers you picked up. If your dreams are true, your mate is a dangerous chick who will try to kill you. But this human female? She's helpless and has no business being in the middle of a bunch of shifters. Humans can't find out about us. What if one of the cubs gets drunk and shifts into a bear? We'd have to kill her."

Garrett rose to his full height, his chest expanding. "Nobody touches her. Period."

Sam's dark eyebrows lifted. "Wow. That was a full-on Kayrs alpha male movement there." He looked at Bear. "And you're so full of crap. You'd never hurt a human female."

Bear lowered his chin. "Maybe not, but I'd still lock her down in Grizzly territory so she couldn't inform the rest of the world about us."

Sam nodded. "As would I. She's human, G. You can't mate her."

Like he didn't know that. "No shit."

Bear grunted. "That's it. We knew he'd go and lose his mind at some point. Here it is. Brain mush."

Garrett nearly swung at the Grizzly leader. "I just want to help her."

Bear snorted. "Yeah. I heard her screaming your name last night. You sure as shit helped her. Like, at least five times."

"You're about to get hit, Bear." Garrett once again gave a warning when he just wanted to act. Was he mellowing? Damn it.

A loud ding came from Sam's backpack, and he drew out a tablet, then glanced down. "It's Chalton."

"He said he'd call. Why do you have my tablet?" Garrett moved around the table and shoved himself between the two males, taking the tablet and standing it up on the worn wood. Chalton Reese showed up, his blond hair ruffled and his eyes serious.

Sam shrugged. "Honor borrowed it to watch a movie last night. Figured you were too busy to ask."

Garrett ignored the dig. "Hey, Chalton. Thanks for calling in."

Chalton nodded. As the chief computer expert for the entire Realm, a coalition of immortal species, he no doubt didn't have time to conduct background checks on a human. But he and Garrett went way back. "I just have a moment. A deep dive on Destiny Applegate was kind of interesting, to be honest."

Garrett sat straighter. "How so?"

"The info you texted about her boarding schools is accurate. So far, everything checks out, but I'll keep looking. Also, the info you sent about her family is true. Parents died and left a fortune, most of which is hers. The loving aunt has put out a hit on the girl." He said it so casually that it took Garrett a second to compute. "Went with one human guy, paid cash, and he hired two buddies. They're on your tail. In fact, the hitman's in Tahoe and should be arriving at the campsite any minute, although I assume it'll take some time to find you all. I'm sending his picture to your phone."

Garrett's phone buzzed. He didn't ask how Chalton had found out about the hit, or how he knew the location of the human hitman. Chalton was the best, and his equipment far outclassed any human computer. "Thanks."

"Sure." Chalton looked over his shoulder and then refocused. "Your girl also seems to have a death wish. I have records of her hang gliding, jumping out of airplanes, bungee jumping, and getting arrested, or rather getting caught up in a bar fight."

The woman was trying to condense a lifetime of risk and living into a few months. Garrett sighed. "Thanks." He was going to put an end to that right now.

Chalton cleared his throat. "I'm also sending all of Destiny's medical records. It appears that she's traveled west since graduation and has seen different medical experts along the way. Before you ask, I've sent the records to our doctors as well. Figured you'd want their input."

Garrett nodded. His friend was the best. "Does it all look legit?"

"The credentials for the doctors all check out so far, but a deeper dive is probably needed," Chalton said. "Do you want me to have a Realm team investigate?"

Bear shook his head. "No. This is Grizzly business."

Chalton's facial expression didn't change, but his eyes sparked. "If this has to do with the nephew of the King of the Realm, I believe it is Realm business. All due respect."

"He's a Grizzly," Bear growled.

"He's probably the Realm's future king," Chalton snapped.

Sam chuckled. "He's also a member of the Seven."

Garrett failed to see the humor. Could one guy have multiple allegiances? Once again, conflicting loyalties pulled him in three directions.

Chalton's eyes narrowed. "Are we finally going to talk about the Seven?"

"No," Garrett said shortly. The Seven ritual had been pure hell; it was a shock that any of them had survived. The plus side was that the ordeal had fused the bones in each of their torsos into an impenetrable shield. The downside was that their enemy had fused his entire body into a shield and couldn't be killed by any weapon. He was Ulric, the leader of the Cyst, the religious arm of the Kurjan people, who were the Realm's enemies. Ulric was currently in a prison worlds away, but it was believed he'd be breaking free at some point. "Chalton? Do you have a couple of scouts you can send out?"

"Consider it done." Chalton typed rapidly. "By the way, I'm supposed to tell you to call your mother." He clicked off.

Bear crossed his arms.

Garrett shut down the tablet. "We don't have time to hunt down a lead like that. Let the scouts do it."

Bear pushed away from the table and stood. "Fine."

* * * *

After a lovely breakfast and then a terrific lunch, at which the triplets entertained her with stories about each other, most often crazy ones about Tackle, Dessie still couldn't get settled. She helped clean up and then looked around for a place to meditate.

Her gaze caught on Garrett, Sam, and Bear talking together by another fire. Even from this distance, she could see the tension in their bodies.

Something told her this motorcycle run wasn't all for fun. They seemed to be planning something. Plus, Garrett had ignored her all day. Well, he'd been busy and hadn't included her.

Shrugging, she moved beyond their now rolled-up sleeping bag, looking for a private place to meditate. Garrett had been more than clear that she wasn't to leave the immediate campground, but she intended to walk around later to look at the other campers. Who were they? She was so curious. But she'd have to wait until later this afternoon, when he'd told her he had some sort of super-secret business to handle.

The perfect spot caught her attention, and she sat on colorful leaves, facing the rocks. Setting her hands in position on her knees, with her thumbs and middle fingers touching, she shut her eyes and breathed in the world. Sounds and smells disappeared first, followed by all other sensations. She'd been meditating since she'd first arrived at boarding school, and the way into Zen had become second nature to her. Her mind was the last to clear, and then the universe went quiet.

Once she dropped into peace, she pushed herself back to that day she'd had the dream. This time, she was merely an observer. The man at the cliffs was definitely Garrett Kayrs. His eyes, his body, his voice. There was no question in her mind that it was Garrett. He was there, and he'd saved her from going too close to the edge and probably falling to her death.

Her eyelids opened, and she stared at the rocks. How in the world was that possible? The only thing that made any sort of sense was that she was supposed to rescue him. Right now, she was torn between knifing him and kissing him again. The muscled male had intended to teach her a lesson the previous night, and he had, but something told her it wasn't the one he'd wanted her to learn.

"Hey, girlfriend," Honor said, coming up on her left. "The rush of the morning is over, and afternoon is usually a better time to use the facilities. I thought I'd hit the showers and think we should go in pairs."

"Good idea." Dessie stood and stretched her back. "I don't have any shower necessities."

Honor grinned, looking even more beautiful today with her hair in several braids. She wore dark jeans and a thick blue sweater, and in her hand was a small backpack. "I found you additional clothing. Also, I have extra toiletries, so don't worry."

Dessie frowned. Why did Honor have extra? Did Garrett regularly pick up women to ride on runs?

Honor slid her arm through Dessie's. "I'm so not going to answer that question on your face."

Yeah, that's what Dessie had thought. Her mood turned even darker, unusual after meditating so deeply. They reached the shower area, which was rather quaint. They showered quickly, and then Dessie changed into faded jeans that cupped her butt perfectly. The sweater Honor handed over was a sweet pink. It was nice of the woman to find her clothing, but Dessie wanted to look more like some of the other biker babes, as she'd heard them called. They wore black and looked tough.

She looked like an assistant to Cupid.

Sighing, she pushed her wet hair away from her shoulders so it could dry, curling down her back. The autumn afternoon was warm, so at least she wasn't chilly with the wet hair. Although clouds were rolling in from the east. "Thank you for the clothing. I appreciate it."

"Sure." Honor pulled the backpack over one arm. "The Grizzlies are always happy to share. Though it was hard to find clothing in your size."

Dessie had noticed the female Grizzly members were all a healthy size. "I'm not loving the 'property' designation on the jacket Garrett gave me."

Honor snorted. "It's dumb but necessary, unfortunately." Over her sweater she wore a deep green leather jacket with the designation on the back. "Speaking of which, put on your jacket. Garrett won't be happy to see you walking around without it."

While Dessie would love to defy Garrett, her butt was still sore from the previous night. Sore and tingly in a way that was more intriguing than annoying, though she'd never tell him that. Of course, he probably already knew.

Three women stepped in front of them. "You Grizzly twits think you're too good to party with the rest of us?" The one slightly in the lead, a redhead wearing a black tank top showing tattoos down both arms, sneered.

Dessie blinked.

Honor pulled her to the side. "Ignore them."

The trio moved right along with them. The other two women also wore tank tops, had tattoos, and looked tough. One was a brunette and the other a blonde. The blonde had a nose ring and a piercing in her eyebrow that was red and looked infected.

Nessa suddenly appeared on the other side of Dessie. The petite mother of three put her hands on her hips. "Is there a problem?"

Dessie's senses went on full alert. It was one thing to defend Honor, who had some decent muscle mass, but another to protect the fragile young mother. It appeared Nessa had forgotten her jacket with the Grizzly emblem on it! "I think this is just a simple misunderstanding, and we should all go our own ways," Dessie said calmly, edging a few inches in front of her friends.

"I don't think so," the redhead spat, her eyes so bloodshot they matched her hair. "I hate stuck-up bitches." She swung at Honor.

Dessie launched herself into motion, blocking the punch and pivoting to kick the redhead in the stomach. She flew back to land on her butt, her head thunking against the shower building. The blonde screeched and lunged at Dessie, nails ready to claw. Dessie ducked back to avoid the pointed tips and then shot in, grabbing the woman by the ears and headbutting her.

The blonde went down hard.

The third woman attacked Dessie next, and Honor clotheslined her, tossing her onto the ground. "Stay down," Honor advised softly.

Nessa looked at Dessie and then back at the women groaning into the dirt. "I didn't get to do anything." Her lips formed a barely there pout.

Heat flared along Dessie's back, and she turned, already knowing what she'd see. The three men stood at the campfire, watching them. Even across the distance, she could see the fury on Garrett's rugged face. She sighed. "I'm guessing that falls under the category of making things more difficult for Garrett?" Something he'd specifically told her not to do.

Then he started toward her.

Chapter Nine

"What the fuck?" Sam muttered at Garrett's side as they strode toward the females.

Garrett didn't have an answer. Nothing close to an answer. Dessie had obliterated two women without much effort, and there was no doubt in his mind she could've taken the third one had Honor not stepped in. He reached them, noting that the downed females hauling themselves to their feet were from a human motorcycle club.

They scampered off quickly.

Dessie turned toward him, her face flushed. She kicked an invisible pebble on the ground. "They started it."

Amusement ticked through him, and he reached for her arm, checking for bruises. Then he glanced at her forehead, which was showing a red mark. "A headbutt isn't usually necessary, kitten."

Relief smoothed out her features. "I was going on instinct."

"Honor? Hang back with Bear and Nessa and pack up our camp as much as you can. We're leaving right away." Sam nudged Garrett. "We have to go, G. It's shocking Jordan agreed to meet with us at all."

Garrett clamped his hand over Dessie's. "True. Dessie? We're going to chat about this later, I promise you. For now, let's go." He started moving.

Dessie turned and hustled to keep up with him. "I'm attending your meeting?" She sounded delighted, her gaze sweeping in every direction as if she were afraid she'd miss something.

"Yes," Garrett said, keeping on the main trail past several camps until he reached the winding river. His hope was that Jordan, the leader of the feline shifters, would sense that Dessie was human and thus wouldn't shift into a mountain lion and try to kill him.

They were met at what could be considered the entrance to the feline camp by two of the three feline enforcers. There were no hugs this time. Mac and Noah looked every bit as dangerous as Garrett knew them to be. Tall, broad, and graceful. Their hair was dark blond, their eyes sharp, and their hands ready to form claws at any time.

Garrett forced a smile. "I take it Baye is in the trees?" Their third brother, the other enforcer, was a well-known sniper, even in the immortal world.

"This way," Mac said, turning and leading the way through a maze of trees closer to the river. The shifters wore ripped jeans and worn T-shirts, and both had knives strapped to their thighs.

As they reached the inner sanctum, a toddler bustled over, his tawny hair sticking straight up and his eyes a mellow honey.

Garrett stopped cold. The kid was the spitting image of Jordan Pride.

Jordan stepped out of a large tent that no doubt held computer equipment. "Lark? Go find your mama."

"I'm here." Katie Pride appeared from a trail near the river, heading right for Garrett. "Hey, G. It's so good to see you." She lifted up on her toes to kiss his chin.

He ignored the stiffening of the male cats around him and hugged her. "I've missed you."

"Ditto." She stepped back and reached down for Lark's hand. "This is our newest. Say hi to your Uncle Garrett, baby." She smiled.

"Hi." The kid studied him, much as his father was doing.

Jordan flashed his teeth. "Honey? We're mad at the Realm, and we're furious at the Seven. It'd be nice if you didn't hug any of them."

Katie rolled her eyes. She'd always been beautiful, but the years had made her even more so. Her hair was liquid gold with darker highlights, her features feline sharp, and her lips a generous pink. "We're still family. Get over this feud, boys." She smiled at Dessie, puzzlement in her eyes. "Hello." She tilted her head and scented the air. "Interesting."

Garrett introduced them.

Jordan stared at Dessie, the question clear on his face. "Why don't you three go pick up the toys by the river?" It wasn't a suggestion.

Katie linked her free arm through Dessie's. "I hope you like toy trucks. So. Tell me how you and Garrett met."

Garrett reached out with his senses to the trees around them. "Mayhem is to the east and Menace to the right," he noted, referring to Jordan and Katie's twin girls, now in their late twenties, who no doubt were excellent snipers with scopes on him right now.

"Samantha and Sidney are just fine, and yes, they both could shoot your ear off for fun. So you might want to watch it." Jordan glanced down toward the water. "Why do you have a female human with you? She's not enhanced."

"Long story," Garrett muttered.

Sam angled his body slightly to the side, no doubt blocking at least one sniper's view of Garrett. "G has taken up altruism. He's going to save her."

Jordan tucked his thumbs into the waistband of his very worn, very torn, very comfortable-looking jeans. "It's nice to find a calling."

Smart-ass. Garrett let his body relax. "Jordan, we need a truce. The feline nation has shown its displeasure at what the Seven did. I promise that the Realm was unaware of our activities. Ulric will find his way home at some point, and we all need to be on the same page."

Jordan's gaze sharpened. "While the Realm was unaware of the Seven's activities, they've chosen to allow the Seven to continue on whatever path they have chosen. So far, they, you, have fucked with the laws of the universe in a way that hasn't been good for anybody. I'm a cat, Garrett. We kind of like the laws of the universe."

"I'm aware," Garrett allowed. "However, it's over and done. The wolf nation and the bear nation are back on board with the Realm. The feline nation will be left out in the cold." He didn't mention the dragon nation. Dragon shifters were still kind of a secret to most folks, and who knew if they would align themselves with anybody, anyway. Bear's half brother led the nation; hopefully, family ties mattered to him.

Jordan crossed his arms, flexing impressive muscles. "It's not the past that worries us, Kayrs. It's the future. This ritual you're all planning to destroy Ulric for good sounds like another fuck-you to the laws of physics, and who knows what disaster you'll bring upon us then. We don't like it. We don't want it. It's that simple."

"The ritual won't mess with any laws," Garrett countered. "Not like the Seven ritual or the one Ulric used."

"Bullshit." Jordan shook his head.

Garrett's heart sank.

* * * *

Dessie helped pick up the myriad of toys as Katie bustled around efficiently. She'd answered all of Katie's questions, while leaving out the intimate details. She wouldn't know how to describe the pleasure she'd found with Garrett the night before. He was bossy and domineering, and for the life of her, she couldn't figure out why she liked that about him. Well, why her body liked it, anyway. "How long have you known Garrett?"

"Forever," Katie murmured. "We're family."

How lovely that would be. "It looks like your family is feeling tension." Dessie took in the body language of the men.

Katie nodded. "True statement." She walked around Dessie to pick up a shovel and small bucket.

"I don't want to pry, but will everything be all right?" The men looked dangerous, and if they started fighting, it would be a disaster.

"I hope so." Katie straightened her back and stared at the men. "I honestly don't know at this point."

Dessie tugged a Frisbee out from under a rock. They'd had Frisbees at school, and she'd practiced dodging them during her training. "Why is everyone so tense?" It wasn't any of her business, but curiosity had always propelled her to find answers. If these people went way back, then why not find a good way forward?

"It's hard to explain," Katie murmured, still watching the men, her body visibly tightening.

At that moment, Lark ran full bore for the river. "I hafta save Sammy," he yelled, barreling faster than any toddler should be able to move and jumping.

Dessie reacted before Katie had even turned around, leaping behind the boy and aiming for the middle of the rushing river. Her ankle clipped a rock, and pain slashed up her leg. Water flew up over her head, and she shut her eyes, trying to cough it out. The cold pierced through her, chilling her instantly. The current was already pulling Lark under, so she grabbed him and tucked her body around him, searching frantically for help.

The rushing water was relentless. Her shoulder crashed into a rock, and she cried out, holding the little boy closer. Even if she'd known how to swim, it wouldn't help in such a strong current. She scrambled to find purchase on the slippery rocks, but just as she almost caught an edge, the water deepened. They went under, and she fought to get back up, her feet hitting rocks again.

Water went up her nose, and she blew it out, struggling to keep the boy above the surface. He clutched her, his small hands digging into her neck. Her ears filled, and her hair floated around them as they careened farther downstream. She had to get to the shore.

The water propelled her into another sharp rock, and pain exploded in her arm. Blood filled the water around them.

She blinked water out of her eyes just in time to see Jordan and Katie Pride run to the edge of the river. The air shimmered around them.

Jordan leaped toward the river, his body fluidly changing from man to a massive mountain lion. A real-life animal with deadly fangs and powerful muscles, bigger than any mountain lion she'd ever seen in pictures, but his eyes looked almost the same as before. Almost. What in the world? Pain tried to drag her under and into darkness, but she fought it. The agony in her arm was so intense, she'd fall unconscious soon.

The lion bounded by them and crashed into the river downstream, water splashing in every direction.

Katie turned into a smaller lion and ran along the bank, her canines dropping and the fur ruffling down her back. How was any of this even possible? Darkness edged in from the corners of Dessie's vision, and she tried to strengthen her hold on the toddler with her good arm.

The current smashed her into the male lion, her shoulders to his flanks. He was like a solid statue in the middle of the stream. Her head pitched forward, and she shoved Lark up so he'd stay above the surface. Lights flashed behind her eyes, and her injured arm exploded in agony. The air burst out of her lungs, and her ears rang. Darkness spiraled in even faster, turning her vision gray.

Then Garrett was there. She didn't even see him coming. He stood tall and sure against the current as if even a rushing river couldn't beat him. With a swift duck, he plucked her right out of the water, along with the boy, and fought the current to carry them to shore.

Dessie blinked, trying to remain awake. Her body shivered uncontrollably. Her arm had gone numb, but an echoing pain dug deep into her bicep.

Katie shifted back into human form, bare naked. She reached for the trembling toddler. "Cats don't like the water, boy. You should know that." She held her son close, her eyes filling with tears. "I never would've thought you'd jump into the river."

Cats? Was this real?

Lark coughed out water. "I saw Sammy in water. Had to save my sister."

Jordan's frown darkened his entire face. "How old was Sammy?"

Lark sniffled. "Little like me." He scrunched up his nose. "But it was Sammy."

Katie held him closer, her eyes wide. "Sam did fall in the river as a young girl. But how does he know?"

Lark shivered. "She was wearing a green dress."

Katie's eyes widened.

Jordan growled. "Weird shit like this has been happening since the Seven messed with the laws of the universe, Garrett. Since two of the three artificially created worlds have crashed, our children are seeing past events in their heads. It's nuts. My kid shouldn't be psychically seeing an event that happened decades ago."

Dessie couldn't quite grasp what they were talking about.

Garrett fell to his knees and gently laid her on the ground. Water dripped from his thick hair, and his eyes had turned from gray to an intriguing blue with silver streaks. A shade she couldn't quite name. Did eyes change colors? The world began to quiet as she turned inward with her pain, but she couldn't look away from his rugged face.

"Dessie?" He pushed her hair away from her eyes and looked her over. His jaw tightened, and his gaze hardened. "You're going to be okay." He stared at her right arm. "We can get you to a hospital. Just hold on."

She shivered and turned to look at her arm. The bone had snapped in two and was sticking out of her flesh with blood pouring in every direction. She screamed and then fell into silence as the darkness finally won. Her last thought before dropping into unconsciousness was that people could turn into mountain lions. Maybe she was already dead.

Chapter Ten

Garrett's heartbeat pounded in his head.

Sam landed next to him, looking at the sharp bone halfway out of Dessie's arm. "Shit. I've never seen a compound fracture like that."

Neither had Garrett. Thank god the woman had fallen unconscious. He looked up at Jordan, who let out a piercing whistle.

"Doctor on the way." Jordan's hair dripped down his naked body now that he'd shifted back to human. He crouched and examined the arm. "This is bad, Garrett."

A female ran up, her hair a dark brown and her eyes a lighter honey color. She knelt and studied Dessie's arm, leaning in to sniff her neck. "I'm Dr. Nance. Shit, Jordan." She looked at Garrett, her lion heritage evident in her angled cheekbones. "This is a human. No enhancements." Confusion blanketed her features. "I can't set the bone here. We need an operating room. This is the worst fracture I've ever seen."

Garrett's gut rolled. "The nearest hospital is three hours away." He moved to lift Dessie.

The doctor grabbed his hand, halting him. "Three hours is too long. She's losing too much blood." She shook her head. "I can tie a tourniquet, but she's going to lose the arm."

Garrett's chest ached with a pain he'd never experienced. Dessie's face had turned stark white, and she lay so still he had to check her breathing. Shallow, but there.

Still on his haunches, Jordan looked across her to Garrett. "Did you fuck her?"

Rage lit Garrett's body on fire, and his muscles bunched.

"Wait." Jordan held up a hand, his tawny eyes serious. "If you exchanged bodily fluids, maybe you could give her blood?" Immortal blood could heal the wounds of other immortals and their mates, and sometimes of enhanced humans.

"She's not enhanced," Garrett said hollowly, his ears ringing.

Sam shook his head. "Your blood will kill her, G. No human can take it. Better her arm gone than all of her."

Did he have a choice? "Maybe just a little will get her to the hospital." Without waiting for an argument, Garrett's fangs dropped, and he bit into his wrist. Blood welled. Holding his breath, careful not to jostle the unconscious woman on the ground, he leaned over and let three drops fall into her slightly opened mouth.

Color instantly washed through her face.

"Whoa," Jordan said.

A cut above Dessie's right eyebrow slowly knit itself together.

"What the hell?" Sam hissed.

"I don't know." Garrett settled his wrist against Dessie's mouth and let more blood slide inside. There was no way a human female could take that amount of blood without seizing and dying, but she was healing quickly instead. "She's not an enhanced female or an immortal." Even now, not one ounce of power emanated from her.

She gave a soft moan, still out cold, and sucked more blood from his body. She jerked several times.

Dr. Nance elbowed him aside and gently reached for the protruding bone, shoving and setting it. "It's close but not there yet. Give it a second and I think it'll find the right alignment without my pushing it harder into place."

Dessie drank more blood, and her legs kicked out.

The bone began to mend in front of their eyes, forming a solid white form. The bleeding stopped. The flesh and then the skin began to stitch together with invisible thread.

Sam growled. "G? I have a feeling your pet here isn't being truthful with you."

Garrett's growl rumbled low. He'd been thinking the same thing, but he wasn't discussing it around the lions. "Shut up, Sam."

"Sure thing," Sam muttered.

Katie returned, wearing a cotton shift with a towel wrapped around Lark as he snuggled into her neck. She tossed a pair of worn jeans at Jordan. "I'm confused." She stared down as Dessie healed as well as any immortal would have after such an injury. Maybe even better.

"Me, too," Garrett said, feeling for the pulse in Dessie's wrist. Strong and steady now. "I need to get her to the Realm doctors." None of this made a lick of sense. He dug deeper for his strength and intuition, all but shoving them into her body. Nothing. Not one vibration or one hint of her being anything other than a normal human female. What the hell was happening, and who was she? Did she even know? "Destiny?"

She slowly blinked her eyelids open, and her pupils immediately dilated. But instead of panicking and trying to sit up, she just looked at him. "My arm."

"It's healing." He stared down at the now smooth skin.

She frowned and turned her head to look at her arm, which only had a red scrape now. "I don't understand."

He helped her to sit and brushed leaves out of her hair. It was time to get some answers from the little minx. "Have you always healed quickly?"

Her mouth parted, and her brow furrowed. "No. Not at all. If I even get a little scrape, I need antibiotic ointment to prevent infection." Her voice was slurred as she regained consciousness. Then her gaze landed on Jordan, who had thankfully yanked on his jeans, although he'd left them unbuttoned. "You turned into a mountain lion." Now she just sounded dazed.

The cut muscles in Jordan's torso bunched. "I don't suppose I could convince you that you hit your head and imagined everything." The lion's tawny hair hung in wet ropes to his shoulders, and threat was evident in every line of his body.

"Sure," Dessie murmured, her gaze moving to Katie. "No problem. Concussions definitely cause hallucinations." Her voice rose slightly at the last.

Katie smacked her mate in the arm. "Knock it off, Jordan. There's no need to terrify her. She just saved your son from drowning."

Dessie shoved wet hair out of her eyes. "I should probably learn to swim before we do that again."

Garrett's throat closed. "You can't swim?"

She shrugged. "Never had the chance to learn."

He ducked down and lifted her into his arms, standing tall. She was wet and shivering against him. Brave little human. Either she was telling the truth and she'd risked her life to jump into a rushing river to save a child, or she was lying to him and had an ulterior motive for everything. Either way, she was courageous, and he could admire that, even if she was working against him. A fact she'd regret.

Jordan partially turned to block his path. "G. We have to talk."

"I'm aware. We're going to get into warm clothing, pack up, and then you and I will have that chat." Garrett stared at the feline shifter leader without blinking. Oh, Jordan had known him as a kid, but those times were over. At the moment, Garrett was a representative of the Realm and most likely its future king. It was time he acted like it, even if he had to kill one of his oldest friends. "I'll be back in thirty minutes."

Then he turned and strode away, carrying a female who didn't belong in his arms but whom he wouldn't release.

Even if she was the enemy.

* * * *

Katie Smith-Pride waited until Garrett and Sam had walked out of the camp before kicking her mate in the ankle.

"Ow." Jordan jumped back, turning to face her, his light brown eyes going dark. "What the hell?"

"I'd do worse, but I have a sleeping toddler in my arms," she muttered quietly, meeting his gaze directly. "It's time for a family meeting." She let out a high-pitched whistle and strode away from the river toward the center of their camp, where they wouldn't be interrupted.

Jordan's long-suffering sigh followed her, but so did he.

She reached the quiet oasis and ducked inside a tent to put Lark in bed. The child was sleeping peacefully after his dunking in the river. Lions didn't like water, and he'd never shown any interest before, so she hadn't imagined the kid would jump right in. Of course, he was her child, so it shouldn't be a surprise.

When she emerged from the tent, her family was waiting. Jordan still stood in his jeans, with his torso bare and his hair hanging around his shoulders. Despite being mated for decades, her mouth watered. The male had some very cut muscles in his torso and arms—sleek and powerful. Right now, the pissed-off expression in his eyes only aroused her more.

Their twin girls flanked him, both dressed in shorts and tank tops, looking like human females out for fun. Sidney had long golden hair with flowers woven through it, which looked strange next to the long-range rifle slung over her slim shoulders. Her eyes were a mellow tawny and her frame petite like Katie's, but she could throw a roundhouse kick better than anybody Katie had ever trained. Amusement was evident on her face, making her freckles appear to dance.

Her twin looked anything but amused. At nearly six feet tall, Samantha had her mother's deep brown eyes and her father's thick, sandy-blond hair. Her face was free of freckles, and an intriguing dimple twinkled in her left cheek when she was amused, which was rarely. Her weapon was still held in her arms, pointed at the ground. "I had a clear shot at Kayrs," she said quietly.

Katie straightened to her full height. "As of right now, we're no longer thinking of war with the Realm. In addition, we're going to realign with them. Today."

Sidney grinned, Sammy frowned, and Jordan showed absolutely no reaction.

Not good. Definitely not good. Katie looked beyond them to the three enforcers spread out to guard the family while still taking part in the discussion. Or at least listening to it. If anybody gave an opinion, it'd be Baye, but even he was silent. "The showdown with the Kurjans and their Cyst faction is coming soon. I can smell it on the wind, and so can all of you. The Realm will need us."

Jordan's chin lowered. "The Seven fucked with the laws of physics when they fused their torsos in that stupid ritual. Demons and fairies can't even teleport any longer because of them, and now shifter kids, including mine, are having visions of past events. Shifters look to the future, not the damn past."

Katie shrugged. "As I'm neither a demon nor a fairy, I don't really care. Plus, Lark and the other children will be fine. We'll figure this out. The final ritual when Ulric returns to this world will happen, Jordan. Let's be on the right side when it does." She had dreams sometimes of the freakishly scary leader of the Cyst nation, and she wanted all the allies she could get before he returned home to do whatever it was he had planned. She couldn't see the full picture, but it wasn't good for anybody.

She went for the kill. "Please, Jordan. Trust me."

Jordan Pride was generally a mellow mountain lion...until he was poked. Currently, he felt as if the entire fucking universe was poking him. Seeing his kid almost drown in the river had shaken him more than he wanted to admit, even though he would've gotten to the kid. But that brave little human had risked her life for him.

If she was a brave little human. Or even human. "Garrett doesn't even know who he's sleeping with," Jordan growled. "Why should we trust his judgment?"

"You're not," his mate returned, her pert nose in the air. In her light blue shift, she looked fragile, and yet she could fight with the best of them. He wouldn't have thought it possible, but he loved her more today than he had when they'd first mated. "You're trusting the Realm and everyone in it." She sighed. "Come on, Jordan. We made our big statement by withdrawing years ago. Now it's time to regroup. Right, girls?"

"Yes," Sidney said, just as Samantha said, "No."

He couldn't help but smile. His girls were opposites until it came to family, and then they were always on the same page. It was hard to believe they'd been in his life for nearly three decades. Oh, for mountain lions, they were young. Even so, he'd made sure they were deadly. He'd need to start training Lark soon.

Noah whistled quietly. Kayrs was back. That was quick.

Jordan leaned over and kissed his mate on her nose. "I'll take your opinion under advisement." While he respected Katie and the rest of his team, he was the alpha of the feline nation, and the decision would be his. His word was law, and it would do them all good to remember that salient fact. So he turned and strode toward the river again, noting that his twins slipped off silently to take positions in the trees.

Hopefully, Sammy wouldn't shoot Garrett.

Katie stayed behind with Lark, and Noah remained to guard them while his other two enforcers kept at a distance to intervene if necessary. It'd be pointless to tell any of them that Jordan was twice as dangerous as any other mountain lion and could handle anything. Plus, the twins liked shooting from trees, and they deserved some fun.

Garrett met him alone, no weapons visible on his body.

Jordan paused close to him. "No weapons? Is that a sign of respect or arrogance?"

Garrett's metallic silver eyes remained steady on his. The kid had grown up good. "Neither. It's a sign of trust. We go way back." His upper lip curved. "Please tell me you asked Sam not to shoot."

Jordan shrugged. "I might've forgotten that." He didn't want to be on opposing sides with the Kayrs family. They were allies, and he trusted them, although he didn't like not knowing the details of the final ritual. "One condition, G."

To his credit, Garrett didn't blink. "Name it."

"When Ulric gets free of this secret prison world the Seven created in another dimension, I want to be your first call." He held up his hand before Garrett could speak. "And when you know anything about the final ritual, the one you think will kill him, I'm on speed dial. No more secrets if you're going to mess with my universe."

Garrett exhaled from his powerful chest. Man, he looked like his father. "It's a deal." He held out his hand.

Jordan shook it, finally feeling peace filtering through him.

Even so, his feline ears heard Samantha's sad sigh from the tree line. She'd really wanted to shoot.

Chapter Eleven

Dessie was back to riding behind Garrett on his motorcycle, the wind in her face and those wild vibrations between her thighs. She held on to his abs beneath his leather jacket, her mind spinning.

Shifters. Real mountain lion shifters existed.

She had so many questions, but the second Garrett had returned from speaking with those shifters, he'd plunked her on the back of his bike and started the engine. They'd exited camp, just the four of them, with Honor once again on the back of Sam's bike.

When Dessie had tried to question Garrett about the lions, he'd handed back the helmet with a terse snap.

"Later," he muttered.

She sighed. He was kind of grumpy, truth be told. A while back, maybe ten years, she'd had a history professor who was always cranky.

Yeah, she'd liked him, too. Not in the same way as Garrett, but perhaps she had a penchant for lions with thorns in their paws. She jumped. Was Garrett a mountain lion shifter? No. No way. She'd know that, wouldn't she?

The wind picked up, and she huddled closer to him, grateful for the Grizzly jacket covering her. Grizzly? Wait a minute. If there were lion shifters, were there bear shifters? Was Garrett a freaking bear shifter?

A light rain began to batter them after several hours of riding. Soon sleet joined the rain, and she shivered, holding him tighter. He signaled, and Sam nodded, both of them heading off the main interstate to a recreation area that was largely abandoned this late in the autumn. A small motel with light blue trim and doors sat just off the road.

She shivered as the rain and sleet pelted her helmet.

Garrett stopped in front of the main office. "Stay here." Without waiting for her answer, he swung off the bike and walked inside, his massive black boots crunching dead leaves. He returned shortly and tossed a key at Sam, who caught it with one hand. "I chose rooms around back where the trees can provide cover for the bikes. Also, there's a pizza place three miles away that'll deliver."

Honor leaned up and nuzzled Sam's neck.

Garrett rolled his eyes. "I'll order a couple, and if you want one, swing by." He gracefully straddled the motorcycle and started it, quickly driving around the back of the motel to park in front of door eleven. After helping her off, he kept her arm, grabbed their belongings, and escorted her into the room.

She gulped, taking off the helmet. It was one thing to be with him in a sleeping bag, and quite another to be in a motel room. While that made absolutely no sense, she couldn't help but feel vulnerable alone in the tidy space with him.

There was only one bed.

She'd slept in a small bag with him the night before.

Even so, that bed loomed large in the tiny area. She edged toward the polished wooden table with two chairs by the window, while Garrett dumped their belongings on the bed and then ordered three pizzas with soda to be delivered. Then he turned and sat on the bed facing her, crossing his arms.

She gulped and sat on the orange cushion of the nearest chair. "Are you a mountain lion shifter?"

"No." He cocked his head. "Are you?"

She snorted and then realized he was serious. "No." She removed her wet jacket and hung it carefully over the back of the chair, acutely aware of his focus. In the small room, he looked oversized and beyond dangerous. "Are there bear shifters?"

"Yes. There are bear, wolf, and feline shifters." He removed his leather jacket, leaving droplets of water on the floor. "As well as dragon, but the dragons think that's still a secret."

Her jaw dropped. "Real dragons. Like they blow fire?"

"They do, indeed," he said. "Are you a witch or a fairy?"

"I wish," she blurted out before she could stop herself. "I'd love to have magic powers. Can you imagine?" So witches and fairies existed as well. It kind of made sense. Most fables were based on some sort of truth. "What are you, Garrett?" It was obvious he wasn't human, now that she knew there were other species on earth. While she should be going crazy or at least freaking out, the entire situation just felt surreal, as if she was in a dream. Maybe she was dreaming.

"You're not dreaming."

Oh. She'd said that out loud. "Did you heal my arm?" There had been such pain, and she'd seen the bone. How had he healed it? Unless he also had magic. "Are you a witch?"

"No. You healed your arm. I just helped by giving you my blood."

Blood? Her stomach lurched. "I drank your blood?"

"A lot of it."

Gross. Just gross. She hoped the pizza arrived soon because now all she could taste was blood. She and a couple of other girls had figured out how to watch movies on the internet before the headmistress shut them down, and they'd watched a scary movie where the werewolf gave his blood to save a teenager. "Are you immortal?" What was this world she'd walked into? Was it a secret? Did all of her time at school mean she didn't know the real world? "Garrett?"

"Yes. Well, mostly. I can be beheaded or perhaps burned. It's time you stopped fucking with me, sweetheart."

The spit dried up in her mouth. Even though he looked relaxed, the guy wasn't truly human, and for some reason, he didn't believe her about anything. She eyed the door but knew she wouldn't escape before he could grab her. "Is it a secret? I mean about the shifters and everyone else who's, well, mostly immortal?"

"Yes."

Wonderful. Now she knew this momentous secret that she wasn't supposed to know. Getting on the back of that bike had been a mistake, and she'd done so with her eyes wide open. Unless she was actually dreaming. Witches didn't really exist. It was impossible.

"Yes, they do," Garrett countered.

She had to stop thinking out loud. "Are you trying to frighten me?"

"Baby, if I wanted you scared, you'd be terrified," he drawled.

Well. No problem with his ego, that was for certain. She covered a shiver by resettling on her seat. Apparently he could scare her, but that was to be expected, considering his size. Although she did know how to defend herself. She eyed him.

His grin was slow but didn't reach his eyes. "Go ahead. You want to fight?"

She couldn't breathe. "Not really."

"Smart girl. Finally." His wrists rested on his thighs, and his hands appeared loose and relaxed. "How did you take my blood without blowing up?"

She blinked. "Blowing up?"

"Yeah. Humans can't drink our blood without dying, and yet you did. In fact, you healed your arm."

Sparks shot through her, and her face blazed. "You gave me blood that you thought would kill me?" She stood, trembling.

"Just a little, and then you took more on your own." He didn't seem fazed by her anger. "Then your arm started to heal, so I figured you could handle it. Of course, that means you're nowhere near human. What's your enhancement?"

He could at least look a little chastised by her temper. "You're speaking Greek to me." She paused. "Hold that thought. I speak Greek. You're speaking an unknown form of Gaelic to me. I'm not enhanced." In any way.

His lids half-closed, giving him a predaceous look that made her want to hide behind her chair. "My patience is rapidly dwindling. What is your enhancement? Are you psychic, empathic, or what?"

Perhaps her head injury had sent her into a coma.

"You're not in a coma." Any amusement had fled his expression.

She held up a hand as if to ward off his anger. "I don't know what you're talking about. I'm none of those things." Her mind reeled. "Why? Why do you think I have gifts like that?"

"Because only an immortal or an enhanced human female could've taken my blood, and you did. So you must be." He cocked his head. "If you were immortal, your wounds should've started healing even before I gave you blood. Though, with you, I'm not sure."

It was like he lived in a completely different world than she did. Of course, she had been secluded at school. "What's an enhanced human female? I mean, why does it matter?" It would be nice to be psychic.

"Enhanced humans can mate immortals and become immortal," he said.

Mate? She cleared her throat. Mate. Well. That sounded sensual and explicit. "What does mating entail?" Oh, she had not just asked that.

His chin lowered in clear threat. "You had better not be fucking with me."

"I'm not," she whispered, unable to speak any louder. Trying to be casual, she retook her chair and crossed her legs.

"Fine. A marking appears on our palm, in my case a *K* for my family surname. The design transfers to our mate during the mating process, which includes sex and a good bite."

She cleared her throat and tried incredibly hard not to think about sex. "That sounds intense." And bizarre.

"It is. Mating means a good bite, a brand, and then being together forever. If an enhanced human mates with an immortal, they gain immortality by an increase in chromosomal pairs after the act."

She shook her head. "This is all insane." Yet she'd seen the shifters turn from human to animal. "A mating mark?"

"Enough about me, Destiny. Where did you learn to fight like that?"

Finally, something she could answer. "At school. Headmistress Louann dictated that all young ladies should be able to both choose a fine wine for dinner and defend themselves from unruly suitors." Yes, it sounded horribly old-fashioned, but Dessie had enjoyed the lessons in fighting.

He blinked.

She winced. For some reason, he didn't like her explanation. "I'm sorry," she said lamely, not sure why she'd apologized. Then another thought careened through her brain. "So we could mate? I mean, if I had an enhancement?" Which she did not.

For the first time, he appeared to withdraw. Not in any obvious way, but she felt it. "No. I've seen my mate, or rather felt her, in a dream. I think she's a very dangerous shifter, and she's trying to kill me. I've felt her on the back of my bike." He winced. "I think she's blond, but I don't know why I think that. Maybe because so many lion shifters are. Or maybe I saw her hair in a dream and I don't really remember it. Who knows?"

What in tarnation? "Your mate wants to kill you?" How did that make any sense?

"Yes. I think so." He looked around the room and then back at her. "Don't look so shocked. It's okay. A good kill attempt is often foreplay for my kind."

Maybe she didn't want to be in his world. Now she was jealous of a murderous shifter neither of them had even met yet. "Perhaps you need better taste in women." Yes, she sounded a little huffy there.

"Perhaps," he allowed. "I should've told you I was expecting to meet somebody else before I kissed you."

"I wouldn't have believed your story," she admitted. Even now, she was having trouble accepting this new reality. "Plus, I told you I just wanted to have some fun and experiences before I die. You and I never had a future." So the hurt in her breast at the thought of him with somebody else was just silly. "Even so, I'd appreciate it if you didn't let your homicidal shifter mate kill you."

"I won't," he promised, his lips twitching. "You're very sweet and disarming, Destiny."

Yeah. That was just super. She was sweet, and his mate was sexily dangerous. "Do you have a timeline for the appearance of this mate of yours?"

"No." His frown cut grooves in his strong face. "Could be tomorrow or next year or next century."

Oh. Well, then. "So we can still enjoy our four weeks?" If she was going to have sexual relations before she died, doing so with an immortal seemed to guarantee a good experience. "I'm very attracted to you."

Instead of calming him, her statement made his eyes narrow. "I'm not going to let you die. My doctors are the best in the world, and we'll see them when we arrive at my home tomorrow."

The hurt in her chest turned to a dull ache. Even her smile felt sad. "That's kind, Garrett, but not even you can cheat death for me. Maybe you and your shifter mate will have forever, but I'm just a human woman with no enhancements." She'd accepted her destiny after the last doctor had read her scan with shaking hands. "It's okay. I'm all right." It was sweet that Garrett wanted to save her.

"We'll see." He glanced at his phone. "That pizza should be here soon. Then you're going to tell me all about your childhood, your family, your schools, and how you ended up walking into that diner where we met. We're going to figure all of this out."

"Of course." She tried to smile, but her limbs felt heavy and in need of rest. Nothing she could say would help him answer his questions, because none of this made sense. "I'll cooperate and tell you everything on one condition."

He stilled. "Which is?"

"You tell me the truth. What are you?" She held her breath.

Slowly, tortuously, sharp fangs dropped from his mouth and then slid back up. "I'm a vampire with a hint of demon in me. So you're definitely going to cooperate, sweetheart."

Chapter Twelve

Dessie froze in place for all of two seconds. Those were fangs. Like, actual fangs. "Nope." She stood and edged sideways, past the chair, aiming with her butt for the door. "No. No way. Nope."

Garrett cocked his head, looking even deadlier, if that was possible. "What are you doing?"

"Leaving." A buzzing echoed through her head as if a hive of bees had taken up residence between her ears. The room tilted, and she reached back for the doorknob, which was cold and a little grimy. "I can handle shifters and Grizzly motorcycle riders. Yep." Darkness edged in from the corners of her vision. "But vampires. I don't think so." It was just too much.

As if on cue, lightning zapped outside.

She jumped and tried to twist the knob without looking.

"I think you might be in shock," he mused.

"That makes sense." Her voice sounded like it had come from far away. Far away, where reality had somehow gone. "Thank you for the ride and for the, ah, the education. The entire experience has been illuminating." She turned the knob, pivoted, and almost walked into the pizza delivery kid. Instead, she yelped and jumped back, her heart racing so fast she nearly doubled over.

Garrett was at her side within seconds, handing over bills and taking the pizza. He shut the door. "Sit down."

She walked as far away from him as possible and sat on the bed. The smell of pepperoni wafted through the room, and her stomach growled. How could she be hungry right now? "I don't want to be vampire feed."

He snorted and put the boxes on the table. "Quick lesson. Vampires don't need to take blood to live. We make our own just like you do." He dug into a bag and drew out paper plates and napkins. "We do drink blood in extreme situations—for example, to heal ourselves or during sex." Frowning, he flipped open the lids of two of the boxes.

Sex? They took blood during sex? "I don't want to be turned into a vampire." She'd read a vampire novel years ago. Now she swallowed over a lump in her throat and casually reached for her bag, which was sitting on the floor.

He shoved a piece of pizza in his mouth and chewed thoughtfully. After he swallowed, he gestured her toward the open boxes. "You need to eat. Also, you can't be turned into anything but what you are, so stop worrying about it. When an immortal mates, the only thing that changes are the chromosomal pairs, if the other mate is human. Other than that, we don't change anybody."

Even so, her time on this fun ride had just ended. "Okay." She drew her knife free and then tugged her laptop bag over her shoulder. "I'm going to go make my own way now. Thank you for everything."

He just watched her while he finished his pizza. "It's storming. Where do you think you're going?"

She shrugged. "I've hitchhiked before. It's okay. I'm fine." She looked harmless, so people would pick her up on the road. It probably wasn't safe, but neither was staying in the same room with a vampire who thought she was lying to him.

"No." His voice was soft. Too soft.

She shivered. "Yes." She kept her head high as she walked casually toward the door. Though she didn't want to stab him, she would. There was no doubt he underestimated her ability to fight, and that was good. Taking him by surprise was the only chance she had.

"Dessie, there are at least a dozen reasons you're not going anywhere, but the only one that matters to you is that I'm not gonna let you. So put your knife away, grab a piece of pizza, and have a seat." He flopped a piece onto a plate and held it out.

She tightened her grip on the handle.

He sighed.

Then the world crashed in. A bald man flew through the window, shredding glass and then rolling to come up on two feet with a gun in his hand. The door burst open, and two more men jumped inside, both with weapons.

Dessie stumbled back, adrenaline bursting through her veins. The first man was the one who'd been following her around town the week before. She'd forgotten all about him until right now. How had he found her?

Garrett pivoted, manacled the man who'd come through the window around the neck and twisted. The guy's neck broke with a loud snap.

The second man fired rapidly at Garrett, while the third swung his weapon toward Dessie. She reacted instantly, slicing his wrist with her blade. He screamed and dropped the gun. He was at least six feet tall with a broad chest, but he moved gracefully like he could fight. His hair was blond, his eyes green, and his beard dirty. Ducking his head, holding his bleeding hand, he charged her. She jumped back and swiped across his shoulder, slicing clean through his denim jacket. Blood spurted as he flew past her.

She danced away, keeping her legs loose as Garrett and the other man grappled. How badly had he been shot?

The bleeding man caught her around the legs and took her down. Her heart pounding, she stabbed him in the shoulder, planted her feet flat on the ground, and flipped them both over to land straddling him.

Something cracked loudly above her head.

She focused on the man beneath her as he pulled his arm back to punch up. Reacting instinctively, she flipped the knife in the air and brought the heavy steel handle down in the center of his forehead, as she'd been trained. His eyelids fluttered shut, and his body went limp.

Gasping, she partially crouched to go help Garrett but stopped cold. Both bodies lay crumpled at his feet, their heads at odd angles. Now that the danger had passed, her hands started to shake. She looked up at Garrett to see fury swirling blue and silver through his eyes. How had she ever thought he was just human? She gulped. "You're angry."

He cocked his head, his fingers curled into fists. "You're empathic?"

She gingerly got off the man she'd knocked out. "No. You don't exactly hide your feelings." Then she looked at the prone bodies. "You killed them."

"Yeah. Humans," he muttered. "They attack, they die." He reached down and hauled up the guy who'd fought with her. "Stay here, Dessie. I'm going to ask our friend a few questions."

Panic seized her around the throat. "I am not staying here with dead bodies." Her voice rose.

A muscle visibly pounded in his neck, and his face looked harder than any granite wall. "Follow me. You can stay with Honor and Sam. I won't be long."

* * * *

Dessie paced back and forth as Honor flipped through the channels on the bulky television set in the room she shared with Sam. "Why aren't you more upset?"

Honor looked up, her brown eyes mellow. "Honey, they attacked you. This new world you're living in has different rules, and you'll drive yourself crazy if you try to hold on to the old ones. Trust me." She stretched her impressive body. "You're pale. Are you okay?"

"No." Dessie inched toward the door. If she wanted to leave, now was the time. But her body kept shaking so hard it was difficult to move.

"He'll just find you," Honor said quietly. Then she smiled. "He won't hurt you."

Dessie rested her back against the wall, acutely aware of the knife in her bag on the floor. "Are you a shifter?"

Honor snorted. "No. Enhanced human and now mated, so I'm immortal." Her smile was genuine. "It's pretty cool, really."

"I'm not enhanced." The idea of living forever was a dream Dessie couldn't reach. Not with her brain tumor, and not without an enhancement. "What is your enhancement?"

"I can discern lies." Honor shrugged. "Came in handy when I was working for Homeland Security. I still use it to help with investigations for the Realm, and sometimes I consult with humans." Her expression softened. "I promise that nobody wants to hurt you."

The door opened. "Except for the three guys who just busted into my motel room," Garrett said, walking inside, bringing the wind and rain with him. His wet hair curled around his ears, and he looked solid and strong with the storm behind him.

Dessie swallowed. "Who were they?"

"They were just freaking humans. What a waste of a night." Sam walked in behind Garrett, went to Honor, and lifted her for a kiss. "Did you miss me?"

"Definitely." The woman kissed him back, wholeheartedly.

Garrett sighed. "They were just human."

Sam snorted.

Apparently there wasn't time to deal with humans.

"Come on, Dessie. Honor and Sam have already forgotten we're here." Garrett took her hand and led her outside, making sure she stayed beneath the eaves as the rain blew in. "I rented the room next to ours and called for friends to replace the window and fix the door tonight, so the management won't know a thing happened when they return to work tomorrow." He unlocked the next door and nudged her inside a room similar to the one they'd had earlier.

She stumbled and righted herself. "Where are the...I mean, the bodies?"

"Gone," he said simply.

"But, Garrett—"

He shut the door and wiped water off his chiseled face. "It's no longer your concern. Forget about it." There was no give in his words or expression.

Her eyes felt gritty, and her back ached. She'd hit the floor harder than she'd thought. "Did you torture that man?" Her legs trembled, so she sat on the bed.

"Not really. He gave it up pretty quick." Garrett crossed his arms. "You fought well. I want to know all about your training. That was more than simple self-defense."

It was her physical education class for ten years. "That one man had been following me in town, although he didn't make a move until today."

He took her measure and then finally spoke. "The men were hired by your aunt to kill you so you can't inherit what your father left for you. She apparently doesn't know about your diagnosis."

"Wait—what?" She blinked, trying to make sense of the words. "You knew there was a hitman after me?"

"Yeah. But just a human one." He shrugged and a droplet of water fell from his thick hair.

Apparently that didn't require her being informed. "You should've told me."

Genuine surprise lit his metallic eyes. "Why? The guy was just human." It was as if the threat was negligible.

Maybe to a vampire, there had been no threat. Hurt flared deep in Dessie's chest. She shook her head wildly. How could that be true? Sure, Cecile had never liked her, but to want her dead? Tears filled her eyes, and she couldn't stop them from spilling over onto her face. "She wanted me murdered?" Her voice trembled, and she pressed the back of her hand against her mouth.

"Yes." Garrett's gaze softened. "I won't let anything happen to you. Those guys just got lucky finding us at the motel because of the storm. Apparently they followed us from the camp and then waited for the storm to search for hotels in the area where we were most likely to be. Smart, actually. They're also the only people she hired, so there's nobody else out there ready to harm you. I'll have her taken care of as well."

"No." Dessie held up a hand. "Please don't kill her." The idea made her want to vomit. "I can't be responsible for that." Although now that she knew what Cecile had planned, she'd claim that money and give it away. "But I do need to go to Texas. I'll leave you tomorrow."

His eyebrow arched. "I'll take you to claim your inheritance after you see the doctors at my home. Deal?"

"No." This was all too much; she couldn't make sense of it. Worse yet, the longer she was around Garrett, the more she wanted him, and not just for a night or a week or her remaining month. It was crazy that she was so drawn to him despite his penchant for violence and casual acceptance that he'd just killed three people, even though they were assassins. He wasn't hers and never would be. Even if a miracle happened and he fell for her, she wasn't enhanced and couldn't live forever. Plus, he had that murderous mate out there looking for him. "I appreciate everything, but I'm on my own now." As she had been her entire life.

He leaned back against the door, so solid and strong it hurt to look at him. "My people have lived on this planet for eons, and I guarantee our doctors are better than yours. I've seen you fight, sweetheart. Don't stop now."

She blinked. Was there a chance she could live? She'd been afraid to allow even a hint of hope into her breast, but what if? She'd seen the scans, and the tumor had tendrils that extended throughout her brain. But vampire doctors might have better equipment. "You make a good point." She threw up her hands. "Eons? How old are you, anyway?" The guy could be thousands of years old.

"I was born in the twentieth century." He grinned.

Okay, well good. That was something. "No more killing, Garrett."

His eyes glittered, now back to their brilliant metallic sheen. "Their next kill was to be two kids in elementary school who are supposed to inherit even more than you just did."

"Oh." Her head started to ache. "Well. Okay." The energy drained out of her. "But if your doctors can't help, you have to let me go to Texas."

"Fair enough." He gestured to the bed. "Let's get some sleep."

She jolted. It wasn't a very large bed.

Chapter Thirteen

Garrett initiated protocol Zuma before driving his motorcycle into Realm territory in northern Idaho. His head had ached all day, and his primal self kept trying to stretch awake with the mysterious female behind him on his bike. Though she wasn't dangerous, like his mate, she had his blood pounding through his veins after sleeping next to her all night without touching her.

The mystery of her drew him.

She'd seemed honest when answering his questions earlier, and he couldn't find any enhancement. She'd traveled west and taken a job with a fledgling newspaper to make some money. It was owned by the family of the moron who'd been with her that day in the diner. They'd been in town for a fall festival, and supposedly Garrett knew the rest.

None of it made a lick of sense.

He caught wind of soldiers as he and Sam rode their bikes toward the mountains and the private lake where vampire headquarters was situated. They flanked the narrow road on both sides, escorting the visitors without Destiny knowing. His family must have been surprised to get the call sign, but they had reacted instantly and appropriately.

Sam led the way through the main gate, which would close once they turned the bend toward the central lodge. A myriad of different tree species lined the way, showing gold, orange, and red leaves. He turned onto the main drag of headquarters and headed straight for the hand-hewn log lodge.

Armed soldiers were all around them, but none could be seen. He felt several of his uncles close by and gave the sign that he was all right. His dad must still be in Seattle with his mom but would no doubt be heading home.

Then he and Sam both parked against the curb. He helped Dessie off and followed her, taking the helmet.

She blinked as she took in the sprawling lodge and the sparkling lake beyond it. "This is beautiful."

"Thanks." He took her hand and walked along with Sam and a silent Honor into the main entrance, which showcased the lake through floor-to-ceiling windows. Late flowers, red and orange, bloomed near the door. "This way."

She limped along, no doubt sore after riding so hard for the last two days. "Where are we going?"

He kept walking and then drew her down the stairs, going left, deeper into the earth, where the laboratories were located. He palmed the side of a door, and it slid open after reading his prints.

"Garrett?" she asked.

"This way. We need to go through a scanner to make sure there aren't any tracking devices on us. I promise it doesn't hurt and will be over very quickly." He led her through sterile yet comfortable halls until he reached his destination, a comfortable-looking examination room. "You and Honor take off your clothes and put them in that bin. There are scrubs for you in the closet." He nudged her inside, and Honor followed, looking over her shoulder at Sam, her face pensive.

"It's okay," Sam said. "Don't worry." He shut the door behind them.

Two guards appeared from nowhere to stand next to it.

Garrett walked into the examination room across the hall, already taking off his clothes. Sam did the same, and they tossed them in a bin to be burned. He was going to miss that jacket, but he had others.

"I'm first," Sam muttered, walking through a door to the right.

"Fine." Garrett followed into the other room as Sam strode right into a tall, green cylindrical-shaped machine, buck-assed naked.

The cylinder hummed and then closed before the outside layer began spinning around wildly. A beep sounded, and then the machine slowly spun to reveal the doorway again. Apparently Sam was clean. Garrett padded into the machine and waited. It started to hum and then spun around him. Cold air flushed against his skin, and then the sensor beeped.

His body relaxed. He was clean. The door opened on the opposite side, and he padded out to find Sam throwing black scrubs at his face. He put them on and walked barefoot out of the quiet room to a control room, where his uncle and aunt waited. Well, his uncle waited, while his aunt manned the machine, typing rapidly.

Besides the door leading to the machine room, there was a double door behind the console that accessed more medical rooms, and a side door that opened into a main hallway.

"Uncle Dage." Garrett hugged the King of the Realm and smacked him on the shoulders. Then he leaned back. Dage looked good. Healthy. His hair was black, his eyes silver right now, and his body tight with muscle.

Dage then hugged Sam, clapping his back with a bone-crunching echo. Good thing their torsos were fused and impenetrable. "What trouble have you two gotten into now?"

Sam shrugged. "Wasn't me this time."

Garrett ran a hand through his thick hair. "I don't know yet." He leaned down and half-hugged his aunt, careful not to spill the grape energy drink at her elbow. It was the king's one vice. "Hi, Emma. I take it Sam and I are free of bugs?"

She looked up, her eyes sparkling. "I love this new toy. Just freakin' love it." Then she stood and hugged him, her head bumping beneath his chin. "I've missed you." She released him to hug

Sam. "It's so good to have you guys home." The queen had long black hair and blue eyes and wore her usual outfit of jeans and a sweater beneath a white lab coat. She sat back down and studied the monitor. "Honor is clean. No bugs, trackers, tracking dust, or anything suspicious on or in her."

The machine started to hum again.

Garrett leaned over his aunt's shoulder to watch the report on the monitor. The beep was loud. "Dessie is fine?"

"Yep," Emma said. "All clear. There's nothing suspicious on or inside her. The Kurjans have new technology with trackers smaller than a grain of rice, but my machine can detect them. We also ran your clothes through a scanner and didn't find anything."

"They'll be burned anyway," the king said calmly.

Fair enough.

Moments later, Honor and then Dessie emerged through the doorway wearing smaller sets of black scrubs. Honor had met Dage and Emma before, so she hugged them both and moved to Sam's side.

Garrett reached for Dessie's arm and brought her forward. "Dage and Emma, this is Destiny Applegate."

Dage scrutinized her and frowned, reaching out a hand for her to shake. "She's—"

"Human," Dessie finished for him, shaking vigorously. She looked adorable in the scrubs, which were at least two sizes too big for her, with the sleeves all but hiding her hands. "Yes, I know. *All* human. *No* enhancements." She released him and smiled at Emma. "You must be my new doctor." Her eyes were bright and her cheeks a lovely pink color, and the hint of tension in her voice had Garrett wanting to cuddle her against his side. But he refrained under his uncle's too-watchful gaze.

Emma held out a hand to shake. She had a couple of inches on Dessie but wasn't much taller.

Garrett cleared his throat. "Dage is the King and Emma the Queen of the Realm."

Dessie paled. "Oh." She gave an awkward curtsy and released Emma's hand. "Your highness."

Amusement passed across Dage's immortal face so quickly Garrett almost missed it.

"Just Emma," Em said cheerfully, sliding her arm through Dessie's and tugging her away from Garrett. "Let's take a look inside your head and see about that tumor, shall we? I have your other medical records but don't really trust anybody's scans but my own." She drew Dessie toward the other side of the room and the double doorway that led to one of many medical bays in the main lodge.

Garrett could see the guards already at their posts when she opened the door. It made sense, considering Dessie was an unknown. "I'll go with you."

"No, I think you'll stay here," the king said mildly.

Dessie looked back over her shoulder. "That's okay, Garrett." She tripped along with Emma. "I'll see you later?" The doors closed behind them.

Dage crossed his arms.

Sam pulled Honor to his side. "Well, then." His green eyes twinkled. "Honor and I are heading to demon headquarters to see my brothers, and we'll catch up with you later. You two have a nice chat." Then he turned and all but fled the room with his mate.

Garrett watched the side door close behind them. Demon headquarters was a distance down the same lake as vampire headquarters. He felt silly in bare feet and scrubs, but he didn't let it show. "I spoke with Jordan, and the feline nation has agreed to ally with the Realm again. We can count on them for anything we need in case we go to war."

Dage's powerful chest moved when he uncrossed his arms. "Nicely done, Garrett. Great job." A hint of relief showed in his argent eyes.

"Thanks."

"How did you manage it?"

Damn good question. Garrett lifted a shoulder. "Best guess is that Jordan wants back in. Second guess is that Katie smacked him on the head and insisted upon it. Either way, Dessie's jumping into a freezing river to save their kid, even though she doesn't know how to swim, put Jordan in an amenable mood."

Dage's chin lifted. "She risked her life?"

"Yeah. She risked her very human life." Garrett shoved a hand through his thick hair. Man, he needed a haircut. "You should see her fight, Dage. She's quicker than some immortals, and she knows some serious moves." His body wanted to go right through those doors and follow her to make sure she was all right.

Dage frowned, throwing the cut angles of his face into darkness. "She's human."

"I know. But she dreamed of me as a kid, or at least she thinks she did." None of it made sense. "I like her." It sounded lame.

Dage cocked his head, fixing his gaze solidly on Garrett as if he could see inside his head. "You're drawn to her."

Heat spun through Garrett's torso. "Yes."

"Huh."

"I know. She's not enhanced." There was no way to explain something he didn't understand himself. "I know we don't have a future, but I need to help her." If he could make sure she lived a long human life, then he'd be content to go on his way. Probably.

"You can't keep a human, Garrett." Dage's frown held more concern than condemnation.

Garrett crossed his arms. "She's not a puppy, King."

Dage held both hands out, palms up. "Fine. Not my problem, so long as she's not a threat to the Realm. You can discuss it with your father when he returns. For now, go check out your new house."

"I have a house?" This was news.

"Yes. We figured you'd stop riding motorcycles and return home with a wayward mate at some time, so your mother insisted we build you one of the houses in the family section of the territory." Dage scratched at a bruise on his neck. He must've been training with one of Garrett's uncles, or even with his dad. "I take it you haven't found this mysterious female who wants you dead?"

"Not yet," Garrett admitted. "It might be centuries before we meet. I don't know." Yet he did know that he'd stopped looking since he'd met Destiny, and that wouldn't do. He had no idea how the little human had slid beneath his skin the way she had, but he needed to get a grip on himself. Emma would heal her, and he'd make sure she was set up safely elsewhere to live her life.

Then he'd find his mate and get on with the job of being a Seven.

His path determined, he relaxed. "It's good to be home." Although he wouldn't be there for long—the Seven were convening in Wyoming in less than a week. But he would hit his family with that fact after they had a nice meal or two together.

Dage scanned him as if reading his mind, which supposedly he couldn't do. "You're in with the Realm now. No more of this Seven business. Got it?"

"I took a vow," Garrett said.

"Family comes before any vow." Dage clapped a hand on his shoulder. "Later on, we need to hammer out the treaty with the feline nation. We can get Jordan on a call while we draft so we're not playing back and forth for the next year." He glanced toward the door to the medical rooms.

The door opened, and both Emma and Destiny walked out, Emma holding several scans in her hands.

"That was quick." Garrett smiled, his shoulders feeling pounds lighter. He'd known his aunt could help. Then he noticed her pale face. "What?"

She glanced from Destiny to him, her gaze wide. "I can't fix this, Garrett."

His head snapped up. "What do you mean? We're the Realm."

Dessie reached him and patted his arm. "It's okay. I already knew the truth."

Emma handed over a scan. "I've never seen a tumor like this. The mass is attached to the corpus callosum with tendrils extending throughout the rest of the brain. I'd have to remove at least half of her brain tissue to get at it."

"No." Garrett planted his feet. Not once had he thought the Realm doctors wouldn't be able to help the young human.

"Yes," Dessie sighed. "It's all right. The queen just verified what I already knew. The tumor is growing and will start to basically shut down my brain so it can't function. I have about a month left."

Emma's gaze darted around as if she wasn't sure where to look. "I'm contacting every colleague I have across the globe, but…"

Dessie took Garrett's hand and looked up at him, her eyes so blue and full of life. "I'm fine. How about you show me your hometown before I head on down to Texas?"

His blood heated. He would not let her die.

Chapter Fourteen

Dessie had known not to get her hopes up again, but if anybody could help her, it was probably the vampire doctors. Though she wasn't any sort of empath, she could feel the sorrow rolling off Garrett as they walked through the light rain past gorgeous log houses that all fronted the bluish-gray lake.

Every once in a while, a couple of men would stroll by, looking like guards patrolling but in casual wear. Smoke rose from several of the houses, and the scent of a campfire carried on the wind.

"I'm sorry," she said. If she'd known she was going to hurt him, she would've refused his ride that first day.

"You're not going to die." He glanced down as if to make sure the heavy leather coat he'd found for her was keeping her warm. Then he took her hand, enfolding it in heat. "I won't let you."

Sweet. That was incredibly sweet—and a little arrogant.

They stopped in front of a western red cedar post-and-beam home with an arched double door.

"I guess this is mine." Garrett glanced at an oval granite rock with numbers etched in it. "Let's check it out."

Dessie stumbled and then stared at the luxurious house. Even the landscaping was stunning, with autumn red daylilies lining the red, gray, and brown pavers of the walkway to the front door. The pavers were laid in a pattern, with a white paver in the center embellished by a crest of some kind. It was a *K* surrounded by intricate and mysterious lines and points. Truly beautiful. "This is yours?"

"Apparently." They walked by a bubbling water feature shaped like a grizzly bear. Golden leaves floated at the base and burnished orange flowers opened to the meager sun around the stones.

Wow. How could he sound so casual about such a lovely home? "If your family is here, why were you riding with the Grizzlies?"

"I was looking for my mate." He reached the door and rapidly used a keypad before twisting the antique-looking knob to open the door on the left.

Oh. Of course. Lucky mate, whoever she might be. While Dessie wanted to meet as many people as possible before she passed on, she had no interest in meeting this mate. If her reluctance was motivated by jealousy for a guy she barely knew, then so be it. She could live with that.

He set his hand to the back of her waist and nudged her inside.

She stepped onto a tile landing and then stopped, stunned. Floor-to-ceiling windows on the other side of a sprawling great room framed the now-calm lake and the mountains surrounding it. While the lake didn't have the cold beauty of the landscape where she'd gone to school, it was stunning and touched her. Deeply. "Lovely," she whispered.

He shut the door and surveyed the room. "Looks comfortable."

Gray couches made for slouching faced a stone fireplace with a plasma television above the mantel. The sofa and end tables matched the exterior of the home. A kitchen lay to the right, and a gray-and-blue pool table, as well as a bar, to the left.

Dessie moved into the living area just as a brunette emerged from what appeared to be the coat closet, flinging herself at Garrett.

He caught the woman and flipped her around in the air, laughing as he settled her and hugged her close.

She hugged him back, and even when he set her on her feet, she held on to his arms, looking up into his eyes. "It's about time you came home."

"I know." He reached for Dessie's hand and drew her toward the woman. "Des? This is my sister, Janie."

"Hi." Janie had the bluest eyes Dessie had ever seen. Next to her brother, she was incredibly petite, but she held herself with confidence. Good humor and curiosity lit her expression, even as she kept one arm around her brother's waist.

"Hi." Dessie held out a hand. "I'm human," she said lamely before Garrett's sister could sniff her.

Janie chuckled. "So I've heard." She looked up, way up, into her brother's face. "We finished furnishing the place just yesterday since you were headed home. If you don't like anything, just let me know."

"I love it all." Garrett's smile seemed more relaxed than it had the entire time Dessie had known him. "I missed you, Janie Belle." He leaned down and pressed a kiss to the top of his sister's head.

Dessie's heart thumped. While Garrett might be an immortal and a killer, he had a sweet side that tore right through all the defenses she was trying to build around her heart.

Garrett looked behind Janie to the closet. "I don't suppose my niece is in there?"

The vampire had a niece? Dessie craned her neck to look inside the closet.

"No. Hope is working in the computer center conducting research for you, I believe." Janie's gaze clouded.

"What's wrong?" Garrett asked.

Janie shrugged. "Nothing. I mean, I think it's nothing. She has another cold, and it turned into an ear infection."

Garrett's expression darkened. "Seriously? I thought we were done with the childhood illnesses that she shouldn't have in the first place."

Now that was just cute. "Is there something wrong with her ears?" Dessie asked.

Garrett drew himself up. "No. It's a long story, but Hope is the only female alive with vampire blood in her, and yet she contracts human illnesses. We can't figure it out."

That was odd. "How old is she?" Perhaps if the girl was still a toddler, she would outgrow the problem.

"Twenty-one in three days," Janie said. "We're having a ball and combining it with a Realm symposium. It's not like we should miss an opportunity to conduct business instead of having fun." She rolled her eyes.

Dessie jolted. "You have a twenty-one-year-old daughter?" The woman, who had no wrinkles, appeared to be in her late twenties.

Janie grinned. "Yes. Mating an immortal has a couple of benefits, even if one does have to deal with a humongous male demon ego with a side of over-the-top dominance. But whatevs."

Dessie loved her. Of course she'd adore Garrett's sister. Why couldn't Janie be a mean hag whom Dessie wanted to escape? No. She had to be lovely and funny, and Dessie would only have a week or so to get to know her. Once again, her fatal diagnosis brought an ache to her chest that would never completely dissipate. "I'm looking forward to meeting her."

Janie patted her arm. "She's very curious to meet you as well. Garrett has never brought a female home. I mean, a woman home."

That should not ignite a flame of happy heat in Dessie's body. Yet it did, and she couldn't help grinning back at Garrett's sister. "I'm very happy I was able to meet you, Janie." The more interesting people she racked up, the more she felt she'd at least lived this life a little bit.

Janie sobered. "Ditto. Also, we do have the best doctors in the entire world. If there's any way to help you, Aunt Emma will figure it out. I promise." She winced. "In fact, I have a message for you two. Em would like to conduct more tests on Dessie as soon as you've settled in, just to make sure she has everything.

I'm assisting her. We're very good." She focused on her brother again. "Mom and Dad had to run to Seattle to help the wolves with something but will be back first thing in the morning. So get settled in, relax, and get ready."

Garrett's sigh moved his entire chest.

* * * *

Following an afternoon of watching Dessie go through medical test after medical test without one complaint, Garrett had had enough. Not only did the woman not complain, she joked with Emma and asked questions the entire time. It was as if she wanted to learn as much as possible before she died.

He wouldn't have it. None of it. His family was the most powerful one on the planet, and they had the best medical personnel. This one little human was not going to die.

"Stop frowning." Dessie grasped his forearm as they walked past the log homes from the medical center. "It's okay, Garrett."

None of this was okay. "We're going to figure out a way to get that thing out of your head." His gaze automatically scanned the forest on the other side of the road for any threats. It was nearly impossible to infiltrate their property, but he wasn't going to let anything happen to her on his watch.

For the first time, he wondered if he could let her go. Once she was cured—and she would be cured—what exactly was his plan? His chest ached, and he rubbed it with his free hand.

There was no way he could be falling for a human who'd only live for eighty more years or so.

If they cured her.

They had to cure her.

She had taken his blood successfully. What if he mated her? Could he give up the fate he'd seen for so long to save her? Was it even possible?

"Garrett," she breathed. "Look."

He glanced toward the nearest home to see two fawns frolicking near some bushes. Their mama was off to the side, watching them. At second glance, Garrett noticed the bushes had pretty flowers blooming. The twins ran over and started eating them.

"They're too cute," Dessie murmured, her cheeks pink from the slight autumn wind. "It's late in the season for flowers. You must've had a warm summer and fall here."

"Maybe." Darkness was already falling, and stars emerged high in the far distance of the sky. He needed to get her inside, where it was warm. "I ordered dinner, so it should be at the house when we arrive." He'd also asked his sister to have somebody find clothing for Dessie, and hopefully that would be at the house as well. She hadn't complained once about having only a few borrowed clothes, and she deserved better. "Are you hungry?"

"Sure." She traipsed along next to him, her eyes wide as if she didn't want to miss one thing on the walk.

He felt a little like a dork, but he drew a package from his pocket to hand to her.

She stumbled, looking down at the hard-bound book. "What is this?" Her voice hushed.

"It's an ancient tome from the demon archives that I think holds some history of the early romances of the people. There's kind of a clue to the code in the back."

She hopped, delight filtering across her face. "Garrett," she breathed. "I love it." Her smile was dazzling. "Thank you."

He grinned. Many women would've wanted jewels, but not Destiny. Books were the way to her heart.

His phone buzzed, and he lifted it to his ear. "Kayrs."

"Hey, it's Max. I've checked out both of the boarding schools and somehow scared the hell out of the headmaster of Stoneton Hills. He wouldn't give me your girl's records, but Chalton said he can hack them. The place is set on fifty acres of rolling hills— with a heavy emphasis on religion. Guest lecturers ranged from priests to nuns to Buddhist monks. I didn't see anything out of the ordinary, to be honest. Just a bunch of kids going to high school and the attached college."

Garrett gave in to temptation and drew Dessie closer to his side, shielding her from the gathering wind. "That's what I figured. Anything on physical education?"

"Yeah. They offer everything from long-distance running to archery for PE, and two semesters of self-defense are required. Seems like a good idea."

Garrett turned down his walkway toward the front door. Lights glowed a warm welcome from inside the home. "Okay. Thanks for checking it out for me, Max. You'd better head home for the symposium. Sarah will kill you if you're not here." If there was anything Max's mate loved, it was a good ball. The teacher liked to get dressed up for some reason.

"On my way, G. Can't wait to see you." Max ended the call.

"Who's Max?" Dessie asked.

Garrett opened the door and ushered her inside the heated space. "Max is one of my uncles. Dage brought him home years before I was born, centuries really, and he became one of the family. He's mated to a sweet woman named Sarah, and they have a little girl they adopted who's adorable. You'll meet them all." It was hard to even think about a stupid party when there were far more important issues in his life right now.

She took off the jacket and hung it in the closet. "I can tell you're upset, and I'm really sorry about that. Everyone dies at some point, probably even you someday." She turned to face him, her eyes the deep lapis of summer flowers. "Not even you can control this, Garrett." Her grin was impish even as sadness flowed from her.

The smell of something delicious caught his attention, and he took her hand to lead her into the kitchen, where the table had been set and some fancy chicken dish and tons of sides had been laid out.

She smiled. "You have a good life here."

He forced a grin. "Yeah. Guess so. Let's eat." He pulled out her chair, which was a light wood with dark gray cushions.

She sat and waited for him to join her. "You need to stop with the gentle calmness. It's not you. Be you."

He frowned and dished out the food. "I am being me."

"You're acting like I'm breakable. I'm not."

The hell she wasn't. Even at full strength and without a tumor the size of a golf ball in her head, she was infinitely fragile. "All right."

"Stop appeasing the dying girl," she snapped, her chin coming up.

"Stop calling yourself the dying girl," he snapped right back, all of his good intentions flying out the door.

She grinned. "That's better."

Unwilling amusement took him. "Okay. Here's the deal. I know Emma will find a way to fix that brain of yours. In the meantime, let's come up with a list of all the things you want to experience. I figure we'll head to Texas and royally mess with your aunt, and later on have some fun together at Hope's party. Then what? I'll take you anywhere in the world you want to go." Just in case.

She sampled the chicken and hummed in appreciation. "That's quite the offer." She seemed to mull it over. "I'd like to see Paris before I die."

Paris it was, then.

Her gaze rose to meet his directly, and a light peach filtered beneath the skin on her delicate face. "I also want to have sex before I die. You like me, and I like you. What do you say?"

Chapter Fifteen

Dessie flitted nervously through the sprawling closet that housed more clothes than she could've ever imagined having. In every color and fabric, and everything was her size.

There were almost too many pieces from which to choose.

The master bathroom was opulent and somehow comfortable with steel-gray towels, a warmed tile floor, and a bathtub big enough for three. She'd spent a decadent amount of time in the shower, with its many spray nozzles, and now drew on a flimsy white nightgown and matching robe that was pure silk.

She felt like a woman, a sexy one, and not a dying and desperate girl. Even so, she gulped.

Why had her school not been coed? She had learned the last couple of months to relate to people, to speak with men who weren't her professors, but she'd never even kissed a man until Garrett. She didn't feel guilty about asking him to engage in relations with her. Even with her inexperience, she knew he was attracted to her.

She was most certainly attracted to him. Just looking at him gave her those butterflies in her stomach she'd read about. He was gorgeous, but it was more than that. Garrett Kayrs was a good man. Or male. He was strong and sure, and he loved his family. There was a gentleness about him that called to her, but if she were honest, it was the edge in him that made her knees weak. The hint of danger and the whisper of violence, both of which she knew he'd never use on her.

He made her feel safe, which she hadn't felt in a very long time, if ever.

Yeah, she was halfway in love with him, and that was okay. It wasn't as if she had the time to explore her feelings. She had to accept them, and this was a good one.

He knocked on the door. "Des? Put on a swimsuit. Apparently we have a hot tub on the deck." His footsteps echoed away.

We? He'd said we. She hurriedly changed into a one-piece blue suit she found in one of the many drawers and wrapped a thick terrycloth robe around herself before padding out barefoot, past the humongous bed that made her blush, to an open sliding-glass door that led to the deck. Garrett was already in a bubbling hot tub, his head back and his eyes closed.

She hung the robe on a hook near the door and hurried to the hot tub, absurdly grateful he didn't look at her in the swimsuit. It was ridiculous, considering his mouth had been all over her body, but even so. She sat on the edge and gingerly slipped her feet in. Heat tingled up her legs, so she slid all the way in, letting the warm water engulf her.

It was divine.

His eyelids slowly opened, and that metallic gray speared through the darkness.

She shivered and then looked at the quiet lake before glancing up at the myriad of twinkling stars. "Do your eyes change colors?"

"Yes. Most immortals have at least two eye colors, and I seem to have a few."

That was intriguing, wasn't it? She settled down and let the warm water soak through her bones. "I like your home."

"Me too." His voice was a low rumble she could feel along her nerve endings. "I've been thinking."

"No. No thinking." Heat bombarded her, flooding her system like a relaxing elixir. "I mean it, Garrett."

He looked up at the cold but sparkling sky. "Dessie, I don't want you to make a mistake."

She moved then, going on instinct. Water splashed as she walked to him and planted herself right on his lap, her legs straddling his. She was tired of not living and exhausted from trying not to die. For now, she just wanted to *feel*. "If you don't want me, tell me now." Perhaps she'd read him wrong.

"You know I want you." To prove his point, he flattened his palm over her entire lower back and pulled her into his body, where his erection was hard and throbbing through his swim trunks.

Her eyes widened, and her lungs stuttered. Okay. He wanted her. Her legs trembled, but she cupped his face and leaned in to kiss him gently. Then she leaned back, keeping her hands in place and smiling when his whiskers scratched her palms. Letting herself explore, she traced the hard edge of his jaw and down the roped muscles in his neck. "I didn't know necks could have muscles," she murmured, tracing her fingers along his collarbone. He was sleekly muscled, not bulky or bulgy. Just powerful and graceful. "I should've known you weren't human."

"Dessie." Even with the hot water around them, his palm heated her lower back. "You need to take a breath."

"I'm breathing." She inched forward and licked her way up his neck to bite his earlobe. "If you don't want to do this, I'll stop pushing you. But I want this. I want you." There wasn't enough time left for her to play games or learn how to be coy. Honesty and this moment were all she had. "But I don't want you to humor me just because I don't have a lot of time left. Don't take pity on me."

He wrapped his hand around her nape and threaded his long fingers through her hair. "I'm not feeling pity. At all." With that, he took her mouth, destroying any need for her to think ever again. The hunger in his kiss, in how deep he went, was proof that he wanted this as much as she did.

She moaned against his mouth, trying to press even closer to him. The hard wall of his chest had no give against her tender breasts, and her nipples hardened to sharp points.

He caressed from her lower back up along her rib cage to brush the back of his knuckles against those aching nipples.

She gasped, and he took the kiss even deeper, holding her easily in place with the hand at her nape. Unable to help herself, she rubbed against him, and shards of pleasure rippled through her.

With a low growl that rumbled from his chest and moved down through her entire body, he banded an arm around her waist and stood, carrying her out of the hot tub and across the deck, then kicking the door shut with one foot. His mouth continued to work hers, and he laid her on the bed, his movements gentle for such a massive male.

He made quick work of her suit, flinging the stretchy material somewhere over his shoulder. Grabbing a throw blanket off the edge of the bed, he wiped the water off her body, taking care of her. Keeping her warm.

Tears filled her eyes, and she reached for him.

His grin was wicked, giving her a small warning. Then he grabbed her ankles, tugged her to the edge of the bed, knelt, and tossed her legs over his shoulders. Then his mouth was on her.

Fast and hard, he went at her, driving her up so quickly she forgot to breathe. She broke with a sharp cry, her body shaking with the release. Even so, he didn't stop. He nipped her thigh and then went at her again with his lips, his tongue, even his teeth. She thought anxiously of those sharp fangs, but surely he wouldn't use those.

Then his mouth enclosed her clit, and she detonated again, crying out his name as the orgasm pummeled her with sharp waves.

He still didn't stop.

"Garrett," she moaned.

His only response was to press two fingers inside her and twist, hitting spots she had only imagined. His focus was absolute, and he seemed as lost as she was in the moment.

"I can't," she whispered.

He paused and looked up, his eyes nowhere near human. "You will." His voice was guttural. Then he lowered his head and kissed her softly before nipping not as gently at her thigh.

Sparks flashed through her, and she shut her eyes, letting her body take over. Or letting Garrett take over her body. He pressed another finger inside her, and it hurt, but pleasure quickly followed. She gyrated against him, climbing again, her body going taut as she crested. Her legs shook so hard with this orgasm that he palmed one thigh to keep her in place.

Finally, she came down with a muffled sigh.

He paused and then stood, stripping off his still-wet shorts. Moonlight drifted in through the windows and door, so he cast a powerful shadow. Planting a hand on the bed, he wrapped his arm around her waist and lifted her up until her head touched the pillows.

She reached for him, scraping her nails down his torso. Even after the three orgasms, or maybe it was four, she felt empty without him. She ached in a way that only he could fix, and she wanted him.

Now.

"Are you sure?" He leaned down and kissed her nose, cheeks, and then her lips.

"Yes." She dug her fingers into his ribs and then slid her hands around his back and down to feel his butt. Even his butt was strong. There were muscles everywhere.

He lowered his body until his forehead touched hers and then positioned himself at her sex, carefully pressing inside her. "You're beautiful, Destiny."

Her breath caught. He was too big. There was no way.

He kissed her again, taking her mind away, and pushed farther inside her. "Trust me."

She stretched to accommodate him, and mini-tremors set up inside her, stealing her fear. He was too much, but she wanted more. She wanted all of him. So she dug her nails into the top of his butt, urging him on.

He reached her barrier, his gaze intent on hers. "I'm sorry." With one powerful shove, he kept going past the obstacle…and going. Pain sizzled through her, and she cried out, pulling her hands free to push against his chest. She had to stop him.

"You're okay," he whispered, finally fully embedded in her but not moving.

Vibrations of pain echoed through her body. "I think I'm not…" She felt as if he'd broken her in two. This wasn't right.

His grin looked rueful. "You are." Then his mouth took hers with heat and intent, driving fire down inside her to alight every inch.

She tentatively returned his kiss, and as her body began to relax, she became lost again. In his taste, in his touch, in being surrounded by him.

By Garrett Kayrs.

He kissed her cheeks, his tongue catching tears she hadn't realized she'd let fall. Her heart swelled. This night would be a memory she'd take with her beyond this world. Maybe beyond the next.

Even as her emotions exploded, her body started to move restlessly against his. Need built in her so quickly, she had to open her eyes. Metallic gray irises surrounded by dark blue watched her carefully.

One of his broad hands gripped her hip, holding her in place. He stabilized himself on his other elbow, so big and strong above her. How was he even real?

Then he dragged himself slowly out of her, caressing each needy nerve.

She gasped and stilled.

His grin was wicked with a side of sweet. He pushed back inside her, watching her carefully.

Delicious decadence coasted through her. Her hands relaxed almost on their own and then explored his chest, tapering down to the ripples in his abdomen muscles. His skin was heated, the muscles beneath sinewy. So much beauty in one person. In a vampire-demon immortal. "Garrett," she whispered.

He kissed her again, his tongue flicking hers.

Then he pushed inside her again, this time with a little more force. She caught her breath, wanting more.

Needing more.

He searched her face, apparently saw what he wanted, and then sped up his thrusts.

The feeling of fullness, of wildness, took her hard. She arched into him, wanting all of him. She needed to have every ounce of him he could give. Her breasts jolted in rhythm with his pistoning, just adding to the incredible pleasure.

His head ducked, and he nipped her ear, his fingers digging into her hip and marking her. Hopefully for a week or so. She wanted to carry his fingerprints as long as she could.

He half-lifted her, driving deeper inside. She couldn't breathe but no longer cared. There was so much pleasure rioting through her, all she could do was grab his powerful forearms and hold on.

His fangs slid into her neck, sharp and intense. Heat swirled around them, along with sparks in the air. He was an inferno, around them and inside her. For a second, just a blink of a thought, she could feel his heartbeat in perfect tune with hers.

Then the explosion blasted out from them both as he drove even deeper, branding her, making her forever his. An agonizing burn flared along her hip. She cried out, tears leaking from her eyes, as her body drained him, taking as much of him as she could have.

Her heart beat so wildly her chest hurt. She whimpered as she went limp, caressing his rib cage and around to his back to hold him as tightly as possible.

She closed her eyes to just feel.

His fangs gently withdrew.

Sighing, she opened her eyes and let her smile show. "That was incredible." Better than she could've ever imagined.

He stilled. Completely.

"What?" she whispered, noting the widening of his eyes.

He lifted one hand and looked at his palm. "I marked you."

Chapter Sixteen

Garrett stepped out of the shower and wrapped a towel around his waist, glancing down at his aching palm. The jagged and deadly marking of his family—a deep *K* surrounded by sharp and wicked-looking lines. *His* marking. His ears were ringing and his heart still battered his rib cage.

He'd marked her. On her hip.

How was it possible? Sure, she'd taken his blood, but she still felt human. Felt human to him. And he hadn't even noticed the marking appearing on his hand before it transferred to her flesh.

He wasn't a male who was caught off guard. Ever.

Dessie had left scratches across his abs, and he fought the natural healing cells in his body to keep the marks there. While his torso was impenetrable from neck to waist, his skin was fair game. To her, anyway. She'd dug right into his heart, and he wasn't sure what to do about that. Well, now she was his mate, so he'd better figure it out.

The idea pleased him. The realization smashed hard into his solar plexus. Yet, what about that dangerous female he'd dreamed about for so long? He searched for guilt inside himself and didn't find any.

Not an ounce.

Either he was a complete ass, or his dreams had gotten it wrong. The woman in the other room was sweet, vulnerable, and kind. The exact opposite of the female he'd tried to find the last many years. And now she was his.

Brushing wet hair away from his face, he strode into the bedroom to see her sprawled out beneath the covers, watching him. "You're awake."

Her grin was cute and a bit sleepy. He hadn't let her get much rest during the night, such was his hunger. He rubbed his chest above his heart. Had he ever felt like this? If so, he didn't remember it.

She sat, holding the covers to her chest. Whisker burn was visible from her breasts to her neck. He'd have to be more careful with her next time. "So. Am I any good at sex?"

Amusement took him hard. She would ask that question. "You are phenomenal at sex," he said honestly. His cock hardened beneath the towel, but she had to be sore. He needed to be a decent guy and not a selfish asshat. "Last night meant the world to me." True story. Protectiveness and something stronger, deeper, washed through him. For her.

Her smile widened, and she shoved her thick hair over her shoulder. "Me too. Although I kind of felt you held back." Her expression was earnest, and her eyes guileless.

He should feel like a jerk for touching somebody so pure, but he wanted her again already. Of course he'd held back. She was so very breakable. "I didn't hold back." That was probably a decent lie, and why worry her? "You were perfect, and I wouldn't change a thing about last night." It surprised him that he meant it. Being gentle wasn't in his nature, but she deserved every kindness and care. It was an old-fashioned thought, but she'd given him a gift the previous night, and he wanted to take care of her.

She shyly pushed the comforter off her legs and twisted her hips. "The marking looked pretty."

His gaze caught on her hip, where his marking was barely visible. "What the hell?" he whispered, moving for her and shoving the blankets away.

"What?" She craned her neck to see the visibly fading lines.

"It was supposed to stay. Forever." He scrubbed a rough hand through his wet hair. None of this was making sense, and the branding on his hand pounded with the demand to mark her again.

She paled. "Oh. Because I'm not enhanced."

There had to be some enhancement, or he wouldn't have been able to mark her in the first place. He shoved anger down in order to think rationally. "How about I make us breakfast and then we'll have you checked out by the doctors?" He turned and moved for the other side of the room, searching for his discarded jeans.

She gasped. "Your back."

He glanced over his shoulder. When he'd undergone the ritual to become one of the Seven, his ribs had been fused together to make his torso impenetrable. While his front looked normal, his back looked like an intricate black tattoo with his ribs showing. "I know. It's a long—" He caught movement from the corner of his eye and pivoted instinctively.

Pain slashed deep between his shoulder and his neck and then splintered out. He hissed in agony as a blade sliced through his upper arm, removing his shoulder and most of his arm. The blade clattered away on the wooden floor.

He turned, dropping the towel, ready to protect Dessie.

She wasn't in the bed.

Air swished as she somersaulted toward him, grabbing the knife and rolling up on her feet. Quicker than a snake, she jumped up and jabbed the knife, *her knife*, toward his throat with all her strength.

He jumped back, and the knife struck him in the thigh as her arm fell. The blade penetrated the flesh and then viciously split it in two, slicing his muscle clean through. Agony speared through him, and his foot went numb. Blood from his artery spurted in every direction. The weapon dropped near his foot. His mind couldn't take what his eyes were seeing. She was trying to kill him?

Still nude, Dessie dove for the weapon and neatly came up, already striking at him with it. He slapped her away, smacking her hand. What the hell was happening? If that thing hit his neck or throat, it could decapitate him. His left arm was uselessly hanging by a couple of stretching tendons, and his leg was already weakening as he bled out. He sent healing cells to the leg and slid back, his eyes on the woman. "Dessie?" He put command in his voice.

She'd gone white pale, and her eyes were dilated. Her brunette hair was a wild mess around her head, and her teeth were bared. Her nostrils flared as the scent of blood engulfed the room. *His blood.* She was all graceful instinct, her gaze on his body, searching. For a weakness? Giving a battle cry, she lifted the knife and charged him, jumping on his knee and all but climbing him. The tip of the blade sliced at the base of his throat.

He grabbed her hand and twisted, forcing the knife away from his flesh. Her wrist broke with an audible snap. The knife fell to the floor again.

As if she didn't feel the break, she fought viciously, kicking and striking, hitting him square in his injuries. She grunted and hissed, a wild woman. As if possessed, she tried to inflict the most possible pain and injury.

He had to get that fucking blade away from her while he still could. Sucking in air, he kicked the knife with his injured leg and hissed as agony ripped up his thigh to his groin. The blade spun around and around across the floor and stuck into the wooden baseboard.

Grunting, she turned to pursue the weapon, spittle flying from her mouth.

Controlled fury rippled through him. His survival instincts were finally taking over from his shocked brain. He snagged her hair and yanked her back, instantly wrapping his good hand around her throat and lifting her into the air. She was facing away from him but kicked back, nailing him in the thigh.

His leg buckled, and he balanced on his good leg, squeezing her windpipe until she clawed her fingernails into his hand. He shook her, trying to evade her back kicks. If he took another blow to his injured thigh, he'd go down.

She screamed and struggled, gesticulating wildly as he choked her out as gently as possible. Finally, her movements slowed. He held tight, waiting until she'd gone fully unconscious before he relaxed his hold on her neck. Slowly, he inched her toward the bed and set her down, keeping his body between her and the weapon. His vision went dark, but he edged along the bed to his nightstand and grabbed his phone to press speed dial.

"Hey, G. Good timing—we just got home. What's up?" Talen answered the call easily.

More blood spurted from his destroyed shoulder. "Dad? I need blood." He hit his knees, forcing himself to watch Dessie and remain conscious until help arrived.

What the holy hell had just happened?

* * * *

Garrett jolted awake as the air popped around him with healing vibrations. He sat in a hospital bed with the covers down to his waist. An IV poured blood into his vein so quickly, his heart rate had to be in the stratosphere. His arm and shoulder were bandaged, and he could feel his muscles and tendons stitching themselves together with painful needles. "Whose blood is this?" he mumbled, looking around as something beeped above his head.

"It's a concoction," came a soft voice to his right.

He looked over as his vision cleared to see three identical pairs of blue eyes staring worriedly at him. "Hi, Mom." He smiled at his mother, winked at Janie, and blew a kiss at his niece. "Hope. I can't believe you're going to be twenty-one." They had various shades of brunette hair and similar bone structure. Even though they represented three generations, from grandmother to granddaughter, they looked like sisters in their twenties.

Except for the fact that Hope had the blue markings of a prophet winding up her neck into her hair. The lines were graceful and danced like fire, and he'd wanted to take them off her since she was born.

It was too heavy a burden for anyone to bear.

"Hi, my wayward son." Cara Kayrs smoothed his now-dry hair away from his face. "The blood is a mix we use for dangerous injuries. It's a blend of your dad's, Dage's, Zane's, and a couple of your witch aunts. It's the best of all blends." Zane was the king of the demon nation, and no doubt his blood was potent.

"Feels like it," Garrett acknowledged, studying his mother.

Her normally brunette hair had streaks of blond in it from time spent on an island earlier that year with his dad, and she looked healthy, albeit concerned. "How are you feeling?" she asked, worry making her pale.

"Like I took a blade to my arteries." He pushed the covers off his legs, his brain finally kicking back into gear. "Where is Dessie?" He had to find her and figure out what the hell had happened. How had he missed that she was not only capable of killing him but more than willing to do so? He kept his expression neutral. Did anybody know he'd mated her?

"She's still unconscious and behind bars," Cara said, her jaw stiffening. "When we got to you, your dad wanted to rip off her head. But I figured we should wait and see what exactly happened." She stood and leaned over him to study his pupils. "You look like you're healing okay. Emma checked you out and just went to see how that woman is doing."

So they didn't know. Had the marking disappeared completely? A growl rose from his gut, and he shoved it down. He needed to talk to Dessie about this before he made the announcement to his family, especially since right now, his family probably wanted the small human tossed in a cell for good. He was more stunned than angry at the moment.

Janie patted his hand. "Your leg has healed already, but it's going to take another hour or so before you should move your arm."

Hope shook her head. "This is crazy, Uncle Garrett. How could a human get the drop on you like this?" No judgment lay in her tone.

His sister winced. "We have to assume the Kurjans are using humans to do their dirty work now. Right?"

Garrett sat up fully and swung his legs to the side. "I can handle this."

"It certainly doesn't appear that way." Talen Kayrs stalked into the room, his dark hair curling over his ears, and his golden eyes beyond pissed. "What the hell, Garrett?"

"I don't know, Dad." Garrett wished he wasn't wearing white scrubs over his legs, but at least he was dressed. He gingerly flexed the foot of his injured leg, and all was well. That was a quick healing. Good.

Dage was right behind him, no less angry. He crossed his arms. "She's human." He cut a look at his brother. "Talen. Human."

Talen blanched.

Fury swept over Garrett. "I'm aware she's fucking human." Except she couldn't be—his marking had landed for a short while. That couldn't happen with any human. He stood and stubbornly refused to fall right back down again. "Now, if you don't mind, I'm going to have a chat with the little human." The small female who'd nearly beheaded him. He didn't know whether to be embarrassed or furious. Perhaps both.

"You're staying right here," his mom said, trying to push him back down.

He gently set her aside with his good arm. "Where is she?"

His dad sighed. "We have her locked down on the third basement level." He held up a massive hand before Garrett could argue. "She stays there until we figure out what happened, and no, we didn't hurt her."

Garrett's mind reeled as he replayed the entire situation in his head. "She wasn't herself." He limped toward the door, trying to walk straight. "I want more tests conducted by Emma, and we need to examine that knife. Our enemies have a new weapon, apparently."

"Already did," Talen said, drawing the blade out of his back pocket. "It's handmade of a steel and silver mixture that's nearly unbreakable. The thing's ingenious. When the knife strikes immortal flesh, the entire blade splits in two. So if the blade is plunged into a neck, it could conceivably sever that neck." He handed it over to Garrett. "The weapon has your girlfriend's name engraved on it, G. From the looks of you, she knows how to use it."

Garrett took a closer look at the knife. Even now, he couldn't see how the blade could separate. The weapon was expertly made. "I want to talk to her alone."

Talen shook his head. "Shit, G. For all we know, she can spit fire from her fucking eyes. Nobody should see her alone, even if there are bars keeping her from striking."

Garrett made it through the door, his chest heavy and his body wearing evidence of their night together as well as wounds from her homicide attempt. "She tried to kill me," he mused, striding down the hallway. What did that mean? He'd had her on the back of his bike, she'd tried to kill him, and that tumor in her head was going to end her and take her away.

"She is not your mate," Talen snapped, on his heels.

Dage nodded from his other side. "I have no doubt there are many females who'd like to kill you, G. They can't all be your mate."

"I mated her," he said quietly, holding up one hand when they tried to protest. "The marking landed and then faded. I don't know why." But he was going to find out.

Talen and Dage uttered the same expletive at the same time.

Why exactly had he come home? Garrett ignored them both. They were worried, and they were pissed, and they were terrible at expressing emotions. Not that he was much better. "Fuck you both and leave me alone." As expected, they ignored him and escorted him down the three flights of stairs to one of the underground tunnels.

By the time he reached the rock landing, sweat was dotting his forehead, and his left side felt like it was on fire.

"Should've taken the elevator," Talen drawled.

"Don't make me hit you with my bad arm," Garrett snapped, in no mood. He gave up shrugging them off and walked down the tunnel to a secured area, not surprised to find Emma taking Dessie's vitals in a small cell with guards surrounding them. "For God's sake," he muttered. "Everyone get the hell out." He inched toward Dessie, who was lying quietly on a cot with her eyes closed and her breathing calm.

As he approached, she stirred.

Dage instantly grabbed Emma and thrust her behind him, protecting his mate as always.

The guards tensed.

Garrett shoved one to the side. "Destiny?"

Her eyelids fluttered open in her too-pale face. "Garrett?" Then all color leeched from her face, and she sat up, grabbing her head. She let out a scream that clawed right through Garrett and then shut her eyes again, dropping her head and shrieking in an agonized tone that gave him chills.

"What the hell?" He moved to her. "Emma. Help."

She tossed him a syringe. "Sedative."

He manacled Dessie's arm and shoved in the needle, plunging quickly. She went limp again.

Chapter Seventeen

Dessie was wrapped up in cotton and comfort. She stretched, lazily coming awake. A rock ceiling was above her. She jolted upright, looking frantically around a stone cell with iron bars. Blinking, she noted the rough cot with its surprisingly warm plush blanket. As her vision cleared, she spotted Garrett sitting on the floor with his back against onyx-colored rocks. "Garrett?"

His gaze was a tumultuous gray, and a bandage covered his left shoulder and arm. He wore white scrubs on his legs, and his feet were bare, as was his torso. Marks from her nails were evident down his ripped abs. "How are you feeling?"

She rubbed her temple, which ached as if she'd been punched. "My head hurts." Swallowing, she winced as her dry throat protested. "Why are we in a cell?" How did she get there? What was happening? Panic tried to take hold of her, but the entire world seemed so fuzzy. "I don't understand." Then she focused more fully on him. "You're hurt. Were we attacked?" Why couldn't she remember?

He scanned her, the open humor of that morning long gone. "You attacked me."

She snorted. "Right. I attacked you." The idea was preposterous. She was half his size and not immortal. Then a throbbing in her wrist caught her attention, and she looked down to see her right wrist bandaged and iced. "What's wrong with my wrist?" She shoved off the ice pack and stretched her hand.

"I broke it," he said curtly.

Why was he lying to her? She studied her hand and wrist, which looked slightly red but unharmed. "It's not broken."

"I gave you blood, and the bone mended. Again." For some reason, he sounded even angrier now.

She couldn't handle whatever charade he was playing with her. This was too freaking weird. "Seriously. Tell me what happened." Why were they in a cell?

"Dessie? You're going to want to level with me. Right now, you're viewed as a threat to the Realm, and I'm the only thing standing between you and a very quiet death. Why did my mating mark fade to nothing and why did you attack me?"

She blinked. Was he joking? If so, this wasn't humorous. "Stop it, Garrett," she whispered. Her hands shook, and she pulled her legs up, turning her back to the wall to better face him. "There's no way I could hurt you, so whatever game you're playing, I don't like it." She smoothed her hair back from her face, wishing for a ponytail holder. "Please tell me why you're in bandages."

He rubbed the dark stubble across his jawline. "Did you know your knife could split in two?"

"Huh?" What did that even mean?

He sighed. "Tell me what you know about the Seven."

"What Seven?" She wanted to leave this cell. Now. She tried to clear her throat, and pain encircled her neck. She gingerly touched her skin, surprised to find it hurting. "I'm bruised? My neck?"

"I choked you out," he said quietly.

Shock jolted through her. "You did what?" That's why she couldn't remember anything? He'd hurt her? Why? No wonder her neck felt as if it had been smashed between rocks. "Did you try to kill me?" Probably not. He would've succeeded.

"You tried to kill me."

"Stop lying to me," she snapped. How could he do this? They'd spent a wonderful night together, and then he'd turned into a sociopath who'd choked her unconscious. Had the mating mark even been real or some fake temporary tattoo? "I want to leave. Now."

The outside door opened, and King Dage stepped inside, scouted the room, and then opened the door wider.

Emma walked in behind him, her dark hair up on her head and her white lab coat askew over her jeans and sweater.

Dessie straightened, and hope unfurled inside her. Although the woman was Garrett's aunt and the queen, she'd been very kind the day before when she'd run her tests. "Emma. Please help me. I don't understand what's going on."

"Me either," Emma said, peering at them through the bars.

Garrett stretched to his feet, looking powerful and dangerous. "What did you find?"

"Nothing new in her blood. No sign of mating you, and there's no marking on her hip in the slightest. In addition, her second brain scan is odd," Emma said, her brow furrowing. "So weird. The tumor has shrunk, and half of the tendrils have pulled back into the main mass. It's pretty much impossible, and I don't understand it at all, but the scans don't lie."

Dessie stiffened, and her heartbeat galloped. "My tumor decreased in size? How?"

Garrett barked out a laugh with absolutely no humor. "Wait a minute. You're telling me that her attempting to kill me actually shrank the tumor in her head?"

Emma looked down at the scans in her hands. "Uh, yes. Well, we don't know that. Maybe it was the mating mark, but since it disappeared so completely, I don't think so."

Garrett looked down at his hand.

Emma cleared her throat. "Dessie tried to kill you, and her tumor has decreased in size, but we have no proof the two situations are related. Although I suppose chemicals could've been released in her body that attacked the tumor when she attacked you." Her voice trailed off in thought.

Enough. Just enough. Dessie straightened her spine. "I don't know who you people are or what kind of game you are playing, but I'm finished with it and want to leave." Her voice trembled, but she met their gazes directly. For years, she'd had teachers try to intimidate her, and she'd learned young that ignoring bullies didn't work. Facing them squarely often did.

Garrett sighed. "All right. Let's do this."

King Dage opened the cell door. "Not in there, Garrett." The man really sounded like a king, and Dessie's shoulders began to tremble.

Garrett eyed her and then backed out of the cell, still facing her. He moved with a limp. Was his leg injured? He lowered his chin and trapped her gaze. "Dessie? Keep your eyes on me."

Yeah, like she'd look anywhere else. This was so weird. Were they really immortals? Had all of this been some sick ruse to kidnap her? Were there kidnapped women everywhere in this subdivision? Her stomach rolled.

To think that she'd slept with Garrett just the night before. She'd been so happy and had felt so safe. What a complete joke. It took her a second to realize he was waiting for a response from her. "Sure, Garrett. I'd be overjoyed to keep looking at your lying, manipulative ass."

His jaw hardened, and he turned around. A black tattoo that looked like a set of ribs covered his entire back. A humming started between her ears. Her blood heated and popped inside her veins, forcing them to jump in pain. A shriek roared through her.

Then nothing. The world went dark.

* * * *

"Shit," Dage snarled as Dessie hit the bars, wildly clawing at Garrett's face.

Garrett stepped out of reach, studying her unfocused eyes. "Is she in a trance?"

Emma tried to move forward and was instantly hindered by Dage grabbing her around the waist and putting her back against the far wall. She pushed at him but didn't try again. "I don't know, but you were right about the trigger."

Dessie slammed herself against the bars, snarling, her hair flying in every direction. She grunted and tried to maneuver her small body between the bars but couldn't come close. She shrieked and started kicking the bars.

"Damn it." Garrett moved toward the door. "She'll hurt herself." Stepping inside the cell, he spun her around and banded an arm over her torso, trapping both of her arms. Then he lifted her up. "Stop it," he commanded at her ear.

Her struggles increased, but she couldn't cause any damage while he was holding her so close. She'd also stopped screaming now that he held her, but frustrated grunts rolled from her chest. He pivoted to face his aunt so she could see Dessie's eyes. "Should we use a sedative, or do you think she'll wind down?" There was no doubt in his mind that Dessie was out of hers.

Emma's gaze was narrowed as she watched Dessie struggle uselessly against Garrett. "I'd hate to sedate her again. With that tumor in her head, I'd prefer to keep her conscious, if possible."

Garrett settled his stance to better balance himself and held on to the human as she fought with everything she had. Without her brutal knife, she didn't have a chance against him. "Dessie, it's time to stop now." He spoke against her ear, keeping his tone as calm as possible.

Her bucking and kicking back were impressive, but he kept her off the ground so she couldn't find purchase. After almost thirty minutes, her movements slowed, and her head began to hang, but she kept trying to free herself, sobbing loudly now. Something in his chest hurt at the raw sound, but he shifted his weight to continue holding her aloft.

Then her sobs quieted.

He kissed her ear. "It's okay. Just let yourself relax. It's over, and you're safe." Risking the pain in his still-healing arm, he lifted his hand and smoothed her sweaty hair back from her face. Her struggles intensified for a second, and he wanted to turn her around to face him, but he couldn't give an inch. "Knock it off, Des." He met Emma's worried gaze over Dessie's head. "How long does an episode last, anyway?"

She shook her head. "I've never seen anything like this."

Dessie's body went limp.

"There we go." Garrett moved toward the cot.

"No," Emma said. "I need to see inside her head. Maybe the tumor has decreased again, or perhaps that just happens when she can actually stab you." She gestured to the outside door. "Or the tumor activity isn't related to her actions. Who knows? I don't, but I want to find out."

Garrett turned.

"I'll take her." Dage opened the door wider.

"I've got her." Garrett flipped Destiny around and tossed her over his good shoulder, careful not to jostle her. He hadn't had a choice earlier, but nothing else was going to hurt her on his watch. She mumbled against his lower back but didn't kick out any longer. His head ached, and his arm hurt like bees were stinging him, but a fresh pain swept beneath his skin and tunneled deep into his gut as she let out another soft sob. Whoever had fucked with her brain was going to die, and it was going to take a long time for them to get there.

Emma looked at his expression and stumbled. "Whoa, Garrett—"

Dage grasped her arm and steadied her. "I'm with you, G."

Garrett strode up the stairs, keeping a hand on Dessie's legs in case she came back awake. She tried to kick out again, her movements feeble. "She's not calming down," he muttered. If she had time to rest, she might even attack again. "I think we're going to need a sedative."

Dage opened the door to the main medical facility, and Emma swept through.

"Let's get her on the table for the scan, and I'll give her a light sedative." Emma hustled toward a counter in the far corner near a machine that was eons more developed than a PET scan.

Garrett laid Dessie on the soft mattress, careful to cushion her head. She thrashed back and forth, her hands coming up to strike him.

Emma smoothly injected the sedative into Dessie's upper arm. The woman went limp with a soft sigh.

Dage reached for Velcro restraints beneath the mattress and gave Garrett a hard look when he started to object. His uncle was right. Garrett nodded and secured Dessie's other arm and ankles, making sure the straps weren't too tight.

Emma fetched a tablet from the counter and a screen came alive behind Dessie's bed. "I need to access all of her earlier tests."

Records began popping up on the screen, and an address caught Garrett's attention. Then another. He straightened. "Em? Would you bring up a map of the medical facilities where Dessie sought help?"

Emma paused. "Sure." She clicked buttons and a map came up with dots. "Huh."

Garrett stiffened. "Well. That's a nice straight line from her school to the diner in California. Where she met me." So much for it being a coincidence. Fury caught him hard and squeezed his chest.

Dage studied the map. "Definitely a direct line. So she was herded toward you." He looked down at the sleeping woman. "Or she knew what she was doing."

Garrett's throat heated but he kept his expression inscrutable. "Send scouts to interrogate those doctors, and I need Aster, her former employer, brought here to me within the hour." The chat was going to be painful if the loafer-wearing jackass didn't give him what he wanted.

Dage pulled out his phone and shot off a quick text.

Emma read her tablet. "Dessie will be out for at least thirty minutes and back in the cell before she awakens." She patted Garrett's arm. "Go ahead and do what you need to do. I'll make sure she's safe."

Two soldiers walked in from outside the hallway, and Dage gave them orders to protect Emma.

"Don't hurt Destiny," Garrett said quietly, waiting for nods from them both. "If she fights you, remember she's breakable. I want her in one piece when I get back."

Aster, on the other hand, was another story. He was about to meet a very different fate.

Chapter Eighteen

Lights flickered behind her eyelids as warmth cascaded over her skin. Dessie awoke in a slightly reclined chair with a heated blanket over her legs. She swallowed and tried to focus. The edges of her vision remained blurry, so she blinked several times until she could see cell bars across from her chair. Weird.

This was a strange dream. She forced herself out of it and jerked her head, awakening completely. She was in a lounger in a cell? Black stone with silver glimmers comprised the walls and ceiling as well as the floor.

"Hi. How's your head?"

She looked up to see the queen on the other side of the bars. Many tendrils of Emma's black hair had escaped her clip, framing her face. It appeared as if she'd had a very busy day. "Dessie?"

Dessie looked down at her wrists, which were strapped to the arms of the chair. Her legs tingled as a wave of fear engulfed her, and she kicked out, only to find that her legs were restrained as well. "What are you doing?" Her voice came out a husky whisper.

Emma stuck her hands in her lab coat pockets and moved closer to the bars. "Do you remember anything?"

Dessie tried to free her arms, but the bindings were too strong. "No. Just last night with Garrett." Her breath caught in her throat. "Where is he?"

Emma opened the door, and two bulky men instantly stepped forward from the shadows behind her. They were tall, dressed in black, and visibly armed with guns and knives. She waved them back. "I'm okay." Then she walked toward Dessie, her steps graceful as she crossed the smooth, black rock floor. "Every time you looked at the, well, the tattoo on Garrett's back, you tried to kill him. Can you explain that to me?"

Kill Garrett? Seriously? "You've lost your mind, Queen." Dessie kicked as hard as she could, but she couldn't free her legs.

Emma sighed. "Okay. While there aren't cameras in Garrett's house, we have them in this cell. Watch this." She dug a small tablet out of her pocket and held it in front of Dessie, starting a recording.

Dessie frowned at seeing herself in this same cell with Garrett. When had she been here before? She couldn't remember it. Was the video doctored somehow? She'd read that people could do that... but why? As she watched, Garrett exited the cell and shut the door.

"Watch your reaction," Emma said, leaning closer.

This was insane. All of a sudden, on the video, Dessie saw herself spiral into a rage and attack the bars. She gasped, shock echoing through her head. Her eyes were wild, and she acted like a rabid animal. Her heart raced, and her body began to tremble. "I don't understand," she croaked.

Then Garrett moved back into the cell and spun her around, lifting her into the air and controlling her. She wound down, looking exhausted.

Emma slid the tablet into her pocket. "Garrett's back tattoo is a trigger for you. Do you know why?"

"No," Dessie said numbly. She wouldn't believe any of this if it wasn't on a video. "I don't remember. Not a second of what's on that recording."

Emma bit her lip. "Do you, um, remember being mated?"

Dessie's jaw dropped. "No. I remember, our, ah, time together, though."

"Guess not," Emma murmured. "Do you have any recollection of being trained or hypnotized while you were at Stoneton Academy?"

"No. None." She tried to think back to her classes, but nothing came to mind. A feeling of vulnerability engulfed her. Somebody had manipulated her mind? Had forced her to attack Garrett? "I don't understand. What's wrong with his tattoo?"

"Nothing. It's not really a tattoo, but Garrett should tell you that story." Emma tapped her finger on her lips, as if thinking. "We should concentrate on you right now."

"Am I mated?" To Garrett? Dessie's body warmed. Why didn't she remember?

"I don't think so." Sympathy lightened Emma's blue eyes. "The marking didn't take and your genetics haven't changed. However, I would like to conduct additional tests."

Nausea rolled through Dessie, and she shifted her weight, trying to keep from gagging. "What kind of tests?"

"Well, let's see what triggers you. We know that seeing Garrett's back does it. What if you just see a picture of his back?" Emma began to pace and continued as if she was talking to herself. "And then there are other people with the same markings. Would you react the same way to one of them?" She started speaking faster. "They're all mated now, so we can't conduct a true A/B testing. Garrett will just have to be A and the rest B. It's too bad they're all mated except for him." She shook her head.

"Emma, this is too much." Dessie had never felt so alone in her entire life, and that was saying something, considering she hadn't had family after her parents had died. Not really. "I'm not a killer. Please tell me I didn't kill anybody." She'd already been in that cell when she'd attacked. How had she gotten there?

Emma patted her arm. "You haven't killed anybody that I know about."

Thank goodness. She'd never imagined she could be so violent. Her mind replayed what she'd seen. "Garrett remained totally in control, even as I fought him so hard. How did he do that?" Not once had he lost his temper or hurt her, and he'd been injured and bandaged. God. Had she hurt him?

Emma's face softened. "Garrett's been an adult since he was in diapers. He's strong and smart, and he'll be the king someday." She must've caught sight of the confusion on Dessie's face because she continued to explain. "When he was just twenty, most of the males in our family contracted a virus we thought would kill them. Most females were weakened from the virus as well. Garrett stepped up that day to lead, and I don't think he's ever taken off that mantle of responsibility. Not once."

Dessie swallowed, and her heart swelled. It was crazy, but she needed him there with her. "He was wearing bandages in the video. Because of me?"

"Yes," Emma said gently. "Your knife is deadly. Did you know that it splits in two once embedded in flesh? That it can behead immortals?"

Dessie jolted. "No. I had no idea." Unwilling tears pricked the back of her eyes. Why would her professor give her a blade that could kill immortals? "Did I hurt him badly?"

"No. He's fine by now." Emma finally stopped moving. "I should tell you something else. The attacks you made on Garrett had an effect on your tumor. Both times it shrank noticeably, and the tendrils retreated somewhat."

Dessie's mouth dropped open. "What does that mean?"

Emma spread out her hands. "My best guess is that the tumor was created on purpose by whoever programmed you to kill." Sympathy darkened her pretty eyes. "So buckle up, sister. Your life is about to be turned upside down by one very pissed-off vampire."

* * * *

Garrett sat on the floor in the medical hallway, flanked by two of the three Kyllwood brothers. Sam, his Grizzly motorcycle-club brother, was on his left. On his right sat Logan, Garrett's best friend and the youngest of the Kyllwoods. He was also a member of the Seven, and they'd forged blood and bone together in their fight to survive the devastating ritual to bond their torsos, creating a brotherhood from pain and survival. At the moment, they were silent, each staring at the innocuous gray wall and the wide window across from them that showed the examination room.

Emma and Janie bustled around an unconscious Destiny, obtaining another brain scan while she was out.

Logan broke the silence first. His black hair was cut short now, and his green eyes were shades darker than Sam's. Both were built hard and tough. "Your woman is fierce when she wants to kill."

Garrett sighed. "Thanks for going in there and showing her your back." Logan's torso was fused much the same as Garrett's. Although Dessie was secured in the chair, the second she'd seen Logan's marking, she'd lost her mind the same way she had earlier. Emma had been forced to sedate her again.

Sam shrugged. "Well, I guess the good news is that her trigger requires seeing the marking on a live body?"

"That's something," Garrett muttered. Dessie hadn't reacted to pictures or drawings of the markings, so at least she was safe from somebody sending her an unwanted email or text to provoke a reaction.

Sam stretched his long legs out. "You know, I don't think I've seen you date a woman under six feet tall in years. You normally like them broad and dangerous."

Garrett just watched to make sure Dessie didn't awaken and find herself strapped to a table again.

Logan nodded. "I guess it's not a surprise. I mean, look at them."

Garrett frowned as his aunt and sister bustled around. Both petite with blue eyes. Just like his mom, who was also a brunette. Just like Dessie. "I thought my mate would be a strong immortal woman I don't have to worry about breaking." He caught himself and glanced at Sam. "No offense. Honor is tough." But she had been a human, which meant no immortal strength or speed.

Logan scratched his ear, which had a clear bite mark on it. Probably from his mate, Mercy, who was a crazy-assed fairy. Garrett adored her. "I don't think you get to choose who you fall for in this life," Logan mused. He leaned slightly forward to share a look with his older brother.

"Shut up," Garrett said mildly.

Logan kicked out his legs to cross his ankles. "Just think about it. You've had dreams for years, and except for being human, Dessie fits the description. She has ridden on the back of your bike, is dangerous, and has tried to kill you."

"I know." Why hadn't his mating mark stuck? Frustration blew through him. "Our life is a tough one." It was only going to get more dangerous, and the fact that somebody had programmed a human to kill him was proof of that. The Realm was still at war, no matter what the leaders of the species wanted. "If I can't get the mating mark to stick and increase her chromosomal pairs, I can't make sure she's protected. She won't be immortal."

Sam shook his head. "I don't understand what was done to her, but it seems like a shitload of a mess. She has to be enhanced somehow. Maybe whoever assaulted her mind somehow screwed with her on a deeper level than we can imagine."

Garrett had already considered that fact. But Dessie was also not telling him the whole truth. There was no way she'd spent years being trained to fight as she had that morning and not know it. He'd have to question her, and it wasn't going to be enjoyable for either of them. His phone buzzed, and he lifted it to see his father's face. "Hey. What have the scouts found?" Garrett asked instead of a greeting.

Talen's eyes were a deep gold in the light by the lake. "The teams have met with each of the doctors Dessie consulted on her trek west. As expected, the medical tests they ran on her were legitimate, but the way each sent her farther west to another doctor was because they were under threat from some soldiers who scared the hell out of them. They steered her toward you, G."

"Human soldiers?" Logan asked, elbowing Garrett to get closer to the screen.

"I think it was Kurjans in disguise," Talen said. "One of the doctors described the males as very pale with black hair and dark eyes, which were probably contacts. Now that the Kurjans can venture into the sun, it could easily be them."

The Kurjans had been the Realm's enemy from the beginning of their species. They were pale-skinned, with purple or red eyes, usually. Their hair was either black tipped with red or red tipped with black, and until very recently, exposure to the sun had killed them. Their scientists had just overcome that weakness. The Cysts were their religious leaders, and Ulric was their ruler.

Sam elbowed Garrett's other side to see the screen. "Has sweet Dessie left behind a trail of bodies?"

"No. Didn't find any murders," Talen confirmed.

"Thanks for checking," Garrett said. None of this was looking good for Dessie. Just what had they done to her? Why couldn't she remember? Or did she remember but didn't want to level with him?

"What did you get from that Aster who was with her when she found you?" Talen asked.

Garrett rolled his neck. Aster had been brought to the Realm, but Garrett hadn't even gotten to hit the moron. Not once. Aster had folded like a wounded fish. "Dessie answered an ad to be a freelance journalist with Aster's small-town family paper, and that was legit. Then terrifying goons, as he put it, forced him to take Dessie and chase a story about the Grizzlies, which was why they'd walked into that diner where I was eating." Of course, even the Kurjans hadn't known how he'd react, if at all. He'd had to let Aster go home unharmed.

Talen frowned. "You fell right into their trap."

"Thanks, Dad," Garrett muttered.

Talen shook his head, his face as sharply cut as any mountain around them. Rugged and strong. "Not what I meant. She's human, and you jumped right in. You kind of mated her. She has to be enhanced, and I think you recognized her."

"Agreed." The female was his, and Garrett would fix this. Even though his dad was the toughest male on the planet, sometimes Garrett forgot that he was also a romantic. "Dad—"

"Or she knows a lot more than she's telling you, which is probably what's happening. She must have said or done something that caught your interest, and you know it. Either way, you'll probably have to kill her," Talen murmured, watching him closely.

The beast inside Garrett stretched awake. "She will not be killed." His voice went demon guttural.

A very rare dimple flashed in Talen's cheek. "Interesting. You're gonna want to smooth things over with your mother before she cuts off Dessie's head, then." He ended the call.

Chapter Nineteen

Destiny felt like a fish trapped in a beautiful aquarium as she sat on a barstool at the kitchen counter in Garrett's lovely home. Guards were stationed outside at every exit. "I thought they wanted to put a tracking monitor on my ankle."

Garrett slid warmed-up pasta across the white granite top to her. He'd changed into ripped jeans, a dark T-shirt, and black socks. "They did. I said no."

She sipped the coffee he'd already given her. A shiny green plant bloomed on the bar. Had it looked that good the other day? "Does everybody do what you say?"

His eyebrow lifted as he dished up his food. "They do when it comes to you." Then he leaned back against the counter and began to eat, one hand holding the bowl and the other his fork. The mood between them was casual and comfortable, as if they'd been together for more than a few days. In the evening light, he looked more dangerous than ever, with his dark hair curling around his ears and his muscled chest filling out the faded black T-shirt in a way that gave her those Garrett-sized butterflies.

She took a bite of the spaghetti, and it was as delicious as dinner had been the night before. Had it only been a day since her entire world had been changed? "Because you brought me into vampire territory?" Should she feel comforted by the shield he was providing? What if he changed his mind? She had tried to take off his head just that morning, apparently.

"You're my mate," he said simply. "You're my responsibility, and my word is law."

Some of that coziness began to dissipate. "Your word is not *my* law." They had to get that straight, even if it meant he stopped providing shelter for her from his people. "I might be a hot mess right now, but you're not my dictator." She'd heard the expression on a television show she'd seen in a motel room on her journey to California, and it seemed to apply to her. *Hot mess* sounded better than *total disaster.*

He kept eating and didn't answer. Almost as if he didn't want to bother arguing with her.

"Garrett?" She glanced at the ancient book he'd given her, which was sitting on the counter. She'd already translated half of it, and it was indeed, filled with romantic fables.

"Eat your dinner, Dessie. We need to figure out our next steps." He reached for a bottle of beer on the counter and drank it down, his throat moving in a way that should not be so sexy. The man was completely healed now, with no bandages or even stiffness in his movements.

She sipped her coffee. "We're not mated." The marking didn't stay on her hip, and she wasn't even comfortable enough to ask him if she could look at his palm.

"We are."

She couldn't help but frown. "Do you boss everyone around?"

He finished his bowl and placed the heavy pottery in the sink. "I'm usually in charge one way or another." He drank more of his beer, his gaze thoughtful. "I guess it's a little different here at home with my family, because my uncle is king and my dad is the strategic leader of the entire Realm."

He took a big drink. "My aunt and sister are our top doctors, and my mom the head botanist. My niece, Hope, is also involved in the business in a scary strategic way. Kid is a complete genius." He shrugged. "The rest of the family have leadership roles as well."

"But people still do what you say," she murmured. Interesting. Fascinating, really. "Do you think you were born to lead or did you have the duty thrust upon you from day one?"

"Dunno." He finished the beer and tossed the bottle in the recycling bin. "Doesn't really matter, does it?"

It was one more insight into the intriguing male, and she wanted to know all of him before she left this life. Even after the horrible day they'd endured. He was that compelling. Perhaps he was even her reward for whatever she'd gone through that had made her a killer about to die. Rewards were nice. She'd take one if it was him. "So Emma and Dage don't have any kids?"

"They have a son named Hunter, who's off on a mission." Garrett's frown was darker than any thundercloud. "He's been gone for almost three years, and I don't like being on the outside of the plan. It's something I am going to remedy just as soon as we get you figured out."

Mission? "How old is Hunter?"

"Nineteen," Garrett growled.

She blinked. "He's been on a mission since he was sixteen? What kind of a mission? Like spreading the gospel?"

"No. He's not spreading the gospel," Garrett said grimly. "He's in danger, and I hate the fact that he probably won't be the same goofy, good-natured kid I knew when he returns. But that's all I can tell you."

The entire situation sounded terrifying. "I don't understand. The king's only child is in danger?"

Garrett stared at her, his jaw hard. "Yeah. The leaders of my people truly lead. Humans don't understand that. Humans send other people's sons to die in war. We send our own."

Her breath caught. "Why are you going to be king instead of Hunter?"

Garrett opened the refrigerator door and fetched another beer, popping off the top with his free hand. "We'll both probably be king, if gut instinct whispers anything. I'll take over for Dage when he wants a break, and then a thousand years or so later, Hunter can take over for me. Maybe Dage will want the gig again after that. Who knows. None of us really want to be king."

She grinned. It was unfortunate that most people in power wanted the power and not the duty. Apparently, the Kayrs family didn't want the power but met their duty. "Can't females lead?"

"Sure, they can. Usually leaders come from the Kayrs family, and we only make males. Well, until Hope."

Something told Dessie Hope had a bigger destiny than just ruling the nation. She sobered. "I haven't had a chance to apologize for trying to take off your head. I'm truly sorry."

"You're forgiven." His words were kind, but his eyes were veiled. There was definitely a distance between them that hadn't been there that morning after their amorous night together. "I haven't had a chance to ask you if you're okay. Not too sore from last night?"

Heat tickled through her face, making her cheeks burn. She looked away from his intense gaze. "I'm fine. No adverse effects."

"Good." He refilled her coffee cup and nudged the creamer closer to her. "Emma said that your tumor decreased in size all three times you were triggered, and now you have another month of life."

She coughed. "So all I need to do to keep living is see your back and attack you. Sounds like a fabulous way for you to live." She couldn't even remember what his marking looked like, darn it.

"We'll get you sorted out without having to resort to anything like that, kitten."

She loved that nickname. Had always wanted one, and it was perfect that her first lover, probably her only lover, had given it to her. "I like it when you call me kitten." Should she? If not, who cared? She liked it. The name made her feel like she was a part of something. Of *them*, no matter how temporary they might be. "I should give you a nickname." What could it be? If she was a kitten, he was a...vampire. Yep. That perfectly described him. "Did you really try to mate me?"

"Yes." He met her gaze directly, no give on his immortal face. "Next time, it'll stick."

She couldn't breathe. Flutters cascaded through her abdomen. "You mentioned our next steps."

"Yeah. I know you went through a lot today, but we need to examine your entire life. Your brain has had some serious programming—enough to mess with your chemistry. To hide your enhancements."

"Or delete them," she whispered, her heart hurting. "Maybe they're gone." While she hadn't decided about forever with him, she wanted the option.

A muscle ticked beneath his rugged jawline. "You must remember something about your time training to kill."

She stilled. "I don't remember anything."

He just watched her, drinking his beer from the long-necked bottle.

Realization flitted through her, landing hard. "You don't believe me." Her hands tingled into numbness, and she started to dissociate, distancing herself from the moment.

"No." He said the word without heat.

Her jaw dropped. "Then why am I here in your home?" She looked around the spacious kitchen, her mind trying to spin through the cotton suddenly filling her head. "Wait a minute. You're not afraid of me at all."

He cocked his head, giving him a predatory look that was all Garrett Kayrs. "Oh, I won't underestimate you again. You don't have access to any weapons, and we've scanned your body and know there's nothing hidden beneath your skin. You're dangerous, and I learned my lesson."

"Yet I'm here." She lifted her chin, wishing she could remember *how* to be dangerous.

"You're here because this is where I want you to be," he said softly.

Her numbing body went glacier still. For the first time since he'd kissed her outside the diner, she felt the danger from him. Toward her. Her attempts to dissociate from the moment and calm her firing nerves were failing. Because of him. The vampire commanded every inch of space around him with very little effort. "I don't want to stay here," she snapped.

"I don't care."

She blinked. He'd treated her with such gentleness since the beginning that his statement made her panic. "You can't keep me here."

"Don't be obtuse. I can do anything I want with you." He finished the second beer, gracefully tossing the bottle in the bin with the first one. "So you're going to want to cooperate with me."

He'd threatened violence before, but she hadn't believed him. Not really. Even the night they'd spent together had shown him to be attentive and gentle. He'd clearly held himself back. Garrett Kayrs might be a controlled killer, and he might be the future king of a species of immortal killers, but he would not hurt her. She knew that. "Do your worst," she whispered.

A muscle ticked in his jaw. "I don't *need* to do my worst with you, baby. I don't even need to exert much effort to gain your cooperation." He stuck his thumbs in the pockets of his ripped jeans. "I have no problem making sure you can't sit down for the next week, and I think you know that's the truth. So how about you promise to go with honesty from right now?"

Anger spread through her veins. If he attacked, could she somehow remember those moves she seemed to know? Did it matter? He'd handled her easily on that video she'd watched. "I've never lied to you." It was the truth, and it hurt that he didn't know that. What kind of life had he led that he'd be suspicious of a woman he'd been intimate with just the night before? One he seemed fine with being his mate. She should feel sorry for him, but instead, she wanted to kick him in the groin. Hard.

"That's a bloodthirsty look you've got in your eye," he mused. "Tell me what I want to hear."

"If I don't?"

His body unfolded from his position leaning against the counter. "Then you're about to have a very difficult night."

She believed him. "Fine. I promise to tell you the absolute truth. And the first thing I want to say is that you're going to owe me a very large apology, and I expect there to be flowers in your hands at the time. A lot of them."

"Fair enough. Tell me about when your parents died." He struck fast and sharp.

She gulped. "I don't remember a lot about them. My father had a deep voice, and my mother smelled like orchids. I didn't know she smelled like the flowers until I went shopping for perfume last month." Her chest ached and warmed at the same time. "Now I know. Orchids."

"How did they die?"

She tilted her head. "I assume you've already investigated my entire life. Shouldn't you know that?"

"Yes. Answer my questions."

She sighed. "Car accident when I was four years old. My aunt came to live with us at that time and then sent me away when I turned six. I've never been back and had no idea there was money for me. In fact, I thought I was going home after my time at Chapel Hill for Girls, but then somehow she found the money to send me to Stoneton Hills for the remainder of my education. Ten years of it." That island off the coast of Maine had been her home longer than most people had a home, from what she'd learned in her sociology class.

"Do you know where she got the money?"

"No." Dessie looked down at the floor, not wanting to see pity in his eyes. If there was pity. Maybe there was nothing there for her any longer, and she didn't want to see that, either. "I figured she really didn't want me to come home." Odd that it still hurt. "My parents were good people, Garrett." She had to defend them for some reason.

He waited until she gave up and looked at him. "I know. From everything my scouts could discern, they loved you a lot. In fact, your trust fund is substantial, about twenty million dollars, though your aunt could only take a small amount each year to raise you. Enough to pay for Chapel Hill but not nearly enough to cover the exorbitant expenses of Stoneton Hills Academy."

She paused. "What does that mean?"

"I don't know, but I think we can assume it has something to do with you being trained to kill me," he said without inflection.

She shook her head. "I just can't explain it, but I'm not a killer. I don't even know how to fight except for the self-defense classes I took, and what I learned wouldn't hurt you." Other humans, sure. But not an immortal. She chewed her lip. "If I die, does my aunt inherit the trust fund?"

"Yep." He glanced at his watch. "I'm going to take care of her shortly, so don't worry."

"No." Dessie jumped off the stool and rounded the counter to grab his arm. "Please don't have her killed. I don't want that on my soul, Garrett."

He looked down at her hand, which couldn't even wrap around his wrist. "Your soul?"

"Yeah. When you're staring at death, that kind of thing matters. I want to go to a good place after this one." Surely he understood.

His eyes softened a bit. "All right. I'll just talk to her. After I go visit the rolling hills of Stoneton."

She released his wrist, instantly feeling bereft at the loss of contact. "Rolling hills? What are you talking about?"

His chin lowered. "At Stoneton. It's on a bunch of grassy hills, right?"

Realization ticked through her. "Oh. Well, the main campus is. I attended the satellite campus on the island for gifted students." By the look on his face, he hadn't known that. She forced a smile. "I'll show you." No way was she letting him leave her in the middle of a bunch of vampires who thought she was a threat.

Chapter Twenty

Garrett barked orders from the back seat of the helicopter, which was exactly where he didn't want to be. While he trusted Logan to pilot the craft, and he knew Sam could fly as well as either of them from the copilot seat, it still didn't sit well with him. But Dessie had looked terrified when he'd loaded her into the special Realm craft, which was supercharged beyond any other helicopter, so he'd sat in back with her. The smirk Logan had given him was going to get his buddy punched in the face.

Later.

"Would you stop snapping at everyone?" Sam drawled through the headset, his gaze at the sun coming up over the East Coast.

"No." Garrett spoke into the mic attached to his headset. "I want the place cleared again." His people had found the island by satellite once they knew where to look. Apparently someone at the school had shrouded the landmass, much as the dragons did their not-so-secret island north of Ireland.

Logan flicked a couple of buttons and banked to fly over the ocean. "We've had two teams clear the land. There's nobody there, and no mines or explosives were found. It's safe to take her in if you want, or you and Sam can rappel down, and I'll keep her up here with me. Your choice."

Garrett looked down at the sleeping woman beneath his arm. Her long lashes lay against her pale skin, and her pink lips were slightly open as she dreamed. She'd fallen asleep nearly an hour into their trek across the country, so he'd put an arm around her to keep her warm.

She held another book he'd gifted her in her hand. It was an older human text from the ancient Greeks, and he'd found it in the family library, figuring it would entertain her during the flight. Her delight had been so sweet. It was difficult to believe that the soft woman leaning against him had been trained to kill.

Possessiveness wrapped around him, swelling within him. Killer or not, she was his.

"Why did you bring her?" Sam asked, looking over his shoulder at Garrett.

"I thought maybe seeing the school or island again would jog her memory about who programmed her to kill us." He wasn't going to guess at an enemy yet. They had so many, and it'd be a mistake to zero in on the wrong faction.

"Then I'll set down over at the far edge near the other copters," Logan said, banking an even harder right.

Dessie stirred awake and peered out the window. "The middle area was where we practiced golf and other sports. It's a better place to leave a craft."

Garrett nodded. "We know, Dessie. Close to the edge, Logan."

Logan turned and glanced at the woman before meeting his gaze. "We good, G?"

"We're good. Just don't crash us into the ocean." Garrett placed his hand over Dessie's, surprised once again by how small she was. How was he going to keep her safe?

For his entire life, he'd thought his dad was a mite over the top when it came to his mom's safety. His mom had been human, and she was still delicate. Garrett had started putting his body between hers and any danger when he'd been just a gangly ten-year-old, and even though she'd tried to shield him, he'd been stronger than her even then. But that was nothing compared to the lengths Talen went to keep his mate safe.

Now Garrett got it. Completely.

Logan landed the copter perfectly, even though the wild wind blasted them. The craft rocked. He powered down. "It's bad out there."

Garrett peered through the front window at the bulbous gray clouds rolling toward them. "We'll be quick." He brushed the hair away from Dessie's face. "We're here."

She looked toward the side window. "Come on, then. I'll introduce you to the dean of students. She always looks like she's sucking on a lemon, and you probably won't like her."

"This place is deserted, kitten." Garrett reached over to zip up her jacket and dug a knit hat out of his pocket to plunk over her head. "There should be gloves in your pocket."

She frowned and pulled them out. "It's not that cold."

"Put them on." He waited until she'd complied before opening the door. "It's fall semester, but oddly enough, there's nobody here." Jumping out, he turned to lift her free of the craft, noting Sam and Logan already taking up defensive positions around them.

The wind whipped at him, and he covered her as he looked around the oval-shaped campus, which was anchored by two stone buildings. One was massive and appeared to be the hub of the school; the other was smaller and much closer to an edge.

She leaned against him and looked at the nearly knee-length grass. "I don't understand. Everyone should be attending fall semester."

"How many people attended with you?" he asked, draping an arm over her shoulder and drawing her toward the biggest building.

"There were twenty-five students," she murmured.

He nodded at one of his soldiers who stood at a post near blooming, bright red flowers. The soldier opened the door for them. "We clear?"

"All clear," the vampire confirmed. "No electricity, though." He handed over a steel-barreled flashlight. "We have lanterns placed throughout, so you won't be in the dark at any point. Guards are stationed at every landing and level."

"Good." Garrett drew her inside to a stone vestibule with a high wall ahead of them.

She gasped. "The crest should be up there." Her hair spun as she looked wildly around. "All of the pictures and furniture are gone."

This was getting odder by the minute, and he didn't like it one bit. "Were you in school with the same girls for all those years?"

"Yes." She moved toward a double wooden door and pushed it open. "This was the cafeteria."

The stone floor was polished, but the space was empty. The smell of some kind of meat hung in the air. "Where are those girls now? They were your friends?" He pulled her away and walked across the landing to a matching door, which led to hallways housing what appeared to be a series of offices, all without any furnishings.

"We were very close," she said hollowly. "The best of friends."

He turned and gently put her against the wall, ducking his head to better see her eyes. "Then where are they, Dessie?"

She blinked, and her eyes grew slightly unfocused. "I don't know."

"But you were the best of friends for years. Over a decade. If you're all out in the world, why aren't you in touch?" He kept his tone calm with a note of command, which she seemed to respond to well.

She frowned. "I don't know."

* * * *

Dessie's head felt as if it was in a cloud. Her temples ached. "I miss my friends." But she couldn't see their faces in her mind. Why not? That was weird. She could feel them, or feel what it had been like to have friends, but she couldn't remember what they looked like. "I, um, I don't remember their names." How was that possible? The more she tried to remember, the more her head ached. She pressed a hand to her temple. "It hurts, Garrett."

He tugged her hat farther down. "Stop thinking about it for now. Let's just search this place, and you tell me what you do remember. Don't push it."

That sounded like a decent plan, considering her brain felt as if it was leaking out of her ears. But there was a hollowness in her chest at the thought that somebody had manipulated her mind. It was the only scenario that made sense. "All right. The classrooms are on the second floor, the living quarters on the third. It's an all-girls school, and most of the professors are women, save for Professor Samuelson, who gave me the knife upon graduation. We did have a few male professors visit for a semester at a time. They were quartered in the other stone building, along with the monks."

Garrett stiffened. "Monks?"

"Yes. The school is affiliated with the Church of the Righteous. We had bible studies as well as secular classes, and the monks took care of the land and buildings but mainly stayed to themselves. Most of them had taken a vow of silence, so only three ever spoke. There were ten of them." She'd never spent much time with the monks, and since they couldn't speak, she hadn't minded.

"Have you ever been in their quarters?" Garrett led the way up to the second floor, which had also been cleared of all furnishings. Their voices and footsteps echoed hollowly across the vacant area.

She shivered. "No. Of course not." It was forbidden for any of the students to bother the holy men. "They were here to find enlightenment and didn't want anything to do with us except during chapel on Sundays. Then they silently sat and prayed, except for Father Thomas, who always gave the sermon."

Garrett looked down at her. "You understand how bizarre that situation was, right?"

She rubbed her nose, noting it was colder than she'd expected. "Not really. This island is the perfect place for monks, enlightenment, and contemplation." It had not been the perfect place for a teenage girl to live. Not at all. She shivered and rubbed her hands down her arms. "It's not usually so quiet here." Although the wind was beginning to shriek in an announcement of an oncoming storm. She used to love watching the skies open up over the tumultuous sea from her small window. "Do you want to see my room?"

"Yes." Even though he still seemed emotionally distant from her, she couldn't help but notice that he covered her with his body, keeping her against the wall. "Show me."

She didn't have enough time left in this life to hold on to anger or hurt. Plus, as bossy as Garrett was, he had seemed fine with mating her and saving her life.

It was a kind thought of his, even though it hadn't worked. She knew herself and understood that she wasn't dangerous or deadly or immortal. There was no way she was the woman he'd dreamed of for so long, even if she had training she couldn't remember.

Yet she took his hand as if she had every right to do so. "This way." They climbed to the third story, and she turned down the hallway, walking along the now-bare stone floor to the farthest door on the left. "In here." She shoved open the door and walked into what had been her space for over a decade. The minuscule room looked bigger with the bed, dresser, and small desk now gone. "I spent a lot of time sitting on my desk and looking out that window." She pointed.

He stepped inside her room, looking too big for the area.

A thrill chased through her at seeing him actually in her room, where she'd imagined him so many times after that one dream meeting when he'd probably saved her life. Oh, she knew it couldn't really have been him. Perhaps she'd seen a picture of him that had sparked her dream. Maybe she was just going crazy—or somehow the fates had shown him to her.

Right now, she wouldn't bet her life on her sanity. Reason had fled the building the second she'd walked into that diner and met her dream man, who turned out to be a vampire with some demon blood. One who'd almost mated her. The idea was incredible. "Do you ever feel like you've just lost your sense of reality?"

He looked out her window at the pounding rain. "Tell me about a normal day here."

She ran her hand along the familiar stone wall, already knowing each groove and divot. "Morning prayer was at five, breakfast at six, and classes began at seven." Truth be told, she hoped never to have a schedule again. "Lunch was at noon, dinner at five, studies until eight, and then a good-night meditation and hot chocolate, warm milk, or apple cider. Then bed."

He turned and leaned against the wall, somehow looking at home against the hard surface. "You'd drink something hot every night?"

"Yes. We'd toast and say something positive about the next day. Something to look forward to for all of us." She'd actually enjoyed that practice. "Is that significant?"

He lifted a powerful shoulder. "Maybe. If you really have no recollection of being hypnotized, then it stands to reason you might've been drugged."

She licked her lips. "There are times I remember being exhausted, even though I thought I'd slept all night." A cold ball of dread dropped into her gut, spreading chills through her body. "If I was drugged, what else might they have done to me? And why?" She shivered.

"We'll find out." He glanced at his phone. "We'll search for any records about the students who attended this part of the school. Unfortunately, you don't have any records at the main Stoneton Hills Academy, so it's doubtful your friends did either."

She jolted. "No records? But I attended Stoneton for years." Or did she? "I can speak five languages, Garrett."

"You can also kill immortals," he murmured. "More specifically, me."

Chapter Twenty-One

The place gave him the creeps. It was cold and barren; the complete opposite of the woman who looked so lost in the small room. She was vibrant and alive, and she must've been miserable in such stark surroundings. Garrett took her hand. "Let's check out the monks' building. What did these men look like, anyway?" Her hand felt small and chilly in his, even through her gloves.

"Like monks. They wore brown smocks and looked like men. They didn't speak. There was nothing remarkable about them."

He hustled them outside and tried to keep her from getting wet in the rainstorm, ducking his head as they ran. The wind slashed at them, and the rain held a bite. The doors of the other building were already open, so he hurried her inside and stopped to wipe off his face.

Sam Kyllwood stood in the center room, which was empty. "Checked out all the rooms. There's a kitchen, several bedrooms, and a couple of offices. Nothing interesting." He swung a lantern in one hand and grimaced as lightning struck outside. Then he looked them over and focused on Garrett. "Did you find anything in the main building?"

"No," Garrett muttered. Somebody had cleared out the entire building. He'd have a couple of teams check every inch of the school, but he wasn't confident they'd find anything.

Dessie released his hand and wandered over to the far stone wall. She cocked her head, her heart audibly speeding up.

"What is it?" Garrett asked.

"I don't know." She placed her palm on a rock in the center of the wall. "I've seen this before."

Garrett and Sam instantly walked toward her and began pushing on the wall. Garrett knocked along the smooth stones, noting a hollow sound. He then traced a series of perfectly aligned rocks to the side, in front of an empty bookshelf. There was something off. He felt beneath a shelf, found an edge, and pushed. A door opened in front of Dessie.

"Oh, no," she whispered. The woman sounded faint.

"Stay here." Garrett took a lantern and ran down rough stairs, finding a wide-open room that smelled like bleach. He turned to look up at Sam. "It's vacant down here, but there's a boatload of electrical wiring. We need to tear this place apart."

Dessie turned even paler but reached for a hand-carved railing and started down the rocky steps.

"Stay up there," Garrett said.

"No." She kept descending, with Sam at her back. With each step, she seemed to get shakier. Finally at the bottom, she gagged and then swallowed rapidly.

It was obvious she was terrified, but she was facing whatever had happened in that room. Garrett couldn't help but be impressed by her. "You don't have to be down here."

She gulped and looked around as if afraid monsters would emerge from the walls. "Yes, I do."

Garrett crouched and gingerly lifted a wire, which was frayed in several spots. "Does this place seem familiar in any way?"

"I don't know." Her voice trembled, and she stumbled to the middle of the room, where bolts had been fastened into the floor in the outline of some sort of table. She crossed her arms. "I don't like how it feels in here." Her voice sounded hollow, and she looked breakable.

He moved to her. Brave little mate. "It's okay. Let's go back upstairs, and I'll have a team scour this area." He'd need them to look for other hidden rooms, although this one was big enough to accommodate any secret activity the monks had wanted to carry out. "Tell me more about these monks." He kept a tight hold on her as they went back up the stairs, trying to take her weight but not wanting to overwhelm her. "I promise we're going to find out what happened to you, Destiny."

She looked up at him, her pupils dilated. Fear? "So you believe me now?"

Did he? She'd fought like a trained warrior the other night and had almost killed him. Was it possible to have those kinds of skills and not know it? He'd met plenty of trained assassins who could seduce a target successfully, and it made sense that his enemies would send a fragile-looking, petite human after him. His guard had been down with her. Very much so. Apparently she was his type. Who knew?

She sighed. "Forget it. Your nonanswer is an answer." Even so, she didn't move away from him.

Logan jogged through the rain and paused at the open door. "Storm's getting worse. Let's go and come back tomorrow to search."

The sound of waves crashing far below echoed up with an energy that had Garrett staring at the mottled purple clouds. "Agreed." He gave a high-pitched whistle, and soldiers began moving toward the three helicopters in the center of what might've been a training field at one point. Then he readjusted Dessie's light blue knit hat. "Keep to my side—we're gonna run."

She nodded.

He took her hand and ducked into the rain, letting the fierce drops pelt his head.

Something whistled through the air.

He paused just as Logan and Sam did the same. A missile from the sea blasted the far side of the monks' building. Rocks and shrapnel blew out, along with a wild firestorm of smoke.

Dessie screamed.

Another blast hit, and Logan flew through the air to land near the other helicopters, his legs on fire.

Garrett grabbed Dessie and tossed her over his shoulder, ducked his head, and ran full bore toward his friend. "Retreat!" he bellowed. "Everyone get the hell off this island!"

Two more missiles zipped through the air, going high and then angling toward the ground. The first struck dead center in the main building, and the next blew up the rest of the monks' building. Heated air smashed against his back, and he went sprawling toward the ground. Grunting, he flipped Dessie off his shoulder, catching her in his arms as he fell to his knees. Pain ricocheted up his legs.

Sam somersaulted next to him and landed near his brother, furiously patting out the fire.

Logan rolled over several times, and the rain extinguished the flames. Blood flowed wildly from his temple, covering his face.

A volley of new missiles pounded the center of the field, right where most pilots would've landed their craft.

Sam grunted and yanked up his brother, setting a shoulder beneath his arm. Garrett went to take the other arm, but Logan waved him off. "I'm good, G. Get to our copter."

Garrett ran for the helicopter while holding Dessie against his chest.

Another missile landed, throwing all of them into the air. Garrett landed on his knees, still protecting Dessie. Smoke billowed up. He looked around frantically to see both Kyllwood men spinning toward the edge of the cliff.

"No!" he bellowed.

* * * *

Dessie coughed out smoke as tears slid down her burning cheeks. Smoke and flames clouded her vision.

Garrett held her so tight against his chest that she couldn't breathe as he careened through the haze to the helicopter. He placed her inside. "Stay here." Then he turned and ran toward the cliff edge.

She tried to gasp in air and then pushed her head out of the craft, trying to see better. Another explosion rocked the island, sending sharp shards of rock to impact every standing object. Pain burst along her arm, and she frantically shook it. The haze cleared to her right, and she could see Garrett diving to the ground next to Sam, who had his hand over the edge.

Oh no. Was he holding on to Logan?

She had to help. Blinking away soot, she brushed burning embers off her hair and jumped out, running toward the men.

Garrett and Sam hauled Logan up over the burning bushes, pulling him free of the cliff.

She paused. Thank goodness.

Several more explosions impacted the small island, and it began to fissure across the middle. "Garrett," she yelled. "The whole island is splitting in two."

One of the helicopters rose quickly into the air, battered by the falling debris as well as the strengthening storm. The wind spread the flaming tree bark, burning her jacket.

Garrett and Sam dragged Logan toward their helicopter, their expressions furious and intent, blood flowing from cuts on their faces.

Dessie turned and hurried back to the helicopter to open the front door.

A low-pitched whistle pierced the storm, and a projectile exploded nearby. All three men flew up into the air and came crashing down—Sam on his head, Logan on his still-burning side, and Garrett on his leg. Even from a good distance away, Dessie could hear his bone crack.

She ran toward him, panic engulfing her.

He staggered to his good leg and gestured her back. "Get into the copter. Now." Fangs dropped from his mouth, and his eyes swirled a sizzling bluish silver through the gray.

She gulped.

Neither Sam nor Logan moved, remaining face down on the shaking ground. They couldn't be dead. She had to figure out a way to drag one of them so Garrett could get the other.

"Now, Dessie," he snapped, smoke all but engulfing him. He then tucked his chin and dove to the ground, grabbing Sam's leg and rolling back onto his feet with the massive demon over his shoulder. How in the world could he do that with a broken leg? Then he leaned down and grabbed Logan's belt before launching himself into motion, dragging the big immortal while limping painfully.

Dessie ran forward and grabbed Logan's shoulder, trying to help move him toward the craft.

They moved agonizingly slowly but finally arrived just as more missiles obliterated the main building, leaving a burning crater in its spot. The fissure widened, and the sound of land splitting apart shrieked through the burning flames.

Garrett shoved Sam inside the back of the copter, leaned down and hefted Logan up, and then shut the door. "Move, Dessie. Hurry."

The second helicopter rose into the air, with two soldiers holding on to the step rails. The ground shook, and new fissures appeared, widening rapidly.

Dessie leaped into the front passenger-side seat and slammed her door, watching with horror as one of the fissures widened its mouth as if about to consume them. Grass, smoldering stones, and small plants fell into the crack as it widened even more.

Garrett careened inside the pilot's seat and rapidly began punching buttons and flipping levers. "Buckle."

Dessie frantically reached for the seat belt to yank it over her head.

Then they were rising into the air. The wind and rain battled them, while the smoke destroyed any visibility. She clutched the side of the chopper with her nails, her throat feeling like she'd swallowed live flames. Her eyes burned, and her body ached with fresh bruises and burns. Hopefully there were no breaks.

Another explosion ripped through the day, and the craft pitched hard to the left.

"Damn it," Garrett muttered, yanking what looked like a small steering wheel and banking away from the island, rising quickly.

She wiped soot off her smarting face and turned to make sure he was all right. A burn mark marred his neck, and blood flowed from beneath his ear. His hands were both burned and dirty, and it looked like his right leg was pointing the wrong way. "Your leg is broken," she croaked out.

"I know." He reached for the headset between them and plunked it on his head. Weird tingles popped in the air around him. "This is Kayrs. Check in. Now."

A groan came from the rear of the copter.

Dessie turned her head to see Sam stirring awake and then jerking back, fangs sliding from his mouth.

"Team B?" Garrett snapped into his microphone, turning the helicopter again.

Sam reached out to shake his brother. "Logan?"

Logan groaned and slowly lifted his head. "What the fuck?"

"Secure here," Garrett said into the headset. "Anybody wounded badly enough to require medical attention?"

"You are," Dessie said, her voice barely above a whisper.

Logan wiped blood off his face, just smearing it with the soot. "Status?"

Garrett turned to look over his shoulder. "Both teams are clear, and we're waiting for a satellite report about launch sites. Several injuries, but all are manageable."

Sam turned to his side and heaved.

Logan smacked his back while lying on the floor beside him. "It's smoke. Get rid of it."

Dessie turned back around to stare at the swollen gray clouds around them. Rain splattered the windows, and the wind tossed the heavy craft around. "What now?"

Garrett pursed his lips as he apparently listened to his headset and then banked left. "Affirmative. Take it over completely—I want all rooms. Get rid of anybody staying there now"—at Dessie's soft sound of distress, he continued—"by paying them off. Give them whatever money they need, so long as they go elsewhere." He lifted an eyebrow. "In fact, buy the establishment. I want all humans gone by the time we land."

She smiled, even though her entire face felt sunburned.

He craned his neck to look out the side window. "Block the road at fifty and a hundred yards out, and I want guards posted throughout, taking three-hour shifts. Lesser injuries guard first, while the others heal, and then we'll relieve each other. We're landing in ten minutes adjacent to the main door. Have things ready." He readjusted a couple of the red dials.

Dessie wiped soot and rain off her face. "What's happening?"

He banked again. "We just bought a motel in the middle of nowhere."

Chapter Twenty-Two

Garrett nudged open the door to Logan and Sam's room at the ramshackle motel, careful not to break the thing in two. The wind and brutal rain beat at his back as he limped inside, forcing healing cells to his damn leg to heal the break.

Logan lay on his back on a threadbare yellow bedspread, healing tingles popping the air around him. "Whatever you paid for this dump was too much."

Sam was on the other bed on his stomach, and he turned his head toward Garrett. "Good news is that it's clean. Sheets, very old carpet, even older drapes...all laundered." His green eyes were dark with pain as healing vibrations came from him. His ribs snapped back into place with audible clicks, and he groaned. "Even so, we should burn it down as we leave."

Logan snorted. "We're a month away from these walls *falling* down. You made some human's decade today."

Garrett eyed the faded green shag carpet and mismatched dresser and bed tables. The place did smell nice, though. Fresh and clean. "How are you two?"

"Not bad." Logan sat up. "Am I needed on guard duty?"

"Not for three hours," Garrett said. His senses were on alert, and his vampire fury calmed as he slid into being a soldier again. "I want to rotate the three of us so two of us are covering Dessie for the night. She's in a hot shower right now." He'd helped her in, and the marking on her hip was gone.

Logan nodded. "Got it."

Garrett popped his ankle back into place and pain ticked up his leg. "I have soldiers posted outside Dessie's door and bathroom window, and all around the hotel. I'll take the first shift, Logan, you the second, and Sam the third. Deal?"

Sam rolled over and sat, the burn marks on his arm blistering and then healing. "Fine by me."

Garrett's phone pinged, and he pressed the speaker button to see the Realm's computer expert on the other line. "Hi, Chalton. What did you find?"

"The weather really screwed with the satellites we have in the area, but it looks like the missiles originated in the ocean floor. We're going to have to scout the destruction to learn more about the projectiles." The sound of typing came over the line before Chalton continued. "There's not enough visibility yet to tell you the status of the island. The last few shots I managed to decipher didn't look good. The entire landmass might be in the ocean now."

Garrett scrubbed a hand through his damp hair. "Were the missiles somehow triggered by our landing on the island?" He hadn't seen any such sensors, but maybe he'd missed something.

"I don't think so," Chalton said. "There would've been some sort of noticeable activity on the island itself that our heat sensors would've caught. The weapons are beyond any human invention, so it's doubtful humans were involved. The shrouding of the island is dragon technology."

Garrett stiffened.

Logan's head snapped up. "You think the dragons are behind this?"

How did that make any sense?

"Dunno," Chalton said. "But it is dragon technology, and they're not known to share. Although somebody could've stolen the specs."

"Or the dragon nation is more pissed about the Seven messing with the laws of physics than we thought," Sam mused.

Garrett didn't have time to battle dragons. "Or there's a rogue dragon faction after us." There wasn't a lot known about the dragons, but Bear was half-brothers with one, so he'd reach out there. "If there wasn't a trigger, then somebody fired those missiles."

"Definitely and remotely," Chalton said. "I need techs in there to tell you more, but somebody wanted you dead. I'll be in touch." He ended the call.

Garrett slid his phone back into his pocket.

Sam wiped blood off his neck. "If somebody aimed those missiles..."

"They wanted Destiny dead as well," Garrett finished for him.

Logan rolled his neck and flexed his hand, which had scrapes down each finger. "If whoever programmed her wants her dead, she's not working with them."

Sam winced. "Or they're afraid she'll break and want her taken out before she can give them up."

"She can't be that good," Garrett murmured, his temper and his intellect battling for dominance. Even if she were, she was his mate, and he'd deal with the situation. But his gut told him she was innocent. "Nobody is that good a liar."

Sam looked at his brother and then back. "Exactly." He held up a hand before Garrett could protest. "I'm going with your gut on this one, brother. But a petite, wide-eyed, fragile-looking human would make the absolute perfect assassin against one of us. Your guard was way down, and she nearly took off your head. I hate to even think it, but what if she has more surprises up her sleeve?"

"Like what? We took her knife. She's human, with no extra strength or speed. Even if she *knows* a thousand ways to kill me, she can't do it." His leg finally snapped back into alignment, and his skin stitched itself together painfully. "I have to go with my gut, like you said. Destiny is an innocent, and we need to figure out what happened to her." Now that he'd made the decision, his shoulders finally relaxed.

Logan shook soot out of his dark hair. "Do we have any experts in programming or hypnotism?"

"I have no idea," Garrett admitted. "We have a couple of psychics in the family, but they didn't see this coming." He didn't want his sister or his niece involved, anyway. Not with an enemy who could turn a human into a killer and then later fire missiles to kill her. "What are the chances the dragons are behind this?" He wished they knew more about the elusive shifters.

"I bet 70 to 30 it's the Kurjans rather than the dragons," Logan drawled. "Although this technology should be beyond the Kurjans."

Sam tore off his ripped shirt and started to heal the wounds on his chest. "Doesn't mean they didn't steal it." He grimaced as his skin stitched back together. "I'm with Logan, G. If your gut is saying to trust her, then I do."

Garrett forced himself to think the entire matter through. "She's innocent, but that doesn't mean she's not dangerous. We don't know what's in her head. The Seven might not be her only targets." Plenty of enemies wanted his sister and his niece both dead, too. "We can't let our guard down around her." Not until he figured out who'd trained her to kill.

In the meantime, like it or not, he was locking her down.

* * * *

Dessie hunkered down in the surprisingly soft bed after finger-combing her long hair into some sort of order. The shower had been small but warm, and with the storm beating at the windows, a sense of safety cocooned her for a brief moment. Though somebody had tried to kill her with missiles, her eyelids were so heavy.

Garrett was out patrolling, and she worried her bottom lip. He'd been injured and in pain, but he'd still headed out into the blistering rainstorm.

Thunder rumbled outside, and then lightning zapped, illuminating the tiny room through the torn curtains.

She tried to decipher the Greek mystery from ancient times that Garrett had given her, but her eyes were too tired. Yet his sweetness in doing so tugged at her heart. He kept giving her books, which was the perfect present for her.

It was like he knew her completely.

She snuggled down, surrounded by the smell of lavender. The furnishings of the room were sparse and worn, but the place was clean and comfortable. And there was a slightly wilted potted plant on the window, a homey touch. She'd given it some water before getting into bed. While she wanted to remain awake until Garrett returned, perhaps a small nap wouldn't hurt anything. Within minutes, her breathing leveled out, and she dropped into sleep.

The storm continued to rage. She opened her eyes to find herself in a meadow with a meager sun shining down. Huh. Interesting dream. She stretched her arms and legs, enjoying the smell of freshly cut grass. Something pulled at her dress. She looked down to find herself wearing her school uniform with its starched white shirt and pleated green skirt.

Ugh. She'd thought she'd burned all of them when she'd left the school. Finally. A fluorescent green butterfly landed on her knee, and happiness twirled through her.

The peaceful ultramarine sky began to yawn.

She stilled as a perfectly round hole with white edges opened up above her, revealing darkness. "Wait, no—" A force pulled her off the ground, and she struck out, spinning end over end toward a black hole.

Nails scratched down her sides, and pain bled through her skin. She cried out, stuck in the darkness, being bitten by invisible teeth.

Then she was falling. Wind bursts swirled around her, and she landed on her butt. Searing torment shot up her spine, rocking her head back. Her vision wavered, and she coughed, trying to remain conscious. Slowly, the night came into focus.

Where was she?

The surface beneath her was rough and had slight edges. Rock? Bending down, she could make out some sort of slate. She tried to stand, but dizziness attacked her, so she remained sitting. Bleeding on the rock. Her arms and legs felt as if they'd gone through a cheese grater.

Tears filled her eyes, and she blinked them back. All right. This was crazy, but it was happening. Planting both hands on the rock, she pushed herself up and compelled her body to act. She stood, her legs trembling. Okay. She could do this.

A high-pitched surreal scream echoed around her.

Debilitating chills burned her arms and legs, but she locked her knees, holding tight. A movement caught her eye. Bubbling and oozing, some sort of thick goo surrounded her rock. Beneath the surface, barely visible, something swam.

She took a step back and then halted, twisting her torso to examine the length of her platform, which was square and only extended about five feet in every direction. Where was she?

Wind whispered above her, and dark clouds parted to reveal two orbs, one orange and the other lapis. Moons? Oddly colored moons? The swish of the liquid hitting rocks came on the wind.

The atmosphere felt heavy, as if filled with anger. She rubbed her freezing arms and winced as pain lacerated her skin.

The clouds slithered away, revealing a shoreline in the distance, with razor-sharp cliffs rising behind the sand.

A figure emerged from an opening in the stone, striding toward the shore and staring at her. She squinted to see better, but her eyes must be lying. The figure appeared to be a male with nearly luminescent skin, amethyst eyes, and one strip of white hair flowing down his broad back. "Hello." His voice rumbled across the murky liquid, and whatever lived below thrashed, throwing up goo.

She retreated another step. This was not a dream. It felt too real. "Who are you?"

His eyes gleamed. "The question is, who are you?" He lifted his hands, and the wind burst against her, dropping her to her knees. Then she began floating toward the shore.

Toward him.

She gulped and looked frantically around for any sort of a paddle. Leaning over, she began to insert her arm into the goo, but air bubbles popped the surface from a creature that felt malevolent to her. She quickly drew back, heat burning down her throat, leaving her mouth bone dry.

He laughed, and the sound reverberated darkly against the jagged cliffs.

She looked for another rock to jump to, but nothing was near. The sky opened up.

The man paused and cocked his head, his scarred face highlighted by the orange moon.

A body fell from nowhere to bounce on another dark surface Dessie hadn't been able to see. A woman flipped over and landed on her feet, her brunette hair blowing back from her face and deep blue markings winding up her neck into her hairline.

"Hope?" Dessie croaked, blinking against the churning wind.

Hope turned toward her, eyes wide sapphires in the odd light. "Dessie? How are you here?"

"I don't know." What was Garrett's niece doing in this horrible place?

Hope faced the terror on the beach. "Ulric. What an unpleasant surprise. I thought I closed those portals."

Ulric's eyes glittered like an animal's in the trees, scoping prey. "You can't close all the portals, my little Lock. Not all by your sweet little self." He bared his teeth, and glistening fangs descended. "We're about to have a very good time." Flipping his palms toward the sea, he increased the wind, and the rocks began moving toward him.

"Not a chance," Hope snapped, lifting her hands and shoving air toward him.

Two winds collided and screamed in fury. Hope's face reddened, but she set her stance, contorting her entire body to shove back Ulric's power.

Dessie threw up her arms. "Stop it. Both of you." The smell of sulfur assaulted her nostrils, and she sneezed. "We have to get out of here."

The winds slowed.

Ulric tilted his head and sniffed the air, his nostrils flaring. "You're not just a little gift from my people, are you?"

"No," Dessie said, calculating the distance to Hope's rock. It was too far for her to jump. "Where are we?"

Hope kept her focus on the scarred being on the sand, while making some odd movement with her right hand. "Do you have any idea how you got here?"

"No," Dessie whispered, her voice sounding hollow.

"Fascinating," Ulric boomed, his smile revealing more sharp teeth.

Hope lifted her hand to the sky. "Out, Dessie. Go now."

Another hole split open the sky and yanked at Dessie, pulling her off the rock. Her scream coincided with Ulric's roar of fury. Stars flashed behind her eyes, and fire singed her nerves.

She awoke in the soft motel bed and sat up, gasping for air.

Chapter Twenty-Three

Hope Kayrs-Kyllwood smashed onto the floor next to her own bed. Her ears rang, and her nose bled. Sighing, she grabbed a tissue from the bedside table and shoved it up one nostril before pushing herself to her feet. The room spun, and she wavered, holding on to the mattress until she regained her balance. A quick glance at the clock confirmed it was nearly midnight.

What was Dessie doing in the hell world? Hope had thought she'd closed off the portals that Ulric could access, but apparently not. Just who was Destiny Applegate?

Hope's entire body ached as if she'd been repeatedly kicked while down, and her hand trembled as she reached for her phone and dialed Uncle Garrett.

"Hey. Why are you up so late?" The sound of thunder rolled across the line along with his greeting.

She wearily sat on the bed, her feet freezing even inside the thick socks she'd worn earlier. "Ulric just managed to pull me into his world again."

More thunder bellowed. "Damn it. I thought the portals were closed."

"Me too." She'd been able to travel in dream worlds for most of her life, off and on, but she didn't have control when Ulric dragged her into his world. The one the Seven had created to keep him imprisoned. "He's getting stronger, Garrett. I don't know how, but it's happening." Someday he'd be free and back home.

"We'll get to him first, Hope. I promise." The vow sounded deadly.

Hope reached for a throw blanket to toss over her legs. "Don't freak out, but Dessie was there also. She was there before I arrived."

Silence met her statement.

Hope bit her lip. "She looked terrified and confused, if that helps."

"How or why..." His voice trailed off into darkness, more guttural than she'd ever heard him. "She has to be enhanced, and that tumor in her head somehow hides that."

Hope wished the mating mark would've stayed. Then Dessie would at least be immortal. "I wish I could help." Even Hope's bones felt exhausted.

Garrett's growl was soft but vibrated over the line, nonetheless. "I'll handle it and inform the other members of the Seven about this development. Then we'll figure out how to close those portals for good. But I need you to tell your folks about this, okay?"

"Why?" She wasn't trying to be contrary. There was no reason to worry them. "There's not a thing we can do about it, G. There's definitely nothing my parents can do, so why keep them up at night?"

His sigh was heavy. "They're already up at night, sweetheart. I am not concealing this from Janie. She's my sister, and I owe her better than that, and so do you. She's a good mom."

"Exactly," Hope said dully. "She's a great mom, and I love her. I love Dad, too. They can't help me, and you know it."

"I don't know it," Garrett snarled. "Janie visited dream worlds before you did, baby girl. I'll give you until tomorrow noon to talk to them, and then I'm calling. None of us are going to let you deal with this on your own. Period."

This made zero sense. "Garrett—"

"I have to go. Love you." He ended the call.

She frowned and blew hair away from her face. A knock on her window had her jumping. She yanked the tissue out and tossed it aside. Her heart raced into her throat, and she hurried to the window, shoving it up. "Pax." Without a thought, she dove through and let him catch her. "You're back."

He easily caught her, so tall and broad now that the cute, pudgy kid he'd once been was hard to imagine. "Why do you have a bump on your head?"

For goodness' sake. "I can't believe you're still skulking around my window at night. We're not kids any longer." A fact that was more than obvious in the ripple of muscle holding her off the ground.

"I know." He sat her on the windowsill, caging her as his hands curled over the wooden frame on either side of her legs. "But I promised you I'd let you know when we returned."

Her world was better when Paxton was in the same town as she was, and always had been. He'd been her best friend for as long as she could remember. "You're safe?"

"Yeah," he said softly, his eyes a burning silvery blue in the soft moonlight. She'd seen those eyes turn a sizzling green, which was probably his tertiary color, something most immortals had. His black hair was shaggy around his ears, thick and wavy, and he'd grown at least another inch, making him more than a foot taller than she was.

A quivering winged its way through her abdomen, but she ignored it. They could only be friends. "How was it training with the wolf shifters?" He'd been gone nearly six months.

"Good." He shrugged out of his dark jacket and slid it around her shoulders. "Terrent has a mean left cross, but that's how a guy learns to duck." His jacket smelled like worn leather and the forest. Like Pax.

She caught something in his voice but couldn't place it. "What else?"

"Nothing." He pulled the coat closed in front of her chest.

Her breath caught, and she covered it with a cough.

"Are you sick again?" He pressed a mammoth hand to her forehead the way her mom had when she was young.

She swiped his hand away. "I'm a vampire. Of course I'm not sick." Not now, anyway.

"Tell me you haven't been meeting our enemies in dream worlds." Now his voice lowered to the perfect vampire-demon growl, which only increased the odd shivers going through her body.

"I haven't, but I went tonight." She placed a hand on his chest, finding solid rock beneath her palm. "Ulric yanked me into his world again, and I couldn't stop him. He also brought a human with him. One who tried to kill Garrett."

Pax slowly straightened. "Huh?"

"I know. I have to figure out how Ulric reopened the portals I'd closed. I fought him this time, but he's getting stronger. There's only one place for us to get information, and you know it." He brushed his knuckles across her chin, and her breath caught in her chest. "I'm going into the dream world again, either with you or not." It had been three years.

Paxton's eyes morphed to that dangerous green, and he fingered the pink quartz necklace he'd given her years ago. She always wore it. "I don't like any of this. The second I say we're out, you bring us both out. Got it?"

Excitement sailed through her. "It's time to bring the gang back together."

His growl dampened her hope. Slightly.

* * * *

Paxton swung into Hope's bedroom the way he'd done a million times before, but they weren't kids any longer. If Zane caught him in her room this time, the demon king would probably just cut off his head. But there was no way he was letting Hope go into that dream world by herself.

Years ago she'd lost the ability, and he'd finally been able to sleep at night. Then it had returned, and now apparently she couldn't control it all the time.

Not for the first time, Pax wondered if he should just offer to mate her. She'd stop getting sick, and then the Kurjans would no longer want her. But he was fairly certain she'd already decided on a different path. He wasn't going to let that happen, but it was getting more and more difficult to make his claim. Shutting the window, he sank to the floor with his back to the wall and extended his feet.

She slipped beneath her covers, although the sight of her in her tight yoga pants and thin T-shirt would haunt him for nights. "Remember when you used to climb in with me?" Her voice was soft. Sweet.

"Yeah." More often than not, he'd had the shit kicked out of him by his father and had run to Hope's house for warmth and safety, not telling a soul. But secrets always came out, and Zane had learned what was happening. Pax's father had been shipped off. Pax had been living with his uncle since. Thus creating a shitstorm of new secrets, considering his uncle led a regime obsessed with preventing the final ritual to kill Ulric. They might be right, but his only goal was to protect Hope. He sighed.

"It's okay, Pax." She sounded sure and so adult all of a sudden.

He knew that he'd been her first kiss, but he had no idea whether he was the last. Had she been dating since he'd left? If so, he couldn't blame her. So long as she wasn't seeing that Kurjan in her dream worlds. "Go to sleep, Hope. Let's get this over with." He closed his eyes and forced his body to relax. He'd trained with many more species than just wolves, nearly dying a couple of times, and he knew how to chase sleep.

He was in the midst of a dream about fishing with his uncle in Alaska, catching salmon, when he spun through the air and landed on a black sand beach near a churning gray ocean. This was new. He caught sight of Hope sitting on a rock outcropping. In this place, the prophecy markings on her neck were a lighter blue than normal. "Where are we?" Usually her dream worlds had a lot of pink and purple in them, including the sea.

"I thought they were pretty." Hope pointed to pieces of a glacier that had rolled onto the sand, where they looked like diamonds against the dark grains.

Behind her was a solid rock wall with a forest of deep green trees to one side. They weren't identifiable. "Nice trees."

"Thanks. Made them up." She craned her neck toward the thick forest. A green book was perched on a branch high up, teasing her like always. It was her book and someday she'd read it, but she could never get close enough.

Pax angled his body in front of hers, watching for movement. There it was. A slight whisper of a tree branch.

Two males strode between two of the trees, and Pax stiffened. "You brought them both?"

She frowned, looking lovely with her deep blue eyes and wild mahogany hair.

Drake reached them first, and Pax noticed the other male was at least an inch taller than he. Damn it. Although Pax was broader across the chest. Drake looked unusual for a Kurjan in that he had black hair and almost green eyes. If anything, he looked less pale than before. His father led the nation.

"Nice tan," Pax drawled.

Drake tore his gaze from Hope. "How kind of you to say so, Paxton. I've been out in the sun. Bless the scientists, right?"

What a dick.

Pax nodded at the other Kurjan, who still looked around eighteen, three years younger than him and Drake. "Vero." He'd met Drake's younger cousin in a dream world eons ago.

Vero had grown to Pax's height and was still pudgy around the middle. He looked at Hope and shook his head. "Why am I here? Again?"

She shrugged. "You must've been close to Drake when I called him."

Vero rolled his odd blue eyes. His hair was pure black with no red, and he looked more human than Drake did. "We're training and caught some shut-eye in a tent. Stop yanking me into your dreams."

"This will be quick," Pax promised, keeping his position in front of Hope. If Drake made a move, he could take off his head. "Hope was yanked into Ulric's hell dimension again. Why?" Ulric was the head of the Cyst, who were the spiritual leaders of the Kurjans. Or their chief assassins. Pax had never figured out which.

Drake's dark brows drew down, and he pivoted toward Hope. "Are you all right?"

She nodded. "Yes, but I'd really like to know how he did that."

Drake reached for her hand, but Pax blocked him. The Kurjan rolled his eyes. "Get out of the way."

"No." Fire lanced through Pax, and he held his ground, his fingers curling into a fist. Yeah. He'd been waiting for this for a long time.

"Pax," Hope snapped. "Knock it off."

Drake's smirk was going to get him punched. Hard. "I don't know anything about Ulric's powers, but I'll find out. Next time, let's meet just you and me." His gaze was possessive as he studied Hope.

"Not gonna happen." Pax had spent his entire childhood learning how to fight Kurjans. To protect Hope. He'd known since day one that was his destiny, and no doubt he wouldn't survive the coming battle. But she would. He'd make sure of it.

"We'll see," Drake murmured. "You and me, Pax? We're gonna happen and soon."

"*Can't wait,*" *Pax said, going with honesty. If Hope wasn't there at the moment, he'd take the first punch.*

Hope hopped off the rock. Tension rolled through the three males.

She paused next to Pax, looking at Drake. "Get me information, and we'll talk. Also, why or how would Ulric bring a human female in with me?"

Drake's lip twisted. "He couldn't."

"He did," Hope countered.

Pax needed to get more information about this woman who'd tried to kill Garrett. "Let's go, Hope."

"Wait." She put her hands on her hips. "There has to be a way."

Vero shook his head. "We've been studying the great Cyst leader, whom your people wrongly imprisoned. There is absolutely no way a human female could be drawn through dimensions to Ulric's hell without being shredded."

"Have your people found a way to banish enhancements? To take gifts away from humans?" Hope asked, going pale.

Drake frowned. "Of course not. If a female was brought through, she's nowhere near human, Hope. At the very least, she's an enhanced female, and some females can hide that. Or, she's a shifter who's learned to mask her nature. We've both seen that happen before. This one probably doesn't trust you or your people and is deceiving you. Open your eyes."

Pax jolted awake on the floor in Hope's room, his ears ringing. "Hope?"

She sat up in the bed. "He might have been telling the truth. What if Dessie is a shifter and not enhanced? We didn't even think of that. I have to call Garrett."

Chapter Twenty-Four

Dessie pretended to be asleep when Garrett returned. When he moved into the bathroom to take a shower, she rolled over to listen to the storm. Where had she been? None of this made sense, and that was becoming her new mantra. Who was Ulric, and why was Hope in that creepy dream world with her? More importantly, how did she even get to that place while her body remained here in bed? She must not have physically moved, because there weren't any scratches on her. Yet her arms still hurt, deep down.

Garrett exited the bathroom, his injuries now healed. She peeked at him through her lashes. He'd tugged on jeans and thick-looking socks. The wide expanse of his chest gleamed in the darkness, beckoning her in a way that made her mouth water. Then he reached for a T-shirt and drew it over his head. "Just to be safe," he drawled.

She swallowed. Did he know she wasn't sleeping?

He twisted on the bedside lamp.

She scooted over and then sat, drawing her legs to her chest. "Is everything okay?"

"Yes. How about you?" His tone was level and his face calm.

She swallowed. "Fine. I was just sleeping." Yes, she knew his niece would tell him about their journey into that terrifying world, unless somehow it was a dream. But she wanted time to think it all through. Without him looking at her like she was a deadly assassin about to decapitate him.

That little voice in her head whispered that his future mate would be an assassin. He'd mated her—kind of. Was it possible they could get the mating mark to stay?

Not that she was ready to mate. "Should we get some sleep?"

"Have you really been sleeping?"

"Yes." She tried to keep eye contact with him, but lightning zapped outside and tree branches snapped, so she looked toward the door.

He curled his hand around her nape and drew her near, compelling her to meet his glittering gaze. "I thought I told you not to lie to me."

Darn it. Had Hope called him in the middle of the night? "I *was* sleeping."

"Then what?" His voice was soft. Velvet soft.

She shivered and goose bumps rose down her back. The quieter he became, the more terrifying he seemed. But whatever had happened to her wasn't resolved yet in her mind, and she didn't want to share. Plus, she was tired of being bossed around. "I am not prepared to discuss the matter with you yet."

His fingers tightened at her nape. "Listen to me, Destiny." His minty breath feathered across her lips. "You're in my world and under my protection, and that means you don't keep secrets. You don't hide danger, and you sure as hell do not lie to me. Tell me you understand."

"But I'm not yours," she whispered right back.

Something dark flashed in his eyes.

Her mouth opened slightly as her breath caught painfully in her upper chest. "You know it's true." While the language was certainly archaic, she'd spent enough time in the vampire holding to recognize the possessiveness inherent in the male members of Garrett's family as well as his friends. "I'll never be yours." Not as a human, especially one who had a shortened life span, no matter how many times she might attack him and shrink the tumor. She took the pang to her heart and kept talking. "So stop telling me what to do."

"You're not mine?" He pulled her even closer, so that his nose was almost touching hers. "Who marked you? Who exactly was inside you the other night?"

Warning radiated through her with a roll of heat. "Garrett."

"Answer me."

"You were." She gulped as her face warmed. "That doesn't mean—"

"Let me tell you exactly what it means." He plucked her out of the bed, sat with his back to the wall, and planted her on his groin, facing him.

Longing smoldered through her, tightening her nipples and spurring her irritation at them both. "I'm not—"

"Destiny." His tone was a low command. One she instinctively heeded. "While we're together, you are mine. In every sense of the word. You understood that when you gave yourself to me the other night. Correct?"

"We're temporary," she said, her gaze dropping to his full lips.

"Wrong." His wrist twisted, and he grabbed her hair, yanking her head back. "My marking appeared. For you. Right now, you're in this, and you're staying in this until we figure everything out, including that tumor in your head. There's no out until I say there's an out. Tell me you understand."

"You won't force me to mate. Even if you could," she snapped.

"No, I wouldn't," he agreed. "But for now, we're sticking together until we figure out what happened to you. Then you can decide what you want to do for the rest of your life."

A part of her wanted to acquiesce, but the other part held on to pride. "I'm not going to be your little sex slave while you dig into my head," she snapped.

His cheek creased with a quick flash of amusement. "Agreed. You can set the terms for us. If you don't want sex as part of the equation, then no sex. However, you're with me for the duration. Period."

Why didn't he just kiss her and make her forget all about this world? "What do *you* want?" She plucked at a loose string on the frayed bedspread.

"Sex. Definitely sex."

"Why?" she blurted. "You're, well, you." She gestured toward his ripped abs. "I'm certain you could have sex with pretty much anybody in the world if you just took off your shirt. Why me?"

"Forgetting the fact that you're my mate?" He studied her, obviously taking her question seriously. "I'm drawn to you in a way I don't understand. Also, you quiet the rushing energy always pummeling through me."

Her body settled. "I bring you peace?"

"Yeah," he murmured.

That was incredibly sweet. Even so, it sounded boring. "Not like the mate of your dreams, who's all excitement and danger?" Jealousy wasn't cold. It was a hot poker between the ribs.

One of his dark eyebrows rose. "Kitten, you're all danger. I've trained to fight my entire life, and I've been in battles where not many survived. Nobody has come as close to killing me as you did the other morning. Nobody."

She sank her teeth into her lip, acutely aware of the rock-hard erection touching her thighs. Her mind wanted to spin away and let her body take over, but she had to concentrate. "What does that mean?" The answer meant something to her heart, based on the little jumps it was taking.

"It means I've been dreaming about you," he said. "You're not human, Destiny."

Her back stiffened. "I most certainly am too human."

"No. You wouldn't have survived the trip you just took to meet Ulric if you were human."

How did that make any sense? Obviously Hope had told him about the dream. "I'm not a vampire."

"There's a possibility that you're a shifter who has lost the ability to shift, but I don't feel that in you. You have to be an enhanced human." His tone was a low growl now.

One that licked along her skin. Like his mate?

Garrett was dangerous and more than deadly, and he had his fair share of possessiveness. Being with him was one thing when it was definitely temporary, just a way to experience life. Jumping into forever was another situation entirely, and she would need time to process that possibility. Plus, there might be a broken heart at the end of this for her. "What if I'm not your mate and she comes along while we're trying to solve the mystery of me?"

His lips pressed together, and he didn't answer.

She nodded. "Exactly. What if whatever the Kurjans did to me somehow made that mating mark appear on your hand? What if I'm a trap?" It sounded crazy, but she'd seen that room where they'd experimented on her.

"That's insane." He held up his hand, showing the vibrant marking on his palm. "This appeared in me, in reaction to you." A possessive glint filled his eyes. "The Kurjans didn't create this reaction."

But what if? "I've watched you. You were all in with the Grizzlies, who you call brothers. You're all in with your family. What if we're just tooling along and your real mate shows up? If you found your mate, then she'd be your total world, and you know that. You wouldn't be able to help yourself." Was that longing in her voice? No. "You'd drop me in an instant, and I'm not going to put myself in that position."

"I don't think you're giving me enough credit, kitten." He seemed more thoughtful than irritated. His fingers started caressing her nape, spiraling desire down to her sex.

She cleared her throat and tried incredibly hard not to rub against him. "You have to be open to the possibility that whatever chemical is messing with my brain, with a possible enhancement, also messed with your mating mark." She had to understand what she might be getting into here.

"Not a chance. My marking appeared because you're my mate, and I'm more than happy to give you time to come to that conclusion." His gaze ran over her face as if he was kissing each inch.

This was all too much, and she needed to think. Time to change the subject. "What did Hope say?"

"You tell me about the dream world, and I'll compare notes."

Fine. Dessie told him about the entire dream, and while his expression remained calm, blue shot through the gray of his eyes. Finally, he grimaced. "That meshes with what Hope said, and I'm sorry you had to go through that."

She shivered. "What about this Ulric?"

"Tomorrow. I'll tell you all about Ulric and the Seven tomorrow." He glanced at the manual clock on the bedside table. "For tonight, we need sleep." Yet he was steel-hard against her core.

"I'm very confused, Garrett." And wet and ready for him, aching in a way that could not be healthy.

His fingers began to untangle from her hair. "Then let's get some sleep and figure out the rest tomorrow."

"But I want you." She ran both of her hands up his chest, humming at the hard muscle beneath his worn T-shirt. "This is all a lot to take in, but one thing I know for sure is that I'm not waiting for the morning to live." She didn't have enough time for that. "I'm tired of thinking about this new world. I just want to feel for a while. What do you say?"

His nostrils flared, and his eyes morphed to a battleship gray. In one smooth movement, he twisted and put her on her back, his substantial body covering her. "I say that's a fantastic idea." Then his mouth was on her neck, his teeth gently scraping down to her clavicle.

He nuzzled his way back up and then took her lips. Fire burst through her. Wild and out of control. She tried to hold on to sanity, but his heated touch took away the world for the moment.

All she could do was feel. His dominance emerged full force when he kissed her with an aggressiveness that consumed her. He took control of them both, and there was no more resisting. No more thinking.

Her sex clenched, and he pressed against her, sending mini-tremors through her entire lower body. The blood thundered in her ears, and her breasts tightened painfully.

He ripped off her shirt and shoved down her yoga pants, the rough pads of his fingers marking every place they touched. Maybe forever. "Destiny." Just one word. Her name. The sound curled deep inside her where she was trying to protect her heart.

There was no protection from Garrett Kayrs.

Frantically, she clutched the bottom of his shirt but didn't try to remove it. There was too much risk of her seeing his back. "Hurry."

"My way, kitten." He shoved down his jeans, and the sound of the heavy denim hitting the floor barely registered in her mind. His body was solid titanium against her, showing no give. No weakness. Just pure strength and power.

She wanted this and him with everything she had. Her body softened naturally against his as his hand at her hair controlled her every movement. Her mouth opened to let him take, and she drew him in, feeling his hand on her nipples, pinching with a sharp bite.

Need erupted through her body, bursting like a supernova and blasting directly to her pounding clit.

How was so much pleasure possible?

Then his hands and mouth were moving. Across her jaw, down her neck, to her breasts. His teeth and fingers bit and tweaked, while his mouth and tongue licked and soothed.

It was as if he knew her body better than she did. Knew just how to arouse her to an unbelievable need.

"Beautiful," he murmured at her breasts. "Stunning," he whispered against her undulating abs. "Fucking mine," he said, his mouth at her core right before he lashed her clit with his rough tongue.

The words barely registered, and then the world went dark as he went at her, his tongue and teeth and fingers taking her over. Those teeth nipped her thighs and then he was right there, his fingers inside her, finding that spot that was all his. He flicked her clit, and she went over, crying out his name.

The orgasm had barely crashed through her when he was driving her up again, his shoulders settled between her thighs and forcing them to open wider.

She gasped, needing him already again. It was too much. She dug her fingers into his thick hair and tugged. "Garrett?"

He looked up, a predator with a treat. "Mine, Dessie."

Chapter Twenty-Five

Garrett made his point and bent back down, taking what he wanted. What she needed. The woman tasted like strawberries with a hint of sweet orange, and he'd never get enough. He forced her high and pushed her over the edge, and her body responded beautifully, exploding with wild tremors against his mouth.

A desperate need took him, so he kept her in place, never wanting this moment to stop. He was out of control, and he wanted her bad, but she had to be ready first.

Her breath burst out of her in little pants, and her body writhed against him. He reached up and played with her nipples, giving her just enough of a tug to pull more heated moans from her. God, she was perfect for him. He loved her nipples. "Hold still," he growled, feeling her body react obediently before her mind could catch up.

She might not like it, but she responded to his commands. There was a submissiveness in her that she'd probably deny to her dying breath, but she instinctively obeyed. He needed that. Needed the idea he could control the danger around them both.

His fangs started to drop, and he shoved them back into place. But he allowed his teeth to scrape the sides of her clit, enjoying her sharp intake of breath. Then he sucked hard, pushing her back to the pinnacle but not letting her go over this time. Over and over he brought her to the brink, memorizing the small sounds she made. Sweet mewls. Soft whimpers. Bossy demands.

All for him.

He primed her until she couldn't help but fuck his mouth. Yeah. She was there. Thunder bellowed between his ears. "Now, Dessie." He sucked her clit into his mouth, using his tongue the entire time.

She stiffened and then arched off the bed, crying out, her body shaking so hard he had to put both hands on her thighs to hold her down. Finally, she murmured and came down, her body jolting with aftershocks.

Then he stood and kicked off his socks. His blood raged through his veins, and a pounding pummeled his brain. He grabbed her ankles and flipped her over, manacling an arm around her waist to pull her up on her hands and knees. He ripped off his shirt. "Hold on."

She tightened her body and gripped the pillows, open to him. She was ready, and he couldn't wait. "You can try to mark me again," she whispered.

The words roared through him. He tried to be gentle, but his hands on her hips were rough, leaving his fingerprints. Her ass was perfect, with round globes, tight and smooth. Pressing at her wet entrance, he shoved in, plowing through tight folds and nearly going mad. Instantly, her body gripped him in silk and fire. God. It was more than he'd ever imagined.

She cried out, her body vibrating around him. "Wow. I mean, I knew about this, but I couldn't imagine." Her words came out fragmented and full of need. "This is…"

"Yeah." Her internal walls caressed his shaft, and lust consumed him. "Feels different, right?"

"Yes." She ducked her head and pushed back against him, widening her thighs at the same time. "You can go so deep."

That was his plan. Her innocence and openness spiked right to his heart. There was no way she was lying now, and her honesty touched him in a way he didn't need at this moment. He pulsed inside her and pulled out to push back in, careful not to scare her.

"I like this," she whispered, her hair a wild mess down her back.

God, she was sweet. He leaned over her and pressed a soft kiss at the top of her spine, his abs brushing her taut ass. One that now carried his fingerprints.

She shivered. "More, Garrett." Her voice was a low plea.

He clamped his hands tighter and then pulled out, hammering back inside her. He controlled her with his hands, pulling her back to meet each thrust, his thighs bracketing hers.

Nothing in his entire life had ever felt this good. He was starting to need her in a way that should concern him, but nothing mattered right now except her sweet body taking him. He fucked her hard, losing himself in all of her.

Pain flared hot and bright in his right hand, and he lifted it to study his palm, his breath catching hard in his chest. The marking was even darker than before. Even more insistent.

Her breath quickened, and her body went taut.

"No." He grabbed her hair and pulled back, forcing her head to come up and her back to arch. "Not yet. Not until I say."

She mewled a sound of protest but sucked in air, obeying him.

Her soft body was tight, gripping him as if she never wanted to let him go. She was fire and silk, all around him, taking his breath. In that moment, she was everything.

His.

He thrust harder into her, and his balls tightened so painfully he saw darkness. If he could make this second last forever, he would. It was past the time of holding anything back, so he hammered powerfully, three times warning her not to climax. How she prevented herself, he'd never know.

He desperately needed this, and he needed her. With her, the rest of the world and its competing pressures faded away. He could be just Garrett Kayrs and not the future king, the Grizzly enforcer, or a member of the Seven.

Right now, he was just hers.

Her body tightened, and she panted, going stiff as she tried to fight the orgasm. If she went over, she'd take him with her.

The place she took him was as close to heaven as a killer like him would ever reach. She was soft and smart and kind, and too fucking brave for her own good. The woman had jumped into a rushing river to save a toddler, even though she couldn't swim. Plus, she held an intuition about people that was inspiring. And impressive.

"Garrett, please," she panted, fighting the hold he had on her head. Then she squeezed his shaft hard enough to nearly push him out.

Explosions detonated between his ears, and flames crackled down his spine to land in his balls. He ground hard inside her and let the marking plant bright on her hip, gently sinking his fangs into her flesh.

"Now, Dessie."

She jerked and then pushed against him, her body clamping down even harder on him, engulfing him in a paradise he hadn't realized existed. Then he released himself into her, his chest taking a hit along with the rest of his body.

He groaned and licked her spine, his cock pulsing inside her. He felt every sigh, every twitch, every ripple in her body. Heat flowed along her skin, nearly burning him.

There was no way he could let her go. She belonged to him, and he had to protect her.

She went limp beneath him, and her arms gave out. Her face hit the pillow, and she moaned, stretching her arms out in front of her. He didn't want to withdraw from her. Not now. Maybe not ever. The feeling of her surrounding him was pure bliss.

He caught sight of the potted plant on the windowsill, which looked like it had grown several inches. Were those small flowering buds on it? Dessie had been correct to give it water. His mom was a botanist, and so was this little sweetheart.

It figured he'd find the perfect woman for him, and he'd be unable to make her his forever. He hadn't known her long, but every cell in his body wanted to keep her. What if that tumor in her head always prevented their complete mating? Was there a way she could live her life with him? Could he watch her grow old and die? The mysterious mate he'd been chasing for so long dropped away for the moment and then comingled into Destiny Applegate. She was the murderous sweetheart on the back of his bike.

He had finally found his mate.

So he kissed each of her shoulder blades and her spine again, pulling her hair out of the way to kiss her nape.

Even in the darkened room, he could see an outline on her soft skin. He paused, and his body went from satiated to alert in a second.

Holding her still, remaining inside her, he reached for the bedside lamp. Light illuminated her beautiful skin. He swallowed, looking at the birthmark that had been hidden beneath her hair. The outline was graceful and extended to the bottom of her hairline, covering her vulnerable nape. "What the fuck?" he whispered.

She lazily turned her head to the side and rested her cheek on her arms. "What?"

He couldn't believe what he was seeing. "What is this?" His voice came out nearly demon guttural.

She blinked and tried to turn her head farther to see him, but he was still on her and hampered her movements. "My birthmark?" Her voice came out tentative this time as she caught his mood.

"Yeah." He pulled out of her body and reached for his boxers, yanking them on. "Hold still." Though he didn't need to, he lifted the light closer to examine the deep red mark.

She tried to move, but he held her still. "It's just a birthmark, Garrett."

No. It wasn't. On Dessie's neck was an intricate Baroque symbol in the shape of an ancient butterfly. "Dessie, this is Ulric's mark. Tell me you somehow just got this last night in that dream world."

She started to struggle, so he allowed her to roll over to face him. "No. I've always had it. Since birth. Why?" The sleepy look in her eyes began to slide away, leaving concern.

He couldn't believe this. A quick glance at her hip showed the *K* marking fading away already. He scanned back up her to meet her eyes. "The birthmark on your neck is Ulric's marking, which means you're his current Intended." Well, that wasn't going to fucking happen. Ever.

Chapter Twenty-Six

Dessie could barely think through the haze of post-orgasmic bliss she was trying to maintain, but the tone of Garrett's voice shot her right into awareness. "What do you mean?"

He stood and reached down to grab her clothing, tossing it on the bed. "Ulric has an Intended born every once in a while who's supposed to help him get free, mate him, and have tons of Ulric-style evil babies. The marking on your neck shows you as an Intended." He paused, his jaw hardening as he drew on clothing. "Who else knows about this?"

The suddenly frigid air prickled her skin, and she hurried to pull the shirt over her head and shimmy into her yoga pants. Her body held whisker burn and love marks from him, but right now his expression was a hard mask. His anger chilled her to calmness, when all she wanted to do was run. "I don't know. It's never been a big deal."

When his chin lowered, she hastened to continue. "I've worn a ponytail at school, so I'm sure everyone has seen it at some point or another. When asked about it, I just say it's a birthmark."

"A birthmark." He wiped a thumb across his bottom lip.

Both his lips had been on her sensitive parts just minutes before. "Yes." Her mind ticked back to the terrifying creature in her dream, and terror rumbled beneath her skin. Should she just run? "So Ulric can mate unenhanced females?"

"No. No, he can't. You're enhanced. I can't see you being a shifter. So whatever they did to your head, to your chemistry, keeps negating my mating mark." Garrett paused and then turned to look at the flowering plant on the windowsill, his gaze narrowing. "Flowers and plants thrive around you, don't they?"

What was he talking about? "I've been told I have a green thumb."

"More likely an enhancement," he murmured. "My mom has the same one, in addition to being empathic." Then he removed a phone from his back pocket. "Turn around and lift your hair."

She blinked. "No." Her entire body tensed as if expecting an attack.

He didn't move, but he blocked the illumination from the outside lights. "We have a drawing of another Intended's marking, and I want to compare it with yours. The symbols within the wings might be different. Could tell us something. I just want a picture, Dessie."

They both knew he could take the picture if he wanted.

She huffed and turned her head, piling her hair out of the way. "Fine."

Garrett leaned in and snapped several pictures.

She let her hair drop and scooted up to sit on the pillow with her back to the worn wallpaper that might've been red roses at some time. "All I wanted was a normal life for the brief time I had left."

Garrett was texting with one hand while studying her face. "I think that's off the table, kitten."

Not if she chose otherwise. At the moment, she was at his mercy. At night, it seemed she was at Ulric's. She could run from Garrett, and there had to be a way to prevent Ulric from invading her dreams.

Garrett's upper lip twitched. "You're not fleeing. Put that idea out of your gorgeous head right now."

She crossed her arms over her still-sensitive breasts. "Tell me more about this Ulric and an Intended. Please."

Garrett read the face of his phone. "Ulric is the leader of the Cyst. They're the religious leaders and the key assassins for the Kurjan nation, who are our enemy by their choice. Kurjans are male only, just like vampires, so they need to mate enhanced females or females from other species."

Her eyebrows rose on their own. "Vampires are male only?"

"Yeah, except for Hope. She's the one and only female vampire." Garrett didn't sound happy about that fact. "More than a thousand years ago, Ulric underwent a ritual in which he killed one hundred enhanced females, took their blood, and made his body impenetrable. His entire body. He can't be killed by any weapon." Garrett glanced at his phone and looked back up at her.

"That monster on the beach can't be killed?" Terror coated her throat and filled her abdomen with chills.

He exhaled as if trying to hold on to his temper. Even so, his cheeks were a dark red. "Not from the outside. So seven immortal hybrids, demon and vampire mixes, underwent a similar ritual without killing anybody, so only their torsos were fused. They altered physics and created three hell worlds dimensions away. Ulric is trapped in the center one. The other two have fallen."

This was insane. Yet she'd been to that hell world somehow, and the description fit. "But you're not a thousand years old," she said, her voice barely quavering.

"No. Two of the Seven were killed, so Logan and I underwent the ritual and became part of the Seven to take their places. We have a way to kill Ulric once he gets home, and he will, because he's getting stronger. It's just a matter of time." Garrett's voice remained level, but his anger rolled through the room, making the air heavy.

"How will you kill him?" Was it by sacrificing an Intended or something equally horrible?

Garrett eyed the door. "Logan and Sam are coming this way, and we're going to study your marking as well as the drawing being sent to me now."

He shot one hand through his thick hair. "One of the enhanced women Ulric killed was a witch and a psychic. She had triplet girls, each marked with a key at birth. Somehow she infused a certain poison into all three of them, which has been passed down through the years in the blood of their descendants, along with the marking of a perfectly shaped key. We take the blood of the three Keys and somehow get it into Ulric, and supposedly he'll die from it. If we don't, he has some unknown plan to end the lives of all enhanced females on the planet. Don't ask me why. He's nuts."

It was all unbelievable. Yet her birthmark did cover her entire nape. She'd caught glimpses of it in the mirror through the years, and it looked like a butterfly with mottled blotches on the wings. "Who are these three Keys?" At least he didn't want her blood to kill the monster she'd met.

"We have two. One is Mercy, Logan's mate. The second is a woman named Grace, who's mated to one of the Seven. We're on the hunt for the third now."

Realization smacked her between the eyes. Now he was starting to make sense. "Oh. You think the final Key will be your mate." There would be symmetry to that outcome, and she'd noticed that symmetry existed not only in Garrett's immortal world but in the universe as a whole. She'd always been able to make such connections and figured it was an affinity for logical relationships, which she'd excelled at in school. His mate would be powerful and have a heavy destiny.

"No. You're my mate." His jaw firmed to the consistency of pure rock.

But Dessie wasn't a Key. In fact, she was the potential mate of the enemy. "This is too much, Garrett."

His eyes softened a bit. "I know."

The door opened, and both Sam and Logan walked in, staring at their phones. They paused and looked at her.

She pulled her legs up and wrapped her arms around them. "Hi. Guess I'm not just human."

Logan almost smiled. "This is insane."

"That's what I said," she blurted out.

Sam shut the door and swiped his screen. "The two markings aren't exactly the same. I mean, Dessie's mark and Yvonne's marking have different symbols in the wings of the butterflies. That has to mean something, right?"

"No clue," Garrett said, also looking at his phone.

Dessie cleared her throat. "Yvonne is the other Intended?"

"Yes," Garrett said. "She's lived with the Kurjans and worked with them for years, waiting for Ulric to be released. She's an evil wench, based on our interactions and research."

Wonderful. Dessie's neck itched.

Garrett peered closer at his screen. "I see triangles, Celtic knots, and symbols for fate and destiny in both butterflies, but none are the same." He looked up. "We'll need code breakers and historians on this. I've already sent the picture of Dessie's mark to the other members of the Seven, and we'll need to vote on whether or not we bring in outsiders. I'd like to consult with the Realm."

How odd that he had family on both sides of the equation. She watched him and wondered how he kept any sort of balance when his loyalties lay in more than one place. Then his words penetrated her foggy brain. "I'm a historian," she murmured. "Ancient history and languages were my emphasis in high school and then my major. I studied current languages to help me with the older ones."

Garrett zeroed in on her. "You've never tried to decipher your marking?"

"They're just blotches," she said. "I never saw anything to elucidate."

Garrett handed his phone to her. "Look closer."

Her hands trembled, but she accepted the device to see what he meant. Her heart stuttered. "Oh." The butterfly shape was the same mark that had always been there, but the blotches on the wings and center had taken shape. They were now crisp. "This is new. They weren't like this before."

"Before what?" Garrett asked, tension evident in his guttural tone.

She opened her mouth and then paused before speaking. "I don't really know." When was the last time she'd really studied her birthmark? Was it possible that the symbols had taken shape during the last few years and she just hadn't noticed? It wasn't as if she looked at the nape of her neck very often.

Sam sighed. "My best guess is that her first interaction with Ulric made the symbols more pronounced. She's an Intended, so her blood would naturally react to his in a way we still don't understand." He cut Garrett what looked like a sympathetic look. "It's probably the same way we react to meeting our mate when the mating mark appears."

Logan nodded. "Makes sense. It's all blood and DNA and reactions, if you ask me."

"Agreed." Garrett held up his palm, showing his beautiful and deadly marking.

Was the marking really meant for her? Dessie swallowed over a boulder-sized lump in her throat. "I don't want to mate Ulric."

"You won't," Garrett said shortly.

She tilted her head, looking at the digital image of the right butterfly wing, which held a circular symbol with thick lines that divided it in quarters. "The top symbol is a Celtic knot symbolizing a shield. The four separate corners depict an unbreakable barrier."

Garrett crossed his arms. "Go on."

She studied the symbol in the bottom of the same wing. This was on her nape? "This bird here is actually a quetzal, which was a revered creature in the Aztec culture and symbolized the incarnation of force, power, freedom, and dominance." She squinted at the three symbols taking up space between the two she'd recognized. "I don't know these. I'll need a library to identify them. Preferably the library that no longer exists on the island."

Sam scratched his neck. "I wonder if there's a sort of code in here? Maybe about the ritual." He looked up at Dessie. "It would make a sick kind of sense that the Intended marking holds the answer to how to kill Ulric."

Dessie's stomach rolled over. She wasn't liking this new world she'd entered but destroying Ulric and freeing herself from his pull held a certain appeal. "I can decipher this. Surely you all have a library stocked with ancient texts."

"We surely do," Garrett agreed. "You're free to roam the entire thing once Emma finishes conducting a few more tests on you. There has to be something in your genetics or blood that we missed."

For the very first time, a small hope began to tap dance in her breast. Was there a chance she had a full life ahead of her? Her body had changed to make the marking more distinct. If that could be altered, what about the mass attacking her brain? Was it possible?

Garrett rolled his shoulder. "I'm getting pressure from the king as well as the rest of my family, and we need that vote from the Seven."

"Ditto," Logan said grimly. He glanced at Dessie. "Our older brother Zane is the king of the demon nation. He's not happy to be out of the loop on this one, and when Zane's not happy, things blow up." He grinned. "Zane is mated to Janie, Garrett's sister. You met her, right?"

Dessie nodded. "You're all pretty much connected, aren't you?" What would that be like? Her only connection in life was her aunt, who'd hired a hitman to kill her.

"You could say that," Sam said, shaking his head. "Too connected sometimes."

She looked at the middle Kyllwood brother. "Sam? You're not part of the Seven, so how do you know all of this? Just because you and Garrett rode together with the Grizzlies?"

Sam rolled his eyes. They were a darker green than Logan's tonight. "No. I'm the Keeper of the circle and have the fu—darn marking to prove it. That means I need to find and protect the locale where this ritual is supposed to take place."

There was something in his voice she couldn't grasp. Couldn't pin down. "You don't want the ritual to happen?" But then Ulric would live.

Sam eyed Garrett.

None of the men spoke.

What were they hiding? Was there a reason these three actually didn't want the ritual to occur? If so, did the rest of the Seven know about their opposition? What exactly was she walking into here?

Logan frowned and leaned closer to his phone, widening the screen. "Uh, take a closer look."

Garrett and Sam did the same.

The atmosphere in the room shifted as they caught sight of something at the same time.

"Holy shit," Sam said, his gaze slashing up to her.

Logan did the same, his focus narrowing.

Finally, Garrett looked up, fire burning in his eyes. Then he barked out a short laugh that sounded feral. "I guess fate has no problem fucking with Ulric as well."

She pressed back against the wall, feeling small and vulnerable under their powerful gazes. "I don't understand."

He handed over his phone again. "Look in the body of the butterfly, between the two wings."

She'd never really studied the weird mark before and usually forgot it was there. Using two fingers, she widened the screen even more to study the oval body and a perfectly clear symbol in the center. "Wait a minute. Is that…"

"Yeah, kitten," Garrett drawled. "That's a key."

Chapter Twenty-Seven

Garrett piloted the craft through the dismal storm because he'd needed to be in control. Dessie and Sam slept in the back, and Logan took point next to him. The rain battered them, and every once in a while, lightning would flash purple through the clouds.

Logan turned a dial in the middle of the control panel and readjusted his headset. "Want to talk about it?"

Garrett glanced behind them to see that Dessie was completely out, snuggled down in a blanket he'd taken from the motel. Sam was similarly sleeping, his head against the window, his body sprawled out. Neither wore headsets so they could sleep. "I don't have anything to say."

"Sure you do. Let it out, G." Logan snorted, sounding like a television shrink.

"Shut up," Garrett said without heat. He and Logan had been like blood brothers the second their siblings had mated. Well, after they'd tried to kill each other. Then they'd undergone the Seven ritual and had bonded in blood and bone and too much pain to comprehend. Plus, Logan felt the pull of opposing loyalties as much as Garrett did. "She's my mate and is certainly enhanced. Did you see the flowers on the windowsill?"

Logan stared out of the window. "Interesting."

"Yeah. I hadn't been paying close enough attention. Every place we've been, any environment she's stepped into, plants and flowers have thrived. I doubt even she knows what she's doing."

"Her college major had something to do with ancient languages. Did she express any interest in botany?" Logan fiddled with the same heat dial and then finally sat back, apparently satisfied.

Garrett nodded. "Just said she had a green thumb. I'm thinking she gardened as a hobby. But she has mystical symbols on her body and studied ancient languages and mythologies." The woman's instincts had certainly led her in the right direction to gain control over her life. "But she doesn't know she has gifts?"

"You think she knows?" Logan asked.

Garrett rubbed his chest. "No. Maybe she was aware at one time, or maybe she never had the opportunity to knowingly explore what she could do. But whoever messed with her head and created that tumor took her autonomy away from her." As well as the possibility of a long life, but Garrett was going to figure out a way to save her. "Whoever hurt her is going to die, and I'm going to make sure it's painful." His blood heated with a vengeance that had him gripping the wheel too tightly. Somebody had harmed his mate, and they'd bleed. He forced his hands to relax.

"No disagreement there," Logan murmured through the headset. "Whoever messed with her head did a good job. All of her markers are human. I still don't get any sense of enhancement from her, even though she apparently is your mate."

"So?" Garrett didn't either, and he'd been trying since the day he'd met her. "What's your point?"

Logan was silent for a moment, no doubt choosing his words carefully. "What if she can't be mated? If they turned her into a human, no matter her skills, you can't mate her." Concern rode his tone. "You have to understand that."

Garrett took the words like a punch to the balls but didn't outwardly react. "You think I could let her go? Even if I can't mate her?"

"Perhaps she was once, a long time ago, able to be mated, but she can't be now. I don't want to see you go all in with this woman, no matter how fantastic she is, and then lose yourself when you lose her." Logan sighed, and the sound was tortured. "If anything happens to Mercy, I'm done. She's it for me, and I knew that when I mated the wild fairy. You and I have always been a lot alike. I'm just saying you should protect yourself now."

It was already too late to protect himself, and he knew it. Not that he would. Garrett banked left to avoid heavy clouds. "You wouldn't have turned away from Mercy. Not for a second, and she tried to kill you."

"She kidnapped me. Killing isn't in her nature," Logan returned. "Dessie tried to kill you."

"That's not in her nature, either," Garrett retorted.

Logan drummed his fingers on the dash. "I know. Dessie is a sweetheart."

"We can reverse whatever was done to her." Garrett didn't know how, but he had the best doctors in the world at his disposal, and if they couldn't do it, he'd find other doctors. In fact, he'd hunt down who hurt her in the first place and force them to tell him how to heal her. "I'm not letting her go."

"I wouldn't expect you to let her go," Logan allowed. "Quick question. Say you fix her. Say her enhancements come back, and she's full-on healthy and available and is no longer triggered to take off your head. For years, you've had an image of your mate in your head. Is it Dessie?"

The fact that Logan just sounded curious and not judgmental kept him from being punched in the face.

"Oh, it's Dessie." His marking pounded on his palm. He'd never felt as drawn to a female as he'd been with Dessie, and she matched the mate he'd dreamed of in every aspect, including trying to cut off his head.

"G? There's a chance you'll have to watch her grow old and die. That sounds like true hell to me."

"Yeah." Garrett looked over his shoulder at the sleeping woman. Her pink lips were slightly parted, and her hair was a curly mess across the blanket. Next to Sam, she looked small and fragile, and every possessive instinct in Garrett's body rose to the surface. The beast at his core, the one he tried so hard to control, snapped his chain and waited. On alert and ready to fight. "She's mine, Logan. No matter what." It was a vow, and he meant it to his soul.

So be it.

* * * *

After a dream-filled night that fortunately didn't feature any hell worlds, Dessie spent the day being poked, prodded, and scanned. The Queen of the Realm was a menace with a needle, and the only thing that cheered Dessie up was the fact that Emma took plenty of Garrett's blood as well.

After a nice lunch of tacos, she sat on an examination table, while he frowned from a seat next to the table. "Why are you taking more blood?" he asked, his voice rumbling with an obvious effort to refrain from snapping at his aunt.

The queen, her intelligent eyes sparkling, withdrew the needle. "Stop being a baby." She slapped a bandage on him.

He winced and pressed his other hand over the bandage. "Geez. Fine. Again, why my blood, Em?"

The queen strode on white tennis shoes over to a marble counter and started organizing vials. "You've slept together, briefly transferred the mating mark, and I want to see if there's any change in your blood. Plus, since Dessie seems to be enhanced, the fact that I can't find proof of that in her blood is driving me nuts. Maybe there's a reaction in yours." She looked over her shoulder at him. "I'm also studying what I can of the Seven, since you altered your very biology with that ritual."

Garrett's frown shortened Dessie's breath. "Em. I didn't agree to that."

"Doesn't matter," Emma said cheerfully. "Your blood is your blood. If I'm examining it, I can't just take out the anomalies, can I?"

Dessie shifted on the plush white table, her legs hanging over the end. She'd borrowed a pair of Janie's jeans along with a white sweater, and she loved the black boots that had been included. Her face heated. "Does everyone know we were intimate?"

Emma grinned and turned back to her whirring machines. "Well, you were both naked when you tried to kill him."

Oh. That was right. "I see," Dessie murmured.

A lab tech entered and handed Emma several printouts before hurrying away, his long black hair in a cool-looking braid.

"These are your latest brain scans." Emma flipped through the papers and then stilled.

"What?" Garrett asked.

Emma read further and then looked at Dessie, her brow furrowed and her eyes soft. "The tumor is expanding quickly now." She read some more. "It contracted a day ago but now is increasing in mass and spreading its tendrils at five times the speed of what your earlier tests showed." Shaking her head, she walked to the counter again. "That doesn't make sense. When she attacked Garrett and Logan, the tumor shrank. But now it seems to have been activated somehow." She turned and paced to the door and back, her gaze unfocused.

Did the queen even remember anyone else was in the room? Dessie pressed a hand to her temple as if she could slow down the tumor. Why was it growing faster? Did that mean she had days instead of weeks left? She looked for help, seeking Garrett's gaze.

His eyes were a silvery blue with a deep blue rim around the iris. Was there no end to the colors of his eyes? "Emma?" he asked.

Emma stopped in midstride and looked at them both. "All right. I'm thinking some sort of chemical is released when Destiny sees the Seven marking, and that chemical both urges her to kill and somehow shrinks the tumor. But now that the chemical has receded, the tumor has taken over."

Dessie opened her mouth and shut it. There was nothing to say.

Garrett stood, his body covering the entire doorway. "So we have her attack me again."

Emma grimaced. "We may have to do that, but I don't like it. It isn't good for Dessie's brain to be triggered and then sedated." She tapped her finger on her lip. "We'd need a controlled environment, and I'd like for her to be under a scanner at the time, if possible. I'll need to do blood work during and after, so you'll have to be restrained, Dessie." Her lips turned down. "I'm so sorry about this. It's your choice, of course."

Dessie felt like throwing up. "I want to fight this tumor." She stretched her ankles. "I also need to fight this marking on my neck and figure out how to stop Ulric from pulling me into his world."

"Hope is meeting with you after dinner tonight," Emma said. "She's fought Ulric before, and between the two of you, I think we can come up with a plan." She paused and turned to face Garrett. "Although, if I know my nephew, there's already a plan coming together. Garrett?"

Garrett leaned over and kissed the top of the queen's head. "I don't have anything to report."

Which wasn't a no.

By the look on Emma's face, she was fully cognizant of that fact. "Garrett—"

His phone buzzed, and he lifted it from his pocket to read the face. Then he quickly texted something back before reaching for Dessie's hand. "Your aunt is searching for another hitman to take you out, and the last thing we need is to deal with humans. She thinks she just hired me, and I'll meet with her tomorrow."

Pain filtered through Dessie, and she tried to hide it. "That woman is determined, isn't she?"

"Apparently. I'll take care of it." He helped her off the table. "We don't have time to deal with her crap, to be honest."

Emma's dark eyebrows rose. "Hitman?"

"Trust fund, inheritance, shady aunt," Garrett said by way of explanation, waving his hand as if swatting a fly. "Humans. More importantly, I'd like to have a chat with Aunt Cecile about Stoneton Hills Academy and how she afforded it, which, according to our background check, she couldn't have. She might be the key to figuring out who messed with your head, Dessie."

"It has to be the Cyst," Emma said, putting the printout on the counter. "They're known to manipulate people."

Garrett nodded. "Best bet, definitely. But we do have other enemies out there, you know. I wouldn't want to guess wrong." He held Dessie's hand and moved for the door. "How long until you have new results?"

"Give me an hour." Emma glanced at her watch. "I take it you're going to make an appointment to see Lily?"

"Lily?" Dessie felt more and more off-balance. Now she could almost feel the tumor spreading throughout her brain.

Garrett opened the door. "Lily is one of the Realm's three prophets and is an expert at hypnotism. We'll see if she can get into your head and find those triggers."

Emma reached for a tablet. "Okay, I'll need a while to set up the right environment to do the tests I spoke about. How about first thing tomorrow?"

"I'm going to Texas in the morning, but we could schedule the tests for the afternoon," Garrett said.

"I'm going with you," Dessie said as he ushered her into the hallway.

He shut the door. "No."

She turned and planted her hands on her hips. Enough of this. "Yes."

"I guess we're about to have our first fight," he drawled.

Her chin went up in direct proportion to her temper. "Take your best shot, Prince."

Chapter Twenty-Eight

The sun rose over the horizon, spreading pink and golden hues across the blue Texas sky. Garrett checked the cheap motel room for any cameras or listening devices. The tweaking clerk with the pimples at the front desk had looked squirrelly to him.

"You've already looked for devices," Dessie said, leaning against the doorframe to the connecting room. A tiny bit of smugness lifted her smile, but she was doing a fair job of hiding it; she'd won the argument, and he'd brought her to Texas. She sighed. "Stop giving me the stink eye. You know I'm needed here to sign the papers so I can get control of my trust fund. I have a list of potential charities in mind that could make good use of the money."

He adjusted the knife at his thigh.

Logan appeared behind Dessie. "We're good in here. No bugs."

Garrett tapped his ear communicator. "Sam?"

"All is quiet out here," Sam said. "I'm stationed up in the trees to the north, and there's no sense of any immortals around. Not many humans, either. What's up with you finding motels in the middle of absolutely nowhere?"

Logan snorted. "At least he didn't buy this one."

Sam's chuckle came through the line. "Yet. It'd make a nice birthday present for you, brother."

Garrett shook his head. "Dorks." He'd planned to make this trip solo, but when Dessie had talked him into allowing her to come, he'd brought the best backup available. Both of them knew to protect her at any cost.

"Interestingly enough, the bushes all around your side of the building are suddenly flowering with bright orange blossoms," Sam drawled.

Was Dessie getting stronger, or had she always had this gift? He'd asked her about it before, and she'd just said she had a green thumb. Considering she'd lived for so long on that island, perhaps she didn't even understand the gift. "Keep an eye out, Sam. We have no clue what we're walking into here," he warned.

"Heads up," Sam said. "Champagne-colored SUV dipping over the potholes and coming to a stop in front of room seventeen."

Garrett had chosen the room because it was at the end farthest from the office. There were no cars parked near, and his was partially hidden in the nearby trees. He jerked his head toward Dessie. "Out of sight."

She moved back, and Logan partially shut the door.

Sam cleared his throat. "I have a scope on a fifty-something female exiting the vehicle. Visual confirmation that it's Cecile Applegate, based on her driver's license. No visible weapons, but she has a handbag that could hold several guns."

Garrett didn't care about guns. He did care about the silver knife that could separate his head from his body.

A sharp knock sounded at the door. He opened it and looked down at Dessie's aunt. The woman was fifty-one but appeared to be in her early sixties; he guessed booze and cigarettes were to blame. Her blue eyes were bloodshot, her thick hair a bottle red, and her body wiry in designer clothes. Without saying a word, he moved to the side and gestured her in.

She faltered and then strode inside, her head high.

"Sit." He pointed to one of two wooden chairs placed with a dusty square table by the door. He didn't want her going past the television set and seeing the partly opened door to the other room.

She clutched her gold-colored bag to her hip and edged around the table, careful not to get her pink linen pants dirty. She wore a matching blazer, a white shell, and enough gold and diamond jewelry to show she was a complete idiot. It was amazing she hadn't been robbed strutting from her car to the room. "Why did we have to meet here?"

He kicked the door shut, enjoying the way she jumped. "Are you wired?"

"No." She frowned plucked eyebrows and held her purse even closer. "Are you?"

"No." He discreetly pocketed a scanner invented by his cousin and pointed it at her. "Do you have the money?" A quick check confirmed that she wasn't wired.

She gulped. "I have half of the money." Her chin was weak, and it shook. It was shocking that she was any sort of blood relation to the woman in the other room. "You get half now and half after..."

"After what?" He remained standing and shoved his hands in the pockets of his black cargo pants just so he wouldn't grab her.

She visibly steeled herself and met his gaze. "You know what. We discussed it on the phone."

All right. He was going to make her say it before he considered his next move. "Lady, I'm not playing games. You spell it out for me, or I'm gone." He let the killer inside himself show, although even at his mellowest, he most likely looked like a murderer to her.

She reared up without moving from the chair. "Fine. I want you to take out my niece, Destiny Applegate. She was released from college and is traipsing across the States. Her last known location was California near Tahoe."

"Take out?" he asked, his blood starting to heat. "That's a nice euphemism. Do you care how I do it?"

She opened her purse. "Not really. Well, I take that back. If you could make it look like an accident, that would be best. I don't want any questions."

Of course not. Questions would be bad. What a useless bitch. "An accident costs more."

She lifted an envelope out of her bag. "No more. I have fifty thousand now and will get you the rest after her funeral." She smiled big, and her eyes looked squinty. "I plan to give her a lovely one. If I recall, she's a pretty girl. Please don't mess up her face. People are so much more sympathetic when beauty dies, don't you think?"

A low growl rumbled up from his gut, and he swallowed it ruthlessly. This woman was a cockroach, and he wanted to step on her. He'd been stupid to allow Dessie to temper his plans. He should've broken the aunt's neck days ago and just moved on. "Why do you want your niece dead?"

She sniffed. "That's none of your business."

Dessie burst into the room. "It is *my* business."

* * * *

Dessie couldn't believe this woman was her father's sister. "Answer me."

Garrett plucked the purse out of Cecile's lap.

"Hey." Cecile started to stand, took one look at Garrett's face, and sank back into her chair. "That's mine."

He rifled through it and then tossed it toward the bed. "No weapons."

Dessie started toward her, but Garrett held up a hand. "Close enough," he said.

She stopped. "Why, Cecile? Just money?"

"Just money?" Pure hatred spat from Cecile's eyes. "You're talking millions. Millions upon millions, actually. And my brother left it all to you. I couldn't touch the funds, even while I was raising you."

"You didn't raise me." Dessie drew on the quiet vampire's strength to keep her voice from shaking or tears from falling. This was her only living relative, and she was a rotten person. "You sent me away for all of my life. I didn't even get to go home for holidays." Many of her friends at Chapel Hill had gone home over holiday breaks, while she was left alone at the school. Then at Stoneton Hills, nobody left the island until they graduated. She needed to remember those girls.

Cecile slowly pulled the envelope of money back toward herself with one red-painted nail. "You were fine at school."

"How did you pay for Stoneton?" Garrett asked, crossing his arms and flexing powerful muscles.

Cecile put her nose in the air and sniffed again. "I made do."

Fury shook Dessie, and she took another step toward her aunt.

Garrett's head swung toward her, and she stopped moving. Steel glinted in his eyes. Even though his anger was not directed at her, her stomach quivered.

"I'm leaving." Cecile stood. "This was obviously a setup."

Garrett turned only his head. "Sit your ass back down, or I'll sit you down." He flashed his teeth. "Please give me a reason to put my hands on you."

Cecile paled. "Listen, you—" she tried to bluster.

Garrett stepped toward her, and she fell back into her chair so fast it nearly tipped over. "I'm done with you, lady. You're two seconds from feeling the air leave your body for good. Stop fucking around and answer my questions. How did you pay?"

Her gaze darted around and landed on Dessie.

Dessie crossed her arms. "I can't stop him, even if I wanted to do so. And I don't. Air is wasted on you. Answer. The. Question."

Cecile grabbed the envelope and put it in her lap. "Fine. Some nice monks came to see me and said that you were very advanced for your age in several subjects. They offered you a scholarship to study at Stoneton Hills, and I agreed. I did you a favor."

It was possible. Obviously, the people in charge of Stoneton Hills had wanted Dessie there. "How much contact did you have with them?"

Cecile shrugged bony shoulders. "I met with them once and was notified when you graduated. That's all."

So her aunt had never even checked in on her. "My father would be so disappointed in you," Dessie said.

Cecile looked toward the window as if seeking any sort of help.

"How much did they pay you?" Garrett asked.

Cecile shook her head.

"Lady, I'm losing it here. How much?" He growled. Like really growled. How could Cecile think he was a human?

"Two hundred thousand dollars a year," Cecile muttered. "For her to get a really good education." Her gaze turned beseeching. "Then this year, no money. When I called, I discovered you'd graduated and just moved on. It took my detective weeks to find you."

"Detective?" Garrett asked silkily. "Or hitman?"

Logan came in through the open doorway and stood next to Dessie.

A blue vein showed in Cecile's forehead. "Who are you people?"

"We're her family," Garrett said shortly. "You wouldn't understand."

Family? It wasn't true, but for the moment, Dessie basked in the feeling that she wasn't alone any longer. In fact, she had more than decent backup at the moment.

Cecile stood again. "I'm finished talking with you now. Either kill me or get out of my way."

Garrett glanced at Dessie.

"No," Dessie whispered. While Cecile was a monster, she couldn't hurt Dessie now that he was protecting her. Garrett didn't need the stupid woman's murder on his soul. "Karma will get her."

Logan leaned down to whisper. "We actually know somebody named Karma, by the way." He stood just in front of her, probably in case Cecile attacked. "Though she's pretty sweet. Not sure she would kill Cecile for you." He straightened. "But I would."

Cecile gasped.

Dessie poked him in the ribs. "Thank you for the kind offer, but no thank you."

Garrett's frown was dark. "Fine. Cecile? Tell me what these monks looked like."

Cecile stumbled and caught herself on the table. "They looked like monks. They wore brown robes with hoods that covered their heads. Just men. Nothing more."

That didn't tell them anything. "Did they speak perfect English?" Dessie asked. "No accents?"

Cecile shrugged. "Not that I could tell. I wasn't really paying attention. They just agreed to pay me every year while you attended their school, and they promised you'd have a good education and life."

Sure they did.

Garrett's expression revealed nothing, which was all the more terrifying.

"Cecile," Dessie said quietly, "I know you're afraid of the men in this room, but I'm the one you should fear. Those dear monks trained me in ways you can't even imagine, and I'm far deadlier than even I thought I'd be. In other words, if I ever see you again, I'm going to break your neck. Easily."

Garrett finally grinned. "There we go."

Logan nudged her with his elbow. "Nicely said."

Cecile inched toward the door, one hand clutching the envelope and the other her neck.

Dessie snatched Cecile's purse off the bed and threw it at her. The woman caught it and shoved the envelope inside.

"Just so you know, I'm giving all of that trust fund money away," Dessie murmured. "I have a list of charities, and it's going to go very quickly."

"Why would you do that?" Cecile spat.

Dessie shook her head, sadness pulsing through her. "You really wouldn't understand."

Chapter Twenty-Nine

Garrett scoped the Texan terrain as he drove the solid SUV into the private airport and parked. Sam and Logan were in the back seat, both texting furiously as they worked. Dessie sat next to him, writing out a long list of charities that needed money. They'd spent two hours at the courthouse, then hit the bank, and now she had access to the millions.

She bit her lip and created another entry in her pink notebook. They'd had to stop at a drugstore for her to buy it, along with colored pens.

"Don't you want to keep any of the money?" he asked, turning off the car.

She shrugged. "I may keep a little in case I live, but really, I don't need much." She tugged off the lid of a light blue marker with her teeth and made a quick scribble. "I want to hit your library once we get home—I mean to the Realm—and then do some research on international charities. I like the look of Polaris, which fights human trafficking."

"The library is all yours." He tucked the rental keys above the visor and tried not to notice how she'd corrected herself. The Realm wasn't even his home right now and probably wouldn't be until he killed Ulric with the Seven. Or by himself, which was his plan at the moment. "Let's get going, Kyllwoods."

They both pushed open their doors at the same time, each still texting with one hand.

"I've got the Seven," Logan said. "They want to meet in person, sooner rather than later."

"Agreed," Garrett said, stepping onto the dried leaves covering the asphalt by the entrance. "Is there any chance they'll want to use the Realm medical facilities now that we have the three Keys?" It'd make his life a lot easier if any testing happened in Emma's lab.

Logan slammed his door and walked toward the double glass door of the small main terminal. "No. No chance."

That's what Garrett had figured. "Okay. I know they're all invited to Hope's twenty-first birthday party. Tell them they should come. It's time to bring the Realm in on this, and it's the only way to get to Hope." Hope was the Lock, whatever that meant. To him, it meant he'd take out Ulric before she had to get involved. He watched Dessie keep writing notes as she walked. Withering purple asters perked up as she passed. Now he had another reason to end Ulric before any ritual could be performed.

Logan sighed. "I have about half of the Seven on board, but Benny's being a dick."

Benny's default setting was dick. "I'll call him later tonight." Garrett paused. "Scratch that. I'll have Hope call him with a special invitation later." The guy was a sucker for females, starting with his mate and twin girls. He also had three sons now, and no doubt they were as crazy as Benny, even though they were toddlers aged one to three years old.

"Smart," Sam observed, still texting. "I had Bear reach out to the dragons about Dessie, and they haven't heard of her. Bear's take is that they're not the enemy who blitzed her island. His instincts are usually spot-on."

Garrett reached for the door before Dessie could. A chill clacked down his back. The wind picked up.

Logan and Sam instantly stilled.

"Dessie—" Garrett swung around and took her to the ground, covering her with his body. The glass blew out as the building exploded. Kurjan soldiers poured from the surrounding trees, knives flashing. "Stay down." He was up in a second, ducking his head and charging the oncoming mass.

Logan and Sam pivoted to fight.

Garrett slid his knife free of his sheath, already slashing with it. One Kurjan pulled a gun and shot lasers at him that turned to bullets the second they hit flesh. The guy aimed for center mass. Garrett flashed his teeth as the bullets dropped uselessly to ping on the ground. "Fused torso, asshole." He stabbed the Kurjan in the gut and yanked, slicing up to his neck. The soldier's purple eyes widened, and he gasped. Blood bubbled on his lips, and he fell to the side.

Another Kurjan, this one with flaming red hair tipped in black, tackled Garrett into the side of the burning building. Glass imbedded in his arm, and pain flashed. Growling, he punched the jackass hard in the mouth, breaking all of the guy's teeth. Then he kept going, rolling them over and punching the Kurjan's pale face until he went slack.

Man, he missed the days when the Kurjans couldn't venture out in daylight. A quick glance at Dessie confirmed she'd scrambled away from the fiery building and had her back to one of the SUV's tires. Blood flowed down a cut in her forehead, and she mopped at it, her hands shaking.

A Kurjan soldier moved for her, and Logan tackled him in the other direction, hitting the ground hard enough to send up shards of asphalt.

Sam flipped a Kurjan over his shoulder and followed the enemy down with a blade to the neck. Blood spurted across Sam's face, and he winced, removing his knife and wiping off his cheeks with his sleeve. Kurjan blood burned skin.

Garrett turned and blocked a knife attack from another soldier. It was a squad of six, and more were probably on the way. He needed to get Dessie out of there, and now. The soldier swung at his neck again, and Garrett moved under his arm, headbutted him, and slammed both hands against the offender's wrist. The bone snapped loudly. The Kurjan yelled and dropped the knife. Garrett grabbed him around the neck and took him down, landing with his knee on the guy's nuts.

The Kurjan shrieked.

Garrett leaned in, his fangs dropping. "Who are you here to kill?"

The Kurjan flopped beneath him. "Her. The girl."

Shit. "Why?"

"Fuck you."

Garrett pulled back his arm and punched the soldier several times in the head until he flopped unconscious. "We'll take this one with us."

He turned and stood just as a Kurjan soldier, bleeding from the neck, approached Dessie.

Her eyes widened. Then she partially sat up, set her knee on the concrete, and bowed. "My Lord," she murmured.

What the holy fuck?

* * * *

Dessie moved into the proper deferential position automatically. Then she caught herself and tried to back away.

Garrett was instantly behind the monk, slashing a blade into his neck. The monk cried out, and his blood sprayed toward her. She held up her arms, and they burned. Crying out, she frantically wiped her arms off on her jeans.

Dessie struggled to her feet, the world spinning around her. The building was on fire, punctuated by mini-explosions every few minutes. Flaming debris drifted down. Orange smoke billowed into the sky, and the ground was littered with the bodies of the monks.

Except they looked a little different from the monks she'd known. Some of these had red tips on their black hair, some had red hair with black tips, and they all had weird-looking eyes. Red or purple. She'd never seen anything like it.

She coughed into her arm, trying not to smell blood. The coppery scent competed with the smoke.

"Dessie. Move," Garrett ordered, hefting one of the monks over his shoulder. "This way."

Her eyes teared from the smoke, but she ran after him, careful to avoid the downed soldiers. Sam ran in front of Garrett and around the smoldering building, while Logan followed behind her, pausing to kick a stirring monk in the face.

The monk went back down, his head thunking on the ground.

She tripped on debris, and Logan was there, lifting her smoothly and running even faster. She shut her eyes against the dizziness and just held on, trying to make sense of what had happened.

Six monks had attacked them, and five were bleeding to death on the ground right now. The final one was over Garrett's shoulder, unconscious, with his long arms dangling in the air.

They reached the helicopter, and Garrett hefted the monk into the back. "Tie him up." He leaped into the pilot's seat and started the propellers.

Logan opened the copilot door and placed her on the seat, shutting it and jumping in the rear with Sam. They quickly tied up the monk with ropes from the far back, binding him completely. His eyelids blinked, and he jerked awake. Logan planted a hard fist against his temple, and he slumped unconscious again.

Then they were lifting into the air.

Her neck hurt, and she rubbed it. Some of the monk's blood must've gotten on her. She blinked away tears and coughed again, her throat raw from the smoke.

Garrett handed her a headset and then banked a hard left away from the smoke filling the air.

She put it on her head and wiped off her face.

He settled a headset on himself and then pushed several buttons on the dash. "Are you okay?"

"Yes." She coughed wildly into her arm again, her lungs protesting. "I'm okay. The monks. Those are the Kurjans?"

"Yes."

She wiped soot off her nose, her head reeling. "Their hair was all black and was cut short on the island. Their eyes were brown." They had to have been wearing contacts. "I didn't spend much time with them." Wetness tickled her cheek, and she wiped it away. It was blood. She was bleeding? "Yet I did, didn't I?"

Garrett's jaw hardened, but his hand remained steady on the wheel.

She looked over her shoulder at the unconscious monk between the Kyllwood brothers. "What did they do to me?" The blankness in her brain was terrifying.

"I'm going to find out," Garrett promised, lifting up on the wheel. "I promise."

She eyed the Kyllwoods. Both were bleeding from various parts of their bodies, and Logan's nose looked broken. The air popped around them. She wished she could heal herself like that. Her forehead hurt and was still bleeding. Grabbing the bottom of her shirt, she lifted the material to press it against her wound as she turned to stare at the clouds.

Garrett leaned forward and turned his head. "How bad is it?"

"I don't know."

"Do you need blood?"

Fatigue swamped her, and bile rose up her throat. "No." The idea made her feel worse than she already did. "Thank you, though."

He turned again. "I don't suppose you recognized any of the Kurjans who attacked us?"

She shook her head and instantly regretted it as pain flashed through her brain. "No. Sorry."

Logan leaned forward. "I took two of the new knives off these guys. You?"

"I got one and a new gun," Garrett said grimly. "They're not very proficient with the knives yet." He cut her a look before twisting a dial in front of him. "Not nearly as good as you are, Destiny."

That did not make her feel any better. Ice washed through her. "How could they train me without my remembering any of it?" Oh, she remembered learning to fight during physical education, but it was nothing like what Garrett had described to her when she'd attacked him. She'd been trying her best to meditate and force memories to the surface, but nothing came. Not even a glimpse of being trained to kill. A burning sense of betrayal countered the chill inside her. "I don't understand how somebody could do that."

Garrett reached for her hand. "I'll find out. We'll undo what they did."

What if they couldn't? What if the tumor couldn't be destroyed? "I remember being exhausted some days. So tired that I could barely concentrate, and I thought I'd slept all night." Now she wondered. What if she hadn't been sleeping? "They must've drugged me." What had happened to her during those nighttime hours? She wanted to turn around and punch the monk.

Garrett straightened and then tapped something on his ear. "Kayrs."

Their communication equipment was as impressive as the exotic helicopter they were in at the moment. The immortals had far-advanced technology.

"No. I don't want her dead," Garrett muttered, moving his headset so he could speak loudly enough for the cool ear communicator to catch. "Just destroy her. I want everything taken away. All accounts, all jewelry, all comfort. Leave her with nothing. Thanks." Then he clicked off.

Dessie crossed her arms, partially turning to face him.

He didn't take his gaze off the tumultuous clouds outside, but he did put his headset back into place. "You said you didn't want Cecile dead, and I promised I wouldn't have her killed. Anything else is on the table, and she deserves it." Then he banked a hard right.

In the back, the monk stirred, and Sam elbowed him hard in the face. The monk passed out again.

Dessie wiped more blood off her face. Life had gotten way too outlandish.

Chapter Thirty

Garrett wiped blood off his hands and exited the interrogation room to find his father waiting somewhat patiently, pounding one finger against a tablet. "Hey."

Talen looked up from where he sat at a table in the long hallway. Stone covered the ceiling and walls, while the floor was smooth cement, and he looked at home in the stark environment. His black hair nearly reached his shoulders, and today he wore dark jeans and a white T-shirt. "I hate these things." He tossed the tablet carelessly at the opposing wall, where it shattered. "Crap."

Garrett grinned, even though his hands were stinging from the Kurjan's blood. The guy hadn't taken long to break, and Garrett still needed to burn off some energy.

"What did you find out?" Talen stood, tall and broad. Danger hovered around him as naturally as if it were a part of him, and in the dim light, his golden eyes looked like molten coins.

"Not much. The guy is low-level and doesn't know anything about strategy or Stoneton Hills Academy." Not that Garrett had expected him to have intel. "His orders were to kill us. Said Yvonne had given the order. She's the current Intended of Ulric." He shook his head, frustration coating his throat.

Talen rubbed the whiskered shadow on his jaw. "How does Yvonne know about her?"

"I don't know. The Kurjans obviously do, and they treat Yvonne like a queen. She surely has access to all of their intel." And the woman wanted Dessie dead. "I think we're going to have to reach out to spies we have in the Kurjan holdings." Although now was the absolute worst time to burn any of their assets.

"Already did," Talen said, clapping him on the shoulder with a hand larger than a dinner plate. "I'll have somebody else take care of the Kurjan. For now, you and I need to talk."

Garrett strode with his father up several flights of stairs to the main floor of the lodge. "I need to check on Dessie."

"She's in seventh heaven in the ancient library with Hope and Janie." Talen's hold didn't relent. "Your mom is making cookies, and we're going to see her. She's missed you and needs more time than the few minutes you spent together the other day."

"I've missed her, too." The library was as safe a place as Dessie could be in the holdings, and he had no doubt there were guards posted in every direction. Dessie would be protected for now. Especially if she didn't go to sleep.

They walked out into autumn sunshine and turned right toward the houses sprawled along the lake. He nodded to several patrolling soldiers. "We've upped our security."

"Of course."

He sighed. "Dessie isn't a threat."

"Sure she is. The woman nearly killed you, and we don't know what other triggers she might have." Talen eyed the trees on the other side of the street. "I know she's not armed, but we're not taking chances. I have several men in the library guarding them. Plus, the Kurjans want her dead, which is a new one on us. They usually want to take women. So there's probably something in her blood they want concealed for good, and I want to know what it is."

"So do I," Garrett said, also scanning the treeline. It felt good to be home and right to be talking things over with his father. They understood each other. "But I won't allow her to be harmed."

They passed several homes, all decorated with autumn colors. A few pumpkins were already appearing.

"I want to know everything about the Seven," Talen said quietly.

"I know. I've forced a vote with the Seven, and I think I'll win. The Realm needs to be brought in, although you know almost everything now anyway." Garrett wouldn't bet against his father and uncle knowing the entire situation, except for the fact that Hope was the Lock. They'd be furious, and he couldn't blame them. "I want to tell you everything, but you need to accept my decisions. All of them."

Talen's chin tipped up. "There's a reason you think I won't."

Garrett didn't answer.

They were quiet as they strode beyond several more lawns littered with crackling golden and red leaves.

"You're my son, and I'm proud of you." Talen paused to retrieve a soccer ball from his driveway. "But if you think I'm going to let you sacrifice yourself to avoid some stupid ritual that shouldn't exist in the first place, then you've lost your fucking mind."

Garrett could admire the calm way his father voiced the threat. Yet he was getting closer to being able to destroy Ulric, and Dessie was his way of gaining access to Ulric's world. They had all three Keys and the Lock now. If he could just figure out how they combined to destroy Ulric, then he could end this thing for good. That opportunity hadn't existed before they'd found Dessie.

Now it did, and he was strong enough to kill Ulric. "The ritual changed me, Dad." In ways he'd never understand. His torso was fused, but he was also able to navigate the universe and climb through dimensions to reach other worlds. It hurt like hell, but he'd done so during the ritual; he should be able to do it again. Especially since the portals were reopening. "I can kill him."

"Ulric? In his hell world?" Talen tossed the ball into a wooden bin by a garage door two houses down. "I'll go with you."

"Can you teleport?"

Talen frowned. "No. None of us can any longer, thanks to the meddling of the Seven." There had been a time when most immortals with demon blood could teleport anywhere on this world, but that had ended years ago when one of the manufactured worlds had fallen. "But if you're making your way to hell, I'm going with you."

There was nobody on the planet Garrett would rather have at his back than Talen Kayrs. Unfortunately, he didn't know how to get himself to hell, so he sure didn't know how to bring another soldier. He sighed.

"Listen. About Dessie—" Talen started.

"I know," Garrett interrupted, noticing the abundant plant life around his parents' house, as well as many new hybrids. His mom did love to experiment. "She's human, and there's a chance that can't be reversed. So I should protect my heart, yada yada."

Talen paused. "Did you just say yada yada?" One of his dark eyebrows rose.

Garrett caught sight of his mom inside the front window. "Apparently."

Talen grasped his arm. "Look at me."

"All right." He didn't need another lecture about Dessie's immortality, but he also didn't want to brawl with his father in the front yard. "I understand what I face with Dessie if I can't mate her. That she'll grow old and die. I don't need a lecture about it."

Talen's gaze narrowed. "Your mom got sick after we mated, and the virus negated the mating mark, as you know. I thought she might become human and die, and it nearly killed me."

Garrett sobered. "I know."

"No. You don't." Talen's grip tightened, and white lines extended from his eyes as his face tightened. "Even if Cara had turned human, grown old, and died, I wouldn't change a fucking second with her."

Garrett paused. "What are you saying?"

"I don't know if this woman is your mate or not. But if she is, you take her as is, even if your time together will be short." He drew Garrett closer. "Don't waste a heartbeat for either of you. If she's the one."

Garrett's chest heated. "Thanks, Dad." Of course his father would understand.

Talen released him. "Besides. You're Garrett fucking Kayrs. If anybody can save that girl, it's you."

* * * *

Cara finished watering her plants and watched her men having a serious discussion on the porch. When Talen became intense, the atmosphere of the entire subdivision changed. It was odd seeing her child with his father and both as adults. So strange that her baby had become a fully adult male, as deadly and dangerous as his father. She hadn't had enough time with him as a child. Not enough fun times with a dependent toddler so happy to see her after nursery school each day.

He'd been thrown into adulthood way too early, and the kid had been born with the Kayrs intensity to start with.

Man, they looked alike.

Both well over six feet tall, muscled chests, hard-cut features. Talen's stamp was all over Garrett, from his wide stance to the stubborn shape of his jaw. But Garrett's metallic eyes and old soul were all his.

The amount of testosterone on her front porch right now would probably kill her hydrangea hybrids. She grinned. The level of immortal handsomeness outside was something to behold. They were both hers. Both would always be hers in one way or another. Even if Garrett mated, he would always be her firstborn son. At the moment, her only son.

Though she was always hoping for more children. It was difficult for immortals to procreate.

The males moved away from the window, but she didn't want to miss anything, so she stepped on the sofa seat and then its back, trying to angle her neck to see where they went.

The front door opened. "What the hell are you doing?" An iron-hard band was instantly around her waist as Talen snatched her off her perch and held her off the ground. He slowly turned her to face him, keeping her aloft.

"Observing." She placed a kiss on his nose, her feet dangling near his knees. "Let me down."

The gold in his eyes flickered to blue. He twisted the same arm holding her, using his hand to catch her hair. Then he yanked her head back and took her mouth. His kiss was rough and hard. Hot. Fire flowed down her throat to her body, lighting every nerve she had. Her body began to burn, and desperation spiraled through her head. The need for him, even after all this time, was brutal.

A sound almost caught her attention. The clearing of a throat. She blinked.

Talen released her mouth and looked over at their son. "Not one fucking second." Then he lowered her gently until her feet found the wooden floor, waiting until she'd regained her balance to loosen his hold around her waist.

Heat flushed into her face. Obviously she'd missed some of the conversation. "Garrett. I made cookies."

Talen drew her back against him, ducking his head so his mouth was at her ear. "No more climbing on things, my short little mate. Got it?"

She rolled her eyes. "I'm immortal."

"You're also not at full balance right now." His breath was as hot as the rest of him, and she shivered.

Garrett's eyes narrowed. "What does that mean?"

Cara sighed. It figured she would have no secrets from her observant mate. "I fell off a ladder the other day trimming the ivy on the south part of the house."

Talen nipped her ear. "After I repeatedly told you not to climb that ladder."

Garrett frowned. "Mom. You shouldn't be on a ladder."

She tried not to laugh. She really did. Her son was the spitting image of his father. "I'm immortal too, you know. There's no need to worry about me. Or frown at me."

Garrett's frown didn't lighten. "You might be immortal, but you're still breakable. Your bones break. Please be more careful." Moving in, he hugged her, his hold so gentle it brought tears to her eyes. He released her and looked down, giving her a glimpse of the boy he'd once been. "I was hoping I could talk you out of cutting off Dessie's head." His grin was impish and his body relaxed.

She slapped his arm. "Very funny." Then she sobered. "I know everything that happened to her wasn't her fault. Janie called earlier and said they were having a lot of fun going through the old tomes in the private part of the library. Your sister is quite taken with Dessie." The last thing she wanted in this world was to see her boy hurt.

Though he wasn't a boy any longer, was he?

She'd had no warning when Janie had mated Zane, and that had turned out better than she could've hoped. "Emma wants to conduct her tests around four this afternoon and said to let you know."

"Good. We need to figure out what the Kurjans did to Dessie and fix it." He flicked a look at Talen. "Then we need to make them pay."

Yep. Definitely his father's son.

His phone buzzed, and he lifted it to his ear. "Kayrs." His body stiffened. "I'll be right there." He shoved it in his jeans' pocket. "That was Janie. Dessie just collapsed in the library. They're taking her to the infirmary." He turned stark white, and fire lit his eyes.

Then he ran for the door.

Chapter Thirty-One

As Dessie slowly came to, she heard a beeping sound. "What is that?" she asked drowsily, forcing her eyelids open to see Garrett sprawled in a chair next to a hospital bed. An IV dripped liquid into her arm, and a plush white blanket covered her to her hips. She was partially sitting up, with thick pillows supporting her. "Garrett?"

He glanced at a monitor above her head. "You passed out in the library." A thick book bound in faded brown leather was open on his lap. "You were reading this, and then you just keeled over, according to Janie."

She couldn't remember the book. Her head ached with the echo of an old storm, and she pressed a hand to her temple. "Let me see it."

"Hell, no."

She jolted at the fury in his voice. He was so good at masking his emotions that she hadn't caught the turmoil beneath the surface. She needed to learn that skill, although now was probably not the time. She tried to remember reading the book and then passing out, but a huge dark hole in her memory prevented it. Why did this keep happening to her? "Is it possible that something in the book shut down my mind?" Just how many triggers did she have?

"Emma thinks so, and we conducted tests to see if you physically reacted the same as with the other stimulus. A scan of your brain showed that the tumor receded slightly in reaction to this possible trigger, but it's still growing faster than before." His voice was matter-of-fact, but the energy pouring from him was anything but calm. It heated the room and swelled into every corner. "Since you're all hooked up now, we thought we'd go ahead with the tests, if you're up to it."

That didn't sound like him. He was usually more cautious with her. Her heart sank, and her limbs began to tingle in warning. In stress. Her adrenaline kicked up several notches, and her breathing rate increased. Stress was going to kill her before the mass in her head did, if she didn't figure out how to control herself. "The tumor is getting a lot worse, isn't it." She made the claim a statement because it was obvious.

"You'll be fine." He handed over the spiral notebook she'd used earlier to scribble thoughts and drawings as she deciphered ancient codes. "Ring any bells?"

She scanned her notations, and her memory came rushing back. But not the moment when she'd passed out. The day had been an adventure with Hope as they compared notes and collaborated on deciphering the symbols. It was the most fun she'd had in ages. Well, except for having sex with Garrett. That had been better than all of her recent adventures put together.

"Destiny?" he prodded. "Do you recognize your notes?"

Oh. She needed to stop thinking about his hard body and how talented he was with it. "Yes. I identified the remaining two symbols in the right wing of my butterfly. This one is an ancient demon glyph that symbolizes movement." She pointed to her drawing of a circle coinciding with another circle, enclosing waves in the middle.

"Okay. Movement could definitely have something to do with the portals." He stood and leaned over her to better see the notebook, his smell of leather and motor oil easing her muscles. Making her feel safe and on edge at the same time. What would he do if she just dragged him down to the bed with her?

"What about this other one?" he asked.

She looked at the intricate lines that appeared to create a stooping tree in the middle of a meadow. "Old vampire lore says that the bending tree will survive the oncoming storm and not break." Her fingers traced the lines she'd drawn. "It's supposed to be a good omen." Which they all needed right now.

"Well, that's something. Have you learned anything about the symbols on the left wing?" His fingers brushed her hand, and she shivered, her body doing a slow roll. Just from a simple touch.

"Not yet." Her voice was breathy. There were four symbols in the left wing. The pattern was symmetrical with the right, but the symbols were different. "Hope was working on Yvonne's butterfly and deciphered two of her eight symbols. One was a protection design from the witch species and the other a weapon badge from the demons. Yvonne doesn't have a key in the body of her butterfly."

"No. You're the final Key," he said grimly. "But I promise you, you'll be protected. We just need your blood—nothing else."

That didn't make sense. A ritual to destroy an ancient immortal psychopath would certainly require more than the blood of three women. She might not have experienced a lot of life, but she was a historian, and she understood that monumental events required pain and sacrifice. Heroes didn't become heroic by sitting home alone and hoping for the best. "Garrett? You're going to need to lose that compulsion to control the world."

"I don't need to control the world." He leaned over and placed a hard kiss on her mouth. A possessive one. "Just yours. I'll keep you safe."

It was an admirable sentiment, but she knew better. How, she wasn't certain. But she had a job to do, and while it had been thrust upon her, wasn't that the way of the world? Even so, her heart warmed that he wanted to protect her. He'd never understand her need to do the same for him, so she didn't broach the topic. Actions would have to speak louder than any declarations.

Emma walked inside accompanied by a small woman with white-blond hair, who wore a lovely, long flowered skirt and white blouse. She had sparkling eyes and wore beautiful, beaded jewelry. A prophecy mark wound up her neck in delicate lines. "Dessie? This is Lily, one of our prophets. She's an expert in hypnotism, and we thought you should give it a try before we assault your brain again."

Lily approached Garrett and gave him a hug.

"It's good to see you, Lily. It has been way too long." He gently hugged her back, all but engulfing her with his size. "How is the Realm's Rebel?"

Lily chuckled and released him. "Caleb is fine. He's meeting with your father and uncle." She smiled at Dessie. "Caleb is my mate, and he's not too happy about being chosen as a prophet. There was a time when he was the Realm's Rebel, but now he has plenty of competition for the moniker." She bumped Garrett with her hip. Her every movement was graceful as she walked to the bed. "Rumor has it you've got a few hot buttons."

"At least two that we know about," Dessie said, wondering how she could ever be that graceful. The woman appeared to be in her late twenties, but her eyes showed decades of living. Maybe centuries. "One of the triggers causes violence, and the other shuts down my brain." She preferred the one that made her pass out to the one that made her attempt homicide. "If we could just get rid of one of them, I'd be forever grateful." Although she was uncertain about hypnotism. She wasn't the type to let somebody else take control of her mind. Not willingly, anyway. The Kurjans had found a way, so perhaps she was now susceptible to it.

Lily encircled Dessie's wrist with her fingers. "I'd say you were trained for the violence, which is triggered by the Seven marking. As for shutting down, my guess is that you were on the right track with your research. Otherwise, why implant a trigger to stop you from figuring out the situation?"

That made sense. Dessie's eyes grew sleepy. She snuggled back against the pillows. "What are you doing?"

"Just relaxing you," Lily murmured.

The lights dimmed. Everyone else disappeared.

"You're in control here," Lily said. "The second you want to stop, we stop. Now look into my eyes. What do you see?"

She saw eyes. Midnight-colored. No wait. There was some blue. Pretty and deep. Dessie's breathing leveled out, and her limbs became heavy. So heavy and warm beneath the blanket.

"All right," Lily crooned. "Take me back to your high school years. Where are you?"

"I'm at Stoneton Hills," Dessie whispered, her body relaxed.

Something shuffled. "Good," Lily said. "You're safe, and you're calm. Whatever happened in the past is gone, and you're just watching from very far away. You're only an observer."

Dessie breathed out.

"You've gone to classes, eaten meals, and prepared for bed. Tell me what's happening."

Dessie wandered into her old room. "I've put on a nightgown and gotten into bed. The room is cold, and I curl onto my side to keep warm." She shivered and then calmed. "I'm so tired. During classes that day, I could barely concentrate on the lecture." Was she getting ill? The fatigue wouldn't leave her, even at night.

"Do you fall asleep?"

"Yes." She watched herself sleep, her body barely moving beneath the bedcovers.

"You're doing wonderfully, Destiny. Now, remember that you're far away. That you are no longer in that bed but are just a witness from years later. What happens?"

Dessie watched herself sleep. A storm kicked up outside, and rain splattered the window, turning the room even colder. "Nothing."

"The girl in the bed knows nothing. You are not in that bed. That means all is clear to you." Lily's voice was soft and held a comforting rhythm.

"I...I don't know." None of this was right. Dessie frowned and tried to look beyond the veil. "I'm not in the bed any longer." The chilly room was gone. Where was she?

Lily pressed closer, and the smell of strawberries came with her. "Where are you?"

She looked around. "Downstairs." In the monk's living quarters. How in the world had she gotten there? She was still so cold. She could see herself on a chair in the center of the room. It looked like a modern dentist's chair—like the ones she'd seen on television during her trek west. "That's me," she said hollowly. "How did I get there?"

"It doesn't matter. You're there now. What is happening?"

She could see the monks. They were all around at different workstations with computers. One full wall held medical equipment. As she watched, the girl in the chair slowly came awake. One of the monks hurried over and pressed a needle in her arm. In Dessie's arm. Then she fell asleep again.

In the present, her heart rate increased. Her blood rushed through her veins; there was a roaring in her head. One of the monks took a large syringe, one much bigger than she'd ever seen, and stuck a needle into the center of her head.

She screamed and sat up in the bed, her temples pounding.

The lights flicked on. Garrett was instantly at her side. "Dessie?"

She gulped, tears streaking down her face. "They injected me with something. Something dark red." Her scalp hurt even now. "Something they put *directly* into my head." It was shocking she hadn't sustained brain damage. Well, more than the damage that forced her to either kill or lose consciousness. She wanted to kill them. All of them.

What had been in that syringe?

Chapter Thirty-Two

Garrett was going to kill somebody. Probably everybody ever connected to the Kurjan nation. He waited for Dessie to finish dressing in the other room after a full fucking day of tests. After the hypnotism, Emma had triggered Dessie three times by having Garrett reveal his back. Dessie had gone ballistic each time, even though she'd been restrained. Then they'd had to sedate her before trying again.

The final test was having her skim through the ancient book until she passed out.

"Hey." Hope walked into the waiting room, her brown hair in a ponytail and a bruise across her jaw. "Where's the book?"

"What happened to your face?" Garrett stood and gently touched his niece's face.

She grinned. "Training. We learned some new demon counterattacks today."

He frowned. "Can't you heal that?"

She looked away.

Shit. She couldn't heal a little bruise? "Hope—"

"I know." She threw up her hands. "I normally can heal myself to a certain degree, but when I have a cold or an ear infection, then my healing powers are all used up. There have been many tests, and Emma is working on it, so can we just move on?"

He didn't like this at all. Hope was a combination of several species, including vampire, and she should be the strongest being on the planet. Instead, she was more human than immortal. "Sure." Ducking, he reached beneath his chair. "Here's the book. She passed out when she got to page seven hundred, near the end, which has a series of symbols I've never seen."

"Excellent. I've pretty much learned everything possible about the geometrodynamics of cylindrical systems in order to solve the mystery of the dream worlds, so I'm your gal when it comes to ancient texts. The humans have made some decent discoveries, but they don't come close to what our people have learned through the years. I'll study this and get back to you."

"Thanks. I'm hoping you can find something."

"Me too." She grinned, looking so much like her mother that she could pass for Janie. "Not for nothin', but Dessie is pretty amazing at deciphering these symbols and texts. It's like she can make connections nobody else can see." Hope tucked the heavy volume beneath one arm. "Maybe that's her enhancement. Or it was her enhancement before the Kurjans got to her."

Garrett tuned in to his surroundings, finding two guards outside the door and small footsteps coming from the examination room. "I think her enhancement has to do with flowers and plants. They all come alive around her."

Hope pursed her lips. "Well, nobody said she couldn't have two enhancements, right?"

Right. If Dessie was so powerful the Kurjans had tracked her down and tried to mold her into a weapon, she no doubt had some strong enhancements. "Good point." He tried not to stare at Hope's bruise. Somebody should talk to her father about her training sessions if she was going to get hurt. "How are you liking the work in the computer hub?" A much safer place for her.

Her smile widened. "I love it. The intelligence gathering is okay, but I'm really enjoying covert ops. I'm running two from here." Then she sobered. "Though I do worry about our assets—especially those who are family."

Garrett kept an eye on the door. Dessie was only a room away now. "Honey, half of the Realm is your family." She was related to both the vampire and demon ruling families.

"I know. Give me a call later, and I'll report in on this book as well as any info I have from covert assets. We've reached out to those in Kurjan and Cyst camps, and I'm expecting to hear from at least five of them by end of day today." She leaned up and pecked him on the cheek before hustling out with the book.

The door to the examination room opened, and Dessie walked out, her hair on top of her head and her eyes weary. She was pale and hitched along as if she'd strained her lower back. She rubbed her hands down her arms as if she couldn't warm herself.

"I'm not taking very good care of you, am I?" he murmured, reaching for her.

She snuggled right into his chest with a small sigh. "I don't think that's your job."

Fire flashed hot and bright on his palm, and he jerked it off her. Slowly, he turned his hand to see the Kayrs marking deep and black, a swirl of lines with a *K* in the middle—back at full power. Wanting to be pressed to her flesh.

His chest heated, and his heart thundered as the beast at his core sprang to life. Snarling and needing to mark her. Again and again, until it stayed. Forever.

She leaned back to look into his eyes and then stepped away. "Sorry about that. I guess I needed a hug." She stilled. "What is that look on your face? What's wrong?"

"Nothing is wrong." He'd been drawn to her the second she'd walked into that diner, and he'd known. Deep down, he'd recognized exactly who she was, even though none of it made a lick of sense at the time. The truly male part of him, deep down in his soul, had claimed her before his brain had caught up. Even so, he hadn't given her a chance to truly decide, and she deserved that. "We need to have a little talk."

"About what?" She rocked back on borrowed shoes.

For one thing, they needed to buy her some of her own clothes. Then they had to figure out the trigger in her brain, because he had no intention of wearing a shirt at all times for the rest of his life. But right now, she looked exhausted. "Let's get you some dinner. You must be starving."

Emma bustled through the door, a tablet in her hands. "Good. You're still here."

Garrett tucked Dessie against his body and wrapped his arm over her shoulders, holding her tight. Her shivering subsided. "What did you find?" Now they could get on with things.

Emma looked up, her gaze concerned. "The tumor is in hyperdrive now—I think its growth rate sped up even more after the book triggered a reaction."

Garrett sucked in air as his blood heated. "Makes sense. If she's getting close enough to learning the truth that the Kurjans programmed her to black out, killing her with the tumor would be the next step. How do we reduce it?"

Emma shook her head. "I have no idea. We've run every test we can find except one, and nothing. There's nothing odd in her blood or genes that we can find."

Dessie sagged against him. "What's the one test left?"

Emma winced. "A biopsy tomorrow. But with an unnatural tumor like this, I can't guarantee the results. We have no idea what'll happen when I poke the mass."

Dessie sighed, feeling fragile up against him. "We know what will happen if you don't. Let's do this."

The beast deep down inside him roared in fury.

* * * *

Dessie finished the grilled salmon with a side of cheesy noodles and sat back, sipping on an excellent merlot in Garrett's breakfast nook. Mellow waves sparkled outside beneath the full moon, giving the night an otherworldly beauty. She wasn't normally a merlot fan, but this one tasted more like a cabernet. Garrett had been quiet during the meal, lost in his own thoughts.

That was all right with her. She went over her day and what she'd learned from Hope. About how the young woman thought portals worked. Plus, the symbols and text from the many chapters she'd read before losing consciousness twisted and combined in her head, creating a story. She'd always been able to break codes that way, and deciphering an ancient text was much the same.

She'd been studying about the portals, and she was almost there. Could almost figure out how to control them. How to open them and, more importantly, how to close them. Was it possible to lock Ulric away for good? If so, the directions were in that tome. While she couldn't cognitively remember those symbols on that last page, her subconscious was working on the puzzle.

"You're quiet," Garrett mused, gaze fully on her now.

She jumped. "So are you. I was just thinking about having my brain prodded by Emma." There was no other option. "Let's hope she has steady hands."

"I think we should try and mate again first, but that has to be your decision. The first time, it surprised us both. The second, you were caught in the middle of passion when you asked. This time, it has to be your decision." He took a healthy drink of his wine.

Awareness tingled through her on the heels of surprise. "My decision?" Was that her voice? Breathy and deep?

He held up his right hand, palm out to show the stunning marking of a jagged *K* in the middle of complex lines. It was beautiful and dangerous in a way she felt to her soul. "This is forever. Even if we have to keep trying every minute of every day, once you consent. But if you do, if you agree to be mine, then it's forever. So take your time and think it through."

"Your marking is beautiful," she breathed.

"It's actually yours," he returned.

She pressed back against her chair and tightened her fingers around the glass. Warning trilled through her along with need. "I may stay human." She couldn't bear to see him hurt as she aged and then died. And what about children? She didn't even need to ask if he could have kids with a human. There wasn't a chance.

He just studied her, his gaze a possessive caress against her skin. "I won't force you, but I want this. Want you. Forever." He reclaimed his glass, his shoulders so wide the chair wasn't quite big enough to hold him. "I knew deep down from our first moment that you were my mate. You had all the qualities of the woman in my dream, not to mention you're brilliant, brave, and beautiful."

"That's a lot of *b*'s, Garrett," she said weakly. Oh, she could pretend amusement with him, but not to herself. She'd been in love with him since he'd saved her in a dream so long ago, and every second with him in real life had only reinforced those feelings. But, in her case, love came with sacrifice, and she wouldn't let him ruin his life because of her. "Can you mate more than one person?"

"No," he murmured, watching her with a heat that spiraled through her body along with a strong sense of caution. "Once mated, neither of us can touch another romantically without contracting a horrible rash." He held up his glass and flashed his teeth. "Welcome to immortality. There's no cheating."

"There's no chance? I mean, if I'm gone?"

"You won't be gone. There is a virus mates can take to negate the bond, usually years from the death of one, but I won't take it. You're it for me, Dessie." His eyes flashed to the bluish silver. "That dream you had of me was Fate intervening, as she sometimes does."

The lump in her stomach wouldn't disappear. She wanted to protect him. "I'm human. No matter what I once was, right now, I'm human. That means we can't mate. Or if we do, it can't last for me, and then you're stuck for life? I don't think so."

"Then no biopsy." He set his wineglass down. Slowly and deliberately. "You are not going under the knife without a mating mark on your ass, even if it's temporary, Destiny. Period."

She reared up. "It's my choice and my ass, Garrett Kayrs."

"They both belong to me—even if we don't mate." He planted both broad hands on the table, looking immovable and so damn handsome butterflies winged through her abdomen as if shot out of a bottle. "The sooner you get that into your beautiful head, the easier life will be for you."

She put her glass down to keep from throwing it at his bossy head. "I'm not afraid of you."

"Then you're not nearly as smart as either one of us believes." He crossed his arms, and the play of muscle in his chest and biceps was impressive. And unintentional. He wore strength and power naturally.

Her mouth watered. While she wanted to argue and protest his high-handedness, it had been a difficult day, and her head hurt. The many sedatives she'd been given also slowed her blood to a sluggish pace. "I fully plan on explaining in detail to you tomorrow why you're a moron who can't win this, but I'm done." Even her vision had gone blurry.

His phone buzzed, and he retrieved it from his pocket while entrapping her with his gaze. "Kayrs." He listened but didn't look away. "She's here now." He handed over the phone.

She pressed it to her ear. "Hello?"

"Hey, girlfriend. It's Honor. I wanted to check on you. Things have been nuts at demon headquarters, so I haven't made it over there yet, but I miss talking to you. How are you doing?"

A lump rose in Dessie's throat. She had a friend she could remember, and that friend had called. "I'm well." Tears filled her eyes and threatened to spill over. "Thank you." Her voice choked on the last.

Garrett reclaimed the phone. "It has been a rough day here, and I think Dessie is done. You're a sweetheart for calling, and

I'll make sure she calls you tomorrow." He tossed the phone near his plate and stood, bending down to lift her. "The bathtub in this place is massive, and there's some bubbly stuff next to it that Janie left for you. You're going to soak in the tub and then go to sleep. Our fight will wait until tomorrow."

It was a brief reprieve, but she'd take it. Why did his holding her against his rock-hard chest make her want to fight on his side instead of her own? She sighed.

He kissed the top of her head. "Let it all go for tonight. You can give me your decision tomorrow. If you don't want to mate, we won't. But you're sticking here until you're cured. Period."

Chapter Thirty-Three

After a delicious bath, Dessie snuggled into the overlarge bed with the wind whistling outside. She fell asleep immediately, awakening when an iron-hard arm banded around her waist and tugged her into so much heat she groaned. Muscle surrounded her, and she dove right back into dreamland, feeling safe and secure in a way she'd never experienced as a child.

The dream started much as before, with her falling and then landing in a grassy meadow. She rolled and came up on her feet, searching for any threat. The day was sunny, and the sky a robin's egg blue. A light wind rustled the grass, and the smell of sugar cookies wafted beneath her nose.

She relaxed muscles from her toes to her head and then back, letting her mind flash symbols and text across her eyes. They separated and then formed a pattern she could analyze.

Fear fissured through her, but she ignored it. Her survival was in doubt, so she had little to lose. She lifted her hands toward the lovely sky, much the way Hope had in the hell dream world. Then she uttered an ancient chant, her subconscious working far faster than the rest of her brain.

Three portals opened up above her.

She blinked and stepped back. They were black with fuzzy edges, and they moved as if alive. Which one would get her home? The experiment had been a success in that she'd opened them; now she needed to analyze what she'd done. What it meant. She wanted to be back in that bed with Garrett's protective arms around her.

Waves emanated from the middle portal like steam off hot asphalt in the summer. She'd seen that happen in a movie the headmistress had allowed them to watch years ago. Then energy zipped out, pulling her off the ground

She fought it, pushing herself down and planting her feet. A creature shrieked from the portal to the right.

Her body grew cold, and her breath quickened. She had to get out of there. The middle portal pulled harder, and she rose into the air straight toward it, her arms flailing and panic seizing her voice. Then she was through, and all sound disappeared. For the briefest of moments, there was nothing.

True nothingness.

She fell, and the scream of the wind filled her head. Darkness surrounded her as she landed on her belly, her chin smacking a hard surface. Pain exploded across her face. Groaning, she rolled over to see two moons, one a dark Wedgwood blue and the other a burning orange. No. She was back here?

Her knees wobbled, but she stood, measuring the distance from her feet to the murk. Something swam beneath the surface, nudging the edge and rocking the platform. She hurriedly stepped into the middle and set her stance, now having about three feet of rock around her in every direction.

Ulric stood on the sand, his legs braced, his eyes glowing through the night. "You've returned, Intended."

"I'm not your Intended," she hissed, looking up at the moons. She lifted her hands and started chanting.

A crash on the next rocky platform made her pause, and the figure of a woman bounced twice. "Hope?" Dessie yelled, dropping her arms.

The woman groaned and staggered to her feet. She wore a long pink dress with what looked like diamonds decorating it.

Her hair was blond, her eyes light, and her waist incredibly tiny. The woman was at least six feet tall. She looked at Ulric and then glanced at Dessie, gasping audibly. "Destiny Applegate."

Dessie jolted. "Who are you? How do you know my name?"

"I'm Yvonne. Ulric's Intended." She looked down at the oozing liquid and then back toward Dessie. "You need to leave."

"Gladly," Dessie said, reciting the incantation again. Nothing happened. Darn it. The chant must vary for each world. She scrambled to put together more of what she'd learned from the book into a new chant.

Ulric laughed, and the sound pounded across the murky waves. "You can't leave, Intended."

Yvonne spun to face him, her hair flying up. "How dare you! I am your Intended." She stepped closer to the inky water. "It was I who created the formula to allow your people into the sun. Me. I have given all of you a new life."

"Thank you for that," Ulric said carelessly. "You served your purpose during your time."

Yvonne hissed. "I am the Queen of the Cyst, and we will mate, Ulric."

"You're old. She's new. It's simple." Ulric lifted a massive hand, and the wind stopped shrieking and started blowing. Yvonne's rock slid over the dangerous liquid toward Dessie's.

The woman turned and curled her fingers into fists. "All right. I'll make this happen without your help. Mate."

Dessie looked frantically around for anything she could use to get away from the woman, but there was only her rock and the surrounding lake of ink. "Stop it."

Yvonne smiled, and her eyes glowed with an angry fire. "You're going to die, new one."

"No. Don't let him win like this," Dessie protested, her hands out. She had to figure out a way to open a portal, but her mind was slowing down from panic. "We're not fighting over him. He's all yours."

"Yes, he is." Their platforms crashed together, and Dessie fell back, landing on her butt. Her head knocked on the rock, and stars exploded behind her eyes. Darkness overtook her, but she fought it, trying to stay awake.

Yvonne came at her full force, straddling her instantly and wrapping both hands around her neck.

Dessie struggled to retain consciousness, fighting to breathe. Pain lashed her throat. She scrabbled to grab Yvonne's fingers and pry them off her neck. More darkness edged into her vision. She stopped fighting and settled into her training. Holding her breath, she punched both arms up and broke Yvonne's hold, sweeping her arms out and pushing the blonde off-balance.

Yvonne screamed and slashed down with her nails.

Dessie blocked with one arm and pushed Yvonne off her with the other, rolling them both until she straddled the blonde. "Stop it." She reared back and hit Yvonne square in the nose. The woman's nose cracked, and blood spurted into the air, landing in the liquid surrounding them.

Yvonne somehow brightened, and her dress was now a bright red instead of pink. How? What was happening?

Multiple creatures began to thrash in the water around them, butting against the platform and splashing goo across the rock. Panic seized Dessie, and she lifted her arms and started chanting.

Yvonne punched her cheekbone, knocking her down. Dessie landed next to the blonde, and the air burst out of her lungs. Yvonne struck her in the temple and then kneeled, grabbing Dessie's hair and the waist of her yoga pants. "Let's feed the fishes, shall we?" She partially lifted Dessie.

Dessie shot her elbow back into Yvonne's mouth, smashing against her teeth. Then she twisted her torso and threw a punch at the woman's temple, shoving hard with her knuckles.

Yvonne screamed and dropped her.

Dessie fell onto her side and flipped onto her back. "Yvonne, wait—"

The woman lunged for her, and Dessie kicked up, throwing Yvonne over her head. Yvonne yelled. Dessie turned and levered up on her hands and knees. Maybe she could reach the woman.

Yvonne splashed into the murk, and the creatures rushed for her in a feeding frenzy. She went under, and the water erupted into wild waves.

Dessie turned and heaved.

Ulric clapped from the shore.

Dessie coughed and then formed the words she'd tried to chant earlier.

Ulric laughed. "You can't leave until I choose, little one."

"Yes, I can." She ducked her head and chanted from somewhere deep in her subconscious.

Letting out a scream, she awoke in the plush bed and sat straight up.

Garrett twisted on a light. "What's wrong?"

She turned into his chest, tears already streaming down her face. "I think I just killed Yvonne."

* * * *

Garrett paced the waiting room in the medical wing of the lodge, his blood so hot it was a surprise steam wasn't blowing from his ears. "You're telling me that my mating her for good might put her in more danger?"

Emma leaned against the wall, her eyes bloodshot. She'd probably been working all night on Dessie's case. "I'm telling you that it might. There are triggers in her head that shut her down, and I'd assume mating a vampire-demon hybrid might be one of those."

"That's insane," Garrett muttered.

"Maybe. What if her blood or body has been protecting her by rejecting your mark? If the mark stayed, what if her chromosomal pairs unraveled? I just don't know yet, Garrett." She reached into her lab coat and tugged out a tie to secure her thick hair atop her head.

He didn't want to hear that. Right now, Dessie was in a session with Prophet Lily, attempting to remember more about her time with the Kurjans. "I can mate her. It's her energy that brought on my marking." Finally.

"True, and it's her energy that makes plants and flowers thrive around her. It's also her energy that allows her mind to take ancient symbols and arrange them into a language." Purple shadows marred the skin beneath Em's warm blue eyes. "But her blood still doesn't show any of those enhancements. If I didn't know of her talents, I'd stake my life on the fact that she was a human. A normal human woman."

Garrett ran a frustrated hand through his thick hair. "So she's in danger if I don't mate her and possibly even more if I do?"

"I don't know but will find out. Give me a little time." Emma hunched her shoulders. "Through the years, we've seen enhanced humans who are able to naturally mask their status, but we've never seen their enhancements completely disappear, especially due to an outside force. This is new, Garrett." The frustration in her voice matched his own feelings.

Garrett studied his aunt. "You need sleep, Em. Exhausting yourself isn't going to help anybody." It was shocking Dage hadn't already forced her to rest.

She tightened her lab coat over her yellow T-shirt. "I don't sleep much these days. Not with Hunter away on mission." He was her only son.

Garrett nodded. "I know. He should be done soon, right?"

She shrugged. "Hopefully. He's undercover, and it has been too long. He's only nineteen, Garrett." Worry darkened her eyes even more.

The door opened, and Dessie walked in, looking ready for autumn in a crimson sweater and olive-green pants. Her eyes were pinched, her stride hesitant.

The marking on Garrett's palm burned so hot it felt like somebody was slamming a flaming poker through his hand. "How was hypnosis?"

"Just fantastic." She pulled her curly brown hair away from her pale face. "I remembered a little more, and they sure liked to inject my head with a red liquid. I kind of remember looking at certain symbols on a screen and then feeling intense pain until I blacked out." She sounded lost. Hurt. Betrayed.

Fury rose from deep within him, but he forced a calm expression onto his face. "That makes sense. Now your body goes unconscious to avoid the pain." He was going to rip the Kurjan nation apart.

Her bottom lip trembled, and she sank her teeth into it. "Any news on the other women from Stoneton Hills?"

"Not yet." He had everyone on alert trying to find them. If they'd been let loose as she had, they might also be looking for him. For members of the Seven. If their conditioning was as strong as Dessie's, they wouldn't even know what they were seeking. "Did you remember any of them?"

"Not this time." She held herself upright as if it took effort. "We tried to focus on the training. Next time we'll try to see more of the school and my daily life there. It's like there's this heavy barrier holding all of my memories down. I can't access them."

"All right. I think that's enough testing for today." He tried to make it sound like a suggestion and not an order.

Both women shook their heads.

"It isn't even lunchtime yet. I want this thing out of my brain," Dessie said, her delicate jaw firming.

Emma took a tablet from her pocket. "We don't have time to waste. Even though we triggered Dessie three times yesterday by looking at your marking, the tumor didn't retract to the same degree as before. At best, we halted its progression for a few hours. It may start shutting down her systems at any time."

Dessie rubbed her nose. "Plus, we only know of two triggers. What if there are more? What if eating an apple makes me suicidal or something crazy like that?"

The worry and pain in her eyes cut him deeply, and the hint of defeat there stoked his temper to a dangerous level. The woman hadn't yet had a chance to deal with the fact that she'd fed Yvonne's ass to some hellish creatures. He kept his voice gentle, albeit guttural. "We'll figure this out, Destiny. Our doctors and scientists are the best."

"I know," she said hollowly.

Emma's tablet dinged, and she read a message. "The surgical room is ready." Then she looked at Dessie. "We could probably wait until this afternoon, if you wanted."

Dessie shook her head. "No. I need to get it over with as soon as possible." Determination crossed her face, sharpening her exhausted features.

"All right." Emma turned toward the door. "Let's do this." She looked over her shoulder at Garrett. "Stay close in case we need your blood."

He tugged Dessie close and kissed her forehead. "You'll do great. I'll be right here."

She slid her arms around his waist and looked up at him. "No matter what happens, I've had a grand adventure with you, Garrett Kayrs. Thank you for that." Rising up on her toes, she kissed his chin.

It took every ounce of willpower he'd ever had to let her go.

Then silence engulfed the waiting room with its plush green chairs. He sank into one and sent a text to the members of the Seven. NEED YOU HERE. MATE IS IN TROUBLE AND NO TIME TO EXPLAIN. COME TO HOPE KYLLWOOD'S PARTY.

He had to get the Keys and the Lock in the same place and draw their blood.

Then he was going hunting.

Chapter Thirty-Four

Hope Kayrs-Kyllwood sat with Dessie as she ate toast while recuperating from the final test. Hope's aunt and mother bustled around, speaking medical jargon. She understood most of it, but her interests had always skewed to subterfuge and strategy. "How's your brain?"

Dessie snorted, still looking pale in the hospital bed. She wore white scrubs, and her hair was piled on top of her head, letting tendrils frame her face. A plush blanket covered her to her waist, and she sat up, now sipping apple juice. "I feel all right, really. I'm still me and didn't turn into somebody else, so I consider that a plus."

Hope grinned. "A definite plus." She'd never met anybody as good at deciphering old texts as Dessie was, and it had been fun scouring the ancient books with her. "When you're feeling better, I'd like to know all about the incantations you found and how you opened those portals in Ulric's hell world." Hope had always done so instinctively but having Dessie's knowledge would only help.

"Later." Garrett stalked into the room, his eyes glowing a multitude of colors. "She needs to rest now. It's after midnight."

The procedure had taken all day and then well into the night. Emma hadn't wanted to probe Dessie's head until they tried multiple tests first, but in the end, there had been no choice. So far, Dessie seemed to have come through it well enough.

Hope patted Dessie's arm and leaned over to whisper, "The immortal is in full alpha-male mode. You're on your own." She stood, punched her uncle in the arm, and swept out of the room. She paused as she reached the waiting room. "Pax? What are you doing here?" Instinctively, she twisted the silver butterfly ring he'd given her years ago for her birthday. The delicate design was always on her right ring finger, reminding her of their friendship.

He finished a text and unfolded his muscled body from the chair.

Man, he'd changed through the years. Gone was the chubby boy afraid of his shadow but determined to be brave. In his place was a warrior, battle experience and all. His eyes were the same. A silvery blue that focused completely and fully on her. "I heard about Destiny and her fight with Yvonne and wanted to make sure you weren't about to do something stupid."

She paused. He'd always been blunt, but lately he was getting that bossy edge inherent in all male demons. And vampires. They were friends, and although a part of her heart would always be his, the sacrifices she'd need to make, not only as the Lock but as a prophet, didn't make a long life likely. He deserved peace and a calm home after his traumatic childhood. No matter how sexy and handsome and downright honorable he'd become. "I'm not planning anything stupid." At least, she wasn't planning to drop into Ulric's world again.

"Good." Pax slid an arm over her shoulders and escorted her out of the lodge. "I brought my bike, so I can give you a ride home." Demon headquarters was a mile down the road.

They walked outside, and she paused, looking up at the millions of silver stars sparkling in the darkened sky. "Don't forget you promised to help me move next week." She'd built a house a few homes down from her parents and was so ready for even that small amount of independence.

"I remember." He led her to a shiny, black-and-chrome motorcycle. "She's new." Pride and anticipation lit his voice. Then he lifted her on as if she weighed nothing and handed her a helmet. "It's the right size for your head. I figured we'd be riding together." He waited until she'd settled on and held the helmet. "Is Dessie okay?"

"I think so. She has powers even beyond mine when it comes to Ulric and his hell world. At least right now." Hope frowned. "There's something odd about the way she took out Yvonne."

"Odd?" Pax's shoulders went back. "How so?"

"Dessie said Yvonne seemed faded and then went bright before she went into the water. I don't know. It's bugging me."

Pax smoothly swung his leg over the bike, careful not to jostle her. "We'll figure it out. Helmet. Hold on."

She yanked the new helmet over her head and slid her arms around his tight waist, feeling like a girl on a date. A rare feeling. What would she do if she wasn't tasked with fulfilling the destiny laid out for her? Probably fall head over heels for Paxton Phoenix. He was strong and good with a deadly edge, and sometimes her dreams about him turned steamy.

But she knew better. Wouldn't let herself go there. So she threw her head back and enjoyed the ride, knowing he'd keep them both safe. Too soon, she arrived at her parents' house, which was already dark. Though her father would know the second she arrived. He always did. She removed the helmet and balanced herself with her hands on Pax's flanks as she swung her leg over the bike. She handed him the helmet. "Thanks."

"Any time." He turned his head, studying her. "Promise me you're not going after Ulric."

She hesitated a second too long. In a surprisingly fast move, he grasped the front of her jacket and yanked her toward him, turning at the same time. Then his mouth was on hers.

Hot and fast, deep and wild, Paxton kissed her until her ears rang. Desire poured through her, and her legs grew weak.

Then he released her. "I'm being patient with you, Kyllwood. Don't make me regret it." He restarted the motorcycle and swung away from the curb, a dark shadow in the moonlit night.

She touched her tingling lips, her body rioting. What had gotten into Pax? Stumbling, she turned and made it to the front door and inside the house, tiptoeing to her bedroom. The space was comfortable and all her, and she was going to miss it when she moved.

Paxton had kissed her. Really kissed her. And she'd kissed him back, wholeheartedly. Confusion blanketed her, along with a too-strong need to chase after him. He wasn't to be hers. It was too much of a risk, and even if she survived the ritual, she was born to bridge the gap between enemy factions.

Hopefully. Peace was a good goal, and sacrifice was part of her heritage.

She shut her door, kicked off her boots, and changed into yoga clothes. After midnight was her best time to meditate. Now that she was stronger, and now that the portals had finally begun to reopen, it was time to get back to work.

Her position perfect on the floor, she let this world spin away.

Shockingly fast, she found herself on midnight-blue sand with a lazy ocean rolling in. It was nighttime, and a full moon shone down, glinting off diamonds in the sand. The green book was now up on a ledge in a mountain outcropping, way out of her reach. As usual.

A figure was already standing near an outcropping of rocks, watching the water splash against the sand.

She walked toward him, and he watched her approach.

"You're getting more powerful," Drake murmured, eyeing the area around them. "Just us tonight?"

It was surprising how easily she'd drawn him into this world. "Yes. I hope I didn't take you from a good sleep."

"No." He stood so tall he cast a wide shadow toward the rocks. His hair was all black but now had a hint of red at the tips, and

his eyes were still that intriguing green. Like Paxton, he'd filled out through the years and looked all male. His face was still pale and his bone structure sharp. Handsome. "I was staring at a computer screen, and now I'm here. That's impressive, Hope."

She felt the compliment to her toes, even though her mouth was still tingling from Pax's kiss. "Yvonne is dead. Did you know?"

His eyebrows rose. "No. How?"

"In Ulric's world. She died, and I think her body was really there." Though that didn't make sense. "He's dangerous, Drake."

"No, he isn't. If your people would stop attacking him and going after us, this war would end." He reached into his pocket and drew out a black box. "For your birthday."

Her breath caught, and she accepted the box, opening it to find a lovely gold ring with delicate lines. She slipped it onto her right thumb, and it looked perfect. "Thank you."

"You're welcome." He brushed her hair back and leaned down to kiss her, his lips cool and his mouth hot.

She shivered and kissed him back, her mind going blank. His mouth was cooler than Pax's and his lips just as firm. Tingles set up throughout her body. He released her and stepped away, smiling. "I'll find out more about Yvonne, but I need to go."

"What do you know about the Kurjans conducting mind-control experiments on enhanced women and creating assassins to kill the Seven?" Even though her mind was mulling over the fact that she'd kissed two warriors in one night, she still had a job to do. He'd denied it last time. Would he do so again?

"Nothing. What are you talking about?" He frowned. "That's crazy."

So he didn't know. That was something, at least. "Okay."

He studied her. "You know we're meant to close the distance between our people, right? You and me?"

She nodded. The prophecy markings heated on her neck.

He lifted his head and looked into the distance. "I really have to go. Let's spend more time together tomorrow night. Midnight."
Then he was gone.

She jerked herself into the real world and unfolded her legs. Holding out her right hand, she looked at the two rings. One silver, one gold.

What was she going to do?

* * * *

Drake fell back into the present, staring at a computer screen as the moon shone brightly on the Pacific Ocean outside his Oregon holding. Kurjan soldiers moved around him, stocking supplies to prepare for Ulric's return. Their seers declared the Cyst leader would be home soon.

Finally, the screen cleared. "Drake. How are the preparations coming along?" his father asked.

"Well, Father," Drake said, noting Vero in the background. He'd wanted to bring his cousin along on this mission, but his father had only wanted the best on the Oregon coast to set up camp for Ulric's return. Vero's good buddy Harold was also off to the side, pounding away on a laptop. Drake didn't like the nerdy kid and never had. He didn't take training seriously. "My source tells me that Yvonne is dead. Is that true?"

Dayne's eyebrows rose. "She's missing, and we haven't figured out where she went. Your source is the Kyllwood girl?"

"Yes. She said Yvonne died in Ulric's world." It was common knowledge that Yvonne could visit Ulric in his world when she slept. It made sense that if she died in that world, she'd die in this one, too, but where was her body?

"Did Hope kill her?" Dayne asked, curiosity glimmering in his purplish-red eyes.

"No." Drake had read Hope's expression and was certain that she hadn't killed. Yet. "The newest Intended is now located in

Realm headquarters, so my guess is that she took out Yvonne. Her name is Destiny." It fit. He had spies everywhere, and two of his men had followed each of the trainees from Stoneton Hills. "What about the other females who were conditioned to seek out the Seven?"

"I'll take care of them," Dayne said.

Drake nodded. Now that one trainee had finally made contact with the Kayrs, they could forget the rest. With one hand, he texted orders for the scouts to return to their respective bases.

Dayne leaned closer to his camera. "You were correct that this Intended would be the one to make contact with the Kayrs prince. There is some poetic justice in that, don't you agree?"

"It stood to reason," Drake said. Fate and Destiny twirled in circles, from what he'd observed.

Dayne nodded. "Do they know about the Intended's training?"

"We can assume so, but I have no direct knowledge of that." Drake settled his knife more securely at his thigh. If the vampires killed Destiny, another Intended would come to light. "I plan to meet with Hope again tomorrow night and will question her. She's cautious about what she says to me, even after all this time."

"She's smart," Dayne mused. "It'll be a pity to sacrifice her, but we must prevent the ritual."

Drake straightened, meeting his father's gaze. "She will not be sacrificed. Hope Kyllwood is the only female vampire in the history of immortals, and she'll be my queen. We'll mate, and our sons will rule every world there is."

"A worthy ambition, my son." Dayne's chest puffed out. He was hundreds of years old but looked thirty with his unlined face and strong body. His face was paler than Drake's, as each generation grew a little darker. If they kept going this way, they'd almost look human in a couple of decades. The formula Yvonne had created was changing their lives for the better.

Walking in the sun was one of Drake's favorite things to do. "We could reach out and offer another symposium once Ulric is free. The Realm does like its peace."

Dayne rubbed his chin. "They won't fall for it. They want Ulric destroyed, and he's the leader of our spiritual nation. We're at war, son."

"Agreed." There was no other way. "After I'm finished here, we need a plan to take the Keys and the Lock." He didn't use Hope's name because he wouldn't allow his father to see any weaknesses in him. "We're still missing one Key."

"We'll find her," Dayne said, glancing down at a notebook. "Our tracking software, which catches vibrations from enhanced females, will lead us to her." He grinned, showing elongated canines. "Is the Realm still trying to figure out how we're finding enhanced females?"

"Probably." Something crashed in the recesses of the tunnels behind Drake. He sighed. "I must go, Father. It was good to see you."

Dayne nodded. "You too, son. Stay safe." The screen went dark.

Drake removed the now empty black jewelry box from his pocket and opened it. Somehow he'd managed to give Hope a ring in a dream world, and it had stayed with her.

It was a start. Taking her was next.

Chapter Thirty-Five

The Seven arrived at dawn. In heavily armored SUVs, they pulled up to the guest lodge at the far end of the Realm property. Garrett nudged Logan, who was next to him. "When did we get the badass vehicles?"

Logan shrugged. "Looks like overkill to me, but I guess if my mate were traveling across several states, I'd want her buckled up." He'd ensured Mercy's safety at demon headquarters for now, being just as cautious as the rest of them.

Garrett had left Dessie peacefully making a mess of his kitchen, with guards at every exit. While he wanted to let her sleep, he needed to be by her when she dreamed to keep her from meeting Ulric. Or to prevent Ulric from yanking her into his hell world. Garrett wasn't positive how to do that, but he watched her sleep for any sort of disturbance, prepared to awaken her if she stirred.

Last night, her sleep had been restful and her dreams peaceful, from what he could tell.

He glanced at his phone, waiting for a text from Emma. Nothing. Impatience rode him hard, but he had no doubt Emma had spent another night working on Dessie's case, so he refrained from texting her again.

The front doors of the lead SUV opened, allowing Ronan and Quade Kayrs to exit and scan the area.

"Your great-uncles are here," Logan drawled.

"I think it's great-great-great-uncles," Garrett returned, his chest lightening. He'd missed these Seven brothers of his.

The doors of the second vehicle opened, letting out Adare O'Cearbhaill and Ivar Kjeidsen.

Garrett grinned. "Guess Benny Reese is the one in the trees with a scope on us." It figured Benny would be the sniper. Unfortunately, Benny liked to shoot first and talk later.

Logan just sighed. "Do you ever feel seriously young around these guys?"

"We are. Comparatively." The Seven were all hundreds of years old, except for Garrett and Logan. They moved forward in unison.

Garrett clapped Ivar on the back. "The area is secure. Call off Benny, and we'll show you around. I promise your mates are safe."

Logan moved for one of the rear doors. "Let them out of the cars, you guys. Give me a break."

Ronan gave a high-pitched whistle.

A shotgun cracked, and a piece of the corner siding flew off the log exterior of the building.

"Damn it, Benny," Garrett yelled. "Knock it off. You're in Realm territory." The shot would've brought guards running if headquarters didn't already have a bead on Benny. It was a good thing Chalton was Ben's nephew. "Get over here."

"Some things never change," Logan muttered, helping Faith and Grace Cooper out of the first SUV. They were sisters, mated to Ronan and Adare, respectively. Promise, Ivar's mate, climbed out the other door, her face buried in a tablet as she solved the mysteries of the universe. She and Dessie would get along perfectly, and he already had a library with a whiteboard set up for her in the lodge. Haven, Quade's mate, followed. She had paint on her hands and in her hair, obviously having interrupted her painting to drive to the Realm. She grinned at him.

The other doors opened, and there were hugs galore as Karma and her twin girls jumped out. She was mated to Benny. She turned to help their three boys out, aged one to three, and each was a spitting image of Benjamin Reese, their father.

Faith hugged Garrett and then stepped back, looking at the guest lodge. "I was told there would be medical facilities?" She was probably the best neurosurgeon in the entire world, which was another reason Garrett had called the Seven. If they decided to try to take the tumor from Dessie's head, Faith would be the surgeon to do it.

He bustled them inside the lodge and got everyone situated before the Seven convened in the secluded conference room three stories down and surrounded by solid rock. The table was mahogany and the chairs large enough to accommodate everyone comfortably. Not one of them was less than three hundred pounds and six and a half feet tall. Since he'd called the meeting, he sat at the head of the table, while Logan sat directly across from him. "I want to bring the Realm in on everything, including the fact that Hope is the Lock."

Logan nodded. There was one definite vote for him.

Ronan looked at his brother. "She's our great-niece as well, but she's the Lock. I didn't spend an eternity in hell to fail now."

"Agreed," Quade said. "But blood is blood, and we'll protect hers as well as the Keys. Right?"

Garrett cleared his throat. "I want the Realm brought in fully. Let's vote." To his surprise, all of his brothers voted aye, agreeing with him. He cleared his throat, hiding his emotion as he texted the information about Hope being the Lock to his family and then looked back up at the warriors around him. "Thank you. With that out of the way, I have a plan."

Logan groaned.

Garrett ignored him. "We have the Keys and the Lock—all I need is their blood. That's it. I take it, find Ulric, and kill him before he has a chance to break free of his world."

"Why you?" Logan asked.

"Because I'm the only one not mated," he answered evenly. Although he did keep trying to rectify that. "It's pretty simple, Kyllwood."

Logan sat back and crossed his arms. "Your mate is currently meeting with the other Keys, and I believe you organized that get-together. You have a mate. You can't die."

"I won't die," Garrett snapped, the marking on his hand burning fiercely. He'd trained for this his entire life. "If I die killing Ulric, then she'd need to be free, anyway." He'd do anything to save her, and killing Ulric was the first step. How was this not obvious to everybody?

Benny sighed and spread his mammoth hands on the table. "What is it about this fuckin' group where everyone wants to sacrifice themselves? How about we kill Ulric and all live? Hey, good plan, Benny."

Quade cocked his head, looking so much like Garrett's dad for a moment that he could only stare. "How do you plan to return to hell?"

"I haven't figured that out completely, but I'm thinking I'll have to undergo a ritual much like the one that made me part of the Seven."

"That's a stupid idea," Benny muttered.

Logan nodded. "Amen to that, brother."

They just didn't get it, but Garrett would do what he had to in order to protect his family, and that now included Dessie.

Even without the blessing of the entire Seven.

* * * *

In the guest lodge, Dessie sat at a table with Grace and Mercy, the other two Keys. They'd all had blood drawn, and now the queen and Faith Kayrs, Ronan's mate, were working furiously at a bank of medical equipment on the far wall. The only device

Dessie recognized was a simple microscope. Everything else buzzed or whizzed or spun.

She swallowed. How was she going to remember everyone's names and who had mated whom? It was a bombardment of new information. She couldn't help but study the other two Keys. Both women seemed kind, but they couldn't be more different. Grace was quiet, with a gentle nature, brunette hair like her sister, hazel eyes, and a sweet smile. Mercy, on the other hand, was all energy. She had one green eye and one blue, elfin features, and dark red hair.

Grace patted Dessie's hand. "Are you all right? We can be rather overwhelming all together."

Dessie exhaled and tried to calm herself. "I am. It's just a lot, and I'm not enhanced. Or maybe I am but don't know it."

Mercy blew hair out of her eyes. "That sucks. I can't imagine how strong you must be to have survived the Kurjans messing with your head. We have a complete dossier on the situation. You're impressive, Destiny."

How kind. She hadn't felt impressive in the slightest. "Thank you." She studied the vibrant woman. "Logan seems like a good male. You were an enhanced human?"

Mercy snorted. "I'm a fairy. We're a million times tougher than any demon." She winked.

A fairy? An actual fairy? "Can you fly?"

Mercy chuckled. "No. I used to be able to teleport and travel to other worlds, and I'm hoping that skill will come back soon. Once we set everything right and destroy Ulric's hell world."

"Oh." Good plan. Dessie looked at Grace. "You're a fairy, too?"

"No. Enhanced human." Grace shrugged. "I see things, especially in photographs, that others don't." She sat back and ruffled her hair. "So. We're the three Keys. Do you ladies feel any different being in the same space?"

Dessie tilted her head and turned her attention inward. "I guess I feel calm? Like a sense of peace."

Grace nodded. "Me, too. Almost like things just clicked into place naturally."

Mercy hopped on her chair. "I guess that makes us sisters, right? I mean, Haven is my half-sister, and Faith is Grace's sister, but the three of us share a sisterhood as well. Tell me you agree." A smile filled her eyes.

"I agree." Dessie choked up. She'd been alone for so long that having sisters warmed her in a way she hadn't realized she needed.

Grace smiled. "Sisters it is." She rubbed at tiny puncture marks on her neck. "Adare didn't want to come here and things got a little wild last night."

Mercy chuckled. "We all have bite marks, sister."

Dessie barely had a scratch. "Does it hurt?"

Grace started. "Garrett hasn't bitten you yet?"

"Not like that." Yet they'd engaged in sex several times. Was he still holding back? "I think he's afraid to hurt me."

Mercy rolled her eyes. "How insulting. Next time he treats you like you're too fragile to take a bite, kick him in the nose. It works."

Dessie found herself smiling with them. It was nice to be around people who understood—at least a little bit.

Emma hustled toward them with vials of blood on a tray. She took out a chair and sat while Faith hurried over to stand behind her. "Watch this," Emma said. She poured three small vials of their blood into a round bowl.

Dessie leaned forward and just saw red. "I don't get it."

"Wait a sec. These vials are your blood—the three Keys." Emma took the last vial and held it up. "This is Hope's blood. She's training right now, but the second Garrett texted me the news about her being the Lock, I sought her out for a quick draw." She gently poured Hope's blood into the bowl.

A bubble popped in the middle of the mass, and then widened, engulfing the whole. The liquid churned and spun, finally settling as if completely mixed.

"Wow," Mercy whispered.

Emma nodded. "Exactly. We have samples of Kurjan and Cyst blood, and we're going to test this mixture on it, as well as any other substance we can find."

Faith rocked back on gorgeous brown boots. "We're also going to make bullets filled with the mixture, dip blades into it, and figure out any other weapons that will work."

Made sense.

Emma smiled. "We're going to need more blood from everyone, so I want you to eat a healthy, protein-rich diet for the next week."

Mercy groaned. "What is up with you and needles?"

Dessie's arm already ached from the amount of blood she'd given earlier that day. Yet if this plan could stop Ulric, she'd eat all the protein in the Realm.

"Are we done for now?" Mercy asked. "I have training in an hour, and I'm ready to kick Logan's butt. It's been too long."

Emma nodded. "Come back after lunch, if you don't mind." She stood and smiled at Dessie. "I'll walk you back to your place. Could use some fresh air, and I might as well enjoy the warm autumn weather. Winter will be here soon enough."

Dessie stood and walked to the door.

Emma paused. "Does everyone have a gown for the party tomorrow night? If not, I have plenty to share."

"We shopped on the way," Mercy said gleefully.

Dessie paused. "I guess I need a dress."

Emma tucked her arm through Dessie's and led her down the hallway to the main door. "I believe Garrett has you taken care of." They walked arm in arm down the walkway, where fall flowers perked up as they passed. "It's so cool how you do that. My sister has that gift as well."

Garrett's mom had that gift. Just like Dessie. The idea warmed her throughout as she glanced at the flowers. "I didn't realize that was out of the ordinary until recently. It's a nice gift to have flowers all around." She breathed in their scents.

Guards patrolled in every direction, obviously on high alert since the Seven had arrived.

"So, I wanted to talk to you." Emma's tone was light, but she seemed anxious.

Dessie sighed. "I wondered if you had the results of my brain biopsy." There had to be a reason Emma was telling her alone.

"I do. It took me all night to identify an unknown substance I found in the tumor. I triple-checked it." Emma slipped on a couple of leaves, and Dessie pulled her tighter against her, holding her up. "Thanks."

"What's the substance?" What if it was some sort of carcinogen ready to stimulate new cancer cells in her head?

Emma swallowed. "The substance has markers of Cyst blood. It's close but not completely the same."

Dessie's throat nearly closed. Her mind rapidly clicked facts into place. Logic had to rule here. "In other words, Cyst blood with environmental factors found in, say, the Cyst of a thousand years ago?" She couldn't believe this.

"Yes," Emma said.

Dessie's chin dropped. "You're telling me that the most likely scenario is that Ulric's blood was injected into my head until a tumor was formed? Then I was programmed somehow, and the tumor took on its own life."

"I think so," Emma said. "We could try to remove it, but based on my experience, there's only one way to find a cure or antidote. I don't have what we need, unfortunately."

"What's that?" Destiny already knew the answer.

Emma turned toward Garrett's home. "More of Ulric's blood, which would counteract or even destroy the mass. We need his blood in a quantity I don't know how we'd obtain, even if we somehow sent a force into the prison world, which we don't know how to do."

So. That was that, then.

Chapter Thirty-Six

"Do you believe in fate?" Garrett nudged more casserole toward Dessie, enjoying the quiet of his home.

"Yes." She sampled the carrots, an ancient book of vampire fairy tales at her elbow. He'd found the volume for her earlier, and she'd been delighted to start deciphering it. Finally, she'd taken a break to eat. "With a name like mine, believing in fate just makes sense. What about you?"

He nodded, his blood pumping faster now that they were alone. Her sweet scent was drawing him in, and all he wanted to do was pluck her out of her chair and take her to the floor. His cock pounded in agreement. But he let his brain rule. For now. "Always have and always will. Do you think we're meant to be together?" He was being as gentle as possible as he steered her where he wanted her to go, but she had a stubborn chin and a sacrificing attitude that wasn't going to make it easy.

She wouldn't meet his gaze. "I don't see as that matters."

Interesting. It most certainly was not a denial. He tamped down his impatience. "Why not?" He poured them both more wine.

She swallowed. "Because I'm no longer enhanced, and the tumor is going to kill me in a week."

"No, it is not. You're enhanced in the way you affect plants and flowers and can rule the outdoors, and you should work on that more. Could be a good weapon for you."

Her eyes widened. Obviously she'd never thought of that. "I look for beauty, not danger."

Yeah, danger was his job. "Plus, you're gifted with languages and codes, and that's an enhancement. So your skills are still there and we just need to draw out more of your true self."

She sighed. "Maybe."

"We're going to figure out how to cure you." There was more—he could tell. "What are you hiding from me?" He kept his voice mild.

"Nothing." She took another bite of the casserole as if it were an effort. Purple smudged the delicate skin beneath her eyes, and her shoulders drooped. The tests had taken too much out of her. "Why are you so suspicious?"

"You're not meeting my gaze." He plopped more of the carrot mixture on her plate.

She shrugged. "I'm tired and don't want to argue."

"What would we argue about?"

Finally, she lifted her eyes. "Seriously? Don't be daft."

He lifted one eyebrow.

"Fine. You think we should try to mate again so you can protect me or whatever. Even temporarily until the marking fades again. Then you want to just toddle off on your own and kill Ulric, and somehow steal a bucket of his blood to save me, even though you don't normally navigate dream worlds." A translucent peach color washed over her soft skin. "Right?"

"I don't toddle." He took another drink of the wine. It was impressive how easily she'd read his intentions, however. "Emma has spent the last two days studying your blood and the tumor. She's now nearly certain that if we somehow successfully mate, it won't make it grow in size, based on the chemicals inherent in it." Which had been excellent news, and he trusted his aunt. Mating would not hurt Dessie.

Dessie placed her fork on the plate. "I know. I spoke with her before you did." She rolled her eyes at him and sounded both petulant and exhausted.

He had different remedies for each. "You're courting both a spanking and a warm bath, kitten."

Her eyes sparked. "I choose the bath."

"Not sure the choice is yours," he murmured. At least she was looking more alive.

She stabbed at another carrot. "You told me that Ulric's body is impenetrable, so there's no way to get his blood. Right?"

His chest ached. "Right." Yet he had to find a way.

Her shoulders drooped. "I know Ulric is evil, but what do you think he intends to do if he escapes from prison?"

"He was put away because he had a plan to end all enhanced females. We don't know exactly what he was going to do, but it involved harming women like you—and my mom, aunts, cousins…"

"That's terrible," she whispered.

Yeah, it was. But now Garrett was wondering if the tumor in Dessie's head was a clue. Was there a plan to create such tumors on a broader scale? If so, the end game was death? "Ulric needs to be destroyed."

"I think I agree," she murmured.

Which was why Garrett needed to kill Ulric. While he'd thought to protect Dessie in case he died in the battle, she also needed to mate for good, or at least for as long as possible, to counter that tumor.

Based on further medical examination, Emma had changed her opinion. She now believed there was a chance that mating would slow down the tumor's growth, and that was Dessie's best option, considering he didn't have Ulric's blood. Even if the mating was temporary. Having the marking even for a short time could both protect her and perhaps make that tumor shrink in size, for a while.

For his part, he needed her. It was that simple. "Do you love me?"

Her mouth dropped open. "We…we just met," she stammered.

Also not an answer. "I'll wait all night for the truth." It was only fair to give her a warning. His people recognized their mate at first glance, even if it was just on a subconscious level. Oh, there was often courting and a dating dance or, in the case of his family, a fast lockdown and mating. But it was always consensual, and right now, Dessie didn't seem to know what she wanted. Or rather, she wasn't willing to tell him. "Dessie?"

"Why haven't you bitten me deep?" she asked. "I've seen your fangs and I've seen what they can do."

He hadn't expected that question. Apparently she'd had quite the chat earlier with the other mates. "I didn't want to scare you. Or hurt you." She'd been a virgin, for Christ's sake.

"Isn't using your fangs a compulsion for immortals?" Curiosity burned bright in her stunning eyes—along with need.

"Yes." He wanted a taste of her more than anything. "We bite when having strong emotions, usually in battle or sex with our mates." Her blush was a pretty pink. He figured it was time to put everything on the line. "You're it for me, Destiny. Thought you should know."

Pleasure burst across her face so quickly he could feel it in his body. "Garrett, that's crazy." But her smile couldn't be contained.

"There's a theory that most immortals are crazy," he said, drinking his wine. "My point is that we might as well be honest with each other."

She took two big gulps of her wine. "Fine. Yes, I have feelings for you and have since you somehow rescued me in my dream years ago. You're the only man I've ever slept with, and I'd like to keep it that way."

That was a fucking good thing. His growl rumbled up from his chest, and he let it free. "I'm not a man, baby. Nothing human. All male."

"Oh." Her lips parted on the gasp. "That's true." She twirled the glass with her fingers. "I've been considering everything you said, and I don't want to be a coward with regard to the future. If you're willing to take a chance that I'll never be cured, then so am I. It's been you since day one for me."

God, she was cute. Adorable. Fucking sexier than hell. "We'll cure you, Dessie. I know it."

Her smile was his reward. "However, I think we should wait to try mating again until we're sure I won't freak out and kill you. I don't even want to discuss it until that trigger of your tattoo is gone."

He caught her meaning, and his chest heated. "You're afraid you'll hurt me?" He was both touched and mildly insulted.

"Yes. I almost took your head off," she whispered. "I'm still really sorry about that, by the way."

Amusement attacked him, and he laughed, feeling it to his belly. "Honey, I know you have skills, but your knife is gone. Plus, now I understand your trigger. I promise you can't hurt me."

She frowned and partially turned her head to the side.

Cute. So cute it hurt. He tossed his napkin down. "All right. Here's the deal. If we were both a hundred percent with no war looming and no problem with your chemistry, we'd mate. You know it, and I know it." He stood and lifted her right out of her chair. "So I'm not waiting until Ulric is dead or until the war is over. I want to help you fight that tumor in your head." He didn't know how to get Ulric's blood yet, and that might take time. Mating would not. She felt slight against his chest.

She gave a half-hearted attempt to push him away. "Garrett, I don't—"

"I know you're exhausted. Do you want to mate me?"

She kissed beneath his jaw. "Yes."

Good. Then timing was irrelevant and it was his job to protect her and not the other way around. "Tomorrow you're going to rest all day, go to a fancy party at night, and then mate." He strode toward the opulent master bath to draw her a tub full of warm water and bubbles. It was good to have made a decision.

His body rioted against him, but he could give her one more night.

Plus, she was going to need her rest.

* * * *

After her bath, Dessie climbed into the big bed and curled her body around her ill-gotten gains. She'd never stolen anything before, but she'd palmed a vial of the combined Keys and Lock blood after tests that afternoon in the lab. Could the vial of blood be considered stolen since some of it was hers?

Male voices came from the living area, and they did not sound pleased. She tuned out Garrett, his father, and the king as they argued about the Seven and the upcoming rituals.

This was absolutely insane and she was going to do it anyway.

She loved Garrett, as crazy as it seemed. If she had a chance to protect him, then she'd take it.

Not sure how much time she had, she sat up and looked at the red vial of comingled blood samples. Holding her nose, she opened her mouth and let the liquid slide down her throat. Gagging, she slapped a hand over her mouth and hunched over. Her entire body shuddered.

Don't think about it, don't think about it, don't think about it.

Blood. She'd drunk blood. Her stomach heaved, and she swallowed rapidly, trying to concentrate on anything but the coppery taste in her throat. Dizziness engulfed her, and mini-explosions rocketed through her head, sparking behind her eyes. What the heck?

This was her last chance to do something worthwhile. Emma hadn't been hopeful that the tumor would stop growing and had even predicted it'd take over Dessie's entire brain within a week, even if Garrett managed to mark her for a short time. There was no way to acquire enough blood from Ulric to make a difference.

So why not try to end his reign of terror as her last act? She could save Garrett and his family, as well as enhanced females she'd never meet. It wasn't a bad destiny.

The vial fell from her limp fingers, and she fell sideways, going under.

Sleep came quickly, even though she was frightened. But she didn't dream. For the longest time, she slept off the exhaustion she'd carried around all day. Finally, just as she relaxed, the dreams started. She was back at school, planting spring flowers with a couple of the other girls. Lyrica and Tyra. Her friends. She smiled and enjoyed the sunshine with them, happy to be remembering them at last.

Then she plunged off the cliff, screaming.

This time she landed on the shore with the orange and blue moons high above. A creature shrieked in the far recesses of the jagged mountains, and the water oozed over the sand as if trying to get to her. She set her stance and tried to breathe the heavy air into her lungs. "Ulric?" she yelled, not knowing how much time the blood had been in her system.

Was it still strong enough to hurt him? Blood could traverse the worlds, when weapons could not. Or was blood the ultimate weapon? The smell of burning lemons mixed with the obnoxious sulfur scent coming from the liquid goo. She tried not to look at the spot where Yvonne had fallen in. Or rather, where she'd pushed Yvonne.

Ulric walked out from an opening cut into the rocky mountain. The orange and blue rays danced over his white hair and his face, highlighting symbols and scars she hadn't been able to see from a distance. She counted them, trying to set them in her memory.

His smile showed elongated canines sharper than any blade. "Intended. You came to me this time."

She forced herself to look way up into his face. This close, he was terrifying. "As your Intended, I'd like some answers."

Something flashed in his eyes. They were an electric purple with red rims around the irises. "Answers?"

"Yes." Her voice shook, but by the way his chest puffed out, he was enjoying her fear. Good. No reason to hide it, then. "What is your plan? Do you truly want to kill all enhanced females?"

"No." He moved closer to her and lifted his nose into the air. "Oranges and...what is that?" He stared at her. "You smell sweet."

Her stomach revolted, and she swallowed rapidly to keep from vomiting on the dark sand. If she was going to get him to bite her, throwing up wasn't going to help.

"You're either very brave or very stupid," he said, his voice echoing off the rocks.

Her chin lifted. "I'm neither." What was that symbol cut into his neck? She angled to the side for a better look. The form was somewhat familiar, but she couldn't decipher the meaning. "If you don't want to kill enhanced women, then what's your plan?"

He studied her, curiosity tilting his lips. "Nobody has come close to me for a thousand years."

"Sounds lonely." She looked up at the glowing moons. "Does a sun ever come out here?"

"No."

She eyed him. "Sounds sad." Was there a chance he just wanted freedom rather than revenge? "I, um, I'm sorry about Yvonne. You must've known her for years."

He waved a gargantuan hand. "She's irrelevant. Just another female. You're special. I know who you are."

"You know? About what the Kurjans did to me with your blood?"

His smile was hard. "Yes. My blood was put into the heads of many enhanced females, and every one of them will kill for me. But I knew. When Yvonne told me about you, about your marking, I knew you'd be the one to find the Kayrs prince."

"Yvonne knew about me?" Something growled from the oozing water, and she jumped.

His gaze swept her form. "Yes. I told her I didn't want anybody but her, and that I just wanted you to be trained to kill. Stupid female believed me. You all hear what you want to hear. But your place will be on the throne as my queen. That I promise."

"About that." She barely kept from stepping away. "I don't want to be your Intended. No offense meant."

His razor-sharp fangs dropped past those canines. "You will be a queen."

"No thanks." She couldn't read his mood. "To be honest, I'm in love with somebody else. It's complicated." That sounded weak. "Did you really kill one hundred females to become invincible?"

He cocked his head, so much taller than her that she felt trapped, even though a wide expanse of sand was behind her. "They were just females. Inconsequential. I had left orders for my brethren to follow my lead, but apparently they haven't done so yet. They'll pay for their disobedience."

She stepped back. "You want to kill more females?"

He lifted his hand to run his fingers through her hair. "Just to create an impenetrable army." He cocked his head. "I do have plans for those who live, however."

There was her answer. He couldn't be redeemed. She slapped his hand. "Don't touch me."

The fangs elongated again, and she sucked in air. This was it. Finally. He grabbed her and yanked her toward him.

His image flickered in and out as if part of an old film. A portal opened up. "No!" she yelled, struggling to stay on the beach just until he bit her. Then she flew out of the prison world and sat up in the bed, sucking in air.

The lights were on, and Garrett was shaking her.

"I'm here." She pushed her hair out of her face.

He looked at her and at the vial on the floor. "What the fuck did you just do?"

Chapter Thirty-Seven

Fury rode the entire room, beating away oxygen. She couldn't breathe. Garrett's eyes had morphed to a heated copper surrounded by sizzling greenish-blue. Yet another eye color for him, and this one seemed heated with temper. The hands on her arms weren't gentle.

"Destiny?" He barely shook her, but she was conscious of his strength. "Speak. Now."

She'd gone from the proverbial frying pan to the fire. "Um."

He released one of her arms and reached for the empty vial, which still had remnants of blood in the bottom. His fangs dropped fast and sharp. "Tell me you did not drink blood and dream your ass into Ulric's prison world in an effort to make him bite you."

She couldn't tell him that. "Garrett—"

He stared at the vial as if he couldn't believe what he was seeing. With a flick of his wrist, he threw it across the room with such force that it shattered against the far wall, dripping blood down the smooth surface. When he turned to face her, a hard determination stamped his face with a fine edge of fury. "Apparently I haven't been clear."

She quivered. "I—"

"Oh no, Destiny. You're done talking." His voice was calm and so gravelly it almost sounded distorted. Like he'd been chewing on nails all night.

She'd done the right thing. "I had a chance to kill Ulric, and I took it."

Then she was out of the bed. With no warning, she found herself planted against the wall with a furious vampire holding her aloft, one hand gripping her hair and the other wrapped around her hip, holding her in place. Her heart thundered, and her lungs just gave up. Then his mouth was on hers.

No gentleness, no persuasion, just raw hunger.

He was rough. Hot. Wet. Lava poured down her throat and exploded, bursting inside her and washing through her entire body. Her nipples sharpened against his rock-hard chest, and desperation consumed her. The need was brutal and far beyond anything in this world. His mouth plundered hers, all fire and fury.

She gasped in need as he took her over and sparks flew through her head. Her clit pounded in a way that was going to make her crazy. She rubbed against him, unable to think, reduced to a mass of desperate feelings. Of need so great a sob of violent pain curled up from her chest.

He jerked her head to the side and scraped his fangs down her neck.

She trembled as the touch scalded her, claiming her in a searing rush of possession. One she felt to her soul.

The sharp points slid into her skin above her clavicle, slicing deep to bone. She cried out, throwing her head back, feeling his fingers tighten in her hair to keep her in place. An orgasm blew through her, razor sharp in intensity. She stiffened and rode out the waves, her mouth open silently.

She'd barely given her last shiver when he ripped her top down the middle and dropped it carelessly to the floor.

He moved to her breasts. Hotter than any volcano, he sucked one nipple into his mouth and lashed it mercilessly with his tongue.

His other hand pulled her head back even more, shooting erotic sparks through her scalp. She couldn't move. Could only feel.

Garrett Kayrs, unleashed, no longer holding back. It was too much and yet, not enough. More. She wanted more. Wanted all of him.

His hand plunged into her pajama shorts, finding her wet and slick. Two fingers shoved inside her, forcing her to ride him. The second orgasm rolled through her, spiking out into every nerve. He tore off the shorts, banded his arm around her waist, and turned.

She found herself on her back at the edge of the bed.

He dropped to his knees, tossed her ankles over his shoulders, and zeroed in where she needed him most. Mouth, tongue, teeth, he went at her, forcing her up so fast she could only scream silently when she crested and her world exploded again. He turned and struck her thigh with his fangs, sinking deep and prolonging the orgasm with his fingers.

She thrashed her head on the bed, reduced to so many firing nerves she expected smoke. He licked her thigh, and it felt as if the wound had healed.

Finally, he lifted his head. His fangs slowly retracted. He slid his palm, the one with the brand, up from her knee to her thigh. She could *feel* the rough edges. The *K* pounded against her, burning her flesh.

She wanted that marking.

Wanted to be his for whatever time she had left.

He stood, his torso bare and so powerful he stole her breath. The tattoo of the *K* above his heart matched the one on his hand. His abs tightened as he slowly unbuttoned his jeans and withdrew his belt with a sharp hiss.

Her body trembled.

Then he shoved the jeans away. He licked his fingers, keeping her gaze as he tasted her. "I want to be clear here. You want me, and I want you, so tonight is happening. The morning isn't going to be pleasant, because we're going to deal with your reckless disregard for your own life, and it's not going to feel good."

She blinked.

"Tonight we're too far gone—I need to finish this."

He caught sight of her clavicle, and fire burned in those hypnotic eyes. Then he pierced her with that same gaze and held up his palm. The marking had darkened and looked alive. "But this is your choice. Just yours. If you say yes, then you're all in. There's no out, so make sure of your decision."

She tightened her fingers on the bedcovers. There was no doubt that he could've planted the marking on her in the midst of passion, and she would have let him. Would have welcomed it. She'd said yes the other night. But now he was giving her the choice, and she knew without a doubt that he'd stand by her decision. He would not mate her again unless she agreed. She swallowed, wanting him more than she ever realized she could want. Could need.

"Yes or no, Destiny?" His face showed no give, and his eyes were hard flints of raw hunger. For her. "Forget the war, forget the uncertainty of your future, forget the entire fucking world. What do you want?" The hoarseness of his voice licked across her skin as if his mouth was on her. "There's only you and me, and it's your decision. It has to be."

He was asking her to jump headfirst into the unknown. Into what could be a pile of pain for her last week breathing air. He wasn't offering to save her; he wasn't offering to save the world.

Garrett Kayrs was just offering himself.

And he was everything.

The world was going to come at them, no matter what, and her health was going to deteriorate whether or not she allowed them both to enjoy these last few days. If nothing else, she wanted to be his for the remainder of her life. Wanted him to be all hers. "Yes." Her voice trembled, and she cleared her throat. "I say yes to the marking and the mating. Even if it's just temporary again."

He changed. In front of her eyes, in a way she'd never be able to describe, he changed as the immortal being at his core rose to the surface. Intensity hardened his already hard features, and his nostrils flared like an animal spotting its mate. He was bigger and stronger, more dangerous than any other creature on earth, already showing the power he'd wield.

She couldn't look away.

The singular energy at the core of Garrett Kayrs was fully on display, and she was transfixed. There was nobody like him, including the king and the other immortals. Her breath quickened, and her body softened even more in response. She tried to regain control of her body, or at least her mind. She held up a hand. "But no to the discussion in the morning."

His smile flashed dangerous teeth. "The morning discussion isn't up for debate. Mate or not, you'll never put yourself in danger like that again." He traced her thigh with one finger. "I'll have your promise on that. Later."

They'd see about that. She sat up and reached for him, scratching her nails along the ridges in his abs. He was hard and throbbing, and she tentatively slid her fingers along his penis, wondering again how that had fit inside her.

He groaned. "You can play later." Bending, he cupped her face and kissed her, his tongue sweeping inside her mouth. Then he lifted her up onto the bed and covered her, kissing her into a frenzy before he spent time on her breasts and stomach, his heated mouth claiming every inch of her. As if he couldn't help himself, he moved down her again and tortured her clit, driving her up but not letting her reach that pinnacle. He kept her on the edge until tears filled her eyes and she was begging, yanking on his thick hair.

Finally, he lifted his head, and his fangs dropped. Right above her mound.

She stilled.

He slid a hand beneath her hips and flipped her over, roughly yanking her onto her hands and knees. Her nails curled into a pillow, and she braced herself, needing him more than her next breath. Breathing was irrelevant. The only thing that mattered in the entire world was him behind her. He clamped his hands on her hips and drove into her.

Hard.

He shoved through her tight body, forcing her to accept all of him. So big and so full. Consuming. She stretched around him, and her breath caught in her throat. She threw her head back and felt the strands of her hair fall on her shoulders. Every inch of her skin was sensitized. His deadly hand was instantly at her nape, his fingers tangling in her curls in that way he had.

Fully embedded in her, he slowly, deliberately, drew her head up, forcing her buttocks against his groin and her spine to elongate. To arch. Her breasts brushed a pillow, adding to the sensations bombarding her.

Then his abs were against her butt and his heated breath at her ear. "Tell me, Destiny. Who do you belong to?" The low, possessive tone rolled right to her sex, and she clenched around him. His fingers tightened.

She couldn't see. Couldn't think. But he was asking for everything. For all of her. There'd be nothing left. A primitive part of her, one she'd never known, rose to the surface. Hot and bright. Barely able to move, she still tried to jerk her head. Then she tightened her body and gripped him inside her with an impressive strength.

His hiss of breath warmed her ear. "Not good enough. Say the words, kitten." It was a command and nothing less. He pulsed inside her, balls deep, holding them both so close to the edge they might get cut. The next twist of his wrist turned her head so she could see him from the corner of her eye. "Now."

The fight against surrendering was real. She instinctively understood. There'd be no going back, no matter what. She'd be in Garrett's world from then on. Oh, she'd be the center of it, but he'd demand submission, and she knew it. "I—I can't," she gasped.

"You will." He pulled out and powered back into her, his hold keeping her from plowing into the headboard. Leaning down, he flicked her ear with one fang.

She shivered. "Garrett." The need hurt. All of her hungered for him. To have all of him forever, as long as that was for her.

"Yeah." He placed a gentle kiss behind her ear, and it shot right to her heart. "I need the words, sweetheart. I'll have them. And you."

Acceptance filtered through her along with a release of fear. "I'm yours, Garrett Kayrs. Always will be." For as long as she had.

The next kiss to her temple was soft. Then he levered himself up, manacled both her hips, and powered into her. Hard and fast, furious in motion, he pushed her over the edge. Before she could catch her breath, she was climbing again, her body at the mercy of his. He plundered her, hammering so fast she could only close her eyes and feel.

Sensations, so many, took her over. Pleasure and pain, wildness and hunger, need and want. They all took her, making him part of her forever. He grunted above her, the slap of flesh on flesh filling the night. She mewled against the comforter, her arms giving out and dropping her chest to the pillow. He positioned her head to the side so she could breathe.

Sparks and fire uncoiled inside her, reaching from her core to her extremities. She cried out, her body shaking, the climax so powerful heat swept through her with burning intensity. Pain flashed on her hip and then sharper agony at her neck when his fangs pierced her flesh. They dug down, forever marking her bone.

Pain and pleasure collided, and she closed her eyes to let the orgasm take her. Completely.

He jerked inside her, filling her.

She mumbled something. Could've been anything.

He kissed her on her nape, right in the center. Right on the Key inside the butterfly. Then he withdrew, and her body jerked in denial. He flipped her over and kissed her, his big body bracketing hers.

She kissed him back, sliding her arms around his neck.

He leaned back and eyed her, his gaze still intense. "Let's handle the discipline now before we go on to round two of this mating. I like you wearing my mark."

She rolled her eyes, stretching against all of that hard muscle. "I made a mistake." Although she'd almost gotten Ulric to bite her.

"Yeah, and you won't do it again," Garrett said, the statement not sounding like a suggestion.

She shrugged.

The world tilted, and she found herself buck naked over his knee. "Hey." The first slap to her butt made her chuckle. The second made her protest. The third made her realize he hadn't been joking. The next round of sex had better be good. Then he paused. "What?" She kicked her legs to gain freedom.

He rubbed her hip, and she stilled at the lovely pleasure. "Your marking. It's already fading."

She'd hoped this time was different, but she should've known better.

There was no way to save her.

Chapter Thirty-Eight

The marking on Dessie's hip faded completely by noon. Again. Garrett tugged on the tie of his tuxedo, his mind at war. Dessie's system was still unenhanced. Brain surgery was soon to be the only option if he didn't figure out a way to get Ulric's blood.

There were few secrets in the Realm, and he'd noticed whispers while moving around earlier. It was odd. People were doubting him—not only due to his ties to the Seven, but now for trying to keep a murderous human in their midst.

For so long, he'd been the golden boy of the Realm.

Now he was being doubted. Not by family, though. He'd always have family at his back.

"The Kurjans have Ulric's blood," Janie said, reaching for and straightening his tie in his living room. "We know they do because they used it on Dessie and the other women at the school. We just have to find it."

If there was any left. If there was, why weren't the Kurjans experimenting on a new generation of enhanced females?

Janie stepped back, looking like a princess in her long silver gown with sparkles everywhere. Even in her long hair. "I can't believe you're mated and Hope is turning twenty-one." Her eyes were clear and her features pale.

Garrett ran a knuckle down his big sister's flawless face. Well, she was flawless to him. "Why are you so pale?" It had made sense that she'd come to his house to help Dessie get ready for the ball because she was his sister and a total sweetheart. But maybe there was something more.

She swallowed, and her eyes glimmered.

"Whatever it is, I'll fix it," he promised.

She snorted. "I'm your older sister, remember? I'm supposed to fix your problems." Her smile faded. "I wish I could. There has to be a way."

He brushed a tendril of hair away from her face. "We'll figure it out. For now, tell me what's happening."

She faltered. "I know things are difficult right now, and I don't want to be insensitive. But you're my brother, and I, well—"

The scent of baby powder caught him. His chest settled. "You're pregnant."

Her mouth opened and then closed. "I am." Joy filtered across her face, followed by concern. For him. She was worried about him.

He enfolded her in a hug, careful not to crush her. "This is good news, Janie." Still holding her, he leaned down to study her happy expression. "What are the odds of another girl?"

She shrugged, and sparkles danced. "I have no idea. Hope is so rare, I think I'd bet on a boy. But again, who knows?" Ultrasounds didn't work on immortal babies because of the protection around them, so they wouldn't know for nine months. "You're pleased?"

"Delighted," he said honestly.

The door opened, and Zane Kyllwood stalked in, his gaze taking in the scene. "You're lucky you're her brother." The head of the demon nation wore a tux with his tie askew, looking every bit as deadly as he needed to be. His eyes were Kyllwood green, his hair black, and his body fighting hard. "Don't squeeze her, Kayrs."

Garrett kept his sister right where she was. "So you knocked her up again."

Zane grinned. "It was a pleasure, I promise you."

Garrett gagged. "Stop. Just please stop." When Janie slapped him on the chest, he released her. "No more worrying about me. About anything, actually. You stay calm and peaceful and take care of my nephew. Or niece."

Janie turned and moved toward Zane to fix his tie. "I swear. You can disassemble and reassemble every weapon known to any species while blindfolded and bleeding, but you can't fix a tie?"

"Maybe I just like your hands on me," Zane murmured, his gaze on his mate.

Garrett gagged again. "Dude. That's my sister. Knock it off." Nothing in this world pleased him more than seeing Janie happy and safe with Zane. He'd die for the guy, but he still didn't need them flirting in front of him. Not that he hadn't basically seen his father maul his mother the other day. What was up with his family? "There's nothing wrong with discretion."

Zane looked right at him and planted a hand on Janie's ass.

Garrett breathed in through his nose and exhaled slowly. His mom would be furious if he bloodied his brother-in-law before the big party. Even so, if Zane didn't knock it off, Garrett would risk her wrath. "I'm not in the mood, Zane."

"Too bad. I am." Zane leaned over and kissed Janie on the mouth. Hard.

Garrett started for him just as the bedroom door opened and Dessie walked out. He stopped cold, his heart thumping. "You look beautiful." True words. He'd bought her a floor-length, sapphire-blue dress with diamonds strewn along the neckline, sleeves, and bust that matched the glittering diamonds that created a *V* at her tiny waist. While lovely, the dress was no match for the sparkle in her eyes or the beauty of her face. She'd piled her wild mass of hair on top of her head, and delicate tendrils framed her heart-shaped face.

His. She was all his.

At the moment, she was staring at him in his tux with wide eyes, and her pretty pink lips were parted in a silent "oh."

He reached for her hand, gratified when she instantly slid her smaller one against his.

Zane cleared his throat.

Garrett pulled her close and turned. "Zane, meet my mate, Destiny Applegate." Her name would be Kayrs soon enough. "Zane is my brother-in-law, and he just knocked up my sister again."

Janie sighed. "Don't make me punch you."

Dessie smiled. "You don't look like what I thought a demon would."

"Give me time," Zane said mildly, grinning. "Although your mate is half-demon as well, you know."

Dessie rocked on her three-inch, sparkly heels. "Yeah, but he seems like it."

Garrett laughed along with the others, even though the feeling of doom wouldn't leave his stomach. They had to fix that tumor. "We should go." He snatched the silk shawl he'd purchased with the dress and draped it over Dessie's slim shoulders, following his sister to their SUV. While it'd be a nice walk, clouds were rolling in, and it'd probably rain. So the SUV would work.

Minutes later, they arrived at the main lodge, where the festivities were already in motion. It appeared that members of the Seven were mingling with the Realm and shifter nations already, so Garrett let himself relax.

His father and uncle caught him in the vestibule. Zane took one look and squired Janie away to the dance floor.

"Nice party," Garrett drawled.

Dage nodded, a glass of scotch in one hand. "Are the Seven going to continue cooperating with us?"

Talen's jaw tensed, and he scanned the crowd outside as more partygoers arrived. "They'd better."

"I'm working on it," Garrett said, wanting to get Dessie into his arms again.

"That's not good enough," Talen growled. "There will be no more secrets."

Then, out of nowhere, Dessie seemed to lose her mind. She pushed away from Garrett and stepped toe-to-toe with Talen, having to tilt her head way back to meet his gaze. "That's enough out of you, scary vampire dude." She turned her head toward Dage. "You, too. I don't care if you're the king of all the dangerous ones. Garrett is doing his best, and that means he's…Doing…His…Best."

Garrett's entire body warmed. Amusement battled with arousal inside him.

His dad glowered down at her. "Listen, you—"

She poked him right in the chest. "No. You listen. Garrett is being torn apart by all the different factions and loyalties in his life, and you're going to stop putting pressure on him. He enforces for the Grizzlies, and they are brothers. He underwent some killer type of ritual and formed blood bonds with the Seven. And you"—she poked him again—"are his family. That means you look out for him and should be the one place in the world where his blood pressure doesn't rise." She rose on her toes but still didn't reach Talen's height. Nowhere near. "Do you understand me?"

Talen swallowed. He might've blinked, but he faced the furious sprite evenly. "Yes. I understand."

She swung toward Dage. "King?"

Dage's lips twitched, but he nodded. "Got it."

Garrett wanted to take her to the ground right there and smother her with kisses. Nobody had ever stood up for him like that. Hell. Nobody in the entire world had ever challenged Dage and Talen Kayrs in such a manner.

"That's better." She turned toward Garrett, her color high and her eyes an impossible blue. "Now. Let's dance."

* * * *

Yes, she'd entirely lost her mind. Dessie hid how hard her knees were shaking as she slipped her arm through Garrett's and entered the main area of the lodge. She'd just yelled at a king and

Garrett's dad. Deadly immortals who could probably break her in two with a pinkie. She swallowed but kept her head high as they walked away.

Then she gasped at the opulent decorations. The main area had been cleared of furniture, leaving a dance floor and many tables arranged around it. Sparkling streamers hung from the far rafters, sending glittering lights in every direction. The males wore tuxes, several looking like they wanted to jump out of them no matter how sexy they were. And the dresses. She could only stare. So many colors and cuts, and so many sparkles. It was the prettiest array of silk she'd ever seen.

Garrett led her to the dance floor and turned her around to face him, his touch gentle. "Sorry about all the tests yesterday."

She was sorry they didn't have a cure. "I know. You can't torture yourself about this. I've made peace with my fate, and I'm okay." While he had some sort of crazy plan to get more of Ulric's blood, she didn't see how. Also, even if a miracle happened and they acquired the blood, there was no guarantee Emma or Faith would be able to create an antidote to the tumor. Especially in the week she had left. "Let's just enjoy our time together. Okay?" It was all she had to offer. They moved, and a slight pain wandered up her back. "And no more spankings." She could still feel his handprint.

He grinned. "You didn't mind the aftermath."

Nobody minded great sex. "Seriously." She stepped on his toe to make a point, but he didn't seem to notice.

He lifted her chin with two knuckles and placed a kiss on her mouth. The touch was gentle and his lips firm. "Don't put your life in danger again, Mate."

Bossy male.

She leaned into him and enjoyed the music, loving the feel of his body all around her. The band in the corner moved into a ballad, and she closed her eyes, just feeling as much as she could.

This night was a dream. No, better than any dream.

Her feet started to ache after several dances, so Garrett settled her at a table with the birthday girl, who was chatting happily with friends, while texting with one hand beneath the table. Hope's smile was genuine, but her gaze missed nothing.

The friends moved on to the cake table.

Dessie leaned against Garrett's niece. "Tell me you're texting a boy."

Hope's lips curved into a smile. "I am, but not like you think." She finished and set the phone to the side. "I have a contact in one of the Kurjan holdings, and he's working on finding any record of where Ulric's blood is kept. Their holdings have increased across the world, so it could be anywhere. It's significant that the Kurjans have spread out so far."

"How?" Dessie looked out at the dancers, her gaze automatically seeking Garrett.

"I don't know, but they're positioning themselves in odd places. Not great tactical locations, so there has to be another reason." Hope waved at her father, who was dancing with her mother. Zane and Janie were an incredible-looking couple. "I'm thinking the Kurjans are preparing for Ulric to return and don't know where the dumbass will land."

Dessie looked at the young woman. She had to be brilliant to have risen to such a high level in the Intelligence branch of the Realm. "You're impressive."

"You, too." Hope rested her chin on her hand. "Sorry the marking hasn't taken, but it will. Trust me."

Bear and Nessa danced by, seeming to be having a nice night out without the triplets.

Dessie finally caught sight of Garrett. He was casually walking around the outer tables. Taking a champagne glass off a tray, he turned his head and gave his father a barely perceptible nod. Talen was on the other side of the room, also casually walking.

"They're scouting for threats," Hope said, yawning.

Yeah, they were. Even while having fun at such a lovely event, they were on alert. It was impressive how in tune the two were, scouting in almost the same formation but looking as if they were just enjoying the party. "I bet they could launch into motion before anybody had a clue."

Hope chuckled. "Without question." She straightened as a handsome guy who looked like a badass warrior approached the table. There was no question he was anything but a demon soldier. "Dessie, this is Paxton. He's my best friend."

"Hi." Dessie nudged Hope. "You said you wanted to dance." She hadn't, but somebody should take that hard-bodied immortal for a spin.

Paxton held out a hand, and Hope took it, following him to the dance floor. They looked good together.

Garrett showed up at her side and tugged her from the chair. "More dancing? I can carry you if your feet hurt."

That was an offer she'd never refuse. The rest of the evening passed too quickly, and it was after midnight when she finally fell into the warm bed, too much champagne floating in her head. She barely felt Garrett remove her dress and pull over her head a T-shirt that smelled like him. She dove right in, sure she could keep the portals closed for the night.

She was wrong.

Chapter Thirty-Nine

No sooner had Dessie fallen asleep than she was falling.

Through heated air, fighting the current, screaming into a voice-stealing void. She landed hard on the sand. Pain burst through her body, and she rolled over, coughing out granules. The orange moon seemed brighter than the blue this time.

That was odd.

"I called you." The voice sent chills through her.

She rolled onto her hands and knees before shoving herself to her bare feet. The sand burned the bottoms, but she ignored the pain. She was only wearing Garrett's long T-shirt, leaving her legs and arms bare. Vulnerable and defenseless. "How?" Last time, she'd brought herself. "I thought Hope closed your portals again."

"Obviously not." Ulric wore some sort of animal skin as trousers, and he'd left off the shirt this time. His hair was in a perfect braid down his back, bisecting his scalp. In the bizarre light, his hair appeared to be in flames.

The champagne rolled around in her stomach.

"We're bound, Intended." His canines glinted. "You and me. You came here willingly last time, which means I now can bring you in any time I want." He flicked his wrist toward the blue moon, and a body fell toward the sand. "My gifts have strengthened lately. Because of you, possibly. Or this world is just beginning to fade."

Hope hit the sand behind Dessie and rolled over with a loud groan. She staggered to her feet, her hair filled with sand. "What the hell?"

"Hello, Lock." If homicidal monsters could look delighted, Ulric did. He looked around at the sharp and lonely surroundings. "I've had nothing to do in here but think for too long, and I've decided if there isn't a Lock, the Keys are irrelevant."

Hope snorted. "Guess you can join Mensa when you get out."

Dessie cut her a look. The woman was joking? A closer examination showed Hope moving toward the liquid, putting herself in position to attack. Dessie caught her nod and shifted slightly toward what might be a forest. They'd have to take him from both sides, and their chances weren't good. Was there still the combined blood of all the Keys in her veins? She'd have to get Ulric to bite her. It was their only chance.

Without warning, Ulric leaped toward her, spraying sand. He landed right in front of her. Grabbing her shirt, he yanked her toward him and backhanded her hard enough to send her spinning toward the trees. Pain exploded in her mouth, and her blood washed across the low rocks.

Hope rushed him, and he hit her in the stomach, throwing her several yards down the dark beach.

"No!" Dessie spun up to her feet, her mouth throbbing.

"Yes." He moved toward her across the burning sand.

She balanced on her back leg and pivoted, landing a roundhouse kick perfectly to his groin. It was like hitting a metal plate. Her foot ricocheted off, and pain burst in her toes as she fell back to the sand. The granules pricked the skin of her arms, raising red bumps.

He threw back his head and laughed. The grating sound echoed back from every direction. "I'm invincible, you stupid female." He leaned down and snatched her by the hair, yanking her up as if she were a useless doll. "You need to bleed more, and then you'll learn your place." Studying her, he manacled her wrist and twisted until it cracked.

She shrieked in pain.

The bone burst free, and blood flowed down to the sand. Dizziness overwhelmed her, and her legs gave out. He let her fall.

Hope ran full bore at him, stopped at the last second, and kicked him in the eye.

He reared back and grabbed his eye, swinging at the young woman. He nailed her in the cheekbone, and she careened toward the now-bubbling liquid.

"Hope," Dessie screamed, grabbing her destroyed wrist.

Hope caught herself at the edge and swung around, barely keeping her legs out of the liquid. She rolled over the dangerous sand and then tried to stand, falling to her knees instead.

Dessie's body seemed to flash in and out and then glowed for a moment. She looked down at herself—she was brighter. While she hadn't realized she'd been muted before, now she was bright. And the pain felt even more real. She frowned.

Ulric's purple eyes gleamed. "I thought so."

Tears coursed down her face. The bone in her wrist was still protruding, and her arm was going numb. The blood kept flowing. "What?"

"Blood. It has anchored you here." Ulric looked at the vast ocean. "When you hit Yvonne and her blood fell on the rock, she became more in focus. She was here in body, not just her mind. Now you are here."

Dessie shrank back. It made sense. Her body was no longer safe in Garrett's bed. She was actually here.

"Oh, God," Hope whispered, crawling to her over the sand. The side of the woman's face was already bruised and swelling. "Dessie."

Ulric rubbed his eye. "You're next, Lock."

Thunder rolled across the bizarre ocean. The blue moon shifted toward the orange.

Ulric paused.

Wind lashed up, spinning sand in every direction. Dessie lifted her good arm to protect her eyes.

The creatures in the muck went into a frenzy, spitting the oozing goo in every direction. Rocks began to fall from high up in the cliffs, landing in the muck, making them squeal in an unholy cacophony.

Hope ducked a flying rock. "What is happening?"

Ulric stared at the spray of blood across the rocks. "What did you do?"

Dessie looked at the bloody sand by her feet. It was bubbling. The sky began to fade to an impossible gray, and then it shattered. Spikes and shards rained down all around them. She moved to cover Hope with her body, but Ulric grabbed her good arm.

He leaned down and sniffed her, his nose touching her shoulder. She tried to shove him, but he was immovable.

Both of his nostrils widened, and he leaned back, his gaze wide. "You did it. You combined the blood of the Keys and the Lock." The rocks began to tumble away. "The world is breaking."

Her mouth opened. Despite the pain buzzing through her, more agony tormented her. She'd caused this?

The wind rose to an unbearable keening.

Ulric grabbed for Hope. "You're coming with us."

"No," Dessie yelled, her mind taking over. She read the symbols on his chest. They were so deep they must've been cut centuries ago. She knew them, knew how to combine these symbols with the others she'd studied. She pushed Hope away. Then she lifted her good hand to the still-shattering sky and gave the last order. A portal opened.

"Dessie," Hope screamed, scrambling to get to her.

Dessie flicked her wrist, and the young woman flew up into the air and through the portal. It closed with a loud snap.

Ulric yanked her to her feet. "You'll pay for that," he bellowed over the storm.

The cliffs blew in every direction. The blue and orange moons collided, and they exploded just like a supernova.

Ulric clamped her to him.

Then they were falling.

* * * *

Garrett double-tested his weapon, fully dressed in tactical gear. One second Dessie had been next to him in bed and the next she was gone. There hadn't been a damn thing he could do.

Talen stalked into the armory, already drawing on a bulletproof vest.

"How is Hope?" Garrett asked grimly.

Talen scrubbed both hands down his face. "She's bruised but alive. Everyone's ready in the control room." He planted a hand on his son's shoulder. "We'll get her back."

She was in a fucking hell world they couldn't reach. Or had she and Ulric dropped out of that world and gone who knew where?

Garrett preceded his father through the labyrinthine, fourth-level underground of the main lodge, reaching the control room, where his family and members of the Seven awaited. Several demon soldiers, including all three Kyllwoods, were also present, as were many of their shifter friends. More soldiers geared up throughout the Realm in preparation for a raid. The control room held computers on every surface and screens on every rock wall. Everyone remained standing, filled with too much energy to sit.

Ivar brought up a map on the far wall. "Based on the position of Ulric's world relative to the other two created worlds, we can estimate where Ulric will land if his world also breaks." Ten places lit up on the map. "When Quade's world crumbled, he fell here." A blue dot showed up. "When Ronan's exploded, he fell here." Another blue dot. "So we can surmise that Ulric will land here, here, here, or here." Bright yellow dots lit up.

Garrett studied the map. "Those are known Kurjan holdings."

Ivar nodded. "Yeah. They have the same intel we do, so no doubt they've been preparing."

Dage stepped forward. "A fact we could've used to our advantage had we been given all of the facts." The king was obviously not pleased at being kept in the dark, and now that Garrett had told them all about Hope being the Lock, he was downright pissed off. As was Talen.

Garrett shook his head. "Logan and I joined the Seven to protect Hope, and you know it. Our entire goal was to take out Ulric before any ritual became necessary." Now that Ulric might have landed back in this world, they would have a chance of battling him. Hopefully Dessie was alive. He had to get to her. Fury roared through him, but he shoved the fire down, going stone-cold.

Talen stepped forward. "We'll send four teams of sixteen soldiers, one to each holding. Both Zane and I have taken our territories to red level, and our soldiers are armed and at all stations. We have to assume the Kurjans will make a move on us right now."

Garrett studied the blips on the screen. Where was she?

Promise, Ivar's mate, looked up from a computer next to the wall. "I have several worldwide disturbances being reported. Earthquakes, rare windstorms, hurricanes…" She bent her head to study her screen more closely. The woman was a brilliant physicist who'd been studying the portals, the worlds, and the escapes for years. "They're similar to what was recorded when both Ronan and Quade's worlds fell. I think Ulric is home."

That meant that Destiny either didn't make it when the world fell or was now here with one of the most dangerous monsters to ever have been born. Garrett stared at the map, trying to figure out where she'd be.

Talen secured a knife at his leg. "Which one do you want to take, G?"

Since Garrett hadn't mated Dessie, not completely, he couldn't get into her head. He couldn't find her on a map. Frustration tried to trickle into his mind, but he shoved it out. "Promise? Which location is most likely to be Ulric's landing zone?"

The woman looked up at him, her dark brown eyes concerned. "I'd be guessing, Garrett."

"I know," he said. "Your guess is better than most scientists' lifelong knowledge."

She looked at the map. "Best guess for me would be Butte, Montana. There's a tar pit there hiding the ruins of an ancient Cyst holding, and it's believed to have mystical properties." She shrugged. "Which, of course, don't exist. However, the physics of the place suggest a boatload of interesting cosmological abnormalities."

"I'll take Butte," Garrett said.

His dad cut a look at Dage. "You're with him?"

Dage shook his head. "No."

Garrett frowned. There was only one reason Dage wouldn't want to go with him. "Is that where—"

"Don't know." His dad cut him off. No doubt there were several warriors in the room who didn't know of the Realm's missions.

Logan stepped up on one side, while Sam took the other. "We're with him," Logan said.

"So are we," Benny said, with Adare next to him.

Bear finished buttoning a loose shirt, no doubt so he could shift quickly. "You're not going without me."

It was good that the warriors on his team had all fought with him before. They knew each other's thoughts and moves. The remaining warriors in the room separated into the four teams, led by Garrett, Talen, Dage, and Zane.

Bear looked at the foursome. "Shouldn't the kings stay behind and defend the kingdoms?"

"Would you?" Dage countered.

"Nope." Bear smacked Garrett on the back. "Let's go get your girl. Knew she was a Keeper from the first time I met her." He sauntered out the door, followed by the rest of the warriors, leaving just the four leaders.

Talen studied him. "I could cover your back."

"It's covered," Garrett assured him. "I'd rather you took the secondary location, just in case she's there. I want one of us at each." He looked at his family. "Thank you." They were going to war after not having fought for a long time, and there was a chance one or more of them wouldn't make it back.

Dage handed him Dessie's knife. "You might need this. Don't be afraid to take off a head or two."

It wouldn't be the first time. "I should've told her I loved her." He had said everything but the words that really mattered.

"You will." Talen clapped him on the back. "Let's do this."

Garrett turned and headed out into a fall storm. The knife would get more than one taste of blood that night.

He had to find her.

Chapter Forty

Dessie came to with a start, the musky smell of elderberries around her. Pain pounded from her wrist. She gingerly rolled over to see swollen clouds covering the night sky. The moon made a valiant effort to pierce their bellies but only lit the top clouds. Where was she?

Coughing out sand, she looked around a tiny meadow. Rocks and trees surrounded her, and the sound of an owl carried on the night wind. Then her gaze caught on a form near two downed spruce trees. Panic chilled her extremities. It was Ulric, and he was facedown. She quietly pushed to her feet, swaying as her damaged wrist protested. The pain was intense.

She gulped and took a deep breath. To the left was a long dirt road. There had to be a town somewhere close, but following the road would be too obvious. Was she even in the States? She had to find help. A light rain was falling, and by the look of the purple clouds, a storm was about to hit. That was good. Anything that masked her scent could only help her.

Turning toward the trees, she crept as quietly as possible between two ancient pines, prepared to find a trail and run.

Two helicopters zoomed above them, shining down blinding lights. Vehicles with mounted lights approached on the road and screeched to a halt. Panicked, she turned to run, only to smash headfirst into a hard body. She bounced back and fell on her butt. Agony ripped up her wounded wrist, and her body heaved.

Figures wound through the trees, their light eyes piercing the darkness. She tried to scramble away. Rough hands grabbed her arms and dragged her to her feet, jostling her broken wrist.

The darkness grabbed her, and she fell unconscious.

Then she was in and out. There was more darkness, some light, and then more pain. Finally, a hard surface beneath her head. She had no idea how long she was out or where she ended up. Finally, the pain became too much, and she forced her eyes open to find herself in some sort of shed. The sides were wood, the floor dirt, and the air chilly. She gingerly sat up and then swayed as her wrist protested.

Rain beat mercilessly against the structure, and water dripped from small holes in the roof. The door opened, revealing it was still nighttime outside. A male Kurjan walked in. His eyes were purple and his hair black, tipped with red. He was tall and broad across the chest, but he looked young. Maybe eighteen. She scrambled away from him and put her back to the wall.

He looked at her wrist and winced. His skin was incredibly pale and his lips bright red. "Who are you?"

She swallowed, and her throat felt burned. If he didn't know who she was, then he wasn't very high up. Could she use that? "Nobody. Just wrong place and wrong time. Please help me leave."

"That wasn't an answer." There was the immortal arrogance she'd expected. His jawline was firm and his features more angled than rugged. If he didn't have purple eyes, he'd probably be handsome. "I asked your name."

"Dessie." Either he knew about her or he did not.

Thunder rolled high and loud outside. "You arrived with Ulric," the male said. "Who are you?"

"She's his Intended." Another male entered, and this one wasn't as pale. His eyes were an odd blue, and he looked almost human. "I'm Vero, and this is Harold. What happened to your wrist?"

"It's broken. I could use an aspirin," she said. If the pain would ebb, she could think.

Vero nodded. "We'll send in a medic." He nudged his friend. "We shouldn't be in here, Harold. What are you doing?"

"I was curious," Harold said. "Go get the medic, and I'll wait here. She's in pain, Vero."

Vero's gaze was somber. "All right. If my uncle comes, say you were ordered to guard her. We've gotten in enough trouble lately." He slid back out into the night.

Harold studied her, no expression in his gaze. "Okay, Dessie. You need to explain and fast. You arrived with Ulric, but I get no sense that you're enhanced. You're human. How are you not dead?"

She held her wrist and put her head back on the damp wooden wall. "I'm enhanced, but it's hidden well." This guy really didn't know much about his people or their experiments, but it seemed as if he wanted to help. She needed help. "It's a long story and one that'd probably get you killed if you knew it, but that's the truth. Will you help me get out of here?"

"You're enhanced." Doubt turned down his lips.

"Yes." The higher-ups knew who she was; this was her only chance to get free. "Please help me."

He dropped to one knee, and his fangs shot from his mouth.

She yelped and tried to shrink away from him.

He bit into his wrist, and blood welled up. "If you're enhanced, you can take a little of my blood. It'll heal you. Trust me." He looked over his shoulder and then pressed his wrist to her mouth. "But you have to hurry."

She didn't see a choice. Garrett's blood had helped her, but he was her mate. Or should've been her mate. She sucked down several gulps, and they burned right to her stomach. The copper taste made her gag again, but she kept the liquid down. The pain in her arm started to dissipate.

He stepped back. "Wipe your mouth," he hissed.

She hurriedly licked her lips. Then she jumped as her bone snapped back into place.

"Good." His shoulders relaxed just as the door opened and another Kurjan strode in. This one also wore the same black uniform as the rest, but he had many more silver medallions on his breast pocket. "Hello, Intended."

Harold stepped closer to the door, keeping his back to the wall. "Sir. We were just getting her medical attention. I hadn't known she was an Intended, but surely the great leader Ulric would want her healthy."

"Yes." The leader cocked his head, looking down at her. He had long black hair, deep amethyst eyes, and a sharp jawline. "I'm Dayne, the leader of the Kurjan nation."

"Dessie."

He smiled, looking almost charming. "I know exactly who you are, Destiny Applegate. I know of the marking on the nape of your neck, and I have watched you for years as you prepared to become an Intended." He winked. "Or an assassin. Could've gone either way."

Everything inside her wanted to kick him. She held her wrist away from his prying eyes, because it no longer hurt. But she wouldn't look yet to see if it was healing. "You were responsible for pumping poison into my brain?"

His smile dimmed. "Poison? We gave you Ulric's blood. If you had any idea what we had to do to get it from him in that hell world, you'd be much more appreciative. As well as regretful for killing Yvonne. She gave much more for our cause than you have."

Gross. Wait a minute. "How do you know about Yvonne?"

He straightened, standing at least six foot seven. "The great leader Ulric is awake and has told me of your story. To think it was the blood that broke the prison world."

She'd vomit about that later. "How do I get rid of the tumor in my head?"

Harold shot her a look of surprise.

Dayne shrugged. "By mating Ulric, of course. He'll give you enough blood during the event that it should destroy the mass in your brain."

Should. She needed more than should. "What of the other women from the college?"

"They're irrelevant."

She pushed to her feet, hugging her injured wrist to her stomach. "No, they're not. If they have tumors like this, then how can they be healed without mating?"

"They can't." Dayne moved aside as a Cyst soldier, smaller than Ulric but still huge, strode inside. "Your medic is here. Then Ulric would like to see you." He turned and moved into the storm.

The medic reached for her arm.

She looked down to see that the bone had set itself, leaving open a gaping wound.

"Stitches," the medic mused.

"No." She lifted her chin. "Just give me a bandage." The wrist was healing, and she'd fight better without more holes in her skin. She might lack size and strength, but if she could call on all of her skills, the element of surprise would help.

The medic shrugged, dug in his pack, and handed over a bandage. "Call me if you need more."

Harold stopped him with a hand on his arm before he could leave. "Are the comms still down?"

The medic frowned. "Why do you care?"

Harold grinned. "Vero and I met a couple of women in town the other day, and I'm not done with mine yet. So, comms?"

The medic rolled his eyes. "Young people. So stupid. No, the comms are not back up and probably won't be until the storm abates. Find a mate, would you?" He left.

Harold lost the smile and leaned against the wall, studying her.

She wound the bandage around her rapidly healing skin. "Where are we?"

"We're outside of Butte, Montana, in the mountains." His gaze sharpened, and he walked toward her.

She pressed against the wall but couldn't move.

Harold pushed her hair away from her neck. "What the fuck?"

Crap. "Um." Should she lie and say Ulric had bitten her? If they knew Garrett had tried to mate her, would they just kill her? Or would Ulric force her to mate for real this time before she could escape?

"Who bit you?" Harold's gaze narrowed, and command flowed from him. When she didn't answer, he leaned in, his nostrils flaring. Puzzlement crossed his face. He sniffed again.

She pushed him.

He inhaled and filled his lungs, slowly exhaling. "Here's the deal, lady. I'm your only friend in this entire camp. You're going to want to make a very smart decision and trust me. Why is Garrett Kayrs' scent all over you?"

Her mouth gaped open. The Kurjan could smell Garrett? She just stared at him.

He grabbed her good arm and shook her. "Talk. Now. You can trust me, but we don't have a lot of time. Garrett?"

What should she do? Harold had healed her, and he seemed like a good guy. How did he even know Garrett's scent? "Who are you, and why do you want to help me?"

He glanced at the door and then back at her, regret twisting his lips. "This is a one-way flow of information. Now tell me who you are, or I'm leaving. You don't want me to leave you."

She really didn't. But she also wasn't dumb enough to trust the enemy, even when they were being nice. Wasn't that the oldest trick in the book?

Harold apparently had little patience, because he flipped her around and tugged her hair out of the way to view her neck. "What was Dayne talking—" Tension rolled from him. He spun her around and planted her against the wall with one hand on her shoulder. "That's Ulric's marking." His breath heated her as he leaned closer and then growled. "You're a fucking Key?" he hissed.

She lowered her chin and glared.

He looked over his shoulder again. "Shit. They have no idea about the Key. Must've appeared after they saw the symbols." He released her and ran a rough hand through his thick hair, making the red at the tips dance. "Garrett found the third Key."

She edged along the wall, heading for the door.

He pinned her with his purple gaze. "You're with Garrett."

She rubbed her neck but still refused to answer.

Harold opened his mouth and started to speak just as Dayne reentered the shed. "Ulric would like to see his Intended now."

Panic engulfed her, and she shook her head, but Dayne grabbed her arm and yanked her outside into the blasting rain. "Let's go."

Chapter Forty-One

Ulric's tent was much more luxurious than the dismal shed. He had a small living area with high-end furniture made for larger bodies. A bedroom was to the left, with a bed big enough for five. He sat on a leather chair with a bowl of fruit next to him that he seemed to be truly enjoying.

Dayne shoved her into a chair across from Ulric.

She studied him. He looked even paler here than on the prison world, and his hand shook on the grapes. A blanket covered his legs, and he kept shivering, even though he wore a heavy sweatshirt. Though he appeared much weaker than he had before, he was still muscular and overbearing. His eyes were no less piercing. In this tent, they looked an even lighter purple.

"Gravity must be different here?" she asked.

"Everything is different here," he said, his voice still booming.

Dayne took the third chair, leaving the sofa empty. "We expect it'll take a brief time for you to regain your strength here at home. The Cyst headquarters has been prepared for you to rest and ready yourself for the fight to come. We'll take you there tomorrow morning when the storm has passed." There was no deference in Dayne's tone. It was pure matter-of-fact.

Dessie cleared her throat. "Who's really in charge here?"

Dayne glanced at her as if she were a nuisance. "I rule the Kurjan nation, and Ulric is the great leader of the Cyst faction, our spiritual guides. As well as yours."

That's what he thought. She slowly began to relax. Ulric was weakened right now and wouldn't want to mate yet. She had a brief reprieve. Very brief, considering that the tumor in her head was growing. Was there a way to ask for his blood? What if she just bit him? "I'm dying. I need your blood to heal myself," she blurted out.

Ulric hadn't taken his gaze off her. "You'll get it. When we mate." He looked over at Dayne. "You say she has a week?"

"Should have. We'll conduct tests on her tomorrow and give you a more detailed timeline." Dayne sipped from one of the two goblets near the bowl holding grapes. "The accommodations at headquarters are much more appropriate for when you want to mate."

Hello. She was sitting right there. There had to be a weapon near. Any weapon. A place like this must have an ammo tent. She needed to find it as soon as they tried to take her back to the shed.

The world lit up outside.

An explosion rocketed through the encampment, and men yelled. Dessie jumped out of her chair, but Dayne shoved her back down. "Stay here," he barked, yanking a gun from his waistband and running out of the tent.

Ulric stood, but it took a moment for him to gain his balance.

Dessie leaped from her chair and ran toward the door, with Ulric knocking over furniture behind her. She burst into the storm and ran right into a soldier, taking a second to recognize him.

"Damn it." Harold wrapped an arm around her waist, lifted her off the ground, and ran away from the tent toward a small copse of trees. He plopped her between two of them. "Stay here. Don't move until I come and get you."

Three helicopters hovered overhead, with soldiers rappelling down, all firing green lasers at targeted buildings. Gunfire erupted all around the camp. Kurjans poured out of tents and ran toward the soldiers who'd hit the ground. The rain blasted down, and lightning lit the area repeatedly.

Her gaze caught on Garrett, who was battling two Kurjan soldiers with Logan next to him. She started to rise.

Harold pushed her back down. "Right now the Kurjans think the Realm is here for Ulric. Stay out of sight until I can get you clear." He shoved a green gun into her hand. "Shoot first, but not me. You're human. Don't forget that." Then he turned. "Vero!" he bellowed, running full-out toward the other Kurjan soldier and hitting him midcenter just as a missile impacted the ground where he'd been standing.

Dirt flew into the air along with flames.

Dessie wiped rain off her face and pointed the gun toward the melee, trying to see if Harold was alive. Then she saw Dayne fighting with Realm soldiers, his knife slicing off limbs. She wanted to scream a warning, but the soldiers already knew.

Garrett fought soldier after soldier, cutting off heads or limbs as he moved through the camp. Blood covered his face, and fury lit his eyes, though his movements were cold and calculated. As if he could feel her, his head turned, his eyes a bright metallic multitude of colors.

She knew the second he spotted her.

His shoulders went back, and he threw a Kurjan soldier several yards to land on his head. Then he swiped and cut, kicking and punching, making his way to her.

Bullets struck all around him, and Logan shoved Garrett to the side, taking the hits. He went down, and Sam ducked and rolled, bringing Logan up over a shoulder to run toward a waiting helicopter.

Paxton Phoenix instantly took position next to Garrett, his face set in lines of harsh concentration as he fought with knives too fast to watch. Garrett kept fighting until he came face-to-face with Dayne.

Dessie's breath caught, and she partially stood.

Dayne struck first, slamming a knife into the side of Garrett's neck. Garrett yanked it out and sliced Dayne across the face, following up with a punch to the nose. Blood spurted from them both.

Then a Kurjan soldier grabbed Dessie and dragged her out of her hiding spot. Panic-stricken, she lifted the gun and fired several rounds into his eyes. Blood washed over her skin, burning her. The soldier fell onto his face and didn't move.

She looked frantically around just as another soldier grabbed her by the hair and threw her to the ground. She kicked out and nailed him in the knees, knocking him down beside her. Pain burst through her along with panic. She didn't have a weapon. A bramble cut into her arm. Was it possible? She flashed back to Garrett's words about her skills. Then she sucked in air and imagined the weeds growing thorns. The sharp edges turned into vines and wrapped themselves around her attacker, cutting deep.

He screamed.

She rolled back and started to run, only to bounce off Ulric. He stood, feet braced, and yanked her back to her feet. She tried to kick him, but he backhanded her, sending her down again. She pictured barbed vines climbing his legs, but they weren't able to penetrate his forged body.

He hauled her back up, his hand around her neck. Then he lifted her in front of him.

She struggled to breathe, staring at the carnage all around. Garrett manacled Dayne's arms from behind, twisted, and forced the Kurjan leader to his knees.

In a move so smooth it looked choreographed, Paxton dropped to a knee, set a blade to Dayne's head, and sliced through his entire neck.

The Kurjan leader's head rolled away into the sopping wet leaves. Garrett threw the body to the side.

He rose, a powerful male in a dangerous storm, blood and bodies all around him. Lowering his chin, he prowled toward her, his gaze only on her.

Ulric shook her.

Paxton moved beside Garrett, and they charged.

Garrett reached her first and tackled both her and Ulric with the force of a blowing volcano. She yelled, her hands grabbing for purchase. They hit the ground, and Garrett shot his arm between Ulric and her neck, forcing her to roll off the Cyst leader.

Paxton lifted her off the ground and ran through the rain to a waiting helicopter. He placed her in the back, where two soldiers instantly flanked her, firing rapidly toward the dwindling Kurjan soldiers. "Stay here." Pivoting, Paxton ran back into the fight.

Dessie wiped blood and rain off her face, searching for Garrett. Ulric grabbed him around the neck, stood, and twisted. Garrett flew through the air to hit the shed where Dessie had been kept. The boards creaked and snapped in two.

"Garrett," she screamed, trying to jump down.

One of the Realm soldiers put her right back in place, turning to fire again toward the enemy.

Garrett pushed out of the rubble, ducked his head, and burst toward the Cyst leader in a frenzy of energy that was too fast to track. He hit Ulric midcenter and lifted him, slamming him down to the ground. Then Garrett punched Ulric in the mouth repeatedly, shattering teeth that flew in every direction. With a fast motion, he grabbed his knife from his sheath and sliced. Blood spurted in every direction.

Three Kurjan soldiers tackled Garrett, throwing him off Ulric.

Paxton jumped into the fray, and blood flew as punches were interspersed with flashing knives.

Ulric stood, blood pouring down his chin. Two soldiers flanked him, and they ran toward a waiting vehicle, loading up and zooming out of sight.

A Kurjan soldier leaped in front of the helicopter, firing green lasers past the guards and directly at her.

Harold came out of nowhere and jumped in front of the lasers, his body taking the hit and shuddering. He smashed onto the ground, and water splashed up from the weeds. He convulsed, and blood burbled from his mouth.

Dessie tried to jump down, but Sam was there in front of her, yanking the Kurjan soldier off the ground and around the helicopter. "No, please. He helped me." The soldiers wouldn't let her out, so she rushed to the other side of the craft and threw open the door. Then she paused.

Harold sat with his back to the helicopter, with Sam's bleeding wrist at his mouth. What in the world?

Sam looked up, his gaze sharp. "Are you all right?"

She nodded, her body hurting as if she'd gone through a meat grinder. But she was alive. The sounds of the fight died down as more helicopters rose into the air and various vehicles spun away. The smell of the storm mixed with coppery blood and smoldering wood choked the air.

Then she was hauled up against solid steel. She knew that body. "Garrett." Relief swamped her so quickly her body sagged. "You're okay."

He held her tight, leaning over her to look at Sam and Harold. "You good, H?"

Harold nodded and pushed Sam's wrist away. "Yeah. Leave some holes in me. I have to make this look authentic." He stood. "Need a solid punch."

Sam punched him so hard he fell back against the copter.

"Sam!" Dessie hissed.

Harold grinned, slapped Sam on the shoulder, and winked at her. "Later." Then he dodged around the helicopter and disappeared into the woods.

"Let's go." Garrett held out a hand to haul Sam inside, where several other soldiers joined them. He sat and pulled her onto his lap, holding her tight. "Are you hurt?"

"I'm fine." She snuggled her nose into his neck as they rose into the air. The storm batted the craft around. "You?"

He kissed the top of her head. "Good."

A cough racked her from the smoke, and she turned her head into his chest. Her lungs felt as if they were on fire. She leaned back. "Harold is a friend?"

"Harold is actually Hunter, and he's my cousin. He's Dage and Emma's kid and a future king." Garrett looked out the window. "Should've brought him home with us, whether he wanted to come or not."

"He helped me. Isn't he young to be undercover?" She'd never forget his kindness.

Garrett gave a short nod. "Way too young. But like I said, we face danger before asking any of our people to do the same. I'm proud of Hunter, but I miss him. Also, I saw you fight—am proud of you. Nice trick with the weeds. Didn't know you could do that."

She thought back. "Neither did I. It just came to me in the moment."

"You did a good job, but I saw you get hit. Do you need blood?"

"I don't think so." Her body ached, and the pain in her wrist throbbed, but nothing seemed broken.

He tugged her head back and took her mouth, his lips possessive and hot. Then he released her. "I have a present for you in my pocket."

She leaned back to see his eyes. There was still blood on his rugged face. "Another book?"

His jaw was hard and his expression fierce. "No. It's Ulric's tongue."

Sam and Logan pivoted in their seats, looking back, surprise on their faces.

Garrett rolled his eyes. "Sometimes thinking through analytically helps things, brothers." He glanced down at his red and bubbling hands. "Although his blood burns hotter than I expected."

Chapter Forty-Two

Garrett sat in the waiting area of the medical wing after sending all of his family and numerous friends away. He appreciated their support but needed quiet. Dessie had been in with Emma, Janie, and Faith for several hours, and they'd banned him. For a moment, when she'd been in pain from an injection, he might've lost it.

Helplessness ate away at him until his insides burned. Maybe he should go after Ulric and get more blood. Good plan. He stood.

His mom walked through the outside door, her hair a mess atop her head. "Hi." She moved in and hugged him tight.

He held on, careful not to bruise her, and dropped his chin to her head. "What are you doing here?"

"Your growl can't get rid of me." She leaned back and smiled. "You were brilliant to cut out Ulric's tongue."

Garrett's hands still burned from cutting the thing off. It was too bad Ulric could regenerate himself. "It was the only way to acquire his blood. I hope there was enough of it to help Dessie." If there wasn't, he'd go back and find Ulric again, and pretty much rip the Cyst apart to gain more blood.

The door opened, and he lifted his head, expecting to see Emma.

Dessie walked out, her face pale but her eyes clear. No longer in a hospital gown, she'd donned a pink sweater and dark jeans that made her look healthy and whole.

He swallowed, waiting. His fingers curled into fists as he planned how to track Ulric for more blood.

Her smile brightened her entire face. "The last injection worked. The tumor is gone."

His heart slammed like he'd taken a blow.

Cara patted his arm. "I'll leave you two alone for the moment, but we're having a family dinner later." She smiled at Dessie and quickly made her exit.

Garrett moved for Dessie and cupped her face. "You're sure."

She nodded, happiness glowing in her sapphire eyes. "Yes. Emma was able to take the tongue and get enough blood for several attempts, and they hurt, but the mass is gone." Reaching for the waist of her yoga pants, she tugged down the side. "Emma and Janie are shocked, but look what appeared, dark and beautiful."

He leaned over to see his marking on her hip. Right where he'd placed it. His fingers traced it, and she shivered. "I don't understand."

She shrugged. "Neither does Emma. But her best guess is that we did mate, and the same cloaking aspect of the tumor that prevented the broadcasting of my enhancement also hid the fact that we'd mated." She hopped. "And I looked at the page of the book that bothered me before, and nothing. So…"

As they'd suspected, the triggers were somehow tied to the tumor. "You sure?"

She nodded, her face pensive.

"All right." He turned and tore his shirt up, letting her have a good look.

She was quiet for a moment and then traced his marking, going rib by rib. "It's beautiful."

"Are you feeling homicidal?" His heart hadn't felt this light in decades.

She snorted. "Not at the moment, but you'd better behave yourself and hope for the best."

He dropped his shirt and straightened, sure he didn't deserve such good fortune. But she did. Without question. Even so, he was planting that marking on her again that night and probably every night for the ensuing century or so. And she was going to continue seeing Prophet Lily and working through her triggers, just in case. Plus, Lily was a hoot. Dessie could use some friends, and Lily would be a good one. That reminded him. "We've tracked down three of the women from your college who were treated as you were, and we'll get them help."

She nodded. "Emma said she can create a copy of the blood cure to use on others. I'm so hopeful, Garrett."

He loved that about her. Her brightness affected everything around her, especially him.

She shuffled her feet. "I know we mated, and you were trying to save my life. But—"

He kissed her. She'd have no doubts with him.

She returned the kiss, her fingers curling into his chest. She broke away and drew in breath.

Damn it. He needed to take it easy on her. The day had been difficult. He brushed a curl away from her face. Her skin felt like silk. "The storm passed, and the sun is out. How about a ride?" He had a jacket and helmet waiting on his bike for her.

Anticipation lit her expression. "I would love to go for a ride."

"Good." He took her hand and led her out of the lodge, grateful to have this time together before everyone descended on them. He put her on the bike, facing him. Then he helped her into the leather jacket, making sure she was warm enough. This was the right place. Where they'd started. "My life isn't going to be an easy one, Dessie." It was only fair to tell her.

Her eyebrows rose. "Are you warning me off?"

He grinned. "No. There's no getting away from me." He said the words casually but meant them to his soul. She'd given herself to him, and he'd protect her with his last breath. "You need to know that Ulric is just getting started, and my job is to stop him. The Seven took vows, and we're at war."

"I understand." She patted his hand. "We'll figure it out, Garrett. It's going to be all right."

It was sweet of her to reassure him, but his first goal in any situation was to guarantee her safety. He'd trained his entire life to do so. "Whatever we go through, we go together. I promise it'll be worth it." He'd be worthy for her. Their story had started with a whirlwind, but she was an old-fashioned girl, and she deserved the dream of happily ever after. So he dropped to one knee and held out a box, flipping open the top. "Marry me."

She gasped. Then she leaned closer and looked at the ring. Her next gasp moved her entire body. "Garrett." Her voice was reverent.

He'd figured she'd like sparkles. The diamond solitaire was probably too big for her small hand, but she didn't seem to care. "You need to answer."

"Oh. Yes." She couldn't take her eyes off the ring.

"I know the way to your heart is through books, but you can't wear one on your hand. So I'll give you this as well as the key to the family library, which has books older than you can imagine. It's all yours." He slipped the ring onto her finger. Yep. Definitely too big.

"I love it," she whispered, holding her hand to the sun and watching the diamond send off sparks. "Both the ring and the key to a library." Happiness flooded her face.

Then she'd keep both. "I love you, Dessie. Completely." He stood and kissed her, finally feeling himself settle. "I've been dreaming about you and hunting for you for so long." He'd taken his dangerous little assassin and made her his. Forever.

She smiled. "I dreamed of you, too." She leaned up and kissed him. "You saved me years ago, Garrett. Whether you remember it or not."

Truth be told, she'd saved him. Now that she was healthy, he could feel her enhancements all around them. And he could feel himself in her. The mating mark was strong, and she was his. Now he'd take her on a nice ride and let her feel the sun and wind on her face before he took her home and double-checked that marking. His hand pulsed in agreement. "Are you warm enough?"

"I love you." She said the words with strength, meeting his gaze. "Completely and forever. It's you and me, Garrett Kayrs."

His entire being felt the rightness of her words. Fate had ruled him for years; he'd been seeking and trying to find her most of his life. He grinned, feeling alive for the first time in way too long.

He tunneled his hands in her hair, cupping her head and kissing her. Deep and hard, he took her where he wanted them to go, enjoying the little sigh of pleasure she gave against his lips. He leaned back and smiled. "I knew if I never gave up, I'd meet you. I held on, and I found my Destiny."

Printed in the United States
by Baker & Taylor Publisher Services